The
Karma
Factor

THOMAS LANE

Waterside Productions

The Karma Factor

www.ThomasLane.com

Edited by Joyce Walker

Cover design by Thomas Lane, Loy Whitman, Ashley Ess

Printed in the USA by DeHart's Media Services, Inc.

First Printing, 2022

ISBN-13: 978-1-958848-21-0 hardcover edition

ISBN-13: 978-1-958848-22-7 e-book edition

Library of Congress Control Number: 2022906242

Waterside Productions
2055 Oxford Ave
Cardiff, CA 92007
www.waterside.com

~

This book is dedicated to those
who have outgrown denial and are
rising up with courage and kindness
to face a world in crisis.

~

According as a man acts and walks in the path of life, so he becomes. He that does good becomes good; he that does evil becomes evil.

—The Upanishads

The Letter

In the spring of 1946, a renegade Tibetan monk named Palden sat at a small desk in front of a fire and penned a letter. It would be copied and sent to thirty-two recipients in all, dispatched to locations around the world. The envelopes would mysteriously appear on doorsteps and in mailboxes and be read by scientists and mystics, artists, poets, and philosophers. The message was simple: Humankind was on a path to self-destruction. In the not too distant future, life would become unsustainable. The cycle must be broken.

The monk had chosen his moment: The war was over. Hitler had been defeated. But tomorrow another strongman would rise again, and the cycle of horrors would repeat over and over until the fragile ecosystems of life were destroyed, the miracle of Earth silenced forever. A new approach was called for, and the call was urgent.

The letter asked the recipients to join Palden in a quest for answers . . . to extricate themselves from their current lives and travel in secrecy to a designated place in the Tibetan Himalayas. Here, amidst the timeless skies and majestic peaks, there would be no distractions, no peer pressure, no preconceived ideas. The work could remain pure.

Palden's plea was impassioned. Western technology and Eastern thought must combine forces! Science and spirit must unite and enter the realm of the human soul. The mysterious phenomenon of karma awaits scientific investigation. Here on the Roof of the World, the answers could be found.

On April 6, 1946, the letters were smuggled across the Tibetan border into India and posted from there. Three weeks later, the invitations began to arrive at their destinations.

Soon thereafter, a sampling of advanced thinkers from around the world began to quietly disappear.

THE EARLY STAGES

New York City
. . . forty-four years later . . .

ONE

In times of crisis, James Early often found himself listening to the background noise of the city, the churning mantra of Manhattan that drifted up from the streets below. Somehow all those harsh single notes—the honking horns, the squealing brakes—could blend together and end up sounding restful, like the wash of the sea.

But tonight, watching her put her clothes back on, the air was charged and full of static. He had his reasons for trampling her dignity, but he hated himself for causing her this moment.

Lit only by the flickering light from the fireplace, Kelli Girard stood with her back to him, pulling on her skirt. Usually, after being together, getting dressed was a graceful act, a physical celebration of her womanhood. But on this evening, her motions were clipped and terse. Right then, the world was an ugly place. On top of everything else, she broke another nail fighting with the buttons on her blouse. She spoke without looking up.

"Come on, Early. This stinks. Throw me a bone here. Say something that makes sense." Balancing on one foot, she leaned down and slipped on a high heel. "You won't even give me the satisfaction of a cliché. There's no 'other woman.' You're not doing the 'you deserve better' bit. Nothing. Just—bang! It's over. And you can't even tell me why?"

She stood up and smoothed down her clothes. "But I'll tell you how it feels. Like you've had your little fling with the secretary. And now it's time to toss her back into the general pool where she belongs. Cold, Early. Really cold."

He remained silent, compulsively rubbing his forehead, pushing back a clump of grey-tinged dark hair. In truth, there was too much to say, but words would trivialize it. And it had nothing to do with her, nothing to do with anything he understood. All he knew was that his mind was finally giving way. The hostile voices and images were crowding him out. And he couldn't access the language to describe it.

Kelli scanned the apartment and began collecting her things. "Let's see . . . toothbrush in the bathroom, coffee mug in the kitchen. Even a picture of me on your damn bureau. All my little inroads." Her lips formed a thin, pained smile. "And here I thought I was making progress. What a crock."

Early finally stood up. At thirty-eight years old and driven, he was still lean and muscular. A hybrid of Irish and Jewish ancestry, his thin, sculpted face seemed overwhelmed by a collection of strong irregular features. Growing up in Brooklyn and living the daily warfare of the streets had deepened and darkened the effect, giving him an intense, somewhat brooding presence. As he turned toward her, his expression remained cloaked.

"You're making it worse. This was never about the big love. We knew that from the start. We're friends, remember? Let's leave it there before we regret the whole thing."

She turned away from him, almost fiercely, then checked herself and sighed. "What's the use? You've got everyone else duped. I hear the talk. By day, the great legendary cop—intuitive, ballsy. Down at the station, a James Early hunch is considered gospel. And, on top of all that, he's a regular good guy. Nothing but hard work and 'go team, go.'"

She squinted at him in the semidarkness. "But after hours? Well, strange things come out to play. Guy's got a flip side. He's doing women, liquor, God knows what else. And here's the sad part. He's working hard at it, but the bad boy thing doesn't fit him. Doesn't fit him at all."

She paused, retrieved her earrings from the bedside table, and jammed them into her purse. "So who's James Early? The jury's absolutely still out."

Early grabbed her by the shoulders. "Listen. I'm bone-tired, and I'm not right. I have nightmares, vicious ones. I wake up sweating, with no memories—just worn out. And the pressure never quits, never gives me a day off. Right now, all I want to do is go sit on a beach somewhere and forget. But I can't. And there's no room . . . no room for anything else until I sort it all out."

He slackened his grip. "I can't care if you don't understand. I'm just asking you not to take it personally."

His words slapped her quiet. For a moment, she stopped her barrage and actually studied him. It had only been five months ago, but no, this was not the same man she had flirted with in a Soho bar. The sharp features seemed worn down, the grey-green eyes colder, more distant. Even his skin looked paler, drawn more tightly across his cheekbones. With his guard down, her sometimes-lover *did* seem ten years older and running very rough.

"Hey Early, it's the twentieth century. You feel messed up—you see somebody. There are medications that—"

"Zombies and junkies. No thanks. I'll take my chances." He mustered his best smile. "I just need to regroup. I'll get through it. People do it every day."

Kelli resumed her packing. Wadding up her negligee into a ball, she tossed it unceremoniously into her overnight bag. "I thought I got in there," she said softly, "but I swear there's an electric fence around you."

He shrugged. It was true—he avoided real intimacy. It was all about sex and liquor—mind-numbing sensation and quick routes to oblivion. That's what had gotten him through the nights. Now even that wasn't working.

The flames in the fireplace had softened into embers—a steady orange sheen bathing the room. As Kelly zipped up her bag, Early slipped on his underwear and trousers, then got her coat from the closet. Taking her arm, he navigated her around the chaos on the cluttered floor. Her traditional comment about the maid's night off went unspoken. At the door, he put his arm around her waist. His six feet towered above her diminutive frame.

"It's better for both of us this way. I mean it." He rested a hand on her shoulder. "Please take care of yourself."

"Whatever." She fixed her collar. "I'm not going to hold my breath, but if you need or want . . . hell, just a friend, call me."

She leaned up against him and gave him a girlish kiss on the cheek. Turning quickly, she disappeared down the stairs into the darkness of the lower landing.

When he could no longer hear the click of her heels, he closed the door softly, then sagged against it, exhausted from his efforts. It was getting harder and harder to hold the surface together while the foundation was breaking into pieces.

Nevertheless, he had done all right. The break was clean. A week or so from now, she would be out drinking and flirting again. She had been placated with a *piece* of the truth—not the whole grisly picture. Much better that way.

He willed himself upright and into the living room, where he collapsed into the armchair in front of the fireplace. Alone now, the fire hissed and danced quietly before him.

His eyes scrutinized the small studio apartment. He was struck by its sadness, struck by the pervading sense of loneliness. The room was inhabited, yes, but not lived in. It hadn't always been that way.

When, as a rookie cop, he had first moved in, he had commanded the space. Within months, he had turned it into a bastion of discipline and masculine aesthetics: dark wood and brick and things in their rightful places. As his condition worsened, however, things unraveled. Chaos was an easy mistress. Now, from the unmade bed to a floor strewn with empty bottles, pizza boxes, and newspapers, no sense of home was being articulated. Maybe it never would again.

Early leaned over and pulled his .38 revolver from the shoulder holster on the end table. It felt like a touchstone; the weight, the cold metal in his hand oddly soothing. The cylinder spun effortlessly beneath his fingertips. Round and round. He lifted it to his ear and smiled obliquely. Chamber music.

With the heel of his hand, he brought the spinning cylinder to an abrupt halt, then unloaded a single bullet. Turning it around between his thumb and index finger, Early examined it carefully. Sexy. A jewel of death.

Rotating the chamber slowly, he emptied the rest of the ammo into his hand until all six bullets lay nestled in his palm. They were asleep now. A family. At peace in their snug metal jackets. Then, as if feeding them to a wild animal, he began to toss the bullets, one by one, into the fireplace.

"Here's one for the sickos. One for the cop killers."

Then two more.

"For all the scumbag lawyers, corrupt politicos. You're the worse. You keep it all going. You're supposed to know better."

Without warning, the first slug hit meltdown and exploded, sending a shower of shattered brick from inside the chimney down onto the flaming logs. The second and third followed quickly as ash and smoke belched into the room.

Early's face remained impassive as he fingered the last two shells. He isolated one.

"For all of you. Your crap. Not mine anymore."

The next eruption came moments later, kicking out a fireball onto his carpet. A chunk of metal whizzed past his ear and tore into the wallpaper on the opposite wall.

The hallway outside filled with the sudden cacophony of rattling deadbolts sliding and doors flinging open and people yelling. Early ignored the commotion. Unaware of the silent tears on his cheek, he leaned closer to the pit of swirling sparks and ashes, the last bullet resting in the middle of his open hand.

"And this one, James Early, is for you. You and all your ghosts. You're broken. Don't know how to fix yourself."

A furious knocking at his door startled him back to reality.

"Hey! Hey in there! Early, you all right?"

Disoriented, the detective looked around. Caustic smoke swirled around the room. Live coals glowed on the carpet and from the side of the armchair. He stared down at the bullet still cupped in his palm. It seemed out of focus. Surreal.

The knocking came again, this time louder.

But now the sounds were far away, in someone else's bad movie. Placing the final bullet back into his gun, he adjusted the chamber. When he needed it, it would be there.

Slowly and deliberately, Early got up, went to his closet, and finished dressing. His plainclothes uniform never varied: white shirt, tie, black shoes. Beneath the grey sports jacket, his revolver and holster pressed against his ribs.

Trench coat under his arm, he crawled through the window and stepped out onto the fire escape. The sudden shift was abrasive. A sharp April wind lashed at his face. A massive city roared below.

Hands gripping the railing, he leaned out into the night. All around, the inky skyline peaked and plunged. Above, the stars shone like dull silver—cold, eternal nails hammered into the night sky.

As the wail of a siren grew closer, Early descended, zigzagging his way down to Seventy-Eighth Street.

One thing was obvious. Whatever forces were conspiring, whatever madness was overtaking him, it was about to hit critical mass.

TWO

Inside an unmarked police car, Detective Sam Jenkins blew into his cupped hands and scowled. *April, my ass!* Patches of dirty snow still crusted the ground while the wind whipped cold and strong along the street of the Lower East Side. Even though it was only eight o'clock in the morning, the yellow light of dawn already seemed stale on rooftops and along the sides of buildings.

Sam was fifty-two, Black, and girthy. For younger cops, he was the rock—a steady hand on their shoulder, a word of advice grounded in a veteran's perspective. Today, however, he felt chopped up, and all the little pieces were badgering him into one truly foul mood. Two kids in puberty, overdue bills, and heartburn—that was just for starters. Then there was his wife, who had made him get up early that morning and attend some church function before he went to work. For all he knew, God was still in her pajamas.

This meant that he had arrived ahead of schedule and would be forced to wait—something he detested. He also absolutely abhorred spending any time at all in the dreary urban blight known as Alphabet City. He hated its rats and its winos. More than anything, he hated the prospect of inhaling the stench of stale urine and watching a junkie shoot up—all while nursing his first cup of coffee.

To some extent, he could blame it on his partner, James Early. As usual, Early had announced his "hunch" at the precinct, and the Red Sea had parted. Seemingly within hours, he had muscled and charmed his way through the bureaucratic machinery, ending up with the court's reluctant blessing and an expedited search warrant. Yesterday, he had simply handed Sam a piece of paper with a time and an Avenue D address. They were going to check up on a guy named Willie Greco.

Outside of some loose ties with the mob, there was seemingly nothing current. There were, however, some explosive items on his rap sheet. Over the last ten years, he had beaten murder charges twice: one first degree, one manslaughter. With Greco, one didn't need to be a genius to figure out his character.

When Sam had questioned Early's rationale, Early's grey eyes seemed to glitter. "He's a dirty string. We're gonna yank on it, find out what's attached. Could be an old shoe, could be a great white. I'm betting there's something pretty ugly back there."

And that was that.

Feeling cramped, Jenkins finally got out of the Camry, stretched his legs, and gazed up at the sky that was beginning to cloud over. Right then, he didn't have the heart to look closely at his surroundings. Poverty, hate, and degradation never got original, and every cliché in the book was right there to greet him. Hardest of all was seeing little kids playing in the rubble, turning into young disasters. Tomorrow, he would care again. Not today.

Even though he was dressed in plain clothes and driving a nondescript car, he sensed he was attracting attention, so he walked quickly toward a gutted building next to Greco's. He'd wait for Early there. At least he'd be standing out of the cold.

Stepping inside, he immediately had second thoughts. Dank and dark, the grip of decay was stifling. From every corner, the stink of garbage and feces assaulted his nostrils. He was about to leave when he hesitated. A fraction before he heard something, he felt something. Turning his head slowly, he tried to peer through the nest of shadows surrounding the stairwell. As his pupils adjusted, he discerned the outline of a figure slumped halfway up the staircase. It seemed to be watching him.

Instinctively, Sam reached for the 9mm Glock inside his coat. One step closer, and his hand slid off the pistol—a small moan escaping his lips. The man in the shadows should have been dreck, should have been some last-ditch addict come to jam one more round of death into his veins. Instead, Sam found himself looking into the bloodshot, tear-filled eyes of his partner.

They stared at each other, then Early leaned back, merging into a sheath of darkness. The quiet, bitter laugh was barely audible.

"Now it gets weird, Jenkins—for both of us. Five minutes later, I would have been outside on the curb when you drove up. I would have had my cop face back on. Back to normal. Nothing to explain. But no, not now . . . " his voice trailed away.

With a commotion of flapping wings, a pigeon burst from its roost, disappearing through a hole in the rafters. Early turned, watching its escape. A faint stream of light seemed to float behind him, highlighting his sharp profile.

"And here's the clincher. Now I've involved you. I've put you right in the middle of it, and that's the last thing I wanted to do. Because now you're forced to do something about it, and I can't let you. I . . . I'm sorry."

Sam was still trying to assimilate. All by itself, the image of his partner was daunting: rumpled clothes, two-day growth, sitting alone in a dark, rat-infested dump.

James wrapped his arm around his knees. "For what it's worth, last night I just started walking. Sometimes that's the only thing I can think of doing. No plan, no destination—just walk. Like a black hole pulling me along. So, I ended up here—about three a.m. When the rats got bad, I walked around the block. When a couple of guys tried to tag me, I showed them my 38. I came back here and sat on these stairs. The sun came up, I was still here."

He shrugged. "Yeah, sure. It's twisted. About six people stopped in, splattered piss on the walls. I've heard fucking and fighting and a lot of rap music. In a bizarre way, it was perfect. I wanted to take a hard look, make some decisions. No frills, no padding. Nothing to cheat me out of having an honest night with myself. Now I'm ready."

Sam vacillated between anger and genuine concern, concern being more central and slowly winning out. His partner had been slipping for a long time; that had been obvious to him. The signs were all there. He had just witnessed the inevitable, and Sam felt ashamed. He should have stepped in earlier.

Sam sighed. "I need to be straight with you, man. If you stood in my shoes and got a look of you right now, you'd see a damn train wreck. Yeah, you'd wonder about drugs. But it's worse than that, James."

He peered across at his friend. "Am I clear? I'm saying you need to get some help."

Early wiped his face with the back of his sleeve. "We'll see."

"No. Just do me a favor. Go home and get some rest. I'll talk to the chief. He'll be fine with it."

Ignoring Sam, Early stood up quickly and started walking down the stairs. "Well, maybe you should call for backup then because I'm going in. The best thing for me to do right now is work. It's a stupid little interview. Don't even need you."

Sam grabbed Early's shoulder. "Don't do this, man. You're not well!"

Early pried Sam's fingers away.

Sam flinched. The touch was cold, as dry as bone.

"I *need* to do this. What will be will be. That's the law."

Steady and purposeful, Early stepped out into the sunlight, paused for a second, then spun out of view.

Sam cursed, then ran to catch up.

They entered the tenement together and started up the stairs to Willie Greco's sixth-floor walk-up, the tension thick between them. The yellow walls were peeling and covered with graffiti. Used condoms and piles of trash littered the landings; the smells of greasy cooking mingled with the odor of decaying garbage.

By the time they arrived at the fourth-floor landing, Sam was huffing and paused to catch his breath. Early stood beside him, distant and quiet.

"Talk to me, man. What is it?" Sam whispered.

Early looked down. "We've done okay, you and me. We're real different, you know. We could've been like oil and water . . . or worse. But we didn't go there."

Sam's worries flared again. He had never heard his partner sound like this before.

"And I'll tell you, the truth is, you're my best, probably my only, damn friend in the world." Early glanced up, then looked away.

Without waiting for a response, he turned and walked quickly up the remaining stairs.

When Sam finally reached the sixth floor, his partner was waiting in front of 6C.

"He's in there. I'll take point."

"I think—"

"And brother," Early pointed toward the bulge of the pistol in his partner's coat, "keep that piece warm. We may need her."

Sam took a step closer. "I have a lousy feeling about this. Let's get out of here."

Early ignored him and rapped loudly with his knuckles. "Greco? Open up!"

"Fuck off!" came the muffled response.

"We'd love to," Early barked back, "but we're the police. Coupla questions and we'll leave you alone."

"I'm busy. Come back later."

Early leaned in against the crack in the door and sharpened the edge in his voice. "Let's go, Willie. We got the warrant. Now move!"

From inside they heard scuffling footsteps, some rustling sounds, then silence. They waited. Early tried again. "Last warning. Let us in, or we break down the door. Your call."

No sound emerged. Sam glanced over at his partner. Early wouldn't meet his eye. After another pause, Sam lost his cool. "What the hell is with you? This is wrong, man. All wrong!"

Early heard his partner's voice, but it was as if he were under water. He felt faint, lightheaded. But he couldn't stop now. Not now.

With a swift step backward, he pulled out his gun. For the first time that day, he focused squarely on his partner, about to give the signal.

Then Sam finally saw it, and a chill spread down his spine. The red-rimmed eyes, the almost unearthly gleam, the quiet, desperate resolve. In Nam, he had seen the same look before a battle—soldiers under heavy stress going in under open fire. They weren't coming back, and they knew it.

Sam lunged, trying to stop him. "James!"

He was too late. Early had already thrown the full weight of his body against the door. Instantly, the brittle wood splintered, locks and hinges ripped apart. Propelled by his own momentum, Early barreled into the room through the jagged opening, Sam at his heels.

In the wavering blue light of a TV game show, Willie Greco sat on a shredded couch surrounded by pillows. He was dark and oily, dressed in a green tank top and jeans. Thin hands twitched in his lap.

His eyes greeted the intruders like two poisoned darts.

"Don't bother to get up," Early said coldly.

"Make it quick," Greco spat out. "I don't feel good an' I got work ta do."

The room looked like it had been ravaged by a hurricane. Half-empty boxes and dirty clothes were strewn all over the floor. Squashed beer cans and stacks of open girlie magazines covered the coffee table. The rest of the furniture was in varying stages of demise.

Sam thought quickly. If there were any chance for violence here, Early would find a way to draw it out. And everything about Greco said he would jump at the bait. A little prompting and he would ignite. Sam was going to have to stand between their sicknesses—between the death wish and the psychopath —and somehow get himself and Early out alive.

Keeping his eyes riveted on Greco, he stepped in front of Early.

"Easy guy, easy does it," he whispered. "We're just going to slide back out of here. Slow. No one gets hurt."

Early pushed him aside. No show of emotion. He was busy scanning the room, making mental notes. Almost completely camouflaged in the brown carpet lay a small spoon, discolored by flame. Although Willie's hasty cover-up had missed it, Early was right there. The needling began.

"Just what kind of work do you do?"

"I got a little business. Nothin' wrong with that. Now ask your fuckin' questions and get the hell out!"

A door leading to another room, presumably the bedroom, was closed. An unmade cot was pushed against the far wall of the living room. Early's inner alarm went off. It was always in the details, the small discrepancies that led to big disclosures. He tugged on the "dirty string."

"Let me get this straight," Early said dryly. "You sleep in this room . . . but you got this other room? Maybe your mother's taking a nap in there. Maybe it's just storage. Mind if we take a look?"

"Suit yourself."

Greco's eyes hardened, and the space between the three men crackled with an electrical charge.

"Sam," Early said, "while Mr. Greco and I have a little chat, why don't you check it out?"

Sam didn't move. "Damn it, James."

But the dance had already begun, the players in motion. Early stepped closer to the punk, his gun angled at the floor—tempting him, egging him on. Willie's face tightened, his body began to coil. Soon they were only a few feet apart. Then a slight motion. Greco's hand slithered like a serpent beneath a pillow. Early inched closer.

Their eyes met—metal to metal.

Somewhere a voice was telling Early to fling himself to the floor and fire first . . . fire the single bullet he had left in his chamber. Somewhere in the background, he could feel Sam's hand pressing on his back. His voice pleading. Now all of that was a blur . . . now all behind him. None of it mattered.

With a sudden heave, he pushed back and felt his partner fall away.

Unencumbered, almost giddy, he launched through empty space out across the threshold where the ghosts couldn't haunt him, where the savage guilt would leave him alone. All he had to do was pay the price.

His gun aimed directly at Greco, he paused for a millisecond before firing into Willie's heart.

In that infinitesimal gap, Willie's finger squeezed the trigger first. The angry nose of an AK-47 exploded. From point-blank range, flame and metal blasted through the pillow and into the wholly exposed body of James Early.

*   *   *

... In a small, desolate canyon in New Mexico, a shower of machine-gun bullets mysteriously flew from a "hole" in the sky and ricocheted harmlessly against the rocks. A coyote howled, birds scattered from their perches on craggy trees, and the sound of gunshots faded away among the hills. ...

The diversion had been successful.

*   *   *

On another plane of existence, two beings conferred. They had just violated the sacred, time-honored rule of nonintervention. Both understood the implications. *The fabric of the karmic web had just been irrevocably changed, altering the spacing between deed and consequence. Now, time itself would be infected and become a rogue element in the mix.*

Saddened, the elder spoke before departing. "Remember, we lick honey from the razor blade. If blood is spilled, so be it. The burden is now on his shoulders."

*   *   *

The canned applause and tinny voices of the game show droned on. Willie Greco lay sprawled across the couch, silent as stone. A frenzy of feathers still spiraled through the air in the wake of the bullet-ravaged pillow—some landing on the furniture, some settling in the hair and against the cheek of the corpse. Lower down, blood oozed from the hole above the heart—the shirt thickening with dark warmth.

Early lay face down in stunned silence beside the sofa. What just happened? He must have blacked out.

Something heavy rested across his back. Dreamlike, he reached behind to touch it and shuddered—a hand. One of Willie's lifeless arms had draped itself across his shoulder. Early slid out from under it and took a deep breath. Then another. Tentatively, he reached down and spread his fingers across the stomach area where the volley of bullets should have entered. No tear, no gash. Only the stiff, unyielding cloth of his trench coat. *How can this be?*

Early slowly hauled himself to his feet. Sam stood across the room, ten feet away—mouth hanging open, eyes popping with hysteria. A strange voltage passed between them: *Are we hallucinating? Crazy? Dead?*

With no place in their minds to channel this, their internal wiring hit overload and began to short-circuit. Spastic smiles bubbled up. Simultaneously, both detectives burst into convulsive laughter.

"Man oh man oh man," Sam wheezed, "I can't handle this."

Doubled over and gasping, all Early could manage was a series of moans. For a while, delirium reigned. Unchecked, their minds pinballed between confusion, denial, and overwhelm—subsiding for a moment, then surging up again.

But while his body shook uncontrollably, Early found himself still looking inward. He had wanted to die. He *should* have died. *What was happening?*

The sound of crunching glass nearby interrupted his reverie. A few feet away, Sam was leaning over, checking Greco's pulse. "Gone."

Then he sniffed the barrel of the machine gun and collected some empty shells from the floor. He studied them in his hand, slowly standing up.

"AK-47 fired—six, maybe seven rounds," he said, trying to mask his terror and amazement. "Mind telling me where the slugs went?"

Early didn't try to answer.

Clearing his throat, Jenkins walked rubber-legged into the kitchen, where a phone hung beside the refrigerator. Somehow he was going to have to make his report to the station. They had two dead bodies. One of them, however, was very much alive.

Literally shell-shocked, Early forced himself back to work. *The bedroom. That was what got Greco boiling in the first place.* Pushing the door open, he took one step into the room and stopped. Nothing had prepared him for this.

"Sam . . . ," he called weakly.

No response.

He tried again, louder. "Hey, Jenkins! There's more. Come check this out!"

Sam hung up the phone. A moment later, he stood beside Early—both staring up into the room. Confronting them was row after row of shelving. On every shelf, neatly stacked, were white plastic bags.

"Not food for the homeless," Early said, trying to stay calm. "Let's have a look."

Unfolding a stepladder that was wedged in behind the door, he climbed up and grabbed a bag from the top of a pile. He sniffed and cautiously examined the powdery contents.

Early descended, his face a poor rendition of deadpan.

"So . . . ?" Sam asked.

"Great White," Early said, the giddy twinkle beginning to emerge in his eyes again. "Heroin. Uncut. A mother lode."

Once again, the strange voltage passed between them. This time neither laughed. The chances of uncovering a stash of this magnitude, under these conditions, were unthinkable. Not even plausible.

"You seal the room. Think I'll go wait for the boys outside." Sam made a hasty retreat.

Early waited until his partner had gone, then wandered back into the living room and shut off the TV. Relieved to be alone, he was thankful for a few minutes of solitude before the next storm arrived. For some reason, he felt drawn to the dead body. As though magnetized, he moved closer and closer to it, then bent over.

Greco's eyes were wide open, the pupils huge and black. Early stared down. It seemed that if he looked into them long enough, a tunnel would open up, wide enough for him to follow. Then he could hunt down the soul, wherever it had gone. The tracks would be fresh.

Where are you, Greco? What the hell are you looking at now?

THREE

By now, the bullets fired in New York had cooled in the dry air of New Mexico—unseen and without consequence. But the aftershock of the mysterious "intervention" was still spreading out along the karmic web. A stone had been dropped. The ripples had begun. Yet most of the world slept on, unaware of any subterfuge in the larger picture. A few "sensitives" around the globe, however, gazed warily at the phenomenon . . . and took note.

One did much more.

In a penthouse suite on Fifth Avenue, the alabaster fingers of an albino psychic flew along the keyboard of a computer. A moment later, a fax was sent across the sea.

In a silent vault full of arcane weaponry, buried below an estate in Ascot, England, a reciprocal machine sprang to life, spitting out instructions on pristine white paper. When the transmission was over, the room returned to its musty stillness.

*　*　*

The Outskirts of London

It was lunchtime, and the women workers clustered about the sidewalks alongside the factory were smoking cigarettes and chatting disinterestedly with their friends. Their dull routine was about to be invaded.

At the end of the block, a car slid around the corner. Slowly, heads turned to follow as the black Mercedes glided stealthily down the narrow street in their direction.

One girl stopped chewing her gum. As she watched, a spark of interest glinted in her bored eyes. "Moves like a bloody shark, don't it?" she said sideways to her friends. "Maybe it wants to feed?"

"*My* lunch break, not his. He can bugger off!" an older woman shot back. "Besides, I'm no fish. I douched yesterday!"

The girls began to laugh—all but the first one. She was already reaching into her handbag for her mirror. After a quick touch-up with lip liner, she pushed back her auburn hair, smoothed out the sweater across her ample breasts, and squared her shoulders. "Eat yer fuckin' puddin'," she flung over her shoulder. "I got thirty-five minutes to kill." With an exaggerated swing of her hips, she left the group and approached the car.

"You stupid twit!" the other woman yelled. But the girl didn't look back.

"She'll find out," the woman said, turning to her friends. "Lord Asshole was here last month. Our litt'l Jeanie was sick for a week. Still can't get a word outta 'er."

Malcolm Raines sat back and guided his dark ship past the row of old buildings toward his prey. Through the tinted glass, he could see a young woman detaching herself from the crowd. *Good, a player. Now the bait.*

He pushed a button, and the passenger window slid down. While he remained in shadow, he offered the girl a view of his bejeweled hand, idly stroking the soft leather upholstery of the empty seat.

Today would just be a tease. He wanted to feel the rush of blood between his legs. He wanted the aching demand for release to fill his mind and body, then hold it there. A fax from the albino psychic had been discovered this morning, suggesting Malcolm speed up his timetable. He paid good money for these advices and had agreed. In a short time, he would be challenged by a far more important target than factory girls. Then he could unleash the full beauty of his violence.

"Hallo in there? Anybody 'ome?" Malcolm turned to see the girl's chest framed in the open window. Her breasts were pushed outward against a tight red sweater, bouncing up and down as she walked up beside the car.

Malcolm smiled to himself, and his heart speeded up. Gently, he patted the seat with his right hand.

"Cat got yer tongue?" the girl asked nervously, trying to get a look inside.

There was a sharp click and the door unlocked. "Get in," he commanded.

Still walking beside the Mercedes, the girl gripped the outside handle and started to lean in to see the driver's face. "Yer manners are—" she began to say.

But the sentence went unfinished. As soon as her crimped hair and weak chin became visible, Malcolm sent the window back up and pressed on the gas pedal. The black car accelerated suddenly and pulled away down the street, flinging the girl to the ground.

In his rearview mirror, he saw the young woman getting to her feet, brushing herself off—her face contorted with anger, her mouth spitting obscenities in his direction. But Malcolm couldn't hear her. Vivaldi was already thundering through the car speakers. He felt righteous. Weakness was so unattractive. Those who *could* be manipulated *would* be manipulated. Those who could control would control. That was the law of the universe. All he had done was administer justice.

As he gunned his Mercedes along the M4, he held the steering wheel between his knees so his free hands could retrieve a crystal vial, a small silver spoon, and a precise amount of cocaine from his glove compartment.

A moment later, the graceful music of antiquity had smoothed out all the creases in his mind, and the chronic pain in his thigh was forgotten. Settling back into his seat, he watched for the exit to Heathrow Airport. Tonight he would fly behind enemy lines and onto American soil. His next victim needed to be a masterpiece.

FOUR

New York City

Danny Santano, the owner of Danny's Donuts on Twenty-Second Street, was having a moment. He stood in the doorway surveying the waving arms, cameras, and microphones of the media surrounding his store, a faint sneer creeping onto his face. This was good. Time for a little payback.

With the door almost shut, he yelled through the last bit of crack, "Stay outta here, all a ya! I'm closed for the next two hours. Go spread your slime somewhere else!"

Outside the store, hands pounded on the windows and pointed to the two sleepy policemen sitting at a corner table.

"Tough luck!" Danny shouted back, fully enjoying the role. "They're not scumbags like you. You gotta problem, call the mayor!"

Bolting the door, he flipped over the Open sign to Closed. Then, moving quickly around the tables, he lowered the window blinds.

"There, a little privacy," he said to the two detectives. "Now, you boys just relax. And use the back door when you leave. Fuckin' media don't know when they're beaten. I'll tell ya, it's been a real pleasure throwin' 'em out!"

"Thanks, Danny," Early called out from the corner. "Owe you one!"

A moment later, the owner was in the adjacent room listening to Italian folk music, cooking up another batch of his famous donuts, leaving the two detectives to themselves.

"Total circus," Sam said to his partner, dipping the final third of a glazed buttermilk into his cup of coffee. "Biggest thing anyone ever saw. They listed Greco's stash, street value, around a hundred mill. That'll get you front-page news any day."

He leaned over the table. "Imagine what they'd do if they knew about the disappearing bullet show."

Early's face clouded. He wiped some crumbs from his chin with a napkin and spoke sharply. "Yeah, well, that's going to stay our little secret."

For a moment, they munched in silence.

Early broke the ice. "DEA's totally mystified. Little Willie Greco with all that smack. Feds are all over it now, running prints, DNA, the works. But nobody knows. Theory number one says Greco was skimming off the top. A bag here, a few bags there.

"Saving his pennies. A little while later, he'd have been by the pool in Acapulco with the goodies on their way to Chicago. Unbelievable."

Sam shifted his weight in the chair, uncomfortable with his thoughts. "Not just unbelievable, it's totally unreal. Totally! I mean, what are the odds?"

Early slowly turned the Styrofoam cup around in his hands. "The whole day was from another planet."

Sam suddenly thrust his face forward, eyes sharp as tacks. "No shit! I mean, damn it, man, those were *real* bullets. And they *didn't* miss. You should be in the downtown morgue, not having your face plastered on every front page and TV screen in America!"

Sam shifted again and took a quick sip of coffee. "That's Bermuda Triangle material. I ain't goin' there. But that's not the hard part. The hard part is asking you why the hell you wanted to die! Why you *wanted* to take those damn bullets! I have no doubt that's what you were doing."

Early had tried to prepare himself for this—to mount some shore story, find a way to deflect his friend's heartfelt worry before it became untenable for both. He hadn't found a way to do that. More than anger or frustration, however, he felt his friend's sense of betrayal. Early had let him down in the most fundamental aspect. He had tried to break his pact with the living.

"I don't wanna bullshit you, so I won't try," Early said finally. "It's over. Let's just let it go."

"Not good enough, man. We're old friends. We go back. I just want you to give it to me straight-up."

Early rubbed the back of his hand across the edge of his jaw, trying to clear his mind, trying to get the language to work for him.

"All right then, try this on for size. It's like you're in a dream. Vague, almost surreal. You're walking around and something doesn't feel right. You've done something wrong. I mean, seriously wrong. After a while, you start getting the idea that you're in some kind of jail, doing time. No prison bars, no guards, nobody's announced it—but man, you're doing time. The real problem is, you don't know what you're in for. You just feel bad. You just don't know what you did."

He sighed. "Pretty soon you're desperate. You want someone to come along with handcuffs. Someone to come up and say, 'Okay, you did this terrible thing. You're guilty of such and such.' The charge is very specific. Bingo—pure joy, man. It makes you happy 'cause it's not grey and nameless anymore. Now you *finally* understand *why* you're a bad person. Ten years of hard labor. Fine. I'll do it."

Early closed his fist and pounded softly on the table. "That would be a relief, Sam. Don't you see?"

"Guilt is one thing. But why do yourself in?"

"The past few months, this whole thing's been building up. Yesterday it hit meltdown. All I wanted to do was shut down the noise . . . be the lynch mob, throw the rope over the limb, and do the job myself."

Sam threw his hands up in frustration. "Jesus, man! You're talking suicide. That's seriously fucked up!"

Early leaned back. For a moment, both detectives sat listening to the faint strains of violin and concertina coming from Danny's backroom.

Sam played with the knot of his tie. "You're not going to like this. I didn't even want to tell you. But last night, I wrote up a report on you. About . . . about your mental state. It's not real flattering. I'm turning it in before I go home tonight."

Early felt the anger surge, then squelched it. There was no duplicity here. Sam always followed his heart.

"Come on. I already admitted that I was—"

"Damn it! Get outta yourself and look at it from my side. I got a wife and three kids. You're supposed to have my back. I've got to trust you're gonna be there for me and make the right call. I just can't mess around with this."

Early grimaced. "I deserved that. I'm sorry. But hear me one more time. This *is* straight, from me to you. We were great as a team before. We'll be great again. I'll *never* pull that stunt again. *Never*. That whole bizarre scene at Greco's forced me to . . . to come to my senses. Now I have a second chance. I'm not about to throw it away. If nothing else, I want to understand what the hell happened in that room. That's the truth. I swear it."

Sam shook his head. "I don't know. You're family. I just hate watching . . . "

Early reached across the table and put a hand on his partner's arm. "Sam, doubt me, second-guess me, be distrustful, whatever, but don't pull the plug. You've seen me hit rock-bottom. Just hang in there with me a little longer. You won't regret it."

Sam continued to stare at his friend, trying to separate truth from fiction. Early had always been a master salesman.

Early proffered his hand. "No report?"

Sam wavered, then slowly clasped it. "No report," he echoed softly.

Choked with emotion, he pushed himself away from the table. "Listen, I gotta get back to the station. Coming?"

Early pointed to his empty cup. "Gonna have one more. By the way, that press conference is scheduled at three. It's supposed to air tonight."

Sam nodded and reached down to pull his coat off the back of his chair.

Early tapped above his heart with a finger. "Hey, someday those bullets will just fall outta here. Then we'll have a good laugh."

Sam didn't smile.

Early watched his partner disappear behind the counter on his way to Danny's private exit. He poured himself another cup from the pot on the warmer while his mind continued to whir, nothing falling into place.

A few minutes later, he drained his cup, placed a five-dollar bill beside the cash register, and left the shop, thanking Danny on his way out. And yet, as he walked along Twenty-Second Street, the central question continued to haunt him: *If I've been given some kind of reprieve, what in God's name am I supposed to do with it?*

FIVE

The Teaser Club

Desda Collins held the cigarette between her slender fingers accented with dark burgundy nails and watched the delicate smoke stream from the glowing tip and circle upward. If not her friend, cigarettes were at least her companion. She liked the vibe—sometimes aesthetic and sexy, sometimes cheap and degraded. As long as she had her cigarettes, she was never really alone.

Desda shivered and drew the gold satin cape closer around her bare shoulders, pushing back her long dark hair. She was next up and sat waiting on a metal folding chair in the wings of the stage. The Teaser Club liked its girls ready and willing. She was neither, but the money made it tolerable. She had started stripping there three years ago when the streets had become too brutal. Twenty-seven at the time, she was old enough to know better but too desperate to care. Working the main room night after night never got easier. She never got used to it. If she ever did, that would be the end.

The music in the background began to fade, signaling the dancer on stage was almost done. Exhaling a final blue cloud, Desda crushed out the cigarette against the side of a bottle of J&B, sparks cascading down to the floor.

There was a thin smatter of applause, and Ginger Michaels burst through the cloth partition wearing nothing but a black cowboy hat and red sequin panties. The rest of her discarded costume was balled up in a wad under her arm.

"Man, it's weird out there. Navy boys or something." She ripped off her blond wig. "Watch your ass!"

Then, noticing Desda's bottle, she added, "Mind if I . . . "

"Help yourself." Desda absently handed her the scotch. "Strange, isn't it? Those guys think they rule, yell a few obscenities, act like they own us. Funny thing, all we have to do is take off our clothes and they become our slaves."

Ginger took a sip and grimaced. Wiping off the mouth of the bottle with her palm, she passed it back. "You know, sometimes you say these things, like I can't figure out why you're here. I mean, you're smart, classy. I see guys, rich guys, coming all over themselves to get to you. Screw the lap dance—you could walk outta here with any one of them. And yet you won't give them the time of day. Hey, I'm eighteen, what do I know? But if some rich dude made me an offer, I'd jump."

Desda regarded Ginger with tired affection, then tilted back in her chair. "No, I don't jump. A lot of guys make me pissy. Especially the kind that ends up in here. Most of the time, the only way I can strip is to keep them at a distance—make believe they're not even there. But sometimes I just feel mean. Sometimes I want to drive them right up to the edge, get them into a feeding frenzy, then walk away. Leave them bleeding. Like they deserve it. Now *that's* evil. It really is, and I don't know why I do it."

Ginger was slightly taken aback. Desda was the mother confessor, the veteran, never fully blending in, never sticking out. Yet here she was getting personal, talking trash, like the rest of them.

Ginger pressed on. "When you were a kid, did you get . . . were you ever . . . ?"

"Abused?" Desda answered, smirking slightly. "No. No, I did that all by myself. Didn't need any help. I was raised in an orphanage by nuns. Catechism, Hail Marys, the whole deal. Believe me, they tried to get me clean as the driven snow. It didn't take. No matter how hard they scrubbed, they couldn't reach deep enough to get to the dirt. It was like it was already way down in there."

Desda lit up again, shaking out the match with a practiced flick of her wrist, inhaling deeply.

"Then . . . oh, I don't know, Kerouac, Coltrane, Hesse. All those old guys. They told me to get honest, to stop living a lie, and I started getting restless. So I ran away. The problem is, the lies always follow. If not today, then tomorrow. The lies always catch up."

Ginger lowered her eyes, scraping at a cuticle with her thumbnail. Now she looked like an overgrown child about to cry.

Desda gently took the girl's hand. "Forget it. I'm just a little burned-out tonight. Hang here a little longer, save up your cash, go to California like you were saying yesterday. Lotta good-looking guys with money out there."

"Yeah . . . well, we'll see."

The young dancer stood awkwardly for a moment, eyes downcast, then fled down the corridor to the dressing rooms.

Desda chastised herself. The girl was fragile. Lost. Still yanked around by hormones. The last thing she needed was a dose of secondhand bitterness.

She sighed and waited.

Then it began: the expectant hush in the room, the voice of the MC announcing her act. Finally, The Stones' "Gimme Shelter"—the faint opening guitar lick snaking through the speakers.

Showtime.

Steeling herself, she stood up—five-foot-five, with a slim but athletic figure. Normally her intelligent blue eyes were ablaze with conflicting passions. As she worked herself into the mindset, however, she mentally extinguished all the underlying warmth.

Past the drawn curtains, the music grew louder and more ominous. The houselights dimmed. Chairs squeaked forward in anticipation. Talk stopped abruptly. New flesh was coming.

With short, quick strides, Desda walked out into the middle of the darkened stage. Breathing shallowly, she waited. Then the overhead spot took charge, driving its harsh light down against her face, bathing her body in light. Immediately, catcalls and whistles erupted from around the room. She could almost feel their fantasies brush against her skin, like the fins of sharks in murky waters. Ginger had been right. Tonight, the predators were out in force. Her shields would need to be up and full-on.

Desda began her final preparations. Like driving a car while daydreaming, she had learned to perform while letting her mind go elsewhere. The pouts, the coy smiles, the slow undulations—they were all programmed in, all handled by auto-pilot. No one ever suspected she was missing in action.

Internally, Desda began to wall off her emotions, to detach herself from the scene. Since she was a child, she had always fled to the same secret hiding place inside herself. A destination. A sensation. Someplace far away. But she could never quite remember where the pictures came from or why they were so indelible.

Focusing in, her mind filled with the familiar images: a crescent moon shining down over snowy mountains, a black sky, vast and full of stars—a sense of peace.

She brought it in, closer and closer, until it surrounded her heart. With opaque eyes, she turned to meet the audience. Time to throw back a kiss. Time to lift her arms dramatically. Time to pause and let them want her.

"Give it good, baby!" someone yelled out.

Desda cringed. The room was *definitely* combustible. Vowing not to give in to them, she forced her pictures back into place and went on with her ritual. Flanked by bass and drums, Jagger's raspy voice cut through the smoky air. Everything under control again, her body began to dance.

The cloak was unfastened, twirled on fingertips, pulled across the groin, then dropped, pooling at her feet. The pelvis thrust forward toward the crowd, grinding slowly. Hands slid along the curve of her breasts, down to her thighs.

As their gutter calls assailed her, Desda felt a spike of anger erupt inside. She refocused. Immediately, the vast black sky was there again, the still air of mountains wrapping around her like a blanket.

The catcalls bounced off, fell away.

Now on autopilot, she separated from herself and dispassionately watched her body move, like a puppet on a string. . . .

The dancer moved mechanically toward the enemy camp, stopping at the edge of the stage, crouching down inches from bloated faces and waving arms. Sweaty hands with dollar bills found the G-string. The dancer held still while dollar bills clustered around the waist. Mission accomplished, the dancer retreated to center stage.

The worst was over. All she had to do was remove her string bikini top, and the ordeal would be over.

Pressing her pelvis against the pole, she arched into a deep backbend until her hair touched the floor. Her hand went behind her back to untie her top. Building the suspense, she held the pose and looked out across the room.

From this angle, as always, she found herself staring sideways into the corner of the bar where the huge TV was stationed. The ten o'clock news was on: a massive drug bust, a dead dealer. The camera zooming in on a detective being interviewed. A close-up of his face—his eyes somehow reaching past the interview, out through the screen into Desda's heart.

For that instant, the fetid world of the Teaser Club receded and there was only Desda and this man. Her heart speeded up, and something buried inside her threatened to jog loose.

Riveted to the screen, she stood up slowly, dropping her hands to her sides. She was no longer part of the act. From nowhere, the thought flared in her mind: *We're not supposed to remember!*

Transfixed, Desda wasn't even aware that the crowd was becoming furious. Rowdy men were standing up, jeering, demanding their payment of skin. Wadded-up cocktail napkins pelted her motionless body. But now she didn't care.

Intangible and without explanation, her world had already begun to shift.

Ripping her gaze away from the screen, she looked incredulously around the dank club, blinking rapidly. *This was wrong! All wrong. What in God's name was she doing here?!*

When the first bottle smashed against the stage, she flinched and stepped back. But now, years of suppressed anger finally boiled to the surface. It was time for her to get out of this mess. She would not leave quietly.

Still holding the pole, she leaned down and tore off one of her high heels. With a cry, she hurled the shoe, hitting the overhead spotlight. Glass shattered, shards pouring down from the rafters like angry rain. In the smoke and stink of burning wires, Desda tore the dollar bills from her G-string. Jamming them into a tight ball, she heaved it into the sea of lewd faces.

The yells became deafening. A chair hit the platform beside her, slid across the floor, and splintered against the pole. Customers were now turning on each other, threatening to unleash a full-scale brawl.

Desda paused, stunned by the fury she had evoked. But before she allowed any second thoughts to change her mind, she plunged ahead. Broken glass glinting in her hair, she kicked off her other shoe and stepped forward, directly facing the crowd.

"Wake up!" she screamed at the livid faces. "Wake up, you fucking idiots!" Hands on hips, she glared for a long moment, then shook her head slowly.

Turning on her heel, she marched off the stage.

An ashtray crashed against the wall, narrowly missing her head. She barely noticed, her mind already spinning toward the future. Her rent might go unpaid, but she would survive. Her life might fall apart—she would build a new one. In all of this, she would land on her feet and never look back. The marathon dance was finally over.

The manager was waiting for her in the dressing room, purple with fury, ready to tear into her. Instead, Desda hurled her body against his, knocking him off balance just long enough to grab her purse and coat. Bursting through the back exit, she raced into the street. Heady with a sense of freedom, she flew toward her car. Somehow, the man on the screen had been the trigger, the catalyst. *What was that all about? What weren't they supposed to remember?*

Pulling away from the curb, she adjusted her rearview mirror. Whoever he was, wherever he lived, now *she* had to find him.

SIX

Poised at the bottom of the subway exit, Early looked up wearily. The imposing flight of stairs seemed to stretch on and on—out past the streets, up into the sky. Climbing slowly, he continued to gaze upward until he reached the sidewalk. It was eleven p.m., and he was just getting off work.

Like the feathers in Greco's apartment, the aftermath of the shoot-out refused to settle down. The Thirteenth Precinct was nowhere close to getting back to normal. Sam was still awkward around Early, the chief uncharacteristically cozy, the media still fighting for table scraps.

The real story was harder to fathom. He was no longer just a cop. No longer a loner with a death wish. In fact, he was no longer anyone he could comprehend. If anything, he felt like a ghost walking through his old haunts, stuck in some kind of perpetual twilight, waiting for the next shoe to drop.

Early made his way uptown to his apartment on Seventy-Eighth Street, between Columbus and Amsterdam. Over the years, Columbus Avenue had rejected its roots and become gilded over by glitz with posh restaurants and high-end coffee bars.

Amsterdam, however, had remained true to its grit. As always, it lived out its passions to the fullest through the food, music, and drama of its people. Here you could find Blacks, Hispanics, Jews, gays, Poles, and Italians all pushed up against each other, all making a go of it.

Early always chose this route whenever he had the chance to walk. Particularly at this moment in his life, he cherished anything that had the stamp of authenticity—anything that had the tenacity to cling to its character despite all reasons not to.

Passing God's Gift pawnshop, he heard a series of guitar riffs and squinted up ahead to see where the noise was coming from. There, assaulting every passing pedestrian with posture and vibe rippling with attitude, was a street musician—indeterminate age, rock 'n roll-thin, with big, mangy hair. A dark-green beret served as his donation hat, aggressively pushed into the middle of the sidewalk—bills and coins expected.

Early suddenly felt his guard go up. There was an intrusive quality about this man.

Walking closer, the two men made eye contact. The hairs on Early's neck prickled upward. Not from a sense of danger, but from the feeling that his personal space had just been frisked.

Once Early was alongside, the wiry guitar player lifted his long fingers from the strings and glared. "It's about time," he admonished harshly, as if Early had been late for a scheduled appointment.

Taken aback, Early was instantly flooded with a push-pull of emotions. The man was trouble, and Early shouldn't engage. At the same time, there was something compelling here.

Keeping Early pinned with his eyes, the musician leaned forward as if sharing a secret. "I'm on to you, bro. Might be front-page news now, but I'm not buying. You got back issues, dude. You getting me?" He paused for a moment studying the detective, then added, "Be ready. The spirit's about to slam dance."

Early stood flat-footed—no idea how to process this.

The musician remained deadpan, then a faint twinkle kicked into his dark eyes. "A little of me goes a long way. Tell me I'm right."

"Who the hell are you?" Early asked testily.

"Me?" he smirked, relishing the possibilities. "I'm complicated. A dash of lightning, some skid marks . . . throw in a saxophone wailing from a tenement window. That'll do for the intro."

He tilted his head sideways to check Early's expression as if making sure he was properly impressed.

Early remained impassive.

The musician waited, then begrudgingly nodded toward his hat on the pavement. "Chill. I'm just another street dude looking for something to eat."

"You're quite a performance," Early said dryly.

"Look, you're no paint-by-number job either," the musician said, resting his arm on the curve of the guitar. "You're messy. You gotta bumpy stairway to heaven to climb. Lemme give you some advice."

Before Early could react, the guitar player launched. "It's all about *change*—not spare change—talkin' 'bout the big bad beautiful stuff. Rubles of the gods."

Exasperated, Early turned to go, but the man caught him by the elbow with surprising strength. "Get a clue. The membrane's thin right now, razor-thin. Check your calendar—you might have made some plans."

An inscrutable look flashed across the musician's face. "Okay, now give me something for my trouble." Then he started to play again as if dismissing the current audience to court a new one.

Early rocked back on his heels. The man was a sideshow. Slowly withdrawing a five-dollar bill from his wallet, he said, "Impressive. But you didn't answer my question. What's your name?"

The musician shook his head with disgust. "Names, labels. You miss the point, man. Your kind always does."

"And your kind always ends up broke, playing for dimes on street corners. "Come on, what's your name?"

"Trakker," he spat out as if cornered and forced to surrender. "Hit the K twice on the way out!"

Turning back to the trickle of pedestrians passing by, he broke into his next song. Early dropped the bill into the empty hat, then patted the musician on the shoulder before walking away. "Get yourself some manners, kid. You'll eat better."

Early continued uptown, walking slowly to his home a few blocks away. In a mind already overcrowded with the unexplained, there was no place to store this encounter—the man or his words. All he could do was add one more question mark to the growing list.

Rounding the corner, home in sight, he stopped, breathed deeply, and tried to reign in the barrage of thoughts assailing him from every side. Instinctively, he looked up to follow the blinking red light of a low-flying jet moving in and out of thickening clouds.

It's all shifting, he thought. Whatever was going on, whatever forces were at play, he was being driven into uncharted waters. He could tear up the old blueprints. Nothing would ever be the same.

SEVEN

Early's Apartment

Two-twelve a.m. The green numbers on the digital clock gleamed in the dark. Glowering, Early rolled over one more time, a whitewater tangle of sheets following in his wake.

A moment later he kicked his legs free and finally sat up. This was ridiculous. After two hours of slogging it out, he still couldn't find the sweet spot—on his mattress or in his head.

Oddly enough, in the whole thorny mess, the prickliest piece belonged to the street musician. Amid the man's razzle-dazzle, there seemed to be a point sticking up. But what was it?

For the umpteenth time, Early ran the encounter. This time, one slice separated itself from the whole. Trakker had said, "The membrane's thin. Check your calendar—you might have made some plans."

So be it.

Grabbing his daybook from the desk, he climbed back into bed. Reading light on, pillows propped up behind him, he leaned back and studied his well-worn black book. Somehow it felt different, lighter than usual. It even seemed to give off a little heat.

Turning the pages, he scanned his appointments. What was this? He hadn't scheduled anything before work. The space should have been blank. Yet something was written there. Adjusting the light, he looked down. One word. A name. *Tibet.*

Early immediately felt challenged. *Tibet? Why Tibet?* An obscure country he knew nothing about. *How did that get in my calendar?* Even more peculiar, it was written in his own handwriting. But *he* hadn't written it!

Feeling somehow betrayed, he hurled the book. It sailed across the room, crashing against the bureau.

But the disturbance continued to escalate. Suddenly lightheaded, Early rubbed his forehead. None of this made sense. Now the latent power in the word was gaining strength. It seeped inside, pulling him like an undertow toward something far away and long forgotten. Poised to resist, he inexplicably let go. Energy depleted, mind numb, his body slumped deeper into the pillows.

Now in the corridor of dreams, he felt himself turning inward, folding backward, slipping between the cracks of amnesia to a place buried in the past.

*   *   *

Memory Dream: Tibet, 1950

His initial impression was that he was being led somewhere by something. Disclosure came in stages. First, the black pupils of fierce blue eyes, then the white fur, then the tail. Gradually, three feet ahead, the form of a white Bengal tiger began to fill out. Soon, the rest of the surroundings became tangible: snow-peaked mountains jutting into a crystal blue sky, thin rarefied air—a world completely devoid of human contamination. Vast and silent, it could have been the beginning of time . . . or the end.

Early found himself following the white Bengal along a craggy path leading down the mountainside. There was no sound from his footsteps, no weight on his feet. In fact, the main thing he experienced was an incredible sense of relief.

As the trail descended to the right, the huge cat turned its majestic head as if in salutation, then loped away, blending back into the glistening white snow.

Alone now, Early heard voices up ahead and followed the sound. A moment later, he came upon a small cluster of buildings hidden away in the rocky cliffs. Jutting out from sheer rock, a stairway led up to a massive wooden door—all eerily familiar, underscored by faint understanding. *He had been summoned to the monastery. The tiger was the messenger.*

Early was confounded. How did he know these things? *Was this a scene from a book or a movie?*

Mystified yet intrigued, he cautiously ventured up the staircase to a courtyard overlooking the valley.

Two figures, an older man and child, sat near the edge of the cliff. The elder, dressed in the traditional reddish robe of a Buddhist monk, was leaning back on his hands, illuminated by morning sunlight against the backdrop of the Himalayas. His shaved head, smooth skin, and fine-boned Asian features gave him an almost youthful appearance—in contrast to the troubled light in his eyes as he gazed out across the valley.

Watching him, Early was flooded with warmth. *How well I know that look!*

Sitting alongside the master, quietly basking in his attention, was a teenage boy with dark olive skin and gentle brown eyes. In his hands was a blue rice bowl that he held with reverence—it was a gift that had just been bestowed upon him. An honor, a moment to savor.

Suddenly the quietude was shattered. A throng of men and women poured out through the doors of the monastery, spilling into the courtyard—faces flushed, talking feverishly. In contrast to the monk, the diversity of style, dress, and culture was evident. There were beards and burkas, old and young, men and women—Caucasian, Asian, Black.

One member of the group caught Early's eye. A leathery face and gaunt frame. *The name, Jori, flickered in his mind, then fell from view.*

Strangely elated, Early's gaze instinctively returned to the young boy and he shivered. *He knew this child. He loved and feared this child. He...*

The words faded as the dream began to shut down, the environment pixelating and breaking apart.

Losing his bearings, Early felt the undertow, spiraling him backward through a network of images: a squad car, the playground in Brooklyn, the bars of his crib ... further and further back ... until a shard from the past freed itself from hostage and hit with urgency:

The child he loved and feared. The jaded cop—one and the same!

But something sinister was connected ... an apparition in the distance, moving closer ...

A second later, Early woke up gasping for air—soaked in sweat, disoriented, his eyes darting around the apartment.

It was just a dream. He was an NYPD detective. Nothing more, nothing less.

EIGHT

The Plaza Hotel

Per request, Cecilly Thompson placed the English beer on a silver platter and walked through the kitchen to the service elevator. A guest named Malcolm Raines was staying in Room 1066, and he wanted his Whatney's *now*! Dressed in her starched white and beige uniform, she stepped into the car and pushed the button, careful not to tip the tray.

Cecilly was twenty years old and had recently emigrated from England to join her divorced mother in New York. She felt privileged to have immediately secured a job at a hotel like the Plaza—an elegant refuge for the rich and famous.

At night after work, she would get into bed with her *Victoria* magazine and savor the romantic images—page after page, dream after dream. In the Plaza Hotel, you might meet the kind of man who could lift you off your feet and set you down in the middle of one of those beautiful pictures.

Malcolm ran his tapered fingers through his dark hair, put his writing quill back into the inkwell, and looked at the TV. His work could wait. These messages were his trademark, bringing instant recognition and terror to the police in a growing number of countries. They called them death threats. Malcolm simply thought of them as artful "letters of introduction."

Right now, however, Malcolm was obsessed with one of his beloved horses. King George was the favorite and running at Saratoga this morning. Totally absorbed in the race, he barely registered the soft knock on his door. Moments later, it came again. Annoyed, he stood up, strode across the thick carpet.

Cecilly waited patiently, holding the tray with the long-stemmed glass and bottle level with both hands. The peephole opened and closed.

The door slid partially open, and the girl's heart began to beat violently. She was staring into the face of dark sensuality itself. He was "Heathcliff" with smooth lips and rich tortured eyes. An involuntary urge filled her. Cecilly found herself wanting to curtsy. Instead, she pushed her trembling tray forward.

"Room service, sir," she managed. "Your beverage?"

But the man had turned away, drawn to something inside the room. Unattended, the door opened wider. Cecilly couldn't resist. Cautiously, she took a step through the doorway into his suite and gasped. She had just stepped into a dream from another century, torn from the pages of her favorite *Victoria* magazine.

Although horses pounded across the TV screen, the sound had been muted. In its stead, the ornate joy of Mozart soared through the room, mingling with sunlight pouring through the windows. And she entered an enchanted garden! On every bureau, mantle, and tabletop, flowers cascaded from porcelain vases; the air thick with their perfume.

To her left was a scene crafted from history: a polished antique desk, a bottle of ink, and a feathered quill pen. Beside it was a sheet of parchment with a few visible lines scrolled in the thin, precise handwriting of a calligrapher.

A fantasy formed in her head. The guest was obviously writing a love letter—probably to a baroness in France or an actress in Italy.

She returned her gaze to the object of her fantasies. He still had his back to her, riveted on the TV. Unobserved, her gaze slid over his contours. He had the body of a lover—thin hips giving rise to a well-developed torso. Of medium height, he wore a black vest over a white ruffled shirt, narrow dark trousers, and shiny black boots. On his hands were soft calfskin gloves.

With her imagination on fire, Cecilly felt her knees begin to buckle. She was going to faint. Managing to keep her tray balanced, she lowered one knee to the floor.

Startled, Malcolm swung around ferociously. Instinctively, one hand snaked behind to the pistol hidden in the folds of his shirt. A closer look . . . and he relaxed.

The servant girl was kneeling in front of him. Her eyes were closed, and an expression of flushed reverence covered her innocent face.

"Have you acquainted yourself sufficiently with my room?" he demanded sharply, his voice disturbing, mechanical—almost inhuman.

Cecily shivered. She opened her eyes and found herself staring into two black pools beneath slanting eyebrows.

"Nn . . . No, sir," she stammered. She had been ready to give herself fully to this man—mind, soul, and body. Now she wanted to run.

Noticing her inflection, he took the beer and glass off her tray. "Where are you from?"

"Oxford, sir."

Malcolm smiled to himself. *Of course, she's English, not American!* Placing a twenty-dollar bill on her tray, he spoke quietly, "Your accent has served you well." He straightened his carriage; his voice modulated again—now commanding and hypnotic. "You are dismissed. You have seen nothing."

Cecily stood up shakily, backed away until she was in the hallway. Closing the door quietly, she walked robotically to the elevator.

By the time she reached the hotel kitchen, she was almost back to her normal cheery self. The incident with the man in Room 1066 would be stored amongst the pages of her fantasies, at least for now, never knowing how close she had come to joining the rusty cans and old tires at the bottom of the Hudson River.

Clicking off the TV, Malcolm returned to his desk to finish his letter. He had been careless, but his luck, as always, was holding. His horse had won. The girl, far too weak and suggestible to cause any trouble.

Letter complete, envelope sealed, he locked it away in his luggage to be mailed at the appropriate time. Next, Bach and a few more lines of cocaine to numb his painful leg.

As he leaned back on his bed, the harpsichord began to fill the air with elaborate melodic stairways until the room was timeless and vague.

NINE

The Akashic Realm

From their outpost in the Room of Perspective, two souls watched the drama unfold with growing concern. The elder, a former Tibetan monk named Palden, spoke first.

"It's moving too quickly. The assassin we hope to contain is preparing to strike again."

Jori, his chief disciple, with a lean face and sad eyes, remained quiet for a moment, recalling the violent intervention: *the roar of Greco's AK-47, the smell of gunpowder, an aftermath of cascading feathers*. In the end, he and Palden had done what had to be done—the detective's life had been saved, and their plan could now move forward. But the center had shifted. Although elements remained the same, the proportions had changed radically, complicating everything.

"I believe you have something in mind," Jori said, already suspecting his master's wish.

Simultaneously, a smile slowly dawned between them—the battle-tested friendship saturated with years of hardship, difficult choices, and trust.

They had come from vastly different backgrounds: a renegade Tibetan monk who left the folds of organized religion to follow a vision and a streetwise kid who found eloquence in the hardscrabble neighborhoods of Brooklyn, rising from poverty to become a celebrated poet. Responding to Palden's plea in 1946, he had joined the mission in Tibet one year later, quickly establishing himself as the master's right-hand man.

"Caution is no longer an option, is it?" Jordi finally inquired.

"No, it's not. But I have a proposition for you."

"Go on."

"Since day one, you've always done what's required. Your record is remarkable."

"That, apparently, was the easier part," Jori rejoined. "Obviously something more drastic is needed."

Palden nodded. "There's also the added complication of the albino psychic. For many reasons, James Early must be activated in the *very* near future. Otherwise . . . well, I think you know."

Jori braced himself for the inevitable.

"We'll need someone closer in to help oversee our project. Someone who finds poetry in the streets of New York City, who might help repurpose our fallen angel." A small twinkle crept into Palden's light eyes.

Jori shuddered. The plot had just thickened dramatically! His lofty perch in the Akashic Realm was too remote to be effective. But returning to the physical plane meant fitting back into a spiritual straitjacket—encased in ceilings and walls, the suffocating constraints of time. Most of all, it meant constant exposure to the relentless atmosphere of discontent emanating from every pore of the human condition. Still, he was the logical choice, and the mission had to come first.

"Then it's decided," Palden said gently. "We'll try a more hands-on approach."

Meeting concluded, both souls bowed, wished each other Godspeed, then directed their currents toward other duties and the work that lay ahead.

*　　*　　*

Thirteenth Precinct, NYPD

Late for the meeting, Early braced himself before entering. Despite the closed door, he could hear Chief Ben Ripley in full bluster, his voice rattling around the room like hail. Apparently a new set of atrocities, New York-style, had blotted out the glow of the Greco victory. At the top of the list was the severed head of a young Asian woman. It had been found neatly wrapped in a hatbox and left outside Gracie Mansion. An event that inspired all major hot buttons: politics, racism, sex, and murder. The deceased's last known address put the case squarely in the lap of the Thirteenth Precinct. Ripley was all over it: appropriately pissed, appropriately horrified, but privately elated, salivating for the big game trophies he would win if he bagged the perpetrator.

Early rested his hand on the doorknob, then pulled it back. He could almost feel the blistering tension in the room through the handle. For the last few days, he had found reasons to be elsewhere. Today he didn't have an excuse. When the chief was on a roll, the script was always the same: pacing around the cramped office like a wounded buffalo, silver hair swirling about his heated face, stabbing the air with an unlit cigarette. Officers Radinski and Jones would be squirming, pulling at their collars, glancing around the room. Sam would be sitting calmly in the direct path of the gale, swigging a cup of lukewarm coffee from his Yankees mug—probably worrying about the local gangs or his teenage kids.

Early sagged and closed his eyes. *Tibet.* And again, that feeling of displacement. His tired mantra started up again. *Just another bad dream.* Everything was going to get back to normal. It had to.

Reluctantly, he opened his eyes again. Through the frosted glass, he saw the quick glow of a cigarette lighter, then heard a Ripley growl. "Hey Radinski, you gotta problem with secondhand smoke? Look for a secondhand job, capiche?"

Early stepped away from the door. No, not today. He couldn't subject himself to Ripley's venom. Looking for comfort, he headed for the coffee bar.

Just then, the door opened, and the officers stumbled out of the room into the hallway. Jones looked like he had been blow-drying his hair in the wrong direction. Exhaling deeply, he gave Early a wry nod. "Barn burner. Missed a good one," then glanced over his shoulder. "Better not let him see you. He'll break your balls."

Sam followed, gave Early the once-over, ushered him quickly away from the chief's line of vision. "Where the hell have you been?"

"Anyplace I could find to avoid *that* in *there*." Early hoisted his thumb back at Ripley's office. "The guy's a complete—"

Sam didn't go for the bait.

Early glanced at his feet. "Yeah . . . Okay. Ripley's always Ripley. I just couldn't go into that inferno today. Just not ready."

"This is *not* new news. Any idea when you'll be rejoining the living, I mean here at the Thirteenth? I'm starting to worry."

"You never stopped."

"Gimme a good reason why I should."

They walked in silence to the staff's coffee bar.

Once situated, Sam raised his mug. "Come on, man. We have a deal. What's going on?"

Early felt tongue-tied. If he told Sam the truth, his already suspect credibility would be in the toilet. As always, humor seemed the best way out. "Usual stuff," he quipped. "Damn UFOs were back last night. Sleepover . . . played a little poker. You know how it goes."

Sam grunted but seemed to lighten in spite of himself.

"Anyway . . . all's fine." Early drained his cup.

Sam looked unconvinced, but both managed a small, tight smile.

Glancing at his watch, Early stood up, ready to return to his desk, but Sam waved him back. "Got a sec? Wanna show you something."

Leading the way to the squad car, Sam fumbled under the seat and pulled out a faded object.

"Found it this morning. Yard sale thing. Couldn't imagine it belonged to you, but you're the only other person who uses this car."

With a shrug, he handed it over to Early. "Not quite my style. Yours?"

Early looked down at a worn blue bowl, held it in his hands, and felt his heart misfire—recognition exploding in his mind.

The bowl in my dream. The gift from the Tibetan master!

Early felt like he was holding a cup of sunlight. "Could be," he mumbled. Freaked out but incredibly pleased, he stared down at the bowl. It didn't dissolve in his hands. Trancelike, Early moved unsteadily back toward the station house.

Sam leaned against the side of the car, shaking his head in bewilderment. Not only had Early departed without saying a word, but he was now moving gingerly up the front steps, carrying that old battered bowl as if it were the crown from some ancient monarch.

Unnoticed, at the far end of the parking lot, a thin, middle-aged man in a brown wool overcoat watched the vignette through the chain-link fence and sighed with relief. The artifact he had planted had found its previous owner. Try as he might, their "person of interest" would find it difficult to refute this piece of hard evidence. The irony made Jori smile. Where miracles had failed, this nondescript bowl might do the trick.

Evening was now encroaching on the late April sky—light fading, wind kicking up, leaves scuttling across the pavement. With one last look, the cloaked figure turned up his collar and walked silently away. His gait was slow and measured, like someone reacquainting himself with the unrelenting laws of gravity.

TEN

The Plaza Hotel

Malcolm sat on the edge of the bed admiring his work. The stock, barrel, scope, and trigger of his customized rifle were disassembled, the pieces arranged neatly on top of a white silk scarf. He enjoyed the ritual of cleaning his weapon, the aesthetics of icy steel against the elegant embroidery of the bedspread. But Malcolm had already done this procedure two days ago. Restless and bored, he decided not to wait any longer.

Wiping his hands on a soft chamois, he made the call.

It happened every time. Before the phone had a chance to ring at the other end, he heard the whispery voice of his advisor, thick with an indecipherable accent.

"Yes, Mr. Raines."

"When?"

"Give me a moment." Pale hands put the receiver down on an ebony desk. Soundlessly, the albino clairvoyant known as WhiteMan, a.k.a. the Albino, dragged his elongated body through the pitch-black room until he found his way to the panoramic picture window. Taking a deep breath, he braced himself for the searing impact. It was his method. His tortured aesthetic. His livelihood. Although the moment was excruciating, it would catapult his perception into the future.

With a sharp cry, he flung the curtains open. Splinters of light ripped into his pinkish eyes. Lips quivered from the pain. Completely vulnerable to the slicing razors of the sunlight, he held his eyes wide open by sheer willpower, despite the rush of tears now cascading down his face.

Moments later, his watery vision of the city—the metal, stone, and glass of the skyline—slipped into a liquid blankness. Then lines and colors . . . then patterns merging and falling apart, repurposing into possible futures. Finally, a single "thread" emerged, disclosing his client's best path forward. This was normal. But what accompanied that strand left the Albino speechless. Faint and incandescent, some *presence* seemed to be moving in opposition to Malcolm's pursuits. And that presence was not of this earth!

Shocked by his perception, he closed the drapes quickly, groped his way back to his desk. Spindly pale fingers gathered around the phone for a long moment before the Albino spoke.

"A complication has emerged," he said in his soft rasp. "Whatever it is you wish to accomplish, you must move slightly sideways until we know more. Find something that introduces a diversion to those who may oppose your plan. Once you have chosen this device, act immediately."

Malcolm shifted the phone to his other ear and began to pace. "But I rushed here! Your fax stated that the timetable had been shortened. Damn it! How can you tell me I—"

"Silence! I tell you what I see!"

The voice paused to let its wrath sink in, then spoke again—this time with a hint of menace. "You know our rules! I'm not interested in your complaints or the nature of your business. I block that perception. Another outburst and I will simply refuse your next call!"

Malcolm knew some of WhiteMan's other clients. The list included kings, CEOs of powerful companies, Mafia bosses, and presidents. Only through rumor did anyone know that the man who advised them was an albino. All paid vast sums for his "forecasts." All instinctively understood. WhiteMan could afford to withdraw his services from anyone at any time.

"I apologize. I didn't intend to be rude," Malcolm said, deliberately evening out his tone. "Is there anything else I should know?"

The Albino rested the phone in the crook of his neck and closed his eyes. While he scanned, his long, thin hands moved absently across the top of his black desk, like two white spiders—darting, inspecting, sensitive to nuance. The ivory fingers came to a brass letter opener, hesitated, then traced along the sharp edge before returning to take hold of the telephone. His lips barely moved as he breathed his final message.

"You need to know that something extraordinary is happening. A trap door has opened along the web, causing a shift." The breathy whisper went silent for an instant, returning with a sense of urgency.

"Proceed with utmost care and implement this information. Call me again when appropriate."

The line went dead.

With the psychic's words rippling through his mind, Malcolm stowed his rifle in its hidden compartment, then sat on his bed for a while before finding sleep.

Later that evening, he awoke emboldened with conviction. WhiteMan had planted a dark seed. Now the seed had taken root, and the dark flower was opening.

Reinvigorated, the assassin ripped up the letter of introduction he'd carefully inked—torn pieces disposed in an ashtray, then lit. He watched the flames undulate—hypnotic and seductive, like an erotic dancer. Holding it like a torch, he walked it over to his desk by the window—the acrid smell of burning paper and smoke blending with the perfume of flowers. The parchment twisted, blackened, until its deadly secret was reduced to ash.

Malcolm took out a fresh sheet of parchment and fingered his quill. A different letter with a slightly altered destination would be written; a decoy, a diversion. Later on, he would "introduce" himself to his actual victim. His impact was never less than profound. He always managed to take their breath away.

ELEVEN

Early's Apartment

The blue Tibetan bowl now rested on Early's mantelpiece like an old trophy, a haunting presence above the ruins of his fireplace—and his life. It represented both hope and failure and was somehow the key to unlocking the dark secret that had twisted and turned inside him since childhood. After madness and vanishing bullets and a life that should have ended, after memories of a past life in Tibet had been confirmed, denial was not going to work. As a cop, there could be no plan B, no backup team. He was on his own. Laying his .38 revolver on the table, removing his badge, Early was going in. He would keep the artifact front and center—poking and prodding, watching and waiting until it revealed itself.

This silent investigation became a ritual. After work, he would stand before the mantelpiece and silently cross-examine the witness. *Why are you in my life? Who's behind it? What do they want?* For the first week, the silence was deafening. It was also becoming addictive.

Day by day, Early's obsession grew. After the daily grind at the NYPD, he was no longer returning to an empty apartment. He was now coming home to something outside his battered world, like a mistress waiting in the dark for him to appear. Sometimes, when sleep was elusive, he would park himself before the mantlepiece, lean close to the bowl, breathe in the scent of the ancient wood, and be transported—escaping from the clawing, sleepless drama of the New York streets below to a moment in Tibet . . . enveloped by the smell of ozone and the quiet, majestic nights stretching out high above the Himalayas.

But the tension between his two worlds was unsustainable and escalating. Early saw the signs and refused to concede. Whatever tightrope he was walking, he had to keep his balance. He had officially run out of options.

Enduring another challenged NYPD day with both Sam and Ripley upbraiding him for lack of focus, Early finally snapped and stormed out. Barging through his front door, he threw jacket on the couch, holster on the bed, and glared at his unloved apartment. Anarchy spewed from every corner—clothes hanging out of open drawers, unmade bed, piles of unwashed dishes. Pissed at everything in heaven and earth, he bypassed his ritual and scooped the Tibetan bowl from its altar, immediately dropping it with a cry. *Was he going mad? It was hot!*

Cautiously, with both hands, he picked it up again. Something was wrong. The bowl seemed possessed. Instead of satin-smooth, the wood felt coarse and grainy—threatening splinters. Peering at it more carefully, he noticed a dark smudge near the bottom, seemingly scorched. How was this possible? It hadn't fallen into the fireplace. It had been on the mantelpiece the entire time.

He ran a cautious fingertip along the rim. Wood against skin. It smelled like ashes. Ashes and smoke. Growing lightheaded, Early toppled into his armchair and looked around. The room was morphing, pulsing with an electrical charge, filling with distant sounds—the crackle of fire under his door, the bark of gunshots ricocheting off the streets below.

Early recognized the symptoms. The membrane between past and present was thinning. The first dream was about to have a sequel. This time he wouldn't fight it. This time he would welcome it.

Hovering on the threshold, he took a vow: *This time I get answers, or I'm not coming back.*

A moment later, the leaden blackness claimed him.

* * *

Memory Dream Two: Tibet, 1952

On a night buffeted by howling winds, inside a monastery carved from the side of the mountain, moonlight streamed down through high windows, highlighting rows of silent men and women. Seated on benches, tight-lipped, staring straight ahead, they waited with dread.

Only days ago, a seismic discovery had catapulted them into hope and triumph. Forty-eight hours later, they had just been ripped from their beds, summoned to the main hall, and told to wait. Plunged into confusion, the devotees turned expectant eyes on their Tibetan leader, who now stood before them—the same man who, years ago, had asked them to jettison comfortable lives to join him in this gutted outpost in the Himalayas.

Palden was a thin, ageless man with smooth skin and sharp features. Although his words were always precise and carefully chosen, there was a penetrating kindness that went straight to every listener's soul. Tonight, his eyes moved with quiet determination along the rows, faces softening when the sage's gaze lingered upon them.

Massive and dignified as a statue, the white Bengal tiger sprawled in the corner of the room, surveying the throng with steady blue eyes.

No longer in denial, Early watched the scene with raw emotion. Hungry for answers, some memories came into focus: a Tibetan child, orphaned at two, he had been adopted by a monk named Palden—an unexpected turn for a sage known for his love of solitude. As both father and guru, the relationship flourished. When Early was six, Palden had uprooted, leaving the safe confines of his monastery in Lassa to become a nomad. Child in tow, he had wandered throughout East Asia tracking his vision: camping out with yak shepherds in the steppe lands, drinking raksi with bandits, tracing the paths of holy men through the peaks and valleys in central Tibet. Guided by unseen forces, he finally stumbled upon a structure embedded in the face of a mountain. A place he had seen in dreams. Here, deep in the wilderness, his mission could be housed in secrecy, and his envisioned crew could tackle the mystery of karma.

Drifting with images from his Tibetan youth, Early's attention was suddenly yanked back to the man who addressed the gathering. At that exact instant, Palden raised his eyes, looked directly at Early, and held for a silent transmission—*an admission of love and regret between father and son . . . a plea for patience as things continued to unfold.* Then the space closed, and the sage returned to his team and the matter at hand.

"You have been summoned because our journey together has reached a crossroads. Everything we stand for—our work, our lives, our commitment to the mission—is about to be tested. So tonight of all nights, you *must* listen with your deathless hearts!"

He gazed about the room, allowing each member's thoughts to settle.

Satisfied, Palden continued. "Most of you joined me in 1947 or '48. We would mine the human soul. We would accomplish the impossible. Karma—how does it work, technically? How can we harness its power? Instead of countless lifetimes, could we find a way of dealing with it ethically and quickly? All of us agreed. We had to find some answers . . . and we have!"

Palden's eyes glittered. Around the room, heads nodded. "In the spring of 1951, like fingerprints, we discovered that all souls leave unique prints . . . soulprints . . . that never change, lifetime after lifetime. We studied. We trained. Bravo! We found our tracking device. Next, we set our sights on a repository of past lives, a library mired in myth called the Akashic Records. Did it even exist?"

Palden paused dramatically, then went on. "Two days ago we got our answer. Hidden in the folds of the cosmos, we discovered the Akashic Realm. And there, rising up like a cathedral of light before us, we established contact. The Library of Souls was real. Alive! We could now proceed!

The gathering shifted in their chairs, reliving the exalted moment.

"We celebrated that dawn, standing on the edge of our valley, toasting the gods of the Himalayas. But now a different moment awaits us. One filled with harsh irony."

The room went absolutely still, the monk's lilting voice suddenly urgent and sharp-edged.

"An atrocity is about to occur. Our *own* unhandled karma, right here in this room, will lead to the destruction of this sanctuary and our mission. Everything we have created, everything we have discovered, all reduced to carnage and ash. Right now, as I speak, the event is approaching."

The members sat in stunned disbelief, then exploded. They rose to their feet, crying out in angry astonishment. *How was this possible? Who would betray them?* Palden remained impassive, then raised his hands for order.

"This act will not be done out of malice. It will be the outcome of a divided love, but the result will be the same. As you know, the Red Chinese have sent troops into Tibet to commit genocide. They have already destroyed places of worship, murdering and raping as they went. They do not know where we are but have heard the rumors. Our scouts are reporting that soldiers have invaded the area. They're now in the vicinity, looking for us. Unless some miracle occurs, they will be led here, bringing their vicious mentality inside these sacred walls. That is the nature of *their* karma. And if this comes to pass, it will occur within the next twenty-four hours. Whoever chooses to remain in this monastery will be dead by this time tomorrow."

Stunned into silence, nobody spoke. Breath became shallow. Hands sought hands, struggling to bear the brutal weight of their leader's words.

The monk resumed, speaking deliberately and with compassion. "Consult your conscience. The time has come for each of you to choose your path. That is the purpose of this final meeting."

In the deathly silent hall, the members drifted apart. Standing, sitting, some praying, each individual was left alone to deal with the shock and horror of the situation, each forced to examine their final attachments to community, to humanity, to life itself.

When it was apparent that his disciples had absorbed and answered the question for themselves, Palden addressed them again. "All of you took vows of unwavering commitment when you first joined this mission. I absolve you from those vows, now and forever. Martyrdom serves no purpose. If any of you choose to leave, do so immediately. For those who remain, we will attempt escape through the Akashic portal. Still experimental, but our best hope. Nevertheless, out of respect, I offer you this last chance to consider all options."

One by one, the members voiced their decision. It was unanimous. All would remain.

Early felt moved by this show of courage. Yet, the sense of dread was creeping back into his heart. Instinctively, he frantically sought out the young boy, his former self . . . now remembered as Tashi. Like the other members, the child was talking feverishly, trying to fathom what was happening. But when Early attempted to lock into the boy's consciousness, he experienced an overwhelming grief. Tashi's mind was flooded with despair! But it wasn't impending death that disturbed him. Early shivered. How could he have forgotten? Tashi was totally absorbed in the image of a dark-eyed girl!

"Then it's agreed!" Palden was saying. "We will greet these assassins as nothing more than a violent harvester—claiming our mortal chaff and freeing our timeless wheat."

He clapped his hands. "Now, to work! I want every physical shred of our research, every book and piece of machinery destroyed. Be thorough and move quickly."

Bowing to his disciples, he retreated into his private library. Once alone, he immediately examined the spiritual logistics required to transport his family through the portal—from certain bodily death to a home for their emancipated souls in the Akashic Realm.

Early watched, feeling the grip of terror grow inside him. *What was Tashi about to do?* From every side, the team, inflamed with quiet outrage, was rushing in and out of every room in the monastery, smashing devices, destroying books. No one from the outside world had ever found their way to this hidden retreat. *How would soldiers find them now? Who amongst them would be this Judas?*

But the boy was distracted and didn't engage. Instead, he quietly removed himself from the whirlpool of activity and crept up the staircase. Once out of view, he raced to the entrance, pushed through the front doors into the freezing night. Above, the immense blue-black sky pitted with brittle bits of stars pressed down against his shoulders. Snowfall had ceased, but the frozen landscape and whipping wind seemed to conspire, pushing him back inside the monastery.

Scared but resolved, Tashi held his ground. The Red Chinese were coming. No matter the consequences, he had to warn her and say goodbye. He would return in two hours. With all the commotion going on, he would be back before anyone even noticed.

With a final deep breath, he fled the monastery. Jumping over snow-covered rocks, Tashi flew along a camouflaged path that zigzagged down the mountainside. A mile down the trail, there would be a dot of light, a small thatched dwelling where a lamp burned in the window.

Her name was Usha, Palden's twelve-year-old niece, and she lived with her mother on the outskirts of a nearby village. For Tashi, Usha was the embodiment of godhood itself: beautiful, mysterious, and kind. Since early childhood, their relationship had been one of graceful discovery—a bond that came easily and felt timeless. But tonight, time was running out, and passion drove him onward. He had to make sure she was safe. He had to see her one last time before he died.

Instead of following the labyrinth of invisible passageways established by Palden, Tashi disobeyed and took a shortcut. For fifty yards, his pounding legs carried him across a stretch of open terrain. In that moment of exposure, he saw something move in the hills—a shadow, a glint of silver in the starlight—then darkness. For a fraction of a second, the boy slowed, considered, then raced on.

Characteristically, Usha was waiting outside her family's hut when Tashi arrived. Feverish and out of breath, he held her for a long moment before any words were spoken. Moments later they were scrambling up a narrow ridge along the mountainside to their secret hideaway—a cave overlooking the valley. It was the only spot in the entire range that offered a direct view of the monastery.

Once inside, Tashi slumped to the floor, thankful and relieved. *He was with Usha. Safe in their sanctuary. Nothing else mattered.* This tiny alcove was their refuge, a world within a world, free from outside influences. Through the years, they had furnished the cave with treasures collected from the valley below that celebrated their friendship: a faded carpet, candles, prayer flags, a snow leopard's jawbone, vulture feathers, and dried blue poppy flowers.

Tashi told Usha the full story—the disaster that awaited the mission and everyone involved; a fate he must return to in the next hour. Desperately, they ransacked their vocabulary for words to express this unthinkable farewell. They could not. Finally, lighting a candle, they lay down side by side, watching the thin flame dance in the darkness. Forcing everything but each other out of their minds and clinging to this moment, they fell asleep.

Morning came too soon, filling the cave with unforgiving light. Tashi was awakened by a scream from Usha. Suddenly hit by the weight of his transgression, he stumbled to his feet and joined her at the mouth of the cave. Across the valley, tongues of flame were licking the monastery, spitting out smoke, spiraling up into the morning air.

Palden's warning! The slaughter. The destruction had come to pass!

Filled with horror, they ran back down past Usha's home, then up the winding trail. They instinctively followed Tashi's earlier footprints, still fresh in the snow. But where he had taken his shortcut, his solo prints were suddenly buried beneath a stampede of other footprints coming from the top of the hill.

Watching the scene unfold, Early felt dots crashing together . . . a storyline emerge. The same starlight that lit Tashi's footsteps last night had also glinted off the barrel of a rifle—a Chinese sentry stationed on that hill. He had seen a boy with a shaved head emerge from a concealed passageway. Suspicions had been aroused. Could this mean the mysterious monastery they coveted was close by? The soldier had hurried down the slope, immediately informing his superiors.

Predawn, troops had been dispatched. Bayonets affixed, they followed the boy's footprints back through the hidden opening and along the twisting pathway until the structure rose up before them like some mythical apparition. At last, the prize! The storied monastery had been found! With torches raised, weapons locked and loaded, the slaughter began.

Bile rose in Early's throat, realizations hitting him like a slap across the face. Now he remembered. Now he knew. Not only had he broken the rules that kept the monastery safe from discovery, but *he* was the traitor! By his own colossal error in judgment, he had completely sabotaged the mission, destroying everything and everybody he had ever loved.

Warily, Early turned his attention back to Tashi and Usha.

Not caring if they lived or died, the two children fought their way through the mayhem—the stench of gun smoke and burning flesh assaulting them; soldiers milling about, firing randomly into the sky in celebration.

Tashi slammed into the courtyard, then came to an abrupt halt. Everywhere he looked, the grey flagstones were slippery with blood, littered with the charred remains of his comrades. Soldiers were carrying corpses out of the building, piling them in heaps, dousing them with gasoline, and setting them on fire. Turning slowly, Tashi recognized a deathly pale face . . . staggered forward . . . knelt down beside Jori. Despite a bullet-riddled body, his eyes appeared calm and filled with distant light.

Tashi stood up, fist in the air, and bellowed with anguish.

From behind came the crack of a rifle. The boy felt a bullet tear into his lungs. He was glad for the searing pain, glad to have the gift of life ripped away so brutally. Before dying, he frantically looked around and found Usha. Surrounded by lusting soldiers, she was looking back at him, calling out with her eyes. *I will find you again. Look for me!*

As these memories faded, horror and shame engulfed Early. The last flickering images of Tibet blackening, disintegrated like paper in a fire.

Then everything began to spin and spin until nothing remained for Early but the hell of self-hatred.

TWELVE

Early's Apartment

For the first time in fifteen years, Early feigned illness. Using his observable depressed state as pretext, he pleaded his case and was granted a short leave of absence. For most of this time, he sat silently in his old armchair—curtains closed, the world at arm's length. He barely ate and refused to turn on any lights. Occasionally, the telephone rang, then went still. Once in a while, he left his isolation to take a walk, staying in the shadows of crosstown streets where he could remain anonymous and unobserved.

As days bled into night and nights melted into dawn, only the imprint of light on his curtains changed. He wanted to deal with his karma. Nothing else.

In the big puzzle, a few of the easier pieces about himself fell into place—the nameless guilt, the sense of being haunted, now all explainable. But this offered little consolation. The horror of the Tibetan debacle was unrelenting and without mercy. Beyond the massacre of thirty-two innocent lives and the profound importance of their work, he now understood he was also dealing with the future of his immortal soul. Ultimately, nothing brought hope or relief. And even if he *were* able to fully face his past, what in all the world could he possibly do to make up for the damage he had done?

*   *   *

Six days into Early's retreat, a dark-haired woman dressed in black leggings and a teal-blue sweater stood in a phone booth on Early's block—telephone in one hand, a lit cigarette in the other. Impatiently she scanned the fifth-floor windows for the hundredth time. Again, nothing. It had taken her a week, but Desda had finally found out the particulars. His name was James Early. He was a homicide detective at the Thirteenth Precinct. Right now she was only a stone's throw away from where he lived.

But the real dogfight had been overcoming her own objections. My God, she was about to *stalk* someone, and a *complete stranger* at that! She had seen his face for ten seconds on a newscast and had jettisoned everything just to find him. Not her style at all. In fact, the whole thing made her furious with herself. Nevertheless, here she was, not knowing what she wanted or even why she wanted. Only knowing that she had to. And so she did.

For the last few days, she had used every conceivable ploy to be unobtrusive in Early's section of town: walking a friend's dog, parking and reparking her car to go to a restaurant nearby, taking slow walks at various times of the evening. There had been no sightings of him. Now her patience was paper-thin and incendiary.

Tonight, out of sheer desperation, she had dialed his phone number, held the receiver, then slowly, haltingly, hung up. No, she needed to meet him in person. After that, she could dismiss the whole thing as nerves or hormones or whatever—she didn't care. But then, God willing, obsessing about James Early would finally be over, and she could get on with her new life.

Ten minutes later, she saw her opportunity and darted across the street. An elderly woman wearing a dark coat and checkered kerchief was pushing a cartful of groceries toward Early's building. Desda had seen her twice before, entering and leaving.

Just as the woman bent down to drag her cart up the small set of front steps, Desda sidled up beside her.

"Here, let me help you." Desda took hold of the cart.

"Well, that's very kind. Thank you."

"No problem. I was just coming to visit my friend in 5A."

The old woman turned sharply and squinted her eyes. "Excuse me for being so nosey. But is he all right? Seems there was some trouble a while back. We all heard gunshots, but no one seemed to know what happened. I just hope he wasn't hurt."

"I'm just on my way to find out. He's an old friend," she lied. "Now, if you let yourself in, I'll help get your groceries to your apartment and then go up and see him."

The neighbor unlocked the door and led the way to her ground-floor flat. After placing the bags on the kitchen counter, Desda said goodbye and began her ascent to the fifth floor. But the closer she got, the weaker her legs became and the less conviction there was to drive her upward. Standing tentatively before apartment 5A, she felt the panic set in. She wanted a smoke. She wanted out. She regretted ever putting herself in this position.

Reluctantly, she pressed her ear to Early's door and listened. No sound emerged. In fact, the silence seemed oppressive.

Summoning her courage, she raised her arm and knocked loudly. Heart in her throat, she waited. Again, the heavy silence.

Desda lifted her hand to bang again, then let it fall to her side. What the hell was she doing? This was sheer madness!

Turning quickly, she fled back down the staircase. At the bottom, she fumbled her way out of the building and onto the sidewalk, fighting tears. *Why was this so hard?* The mere prospect of meeting him filled her with a violent tangle of emotions.

Nevertheless, as she headed to the subway, she began to work on her resolve again. She was not a quitter. Somehow, someway, she would find the strength to face this man. Without breaking stride, she tore through her handbag and lit another cigarette.

Plowed deep in thought, Early tried to extract himself. That sound—had someone just knocked on his door? He raised his head slowly. Who would have done that? Certainly not his neighbors. After the pyrotechnics in his fireplace, he was probably considered a loose cannon—or worse—and they left him alone. If not them, then who?

Unsteady, he rose to his feet and rubbed his eyes, the air slow and dense around him. Finally he looked out through the peephole on the door. Nothing but the yellow glare of hallway light.

A new set of questions formed in his mind. Was this the invisible hand again? Was he being prodded out of his doldrums to *do* something? As if on cue, he heard a noise and turned. Outside his apartment, in the alien land of people and activity, a firetruck was clanging and wailing its way down the street. For the first time in a week, he felt curious: *Where was it going? Who was in danger?*

Feeling a thin connection forming again between himself and the living, he made his way across the dark room and pressed his ear against the window, listening.

All at once, there was a world again. From below came the sound of a car door slamming, footsteps, a conversation between a man and a woman. Somewhere a radio was playing a song from the sixties, then faded away down the street.

With a sigh, he pushed open the curtains and moonlight streamed into the desolate room. Particles danced in the silvery illumination, dust glinting like diamonds. Early stood and watched, oddly moved. Slowly, tentatively, he put his hand into the stream of light as though testing the waters.

*   *   *

Two hours later when the phone rang, Early decided to join the living and picked up. "Yeah?"

There was a pause, then Sam's voice, tense and gruff. "Man, I was sure you were playing hooky, but you sound half dead."

"Touch of the flu. You don't sound so great yourself. What's up?"

"Well, get it together 'cause we got an appointment in forty-five minutes."

"At this hour? Where?"

"Billy Burwell's. *The* Billy Burwell. He got a death threat in the mail today. Ripley handed me the file a few hours ago, and this is the only time they can see us."

"Who the hell would want to kill *him*? Jesus, he's 'The Natural.' Best thing that happened to America in decades."

"That's the problem," Sam said quietly. "He's in the Hall of Fame. He's also just made it to Quill's hit list."

Early sat down heavily. "Quill? I thought they just operated in the UK?"

"Most say it's one guy. Interpol's all over it. Seven murders later, nobody knows a damn thing. But every time, it starts with this kind of threat, handwritten on parchment. Billy just got one."

"I thought the targets were businessmen. Why a ballplayer?"

"*American* businessmen," Sam corrected. "Quill apparently hates anything to do with the States, and Billy's an icon here. But we're all just guessing."

"Sounds like FBI territory."

"Yeah, but the Burwells live in Gramercy Park. That's *our* turf. I want to get there first."

Early untangled the phone cord and sighed. " Okay, let's do it."

"I tell you, Burwell's special. If anything happens to him under my jurisdiction, I'll . . . " Sam's voice trailed off.

"I know," Early said. "I watched him single-handedly beat the Dodgers in the World Series two years in a row when I was a kid. I also know he's about as decent as they come."

Then he glanced at his watch. "Give me . . . about thirty-five. I know the address."

"Good. Meet you outside the house."

After hanging up, Early stood for a moment, pondering this new turn of events and the timing. He had to take the meeting. He owed that much to Sam and the NYPD.

Reluctantly, he changed into his work clothes and threw on his shoulder holster. He needed to do something. He just couldn't see how being a policeman was going to stay relevant for much longer.

THIRTEEN

Gramercy Park

It was raining when Early spotted Sam's Camry squeezed in between a Jag and a new Volvo a block away from the Burwells' brownstone. Early had parked on a cross street and walked to the square—a private park surrounded by well-appointed townhouses. Ripley's men were already in place: a nondescript car parked opposite the home, windshield wipers parting the curtain of rain revealing glimpses of tired faces of undercover cops on stakeout.

Early knew the drill: a thermos full of tepid coffee, a long night of unrelieved tension, and the feel of morning light grinding like glass against bloodshot eyes.

"We're expected," Sam said briskly when his partner joined him at the front gate. As they walked up the pathway inside the fenced yard, Sam didn't raise his eyes. "If you're really sick," he said slowly, "I'm sorry to drag you out here. If you're not, we gotta talk."

Early punched his arm lightly. "We will. Let's go meet your idol first."

"Yeah, let's do that," Sam said dryly.

They passed a handful of security guards stationed around the grounds. Early knew most of them and nodded. This was a headline case, and Ripley was all over it.

Standing in the alcove under the porch light, the detectives instinctively straightened ties, brushed raindrops from their trench coats. In the line of duty, they stood in front of many important doors. In this instance, however, it was difficult not to feel like they were out of their league. Not only were they seeing a legendary Hall of Famer, they were also going to be in the presence of a woman who was splashing her way through the polluted waters of politics, seemingly toward the White House. In the growing eddies of frustration around the country, the name Ellen Burwell was moving rapidly from the back of the mind to the tip of the tongue.

Sam pushed the doorbell, a dog barked . . . the two cops glanced at each other. While waiting, Early stamped some mud off the bottom of his shoes and thought about this remarkable couple. Like every other boy in America, he had grown up with Billy Burwell as an iconic figure in the national landscape. Many years later he remained a legitimate hero, untarnished and still shining.

His wife gave off a different hue and had a wider purview. Early, by habit, was not a political creature. He usually just gave the front page, charged with the noise of disaster and corruption, the "glance, get disgusted, turn the page" treatment. But, like many other citizens, he tended to linger wherever the media covered Ellen. Coming off the page, pushing out from print or image, she had a presence that made contact and commanded attention.

When she had first announced she was running for office, the press, out of respect for her "beyond reproach" husband, had given her a polite public nod . . . and privately licked their lips. This little woman was going to step out of her Norman Rockwell world and enter the smoke-filled backrooms. Sure, she would reform the long-time political hoods with a bit of bipartisan cheerleading. Yes, indeed! *This was going to be rich!*

But the Cinderella candidate had fooled them all. Standing up on her own terms, she had started to talk intelligently, with courage and insight, about the plight of the nation. The public had warmed up quickly. The consensus was that she was smart and actually paying attention. Billy was already considered family by millions of Americans—Ellen had simply joined him. Soon she might be asked to sit at the head of the table.

She was charming and tough. But most of all, there seemed to be little posturing, little discrepancy between who she was privately and what she stood for publicly. She spoke her mind and seemed fearless. This made her both beloved and controversial. Nevertheless, following a series of small jumps up the ladder, she suddenly was viewed as a heavy in the New York State Legislature. Four years later, she was elected to the Senate on the Democratic ticket. Going from PTA member to headline news had taken Ellen Burwell all of eight years.

But what Early remembered most about her had happened two years ago. Shocking everyone in the entire political arena, she had resigned from the Senate! And not because of misconduct or scandal. She had called it "irreconcilable differences" with Capitol Hill. This move had startled the pundits but left regular citizens applauding her integrity.

As was her trademark, she announced her decision directly and without fanfare to the American people. Early had made it a point to watch the broadcast and recalled it vividly.

She had faced the cameras without leaning on the podium, economical with her gestures and words.

"If a ballplayer feels like he doesn't have the heart to dive for a ground ball hit into the gap, he should retire. If a singer cannot give her all on every note, she should get off the stage. And if I, as your elected official, feel that I can't be effective with my work and truly represent your interests any longer, then I should resign. I am doing so tonight."

The assembled political world had stood in stunned silence. Even the political hacks and spin doctors were momentarily caught off guard. For a media moment, not even they dared to run their cold, dirty hands over her heartfelt speech.

She had continued. "After seeing the inside of our government, *your* government, firsthand, I have no other choice than to acknowledge that Capitol Hill has lost sight of its obligations to you, the American people. Many of my colleagues feel the same way. But it's something that must change."

She had then begun speaking more intimately.

"Institutions are built with human hands and hearts. Once established, they become numb, a kind of machinery programmed for self-preservation. That's what seems to be in play with our two-party system waging endless war with each other. Some legislators are good at it. I'm not one of them. And for me, it raises questions, a lot of questions, that I can't answer right now. Maybe some of you understand what's gone wrong. For me, it's a work in progress. And, as a public figure, as my own person, it's something I need to sort out."

In closing, she had turned with genuine sadness to look at her family standing to her left and then back at the camera. "When my husband decided he and the curveball were no longer friends, he turned in his spikes—out of *respect for you*! He couldn't ask you to pay to see him play when he didn't believe in his own performance. I, in my own fashion, am doing the same tonight. Thank you for listening. May God bless you all."

For the next few years, she had remained out of the public eye. When she re-emerged, she did so without party affiliation but with a message forged from her personal experiences—traveling, studying, and gathering different perspectives. Her plans? She was going to continue to develop her skills—listening and speaking with clarity to anyone who wanted to engage—and see where it led. If you believed the snap polls, it was leading straight into the American heart.

The metallic scrape of door bolts brought Early back from his thoughts. Billy Burwell, now in his early fifties, stuck his silvery head out into the night air and scanned the two detectives.

Visibly awed, Sam cleared his throat and flipped open his wallet to show his badge. "Good evening, sir. Detectives Jenkins and Early, NYPD."

"Oh yes. Glad you could make it," Billy said. He glanced at the IDs, then flashed his boyish smile. "Sorry about the hour. Come in, come in!"

"Up here," he instructed, leading a charge up the staircase, effortlessly taking two steps at a time. Sam paused for a moment, watching the six-foot-two frame of "Kid Diamond" glide to the landing and disappear into the house.

"I'll bet he could still cover center field and hit two-eighty," Sam said wistfully, under his breath.

Early was not quite as mesmerized by Billy's presence. He had noticed the butt of a handgun sticking out beneath the man's sweater. "Let's just make sure he lives," he said quietly.

When the policemen entered the upstairs living room, Billy was talking in muted tones to his wife. Surrounded by stacks of books and reports, she sat at the dining room table. Almost imperceptibly, she scrutinized the visitors, then nodded to her husband.

"You folks make yourself at home," Billy called out. "If it's okay with you, my wife'll join us. We've both had cranks before, but according to what we've heard, this Quill threat is no joke."

"No joke at all," Early said solemnly. "Thanks for seeing us. We're both honored to meet you."

Ellen's demeanor went from guarded to gracious. She was a petite five-foot-four, brown-haired woman in her late forties, with classic features and a sturdy chin. Dressed in a bulky black turtleneck sweater and jeans, she took off her reading glasses and rose to greet them. Her brown eyes were troubled as she shook their hands. "Since we got the letter, we've become a little more cautious. I'm sure you understand," she said with a sigh. "Now, would either of you care for something to drink?"

Both detectives declined, then sat down stiffly on the couch.

Billy took the lead. "We're all busy. And I know you men would rather be home with your families than talking to us." Making sure his wife was seated comfortably, he plopped down in a weathered armchair across from them. "Let's get started."

Early usually took charge in these kinds of meetings. But after the preliminaries, he handed the floor over to his partner, indicating he had been ill and out of the loop for the last few days. Sam started off awkwardly, his voice tight and thick with apologies—reports from Interpol and Scotland Yard had just been received and were sketchy on details. With thinly disguised discomfort, he attempted to navigate between giving the Burwells reasons to hope and being the harbinger of utterly terrifying news. The truth was, Billy was being stalked by a killer who never missed, who had never been seen, who left no clues, and who was wanted in Europe for multiple murders.

None of this was said directly. But nobody was fooled. As Sam concluded his opening statements, Early glanced at the celebrated couple. Their faces told the story. Sam's performance had been courteous but ineffectual.

Pulling out a xeroxed copy of the death threat from his briefcase, Sam placed it on the coffee table. Billy sat back, Ellen leaned forward, and Sam continued.

"It's not much, but here's what we know. The letter you got is almost a carbon copy of the other seven that got turned in, mostly from the UK. Same heavy paper, same handwriting. Experts say he uses a quill pen, which is where the name Quill comes from. His big thing is America. According to him, the US is the evil empire, spreading filth and poison around the world. Truth is, we don't see him as a serial killer. We see him as a guy fighting a private war."

Ellen lifted the letter off the table and pointed to the middle paragraph. "Right here, he refers to us as 'the former Colonies.' Says we're 'corrupting the aesthetics and traditional values.' What's this all about?"

"Nobody knows. The shrinks are coming up with profiles on this guy all the time. It's not helping. All we really know is that he's got some agenda to save civilization by taking America's fingers off the map."

Billy leaned back and sighed, suddenly appearing older and tired. "No offense intended, but I don't like the odds. From what I read, he's seven for seven. Who were the other victims?"

"All of them were Americans trying to set up distribution lines for US products in the UK. Fast-food chains, car dealerships, retail clothing outlets—those types of operations. They all—"

"Then why me?" Billy interjected.

"Yeah, I know. My personal belief is that . . . well, a lotta folks feel you're the walking success story of the American dream. I believe that myself."

Billy didn't respond, but Ellen finally looked up from the assassin's letter. "What's this part about leaving Billy 'dead and suitably framed for all posterity'?" she asked, trying to keep her hand from shaking.

Sam grimaced. "Apparently, he thinks of himself as an artist—like a painter or photographer. Before he strikes, he frames the victim in a setting as a message for the media, then kills. The owner of a denim company was found suffocated beneath a pile of blue jeans, stylistically arranged. That kind of thing."

For a moment, everyone was quiet, the threat of evil growing stronger and more visceral in the room. Outside, rain splattered down against the windowpanes, wind gusting branches against the side of the house.

Billy broke the silence. "Okay," he said, staring numbly down at the floor. "Honestly, I feel like we're sitting ducks for this guy. What do you suggest we do?"

Here, Early could do his part and took back the reins. Over the next fifteen minutes, he tried to cover his own misgivings with strong talk of security, precautionary measures, phone monitors . . . local and federal officers totally committed to their safety. Again, nobody was fooled.

Billy finally slapped his thighs and stood up. "Thank you for your valuable time," he said. "I'm sure you'll work hard and everything will be all right."

As they got ready to leave, Sam glanced, almost shyly, in the ballplayer's direction. Ellen knew the look and nudged her husband. "Billy, how about an autograph for Sam? He's probably got kids, and he's far too considerate to ask. How about it?"

Sam blushed and protested, but they all managed to laugh.

While Billy was signing an old photograph for Sam's son, Early had a moment alone with Ellen. During the evening, he had watched her carefully, intuitively drawn to her for reasons he didn't understand but somehow trusted.

"Mrs. Burwell, forgive me . . . I just wanted to say how sorry I am that we're here under these circumstances."

Ellen looked up and nodded.

"I also want to thank you for your service. You're dragging a lot of us out of apathy. First time for me in years."

She thanked him with a tired smile. "That's kind of you to say. And I don't mean for this to sound like I'm descending into clichés, but I thank *you* for what you do. You save lives every day. I just talk."

"Yeah, but the things you say are important. You work hard for those words."

She brightened slightly and gestured toward the table covered with books and paperwork. "Pardon the mess, but that's where those words come from. Mostly philosophy, I suppose, people . . . cultures, similarities and differences. Can't fix something if we don't really understand what's broken."

Early took a chance. "Are you familiar with karma? I mean, the concept?"

Ellen paused and narrowed her eyes. "You're an unusual policeman," she said, then considered the question. "I'm a Christian. But if you're asking me if I believe that actions have moral consequences—absolutely. I suppose it's . . . it's what we're all trying to deal with."

Early felt elated. But before he could speak, Ellen suddenly cupped her hands around his, a look of panic crowding her eyes. "Please. You have to stop this madman! Billy is . . . " She looked away, unable to finish.

"He's going to be okay. I give you my word."

She squeezed Early's hand, then rejoined Billy, who was still talking baseball with Sam, and put her arm around her husband's waist.

Early felt a pang of guilt as the two detectives walked down the stairs and stepped out into the rainy night. How could he promise anybody anything when he had no idea what he was doing? All he knew was that his days with the NYPD were over, and this news was going to be hard on his best friend.

They stood beside Sam's car, both relieved that the meeting had gone relatively smoothly. Sam was first to speak. "Don't know if we accomplished much. We're at least on the same page about security. That's a start. But God, I can't stand the thought that someone is gonna try to take out a guy like Billy. What the hell is wrong with this world?"

"I don't know, Sam," Early said sadly, shaking his head. "He's world-class. They both are. The whole thing makes me sick to my stomach."

As the passing cars flashed headlights into their eyes and the cold rain continued to saturate the night, Early turned up his collar.

Bracing himself for the fallout, he looked at his oldest friend's troubled face and began. "Sam, listen, whatever happens, I . . . I want you to keep me posted on this case. I . . . I know I can help."

"What's that supposed to mean?" Sam asked warily.

"I don't want to drag this out, so I'm telling you tonight. I'm leaving the force, giving Ripley my formal resignation tomorrow. I wanted you to be the first to know."

Sam sucked in his breath. The bewildered look in his dark eyes fractured as the hurt moved forward. "I knew it was comin'. Just didn't know when. Jesus, man, would you please tell me what the hell is going on with you?"

Early winced. "I'm sorry, Sam. I know I've been shutting you out. The problem is, I still don't understand it myself. My timing's bad, I know. But I just gotta get off the treadmill for a while."

"What about Burwell?" Sam shot back. "You just gonna walk away and let him get killed?"

"No, I'm not," Early said, fighting for the right words. "Honestly Sam, I got nothin' to stand on here, but I think I can do a better job *not* being a cop. Don't ask me why."

Sam fiddled with the belt of his raincoat, the drops collecting like silver beads along the top of his coarse hair. "Yeah . . . ," he exhaled slowly. Folding his arms, he turned to watch a yellow cab cruise down the street then vanish around the corner. "I got nothing to say. I just hope to hell you know what you're doin'."

Early felt the big sadness well up inside him. He would miss Sam intensely. Over the years, a lot of side-by-side history had gone down between them. Through the good and bad, Sam had always been there for him, steady and true. For his own peace of mind, Early had to hope that somehow whatever he finally decided to do would benefit Sam as well.

"I don't know what to tell you. Let's just call it a hunch . . . my biggest one yet," Early said, with a hint of a smile. "We'll stay in touch. I just need some time."

"Sure, man," said Sam, looking away into the distance. "Just don't disappear on me."

"I won't. I promise."

Early gave him a fierce hug. Then, lowering his head, he slowly walked away.

Sam got into his car and sat down heavily behind the wheel, slamming the door shut. He buckled his seat belt and pushed the key into the ignition. But he didn't start the engine. He didn't turn on the lights. Instead, he put his hands over his face and cried.

FOURTEEN

Coney Island

In an austere room lit by candlelight, Jori bent over a rickety table, added a sentence to his journal, then leaned back in his chair and listened to the crash of the sea in the distance. For him, the ocean was the great rebel, the great passion, the eternal struggle for freedom. He was always inspired by the sound of its voice.

His "reentry phase" was almost complete. Slowly, spirit was relearning how to seduce matter into compliance. Later tonight he would need this skill.

Coney Island was an ideal base for his operations. The ravished community offered him complete anonymity. It was also a constant reminder of the deep valleys that surrounded the tiny peaks of mortal life. For an awakened soul, it was essential to keep that in mind.

Many years ago, this amusement town had been an immense playground where New Yorkers came to splash and kiss and show off their muscles. Now the wind blew through desolate streets. The few rides that remained were corroded with salt, creaking with age. The rusted rails of the grand Cyclone roller coaster now looked like the bones of some prehistoric creature. But the young gods had migrated elsewhere, leaving the town alone to nurse the memories of its glory years, murmuring quietly to itself in the crumbling language of decay.

This suited Jori perfectly. Here, his true identity could be easily disguised, never questioned, barely noticed. For all intents and purposes, he was just another faded writer come to dream, drink, and die. It didn't matter to anyone if he walked slightly behind the times in a brown overcoat, preferring to be alone. This seemed to fit Coney Island's unwritten law. A stranger had the right to remain a stranger as long as he paid the rent and kept to himself.

Sighing, Jori returned to his journal, documenting the tangled theater of the mission—its tides and events, characters and karma—all roads leading to this moment of pen and paper in a cottage by the sea. But after two more entries, he pushed his chair away from the desk. He was through for the evening. At least for now, he was not dissatisfied. James Early, his earthly ward, was making progress. Nevertheless, the danger was visceral, the urgency growing. As before, Palden had cautioned Jori. *We continue to lick honey from the razor blade. Each time we disturb the status quo, we court disaster. If there is sweetness, it will always mingle with blood.*

In this instance, there was a wild card in the game, a person who could be a huge asset to the mission *if* he played by the rules. Jori was to make the initial overture, observe the reaction, then act accordingly.

In preparation, he blew out the candle and lay down on the woven mat where he rested his body during the night. Closing his eyes, he filled his inner space with calm, letting go of his surroundings. It was time to make his visit.

Spanish Harlem

On an equivalently thin mattress, in a section of the city where the streets still pulsed with life at four a.m., a man lay asleep in a darkened room. Despite the cold night and hard floor, he slept without a pillow, only a sheet covering his naked body.

Suddenly, as if poked by an invisible finger, Trakker opened his eyes and sat up sharply. *Someone was in the room.* After flicking his attention around, he located the source, then relaxed. *Nothing dangerous. Quite the contrary. The intruder's presence was as smooth as starlight.*

Jori, dressed in street clothes, stepped out from the shadows. Reflecting the dim light from the street, his eyes shone quietly in the dark room. In traditional Tibetan greeting, he placed his hands together in front of his chest, then lowered them to cover his heart, meaning . . . *I come in peace*.

"Hello Trakker," he said, warm but unsmiling.

The musician stared back. Then he put his arms under his knees, rocked backward, and grinned. "Well, well, well! What have we here?"

Continuing to study the apparition, Trakker shook his head in wonder. "My system rocks, man. It's not every day an Earth Grad glides through one of my walls."

"Thank you," Jori replied nonplused.

Trakker ran a hand through his dark eclectic hair, still pondering his guest. "You're one of Palden's Tibet boys, aren't you? Don't know what you're up to, but the vibes coming outta that realm—pretty intense."

Jori allowed a small patient smile. "Let me know when you're through."

"I'm never through. And you go on forever. It's gonna be a night to remember."

Pleased with his repartee, the poet gave himself a slight, private nod of approval, then wrapped the sheet around himself like a toga. Standing up, he grabbed his guitar from its stand near the doorway and returned to his bed. Sitting cross-legged, he strummed idly for a moment before resting the instrument across his lap. Then a slight scowl began to appear.

"Your oh-so-patient act is not playing well here," he said testily. "You got something to say, put it to words."

"Then words it is." Jori took a step forward. "You're quite a treat. But I do have a request."

"Yeah, well, I don't do requests."

"Hear me out, if you will," Jori said, then came to the point. "You have the *gift*."

Trakker shrugged. "My wiring's weird. Get cross talk from every sector. Sometimes poetry, sometimes gibberish. You get used to it."

"I'm sure. But I would like to 'impress' you into service. Would you be interested in using your talent to help us?"

Trakker shot him a sharp glance. "Me, help you? Come on!"

"The request is sincere."

Genuinely perplexed, Trakker shook his head. "What would the smooth and the holy want from a toxic crude like me?"

"Good karma. That's our currency. We have a new recruit. The cop who got some front-page news a while ago. You talked to him on a street corner."

"Yeah, okay. What about him?"

"His name is James Early. There are a few things regarding him that you could help us with. My . . . status . . . has some intrinsic limitations. You, on the other hand, are a resident here and free to operate. You could help us enormously."

Trakker picked up his guitar and started playing again, bending notes to sound like a sitar. "This guy . . . he's moonlighting for you folks? That's way interesting."

"We're . . . negotiating," Jori said, then crouched down so he was eye level with the poet. "But back to you, let me ask—do you understand your gift?"

Trakker was caught off guard. "What's to understand? I . . . I fall forward. Play it as it lies. That's it."

Jori laughed. "Well then, you are in for some surprises. Work with us. As you would say, the gods have deep pockets. You could end up a rich man."

"Whatever," Trakker said. "With me, the future rolls like a Coltrane solo. I never plan. But you guys got style. Maybe I'll do you one."

The musician's words seemed to hang in the air for a moment, the room and streets outside strangely quiet.

"So be it!" Jori said with finality, inwardly smiling. Considering the elaborate bouncing stitchwork of this soul, Trakker's response sounded like a firm commitment.

Jori stood up and motioned farewell. "Thank you again. I will be in touch."

Trakker watched the image of his guest grow dimmer and dimmer as if attached to a rheostat. In the vacated space, the molecules danced like fireflies, then faded to black.

Gramercy Park

Ellen Burwell stood with her arms folded loosely across her chest, gazing out her second-story window at the coming of night. "I love this hour," she said softly. "The fading light . . . it always tugs at something inside me."

Billy put the newspaper down and joined her by the window, watching the leaves in a nearby elm catch the last drops of sunlight. "Bittersweet, isn't it?" He rested a hand on her shoulder. "Never liked it much as a ballplayer. Hard to track the ball. Stadium lights not much help. Like a twilight zone, literally."

"Forgive the melodrama, but that's how I feel these days," she said, the stress lines deepening around her eyes, "wondering what's out there, wanting to keep you safe, knowing you have to live your life. I try to dismiss it all, but . . . "

"I know." Billy squeezed her arm. "Just remember, they used to say I could outrun a speeding bullet. If it comes to that, I still will."

Ellen sighed, looked up into his face. "Any news?"

"Nothing worth mentioning. Everywhere I go, the FBI swarms around me like flies. It's almost comical. Last night at the gym, I was taking laps, and I accidentally bowled over one of their agents. The poor guy gets up, brushes himself off, then apologizes to *me*!"

"Bet you hate it. Being watched like that, every minute of every day."

"Sure, I guess it's . . . " framing her face in his hands. "Sweetheart, please, let's not do this. We'll be okay. We're just hitting our stride. The kids are out of the house, you're going gangbusters. These should be our best years."

Billy kissed the top of her head. Looking down into the park, he pointed his finger toward a lone figure sitting on a bench near the fountain feeding the birds. "Look! It's ol' graybeard, Reverend Spencer. Bible and bread crumbs. Must be twenty pigeons tonight. Ninety-two years old and never misses a day."

Then he did a double take. "My God, I think he just tipped his hat to us!"

Ellen smiled and glanced at her watch. "Okay. It's six-fifteen. Let's see if . . . yup, there he goes."

Both watched as the old man got to his feet, then hobbled out of the park.

Ellen shook her head. "You can set your watch by him."

They both laughed, then grew silent. For a long moment, they were a harbor again—a circle of warmth and safety—hoping that the storm around them would pass quickly without inflicting damage.

It was not to be.

In the middle of the park, a small ticking package tucked inside a knothole received its signal and obeyed promptly. With a deafening explosion, an incendiary bomb blast roared through the park. The ground shook as smoke and flames mushroomed into the sky. Orange tentacles blistered through the foliage, scorching everything in their path. Leaves burst into fire, turning trees into huge torches.

The shock waves from the blast rocked the rows of houses directly bordering the park. The Burwells' front window shattered, hurling the couple backward onto the floor.

Billy, stunned and bleeding from a cut on his forehead, sat up slowly, spotted his wife, crawled to her side.

"Ellen! Are you all right!?"

She didn't answer immediately. Finally, pulling a shard of glass from her arm, she met his gaze. "Yes. I think so. You?"

"A few scratches, nothing serious." He helped her to her feet. They turned to each other, the same question mirrored in their eyes. *Were we responsible for this? Had Quill just sent us a message?*

Before they could articulate this, their team of security men came pounding into the room.

Malcolm sat in his car, watching his rearview mirror suddenly flare with orange flame, and smiled with satisfaction. Mission accomplished. Then, systematically, he quietly began covering his tracks.

The remote control for the firebomb went into the concealed pouch beneath the front seat. The Reverend Spencer costume was next. The wig and beard, placed in a plastic bag on the passenger seat. The makeup, removed with cold cream and handkerchief. Later, all these items, plus the disgusting grey suit, would be burned. The stolen gate key would be kept as a memento.

Now he could enjoy the impact of his performance.

Even from this distance, the car had vibrated with the impact, the rush of heated air pressing against the windows. Now, fire alarms were sounding, and frightened residents were pouring out into the street. It was theater. Beautifully orchestrated chaos! With a mock salute to the blazing gardens of the high-toned park, he slowly drove away.

The stately music of Telemann swept through the car, touching him like the fingers of God. He had accomplished this event with his usual style: precise, effective, and mysterious. Next Sunday, when the bell in the old Gramercy Park church didn't ring, the bell tower would be inspected. There they would find the ancient preacher's body—lightly seasoned with his own bread crumbs, still clutching the tattered Bible to his heart.

More importantly, the assassin was now beginning to feel more intimate with his prey, a necessary step to reach the desired climax with his art. The timing had also been spectacular. His binoculars had been glued on the Burwells' windows, drinking in details when the bomb had gone off. They had been worried before. Now they would be terrified. Part of his craft involved helping his victim cultivate a profound appreciation for the aesthetics of pain.

FIFTEEN

The Garden Apartments — Brooklyn, NY

Ida Early rested both arms across the top of her walker and peered at her son with a look that only a mother can do properly—a twinkle and a reprimand folded neatly together into one.

"Well, it's good to see you, but I still have nagging rights—even if I am seventy-two years old and live like a ghost in this old cardboard box."

The "old cardboard box" was called the Garden Apartments and had been her own stubborn choice. Being located anywhere more than five blocks away from the neighborhood where she had been born, married, and worked her entire life would be "untidy," which meant unthinkable.

But the retirement home, with its rundown mismatched furniture and sickeningly cheerful floral print wallpaper, always made Early flinch. She would bat away his concerns by saying she wanted to go down in her own dust when she died, not in a room that smelled like disinfectant. "Anyway," she would voice matter-of-factly, "I don't care what's around me anymore." Then she'd touch above her heart and say, "Only what's in here." Early couldn't argue.

She was a tiny woman, measuring a little more than five feet in her slippers, who still had plenty of snap in her delivery. As Early sat patiently on her living room couch a few feet away, Ida studied her only child with the thoroughness and care of a gardener looking for any trace of damage on a prized rose. She had no idea of the dramatic changes in his life, only that he seemed dramatically different.

"You're a considerate son, James, and I know you're decent enough to ask, so

I'm just going to say up front. No! I don't want to talk about my health! It's rotten and it's boring, so let's move on. I want to talk about you."

Then continuing to regard him with concern, she spoke firmly. "You, of course, didn't tell me a thing, so I had to read about you and the drug bust in the newspaper. You're a genuine hero. That's the truth. And you're doing the world a favor by doing what you do. But, James, I'm going to be straight with you. You don't look so good. You're thin . . . got that world-weary crust. Help me understand, son, or don't even bother speaking." Having made her pronouncement, Ida leaned back in her chair and waited. The floor now belonged to Early.

The startling directness of the woman always made Early feel at home. If her language were sometimes harsh, it was also accompanied by incredibly warm eyes. Mother and son had a longstanding agreement. When asked a question, take your time, but then answer completely and honestly. This time, however, Early held back. He didn't feel ready to discuss his wild spiritual odyssey. Not now, maybe never. He would have to approach the subject indirectly by getting her to speak. Given his recent transformation, there were some things about his past he wanted to clarify—for both of their sakes. That was why he had made the trip tonight.

Without a doubt, his mother had always been his pillar of strength. Her husband, also a policeman, had been killed in the line of duty when Early was only seven years old. Suddenly alone, Ida had quietly taken off her apron, hung it on a nail behind the kitchen door, and entered the job market. The small pension she would receive from the government would never be enough to get her kid through tough economic times, let alone college.

Working a fifty-hour week as a seamstress in a local dress shop, she had managed to support herself and her child. Despite the challenges, a deep connection with her son remained her number one priority. Sometimes overbearing but always straightforward, she had encouraged his strength and ability to laugh—despite the empty chair at their dining room table. Years later, when Early had announced that, regardless of her protests, he was going to join the NYPD, she had made a pronouncement of her own. She was going to be an artist.

And when James left home, she had done just that—taking classes and turning her living room into a studio. Soon she was painting pictures of her beloved neighborhood. She wanted to capture its fading dignity before it vanished from the New York landscape forever. Amid the changing culture, she singled out and rendered aspects of life from pre-World War II Brooklyn: train cars, parts of buildings, and tenacious shops. Occasionally she painted a face that had retained its character, somehow preserved beneath the dehumanizing layers of modern life.

Ida liked to portray herself as a temperamental "old bird," a devout loner. She would engage in friendship only if she decided the person was "capable in the heart," a rare review she bestowed upon only a few. Her son, however, received everything she had to give. He was one of the only reasons her faulty heart continued to beat.

As the grandfather clock ticked steadily onward in the hallway, Early continued to stare down at the threadbare green carpet. Despite the mother and son bond, there was a new and growing gap between them. Early had just opened Pandora's box of past lifetimes, spawning new perspectives on relationships and family and karma—all needing reinspection. Sitting in the presence of his oldest friend in the world, in this moment of transition, Early felt emotions stirring. For some reason, he wanted to do something for Ida tonight—assure her of something, help them both come to terms with something nameless in the past.

Watching her pensive son, Ida began to feel alarmed. She scratched the inside of her neck, smoothed the sleeve of her black-and-white checkered housedress. "Not to break our rule here, son, but you won't find the words on the floor. Talk to me, or I swear I'll paint your portrait. Then you'll really see what I'm looking at. It's not so pretty."

Early shifted his weight, leaned forward on the couch. "Yeah, recently I've started to look at things a bit differently. If it's okay with you, Ma, I've got some questions about the family. I mean, Dad getting killed . . . even before that, things about me growing up. Would that be okay?"

Ida suddenly brightened. "You have no idea, son! I'm thrilled. You changed like day to night after Tom got shot. I didn't know if you lost something or gained something. Maybe both. But I've wanted to talk about it for years. I had to wait. It had to come from you."

Early rubbed the palms of his hands along the thighs of his jeans. "Tell me. I'd really like to know."

Ida moved her walker next to the couch, turned it around, then carefully slid down beside her son. Leaning back into the cushions, she began. "Well, you were a complete surprise—for both of us. We were poor, working-class folk. Suddenly we had this gentle, almost religious kid on our hands. Most of the time you were quiet, played by yourself. You'd sit in this funny position, one leg sorta tucked on top of the other. Then you'd close your eyes, not say a word for a long while. One time, you told me you were trying to protect us. But we didn't know what you were scared of. We bought you things—toys, games. Sometimes you played with them, but mostly not."

Ida sighed, uncomfortable with the memory. "You were not a happy kid. You always had those nightmares, bad ones, especially when you were real young. We tried to get it out of you, what they were about, but you acted confused, like you couldn't remember. We felt pretty desperate. Thought about a psychiatrist, but oh . . . I don't know. Nothing seemed quite right, so we kept it in the family.

"The real problem was, well, you didn't seem to like yourself. Heartbreaking to watch. Nothing we tried did any good. You never complained, but sometimes . . . oh God, I thought you were the loneliest little boy in all of Brooklyn."

Early felt a rush of sorrow as vague recollections stirred inside him. His mother, however, rambled on, seemingly unaware of his presence—her words coming out slowly as if pulled from an old treasure box where painful, beautiful things had been stored from long ago.

"Sometimes you'd do things that amazed us. Even when you could barely walk, when Tom and I would fight, you'd wedge your tiny body between us and kind of . . . well, snap us out of it. Then we'd both feel foolish, and the three of us would hug. It was uncanny."

"Did I talk about anything that . . . I mean . . . anything that was strange?"

"All the time! You'd grip my fingers in that little hand of yours, so tight, and talk about, oh, I don't know, magic things—a snowy place, maybe like a castle, far away. And when Rabbi Jacobs used to visit, you'd get so excited! I always felt you wanted us to understand something. And we tried. God, how we tried. But nothing made much sense to us."

She shook her head. "Don't get me wrong, James. You were a complete joy. So patient! The other kids gave you a hard time. Teased you 'cause you were so different. You didn't seem to care, but you never backed down."

Early smiled at this.

"Darn right, you should be proud. You could have beaten the pants off any of them. You grew big for your age, and very strong, but you only fought when you had to. We didn't know if you were going to be a priest or a wrestler!"

Ida paused for a moment, remembering. "Most of all," she added thoughtfully, "it seemed you were trying to work something out with yourself. Unfortunately, we were no help at all."

"Then what happened?" Early asked.

"Well, as I said, when Tom passed away, you changed. You became all boy—sports, girls. You started dropping that sweetness. You got pretty wild, maybe even a little mean streak, but I never really knew. You said you wanted to get rid of the bad guys, guys with guns, like the punks who took your father away. Do some good in the world. And that's just what you've done. I'll tell you, though, you became a completely different kid and never looked back—'til now."

Ida turned sideways on the couch, her eyes slightly moist. "You were, and still are, a son I'm proud of. Always will be. I just want you to be proud too."

Early lowered his head. "I'm trying, God knows."

Ida watched him, heart brimming over, unable to say a word.

Finally, Early reached over and took her hand—dry and brittle yet still warm, like driftwood baking in the sun. When he looked at her, he saw the soul of a young woman—still luminous inside the aging exterior. For a moment, the harsh lines on her face, the coarse silver hair, seemed like a tragic and unforgiving frame for the noble soul he knew as his mother.

"I'm putting the pieces back together now," James finally said, pushing against the swell of emotions. "I want you to know, I understand my nightmares now. The things troubling me back then had nothing to do with you or Dad. I—," he paused, wanting to tell her everything, but somehow at a loss.

She squeezed and released his hand. "You don't need to explain, son. I'm just glad you're working it out. You're made of fine, unusual stuff. Whatever you're doing, I know it takes a lot of courage, so I'm going to worry. As your mother, that's my right. The fact that you came by to talk to me, *that* makes me happy."

Early stood up. Leaning down, he kissed her on the wrinkles of her cheek. She reached up with a frail hand and held his face against hers tenderly. Gradually, she softened her grip and let go. After thirty years, a sharp piece inside her had finally melted away.

"Thank you," she said, getting back up with the help of her walker. "It helps me to know that you're going to tie it all up. Now I can die in peace."

Early objected. "Don't talk that way! You got plenty of life inside you. You—"

"Shush!" She put her finger on his lips. "When Brooklyn's had enough of me, serves me that eviction notice, I go. End of story."

Ida began to rattle her walker toward the door. It was her signal that she was tired and wanted to be alone. In the doorway, she reached up to pat his broad shoulder. "I know it's tricky stuff, James. You'll do fine, but I'm going to wish you good luck anyway."

Early put his arm around her thin body. "It's all tricky, Mom. What I'm going through, what you're going through . . . it's nothing but work. If you need *anything*, call me."

Early walked away with a poignant sense of accomplishment. Standing beneath the steel girders of the elevated train, he looked up through the metal and concrete, out beyond the rails. Somehow the night sky seemed closer. In some profound way, he and his mother had reached across a nameless divide tonight and touched, soul to kindred soul.

Ida lingered by the door for a moment, turning a few things over in her mind. Decided, she hobbled over to her desk and pulled out a newspaper clipping from the top drawer. It was the most recent picture she had of her son—a photograph taken the day after all the heroin had been found in the East Village apartment. Propping it up on the ledge of her easel in front of a blank canvas, she stepped back, visualizing the painting. Yes, now she could work with the photograph. Now she had the full perspective. Sorrow was well represented in the face, but now she could see the depth and clarity beginning to push forward into her son's eyes.

Tomorrow she would start painting his portrait. A slow smile crossed her face. Then, truly, the circle would be complete—and her work would be done.

SIXTEEN

Fifth Avenue — WhiteMan's Penthouse Suite

The Albino stood before his huge picture window, wincing with pain—the barrage of afternoon sunlight, like needles, piercing his mind open. Lines and colors, shapes and contours . . . shifting, turning, obscuring his client's reading. A moment later, he had what he needed, chaos fusing into simple calculations. With a muffled scream, he wrenched the velvet drapes shut. Blessed darkness!

Instantly the room became womb-like again: silent and self-contained. The psychic hunched over, dabbing the torrent of tears that streamed from his raw eyes with a silk handkerchief. When the pain finally settled into a dull throb, he hobbled to his desk and picked up the telephone.

The raspy voice spoke, like wind through dry leaves, "Mr. Raines. For now, remain on the path of diversion. Your situation is still encumbered with 'unfriendly intangibles,' the same ones of which I spoke in your last call. They appear to be growing more solid and seeking to attach themselves to your operations. If unchecked, they will infiltrate and remove you from your power. You are staying one step ahead. Continue to do so!"

Malcolm sat down on the corner of the bed, his foot tapping impatiently. Even for WhiteMan, this advice was extremely veiled and obscure. Despite growing agitation, he kept his voice even. "This is not exactly what I wanted to hear. I need to know more."

The Albino closed his eyes, re-examining his impressions. As was always the case with his clients, his perception was selective—noting tendencies and patterns, careful to avoid, at least outwardly, any knowledge of specifics. If they used his information to rob, rape, or murder, that was their business.

A long moment later, the throat was cleared and the voice whispered again, "The party you wish to entertain will be most inclined to receive your offer in a setting of celebration—a business headquarters, or perhaps a place of worship. If your venture is to be successful, the altitude you assume must be high and above reproach. Again, I caution you, there are formidable elements that hover about your endeavors. At all costs, maintain your slight advantage."

Malcolm listened intently, watching the stiff movement of the second hand on his Rolex tick around the circle of the dial. "As you mentioned, the timing is important. When do you suggest I conduct this meeting?"

"In the past, you have expressed a desire for maximum impact and spectacle. In this particular case, you have an extraordinary opportunity to do so. Go over schedules and timetables. Find a place of meaning and attraction that plays well for your 'prospect.'"

Malcolm stood up, his mind already beginning to translate the psychic's words into a bold idea. "Thank you," he said, now with more excitement. "Is there anything else you wish to tell me?"

WhiteMan hesitated. Indeed, there was, but not for now. "Not at this time. Tailor my general suggestions to fit your requirements. And use your faculties of observation assiduously. I am becoming fascinated with your progress—and your obstacles. After you have completed the task, please call me again with your news."

The dark Englishman put the phone down quietly, a plan of action beginning to emerge. He had done his research: the articles had been read and the videotapes studied. He knew every detail, particularly the patterns of motions that his subject tended to manifest under stress—an important knowledge to have when Malcolm's finger was poised on the trigger.

The assassin stood by the window looking down at the clogged streets and the knots of pedestrians dwarfed by the towering buildings. *Manhattan . . . soon I will give you unforgettable theater.*

While his client began to work out his lethal plans, WhiteMan remained pensive at his desk. *What was happening?* This new presence lingering around Raines had not dissipated at all. In fact, it had grown! He should have reversed his earlier advice and told his client to move directly and immediately to his main objective, then race back to his hiding place in England. He hadn't. *Was it possible that he, the great psychic, was becoming caught up in this invisible web as well?* He had never seen such a resilient and weightless "texture." Its fabric had no time in it! Its weave intricate and strong, yet very, very old.

WhiteMan took a shallow breath. Although the signs were subtle, the implications were staggering! Unquestionably, some element was tampering with the equilibrium of forces.

As he leaned forward, his fingers began to stir again. Seemingly independent of his thoughts, one of the Albino's hands moved restlessly along the top of his desk, encountered something, then moved vertically up the side of the object. A photograph in a metal frame. Fingertips played about the surface of the picture. The psychic glanced down: his deceased mistress holding their gifted twins. Idly, he wondered about his two children. He hadn't seen them in more than twenty-five years. By now they should be completely out of his way—either emotionally crippled or dead.

Suddenly, one of the fingers snapped back as if it had just been bitten. WhiteMan squinted at the image of his offspring. *No, not dead at all. One of them, apparently, was very much alive!*

Early's Apartment

It was Early's last day at the Thirteenth Precinct. Knotted with emotions, he had placed his badge and firearm firmly on the chief's desk and stepped back from a life that had consumed him, absorbing the fallout from his fellows. Sam had given him a searching look, then sadly walked away. Ripley threw a tantrum, then flung his hands into the air and stomped off. The other officers had been less emphatic, offering bewildered handshakes and best wishes. But it was a wrap. Done. As of today, James Early's fifteen-year tenure with the NYPD was officially over.

The initial twenty-four hours had been rough. He was no longer defined by clock and procedure. It was all up to him—the big and little choices and all the complicated avenues in between. But Early was only intimidated by this vacuum for the first day. A modest pension in place, he began to set up his beachhead. He was now a man with a mission.

On the second night of his retirement, he came home from the library with an armload of books: Tibetan history, Eastern philosophy, and two primers on quantum physics. In Palden's words, philosophy and science must be melded together. So be it. Early would pick up where he last left off. This time, no matter what happened, no matter how dangerous it became, he would try to keep a spiritual perspective as due north on his inner compass.

Hours later, he looked up from his studies. It had been subtle, but he had just felt that odd sense of something invading his space. Scanning, listening . . . nothing. Only the backwash of the city outside. Then a noise—a creaking floorboard from outside his front door, followed by silence. No knock, no buzzer.

Moving soundlessly, he bent down beside the doorway. The crack of light from the hallway was being interrupted by something . . . or someone. Early peered through the peephole: soft blackness. Something was obstructing the view as well.

Adrenalin pumping, he retrieved his revolver from the desk drawer and returned to the doorway. In one fluid motion he unbolted the locks, threw open the door, and leveled his gun. In a similarly fluid motion, a hand flashed out and chopped Early across the wrist, sending the gun skittering across the floor.

"Won't be needing that, cowboy," Trakker said as he burst past him into the room, ringlets of hair flaring like a dark, electrical storm. He was dressed in a torn bomber jacket, black jeans, and old battered boots. Slung across his back, like a quiver, was a guitar in a black cloth case.

He didn't get far. Two steps later, the musician suddenly found his arm in a viselike grip, forced behind his back. An instant later, he was facedown, nose pushed against the floor. His guitar, stripped off his back, now lay beside him on the floor.

Early straddled him, one knee pressed against his back. "Well, well, the spare-change guy with the bad manners." He clucked his tongue, enjoying this odd turn of events. "Before we get started, let's get something very straight. You may be a big hit on Seventy-Second Street, but you're outta your league here—and in a lot of trouble. State your business or I haul you in for B and E!"

"*Your* 'league' is spiritually anorexic. Dinosaurs with derringers," Trakker said through clenched teeth. "All you're doing is proving my point, man, big time. Now show me a little IQ and let me up."

Early shook his head. "My translator's got the night off. Speak English."

"English is just the spin of a ball, man. Learn mine."

"Meter's running," Early said impatiently.

Trakker tried to push his body off the ground but immediately felt his torso crushed to the floor.

"One more time!" Early said roughly. "Tell me why you're here!"

With effort, Trakker slowly craned his neck around so he could see his captor.

"You got benefactors, damn it! I've been sent to help you," Trakker blurted out. "Now off!"

Early assessed, then relinquished his hold. None of the last few weeks made sense. Why should he expect anything to be different now? In truth, the poet's previous advice about the calendar had been eerily spot-on.

"You got two minutes. The riddles go, a real dialogue occurs, or you and your show go downtown. Understand?"

Trakker slowly got to his feet. Dignity ruffled, he brushed off his jeans and adjusted his coat. Then he lifted his guitar from the floor as though it were a museum piece. After inspecting it carefully, he leaned it against the couch. By the time he turned to face his captor, his bizarre package of rock 'n roll, street urchin, and rebel prince had reassembled itself and was back in place.

He studied Early for a moment, a twinge of begrudging respect creeping into his eyes. "You're green, but maybe you'll do okay," he said, rubbing his sore arm. "Now just relax. I gotta look around for invisible ink."

Trakker surveyed the apartment, his eyes lingering here and there as if inspecting the air.

"You're clean enough," Trakker finally announced. "Not talking about dust balls—talkin' cold spots, ghost linkage, psychic noise, interference. That kind of thing. You're going dimension-hopping tonight. Want it smooth as cognac. My rep is at stake."

Early's tolerance finally hit zero. Grabbing the poet by his wrist, he pushed him down onto the couch, then dragged his armchair over and sat down across from him.

"Enough! Now tell me who the hell you're working for and what this is all about."

The musician barely glanced at him. "No deal, no details. Let's just say I'm fulfilling a request for your upstairs neighbors. Get used to me. I've been appointed to your karmic loop."

He looked at his watch as if he were going to catch a plane, then pointed a long slender finger directly at Early. "In fifteen minutes, the monkey rides the crocodile up the Ganges. The Big Dog is waiting."

Early started to interrupt, but Trakker waved him off. "I've heard you've had a few memories. Tonight's no little flashback. You're going live now—gonna parachute *up* through a hole in space . . . a freak in the fabric. This means you leave the earth plane for a while. Go where the dead go. They don't get to come back without a round of amnesia and face-lift—you will. But only if you stop pouting and start playing."

Quickly considering the fact that he had nothing left to lose, Early finally shrugged. "Okay, I'm in. Do what you do. Just remember, you're on a short leash with me. Real short."

Trakker turned off the overhead light, then took a small candle in a brass holder from the inside pocket of his jacket. Placing it on the coffee table, he lit the wick with a flick of his Zippo lighter.

The flame sputtered, then held. As Early's eyes adjusted, the room immediately became drenched in shadows that leapt and bobbed around the walls in the weaving light.

"Here we go," Trakker said. Then the timbre of his voice changed. He was now formally giving instructions.

"Jumping dimensions is like cosmic skateboarding. You gotta know the hills and curbs. Sometimes there's traffic—a bad news bus or phantom barnstormers—so you gotta change direction on a dime. This time, I'm gonna handle that stuff for you. Once you're launched, I'll push you in the right direction."

Early looked at the rascal poet. Putting his faith, maybe even his life, in this man's hands seemed absolutely insane. And yet, under all that smoke screen of jittery verbiage, there did seem to be someone home, possibly someone very astute.

Early slowly nodded his head. "All right, fire away."

"The trick is . . . *go simple*," Trakker said with an enigmatic smile. "So simple that you forget all about the li'l ol' James Early storylines. Return to your *original* stuff, the pure stuff before you bought into the big masquerade."

He inched closer to Early, a lingering scent of cigarettes and jasmine. "Let go of gravity, man, yours and everybody else's. And all those shoulds and shouldn'ts? They're paperweights! Lose 'em, dude, and be amazed!"

Early settled into the couch. If nothing else, this would at least be entertaining.

Trakker sat for a moment letting the wail of a siren on the streets below dissipate. Then, lifting his guitar from its case like a sacred object, he secured it in his lap and began to play.

At first the music was slow, thick, and hypnotic. At the same time, Trakker seemed to slip into a trance, shamanistic, doing something to the space without using words.

Early's mind began to fragment, losing sense of time and place. Then the tempo picked up, faster and faster, kicking up the adrenalin but somehow quieting the mind. In the background, he heard the musician tapping out exotic rhythms with his feet.

All around him now, his apartment was shredding, objects relinquishing their authority and definitions. Soon a fleet of golden balls appeared, moving in slow circles in the air.

"It's the dance of illusions, flatfoot. Stay loose!" he heard from somewhere in the chaos.

The music played on. Then, with a soft jolt, everything unplugged from solidity and became a tumbling mosaic of energy—turning and turning, growing thinner and finer like spun gold.

In the middle of the room, Trakker's face appeared to rise above the upheaval, like a moon coming out from behind a cloud. Early saw the dark eyes directly in front of him, growing larger and gleaming with strange intensity.

He seemed to be smiling.

Finally Early stopped trying to protect himself, stopped trying to stuff this experience into any of his logical files. With nothing left to analyze, he lifted his mental foot off the brakes. Immediately he began to feel like he was floating.

From down below he heard, "You're out on the plank. Now stop caring . . . and leap!"

Early surrendered his last bit of concern, and a wave of peace washed through him, filling up all the crevices of his troubled soul.

In the distance, he heard Trakker's voice one last time. "You're across! Surfing the Big One, baby! Arrivederci, tough guy!"

Trakker's music grew softer and softer. In its stead was the sound of a soft whistle, like a wind chime moving at the speed of light.

Swaddled inside a warm current, Early flowed into "elsewhere."

SEVENTEEN

The Akashic Realm

Neither now, nor then. Neither here, nor there. Without form or known destiny, Early was swept onward—the atmosphere growing thin and cold, like mountain air. But the sensation was different from his memory dreams. This had the elegant feel of being carried by something ethereal as light itself, as massive and gentle as the lapping waves of the sea.

When finally set down, Early's entire being felt blurred, along with an odd, comforting sense of returning home. Images from his previous lifetime in Tibet filled his mind, this time when he was a young child in the early days when the monastery was first discovered and became the unlikely home for his spiritual family: Palden, his sister, and her young daughter, Usha. They had lived each day without fear or doubt. A joyful time when the future lay ahead, resplendent with the full range of possibilities. Then came Palden's letter—his call to action that initiated the mission—and everything changed.

Early shook his head to clear his thoughts. With partial vision, he recognized the empty room made of shifting energy encased in a space hollowed out from the mountainside. And yes, this had been his playing grounds when he was a young boy, so very far and long ago.

For a moment, he thought he heard voices—exciting talk, becoming frantic . . . then no sound at all. Finding his way to a staircase, he climbed to a landing near a wide front door. He thought he heard a burst of gunshots and yelling. Then silence. He pushed the door open and was met by soldiers, machine guns blazing, flames erupting, corpses . . . then nothing.

Early shuddered, rubbed his eyes. Stillness and relief. Time was playing tricks on him. He now stood in the peaceful courtyard of the monastery, bathed in gentle light with its own quiet cadence.

Gradually, however, he became aware of another slower rhythm. A chill passed through him. It was the sound of breathing. Someone else was there and watching! Without warning, words formed inside his head. Don't try to perceive with earth muscles. You are now in an illusion that employs an extremely subtle wavelength.

The voice was precise and warm, but the message was delivered with the underlying sharpness of a man accustomed to authority.

Early exhaled and tried to upgrade his perspective. As the uncertain landscape gradually dissipated, he discerned a lone figure sitting on a bench in the courtyard. Slowly, dramatically, the person turned to observe him. Early immediately filled in the rest of the picture—the hazel eyes, the high cheekbones. Electricity spread throughout his soul as the man rose and strode toward him. "Oh my God!" Early cried. He was looking at the face of his beloved father and mentor. The graceful soul of Palden now stood three feet away.

"Hello Tashi, my son. Be comfortable. I am not your judge."

Early stared as the broken pieces of his current life began to fit together. Now it all made sense! Since day one of his difficult childhood, hadn't all his winding roads led inexorably to this confrontation? Who else could have orchestrated this incredible series of events?

Palden watched with a hint of whimsy. "Who else indeed?" he said mildly.

Transfixed in the brilliant simplicity of his former master's steady gaze, Early didn't want to speak. He wanted to absorb the absolute "thereness" of the man. Palden's appearance seemed unchanged from his Tibetan incarnation. The same fierce yet compassionate alertness poured through his eyes. His frame still slender and wiry with small-boned features and almond coloring. His head was shaved, save for a silvery plume of ponytail that now flowed down from the back of his skull, almost touching his shoulders.

Early's mind finally stopped squinting at the scenario. As much as he wanted to bask in the moment, Palden was also associated with his betrayal and its horrific aftermath. There could be only one reason for this reunion. Early was the prodigal son summoned home to be upbraided.

"Thank you," he finally said, fighting to stay one step ahead of his emotions. "Thank you for . . . finding me again. Your niece and I . . . we never meant to . . . "

As Early clenched down on the torrent of grief, Palden remained utterly still, enveloping the man's sorrow in his presence. Early immediately felt quieted, the frantic urgency behind the gush of words suddenly gone. All was understood.

"Karma is an instructive thing," Palden said matter-of-factly, "if a person has the courage and stamina to listen. Regarding your role in the desolation of the mission, there are many layers that make up that moment. More than you can possibly know. And you are mid-process. All I will say is pay attention, practice curiosity—but not inquisition. Anything beyond that is spiritually unproductive."

Early accepted the words but wasn't ready to feel exonerated. One thought persisted. *Could the visionary Palden have known, even before the mission, that this was all going to occur? Was it all a play within a play?*

These thoughts intrigued him but were pushed aside. He had betrayed a profound spiritual trust. If there were any possibility of redemption, he would grab it and be eternally grateful for the second chance.

With renewed hope, he spoke earnestly, "Then I won't beg you for forgiveness. But the fact is, I've done damage. Extraordinary men and women died because of me. I know I can't undo it, but I . . . I mean, somehow, I have to make this right."

The sage said nothing, listening and watching carefully as his disciple struggled with the pain beneath his words.

Early brushed away a cluster of tears from his cheek. "Police work was something I needed to do. But it was never enough. Not close. I've had time to think about it—a lot. Putting criminals behind bars doesn't solve anything. Just sweeps the dirt under the carpets 'til next time. It's about solving karma. That's the real battle."

Palden knew his pupil well. "And I know you will immediately want to swing your sword—even before you understand your foe. It's passion's way," Palden added. "In time, you'll learn that patience is not just a virtue. It is also the hilt of your weapon. I can only say, should you choose to align with our mission, you will need to be fully armed."

These words were music to Early's ears. Battles were familiar turf. Maybe now he could get to work. "I just need to know what the plan is."

The sage nodded appreciatively, as if the first milestone of their meeting had been passed.

"Then you shall!"

Palden placed an almost weightless hand on his disciple's arm. The physical connection made Early's entire body prickle with energy.

"Come," he said, leading Early to the walkway that crept along the cliff. Palden bent down, picked up a stone, and tossed it into the air. It refused to fall, unexpectedly hovering in the air before drifting upward and disappearing from view.

"No tricks. No magic. Simply a reflection of the subtle nature of the Akashic Realm," Palden raised his hands in the air. "Feel it! Nothing but intentions and light . . . unequivocal space that has no pretense of solidity or reality as you know it. It is elastic and can assume any shape or essence, like this one of Tibet." Palden glanced at Early, making sure he was following. "I will tell you that you are currently in the illusion that also houses the venerable Hall of Records, or Library of Souls as it is sometimes called. Although you cannot perceive them, there are many other beings and constructs that inhabit this plane.

"When we were forced to abandon our monastery in Tibet, this realm is where we came to pursue our work. In simple terms, our karma project has been assimilated into a vastly older and broader system called the Akashic Records. These records were established at the beginning of time by the Ancients. We are extremely blessed to have been allowed to continue our project here."

Early shook his head in wonder. As heady as it was, what he really needed was to know what to do.

Palden was pleased. He had been waiting for Early's burst of adrenalin. "Good. Then let me tell you what you already know. The woeful condition of our world is the direct result of the lack of vision, lack of self-knowledge. Most of the leadership today is born of anger and ignorance. This absence creates a climate where the greed of self-interest can easily outperform basic human goodness, destroying the balance. I have called you because the balance needs to be restored. I believe you can help us."

Early felt strangely liberated. "Just tell me what I can do."

As if in response, Palden turned and set off without a word, moving quickly along a craggy pathway over snow-crusted rocks and ice, descending toward the village below. The significance was not lost on Early. It was the same path he had taken as a young Tibetan boy when he disobeyed the lockdown to warn his beloved Usha. He suddenly felt the weight of his guilt again for taking the lives of so many brilliant souls.

In sync with Early's mind, Palden came to a halt at the precise fork in the path where Early had made the fateful decision. The sage pointed to the bluff over-looking the clearing. "Right there. That's where the soldier saw you when you took the shortcut."

Awash in shame, Early sighed and lowered his gaze. Once again he was haunted by the question: Palden had never left the monastery. How did he know this?

"You acted out of love, James. But karma moves in mysterious ways. Right and wrong are often accomplices, acting out motives that are not clear-cut at all, especially when one can see the whole context."

Agitated, Early spoke with heat. "Please, tell me what you want me to do!"

"Then hear me with your heart. Our challenge is not to handle all the criminals on Earth. It is to shift the ratio between the urge to survive and the desire to self-destruct. Despite all the degradation, your world is also graced with a handful of brave souls who have extraordinary karma. Unlike most of the population, they do not tread water. They do not shy away from problems. They find solutions. They confront evil. They don't do this out of pride. They do it because they are called to service. They do it out of love."

"Above all, they relentlessly pursue an inner vision that inspires, that seeks to liberate us from the numbness of our current state. The problem is, those same people are also subjected to constant attack. Some get crushed along the way. Often, they simply don't live long enough to accomplish their dreams."

"Fifteen years as a cop. I saw it on the streets every day."

"Yes, but imagine if those extremely capable and compassionate souls were allowed to succeed. What if a new kind of leadership came to pass?"

Palden paused, letting it sink in, then spoke again. "This is the essence of our mission. This is where you come in."

Early pondered for a moment. "My job, then, would be to protect them, keep the sharks away."

"Yes, but very, very specific sharks. Otherwise you would be completely overwhelmed and, ultimately, ineffectual."

"How will I know them?" Early demanded.

"If you are positioned correctly, they will find you. Wherever a soul is making significant inroads in the culture, awakening a civilization to its true potential, you will notice the telltale frenzied waters."

For the first time since the start of their dialogue, James Early smiled broadly. "When do I start?"

"You already have."

Early scanned frantically. Then his eyes widened. "You mean the Burwells!"

"Yes. And you will be assisted."

"Trakker?" Early asked with disbelief.

Palden shook his head with mild amusement. "No. The soul you mention is still very enthralled by the sound of his own voice and his . . . angular persona. Perhaps someday, but not now."

"Then who will I be working with?"

"Don't worry. He is an old friend and will make himself known to you in the very near future."

Relieved, Early finally asked the question that had been burning inside him during the entire conversation. "Usha. I feel responsible for . . . her condition, her karma. I want to help her. Do you know—"

Palden interrupted. "Your concern is understandable. Your paths, in fact, crossed long before your time in Tibet, as you will discover. Nevertheless, as in your case, she will have to find her own way back. Considering her strength and tenacity, we have every confidence that she will."

Early relaxed slightly. This good news gave him cause for hope. But just when he was settling into a moment of peace, Palden moved a step closer, suddenly towering above his pupil.

With a raised voice, the sage's words came shrill with warning, "Make no mistake about this. It's dangerous work! Know from the beginning—this is an experiment. Our mission can fail! You may be killed and thrown back into the sea of karma where we cannot help you!"

Suddenly Early felt the crushing weight of this obligation but fought back. "I've taken my vow. I won't betray you again."

"Then hear me with every pore of your being. No one, I repeat, no one must ever know of the existence or whereabouts of these karma files. In the wrong hands . . . ," his voice trailed away.

They stood for a moment in silence, in the snow on the pathway, as the Tibetan skyline became shrouded in evening. Somehow both understood that their moment together was over. Palden's eyes shone mysteriously. "I leave you in the care of time. Make the most of it."

With that, the sage embraced his pupil, looked into the depths of him with kindness, then was gone.

Early looked out across the valley. Like a tide pulling back, he felt the encasement of light that had surrounded him begin to peel away, revealing a panoramic view of the eternal theater of the night sky. Lit by a billion stars, a blue-green planet drifted up before his eyes. Seemingly within a stone's throw, the earth spun quietly on its axis—a glowing gem, a fragile beauty.

As Early opened his heart, the vision of his silent homeland touched him, more than ever before. Inevitably its hardships and promises would grow inside him until it was part of his own soul.

It was then that he felt the winds of space breathing against his face, his life calling him back, drawing him downward into the earth plane and a small apartment on Seventy-Eighth Street.

Thick and only vaguely aware, Early felt a pair of hands gripping beneath his arms, dragging him onto his bed. Laces untied, boots yanked off. In a distant and unreliable corner of his consciousness, he registered Trakker's voice saying, "Sleep it off, space boy. Your valet is officially outta here."

But Early was already drifting in his own sphere. For the first time in years, he was opening the gate into a landscape of hopes and dreams, beginning the search again for the deep abiding trust in life and its infinity of possibilities.

The Puzzle
Calls Its Pieces

ONE

Yankee Stadium

It was a balmy spring evening at the ballpark and a time for celebration. Sam Jenkins, however, was in a lousy mood. With peanut shells crunching underfoot, he paced behind the Yankee dugout like a dog on a chain, trying to hear one of his men on his handset.

"Look, Banes, the connection stinks. Just keep your damn eyes peeled," he barked. "You got rows K through P to cover. Report anything, anything, you hear me?" Flicking off the switch, he went back to his watch, perspiration dampening his shirt.

It was Old-Timers' Day at the stadium—an annual tradition where former greats play an exhibition game. For Sam, it was an event that courted catastrophe. Thirty feet away, Billy Burwell was taking batting practice—larger than life and totally exposed.

God knows, Sam had tried to dissuade him from coming; they all had. But Burwell had his fans and his obligations and had accepted the invitation anyway. Now it was Sam's nightmare.

Despite stadium officials being on alert and the combined forces of the NYPD and FBI in every strategic position available, it was still the worst-case scenario. There would be tens of thousands of unknown faces in the stadium. Only one of them needed to belong to Quill.

Sam's radio squawked again, and he plastered it to his ear. "Yeah?"

"Sullivan, sir. Got a Caucasian male, mid-twenties in the bleachers with a bowie knife, I— "

"Kid's stuff, but get him outta here—fast. Then keep looking." Sam angrily clamped the handset back onto his belt.

Unconsciously, he patted under his left arm to touch the hardness of the Glock beneath his blue blazer. Today, he hated the fact he was wearing it. Baseball was the national pastime. People came here to forget the violence that plagued their city, not be reminded of it. And who in the world wanted to be looking over his shoulder while the game was in progress, afraid some psychopath was going to snuff out one of the greatest players who ever lived? Not Sam. On top of everything else, he was a Yankees fanatic.

While keeping one eye on his charge, he glanced around his surroundings.

Yankee Stadium, the Bronx, a soft May twilight. A place where time stood still. It was here, on these green manicured fields, that a few immortals had come to work their magic and give back the glory. Ruth, Gehrig, DiMaggio, and the lovable Berra—reaching out to kids in the ghetto and presidents in the White House. For Sam, those baseball legends were part of his roots; a matter of the heart. Now, those larger-than-life characters had been whittled down to memorabilia, selling for more money than they ever made as a player. The fans still cheered, the balls sailed, and the flag waved. But, somehow, the soul in the middle of it all had been squeezed out.

The policeman shook his head and once again, systematically, his eyes swept up and down the festive aisles like a flashlight, skipping across the sea of faces. If it came down to spotting the sudden, unlikely motions, it would probably be too late.

As the national anthem played, Billy stood quietly in a line with his teammates, ball cap held above his heart. Clothed in his old familiar uniform, he felt younger and more at ease with the world.

When the ode to stars and stripes was over, the pregame rituals concluded, he jogged out to the outfield. For the moment, he could forget the insidious webs of politics. Now, all was reduced to splendid simplicities: the smell of freshly cut grass, the buzz of the crowd, and his physical instincts. Billy dug his spikes into the ground and felt happy. This was who he was. This was *his* turf.

Up near the light towers where the huge panels of floodlights blazed down, Malcolm crouched in Zen-like stillness with his customized Remington .280 rifle. Wind-bitten in the night and sun-scorched by day, he had held his position for the last eighteen hours hidden in the shadows of the massive light tower used for lighting night games. Thanks to his generous "contributions," a small scaffold-like platform used for cleaning the lights had been left at his disposal, and he had used it to ascend to the upper levels. His money had other magical properties as well. It would ensure the eyes of certain security men would remain turned in the wrong direction at the right times and mouths would stay sealed. In fact, outside of a few seagulls, no one would ever know that a lone human figure had once hidden in a darkened corner of the rooftop . . . and gotten away with murder.

Looking out through the scope of his rifle, he found his target: Billy Burwell innocently doing knee bends in center field. He pounded his glove. He doffed his cap. A sacrificial lamb.

Malcolm was energized by the artistic challenge. WhiteMan's cryptic instructions had inspired his genius. He had found a place "high and above reproach." He was "entertaining" his victim in "his place of business," a place where "he is celebrated." And, for most of the fans, Yankee Stadium certainly qualified as "a place of worship."

Malcolm returned the weapon to his side, running his gloved hand along the smooth metal of the long hard barrel. Soon fifty-thousand Americans would experience his lethal prowess. He was prepared to wait.

It was now the third inning. The Yankees' Old-Timers were at bat and losing to Cleveland, 3–2. Dusty Sullivan had just doubled and danced around second base. He clapped his hands, then pointed across the infield toward his old friend in the on-deck circle. "Your turn, Kid Diamond. Bring me in!"

From out of huge speakers came the words, "Billy Burwell!" and the legend stepped up to home plate. The crowd rose to its feet and shouted a hero's welcome. Balled up wrappers and paper airplanes filled the air and rained down like confetti. As the organ pumped its battle cry, the fans yelled back, "Go! Go! Go!" Even Sam, sweat-drenched and anxious, had to smile. *This is the stuff!*

On the second pitch, Billy lined the ball into left field and raced smoothly to first base while Dusty staggered around third base and scored. Yankees three, Cleveland three. Everyone who followed baseball knew what would happen next. Billy had stolen more bases than anyone in Yankee history, and the circumstances were right. Soon, he would be off—running like the wind, sliding under the tag for another steal. As was his tradition, he would always pause a heartbeat longer, then spring back to his feet with his right fist raised in the air. More than anything else, that was his signature.

Two pitches later he was off, furiously pumping toward second base. All eyes were glued on Billy. There was a slide into second, a spray of dirt, a tangle of ball-players, and a flying cap. The crowd yelled in approval. Of course he was safe! It's Billy Burwell!

The catcher's throw had been high and wide, and the shortstop was forced into shallow center field to retrieve the ball. As the dust settled, Billy lay momentarily alone, stretched out in the dirt as if posing for a cover shot.

At that precise instant, high above the spectators, a finger moved a fraction of an inch. As planned, the small thud made by the silencer was drowned out by the roar of the crowd. Nobody saw. Nobody heard.

The fans waited for the final phase of the routine. It was time for Burwell's victory leap. But Billy remained motionless, facedown on the ground. Cleveland's shortstop stepped closer and stared down. A dark stain was spreading out around the numbers on the back of Burwell's jersey.

"Christ! He's bleeding!" he shouted. Bending down on one knee, he touched the body. No response.

Suddenly there was chaos. Other players began to converge. An umpire trotted over. The manager and team physician scrambled up the steps of the dugout and ran onto the field.

Sam felt the punch to his gut. He immediately leapt over the rail and onto the field, his walkie-talkie already out. *No!* he screamed silently. *Oh please, God. NO!*

New York County Hospital

It was midnight when Sam and Early barged through the doors into the fluorescent shock of the New York county hospital. Despite the gloss of comfortable furniture, plants, and smiling attendants, the scene radiated anxiety and disaster. Slumped on couches, pacing the hallways, people waited in limbo—all pleading with destiny for their loved ones to be given one more chance. Silently, Early did the same.

With the cloying scents of ammonia and antiseptic in their nostrils, the two detectives strode briskly across the white tiled floors and into the elevator. Squinting against the harsh overhead lighting, Early tried to get his bearings, tried to make the world stand still for a moment so he could catch his breath. The pace had been dizzying.

Two hours before, he had been lying in bed, recuperating from the massive dose of new truths posed by Palden. A phone call from Sam had jolted him awake. *Billy had been shot. Intensive care. Status: touch and go.* Early was no longer under the auspices of NYPD. Nevertheless, Sam had called him in, wanting him on the scene. For Early, it was a chance to have Sam's back, be there for him as a friend. He had also given his personal oath to Ellen to protect her husband. There was much more, but those were reasons enough.

Early had flung on his clothes, bolted down the stairs, and grabbed a passing cab.

As he watched the elevator numbers decrease, Palden's words resounded in his ears. *The specific sharks would find him. The telltale frenzied waters.* Didn't this qualify? Certainly Quill *had* to be a candidate. But if that were true, why wasn't the assassin going after Ellen? She had all the credentials. She was a political mover and shaker, a visionary. Yet, the death threat had found Billy . . . then the bullet. So much for theories.

The waiting area was a madhouse. Billy Burwell's wounded presence was big news and a feeding frenzy for the paparazzi. Doctors and nurses tried to function in the traffic jam, elbowing their way through the throng of media and gawkers. The signs of a long, tense night ahead were everywhere: the puffy eyes, lowered heads, and hushed talk. Plainclothesmen and security guards stood somber and watchful, monitoring elevators and stairways. In the back of everyone's mind, a disturbing thought lingered. The assassin might not be finished. He might even strike again tonight.

In the middle of all this commotion, the centerpiece remained as still as ice. Billy Burwell lay on an operating table, a small hole in his chest. He was fighting off death's pitches. He was clinging to his own national anthem, cap in hand, now before God. *A few more innings, please. Another turn at bat, another chance to return to the field and play among the living.*

Ellen Burwell sat with her two children in a row of cushioned chairs, one arm draped around the shoulder of twenty-year-old Michael, one hand interlaced with the fingers of eighteen-year-old daughter, Melissa. Ellen had come directly from the ballpark and had been in the hospital since seven o'clock in the evening.

Clad in jeans and a wrinkled shirt, she alternated between consoling her family and tending to her own personal hell. Despite the raw redness around her eyes, she still managed a faint smile of recognition when the team of Jenkins and Early appeared. She made a feeble effort to get up.

"Don't," Early said, coming to stand beside her. "Is there anything we can do?"

She shook her head. "It's between Billy and God now," she said. "My husband is a fighter. If there's a route to survival, he'll find it." Speaking softly, she thanked them for coming and introduced them to her children.

Sam's eyes became watery again as he began to blurt out his apologies. Ellen stopped him. "I know what you went through to try to prevent this from happening. It happened. Maybe later, but right now, I can't find the room for blame. It was *his* choice to play. It was *my* choice to marry a man who takes risks."

The five people sat in silence as the struggle for life raged on in another room. Words rarely passed between them. All they wanted to do was stand beside Billy on the battlefield and, somehow, help him fall back toward *this* world. They would pray and they would love. They had no other weapons.

Hours later, a man dressed in surgical garb came into the room. His scrubs were rumpled, his expression unreadable. All eyes lifted in his direction, desperately scanning his face for clues.

"Mrs. Burwell, I'm Doctor Salinger," he said and squatted beside her. "Sorry you've had to wait so long."

Ellen sat up and squared her shoulders. "Is he going to make it?"

The doctor allowed a tiny smile to intrude upon the reserved formality of his profession. It was a smile that brought sunlight back into the room. "We have every reason to think so. Good luck seems to follow your husband. We've successfully removed the bullet. It did nick the aorta but completely missed his heart and lungs."

Ellen's head dropped forward onto her chest, her relief palpable. Her hand reached out blindly to grip the surgeon's hand. "Thank you. Thank God!" she mumbled and began to cry.

Quietly, Dr. Salinger went through his customary litany against overoptimism: there was some muscular damage, it would take time to heal, there might be complications and further surgery required. They all listened gravely, waiting for the final verdict. It came. In all likelihood, Billy would be able to resume a normal life in the future. Michael leapt to his feet and gave the doctor a thundering high five.

Early linked arms with Sam as they walked back to the car. "Close one."

"No shit!" Sam said, relief written all over his tired face. "Quill doesn't miss. This time he didn't get it all. Talk about dodging a bullet. I mean, Jesus! I feel like *I* just got pardoned from death row."

He stopped walking, turned to Early. "You know, if Billy had bought it, I swear to God, I would have tossed my badge. That's how bad I felt. Then there'd be *two* old fools wandering around town—playing checkers and dunkin' donuts at Danny's."

"The continuing adventures, huh?"

"Whatever. Right now, all I want to do is get the fucker who did this thing."

Early nodded soberly. "Amen to that."

They climbed into Sam's car, both of them feeling depleted. As they pulled out of the parking lot, Sam changed the subject. "By the way, you just loafing now, or you got a new job?"

"Sort of," Early said, not knowing how to respond.

"Sort of what?"

"I . . . well, I'm going into a kind of private practice," Early tried.

"There you go again—'kind of private practice,'" he mimicked. "You mean PI?"

"Yeah, that'll do."

Sam stopped for a red light and shook his head. "I'm always pulling teeth with you! Shit, man, you got clients or what?"

"I'm working now, as we speak. I'm right beside you on this case. And don't forget it!"

For most of the journey home, Sam attempted to pry answers and information from his former partner without satisfaction.

Eventually they laughed and blew off steam in a way that only old friends can do. As the new sun was beginning to lighten the harsh edges of the New York skyline, they said goodnight.

"You are one strange dude, James Early. I put you in my doghouse an' you keep slipping out. Houdini! Anyway, thanks for coming along. And stay in touch, or I'll sic my wife on you!"

"I could think of worse things. Hey, thanks for the lift."

Once inside his apartment, Early dropped into his armchair and began to think about the case in new expansive terms: the underlying subtext, the real motives. Seemingly, all roads led back to one key principle. Karma.

After much thought, Early finally got up, turned off the light, and headed to bed. Somehow, someway, he had to get to the bottom of Quill. *Was he done, or would more blood flow?*

As he began to surrender to sleep, one thought stayed awake: Someday he would know this monster like the back of his hand.

TWO

The New York Public Library

It was supposed to be a quick errand. Early rode the downtown bus, a pile of library books bouncing on the seat beside him. For a man who hated to wait, the last few days had been almost intolerable. Palden had said Early would not be operating alone. But who would help? And when would they arrive? With a sense of defeat, he had turned to the mundane to provide diversion: grocery shopping, paying bills, doing laundry. The list also included a trip to the public library, which he was now finally doing.

As the RTD bus rolled along, he stared out the window at the passing cityscape, his mind drifting elsewhere. Some truths were harder to deal with than others. Recently, one had given him no rest and seemed to press in on him whenever he wasn't preoccupied. The fact was, James Early was terribly lonely. On God's green earth, where was Usha now?

Since recovering memories of his last lifetime, and his incident with Palden in their secret sanctuary, his thoughts had become increasingly laced with images of her. Painfully, he had recalled their last instant together many times. Just before he died, he had seen her surrounded by soldiers. Without question, they would have mauled her, shredded every ounce of her dignity before taking her life. What were the spiritual consequences of *that*?

Sometimes when he couldn't sleep, he would allow himself to fiercely miss her. Throwing on his old clothes in the middle of the night, he would become the ghost of Amsterdam Avenue and walk around his neighborhood—talking to her in his heart, praying she would find her way back to him.

At Forty-Second Street, he got off the bus and walked toward Fifth Avenue. The main branch of the New York Public Library lay straight ahead. Climbing up the broad outside steps, he passed between the two stone lions, the twin sentries who had maintained their silent vigil for nearly one hundred years. Once inside, he paused. As always, the grandness of the high vaulted space filled him, the hush of thought and written word a counterpoint to the urban angst of the city. It had once been called The People's Palace. The name still fit.

He was just about to set his books down on the return desk when a hand gripped his shoulder with a touch so light yet firm that his skin tingled. Whirling to inspect, a tall gaunt man wearing glasses and a library smock stood beside him. Directly behind was a cart loaded with books.

"Here," he said, indicating Early's armload, "I'll take those."

Early scanned him quickly, then handed him the books. The face seemed uncannily familiar, yet he couldn't quite place it. The librarian put the volumes in the cart without appearing to notice the titles. He spoke in a clear, reedy voice.

"Tibet *is* an interesting place. A place you can never completely leave behind."

Early stopped dead in his tracks. The man slowly removed his glasses.

For a timeless moment, it was Jori and Tashi again!

Spontaneously, the two grabbed each other by the arms. Separated by death on the mountainside of a remote Asian country—reunited half a century later in the feverish modernity of New York City—both men were moved, amazed by their extreme good fortune.

Early wanted to apologize, wanted to thank. But Jori had immediately returned to his duties, or so it seemed. Pushing the cart ahead, he called out over his shoulder, "This way, please."

Early hastened to keep up. Soon, shock was replaced by a resurgence of hope.

This *must* be the help that Palden had promised. If so, he couldn't be in better hands.

With the cart bumping in front, Jori led them on a turning and twisting course through doorways, along corridors, down hallways—ending up beside a seemingly inoperative elevator in a deserted part of the building.

"For the time being," Jori said, his voice husky with exertion, "I will play the White Rabbit, you will be Alice—curiosity a little stronger than doubt and fear. I know there is much to say, but right now we're all under time constraints and need to keep moving ahead. Today I want to introduce you to your new 'situation.' A secret that no mortal can share. This was already made emphatically clear to you, was it not?"

Early nodded.

"Then on we go." Jori opened the scissor gate and stepped into the elevator, beckoning Early to join him. Soon they were creaking downward into the bowels of the library.

Early couldn't contain himself any longer. "I'm incredibly glad you're here. It's been one damn thing after the next."

"It's about to get worse," Jori said drolly. "This freight elevator is rarely used but goes down underneath the library to storage areas called the stacks."

In silence, they both watched the floor numbers on the dial. The last number was five . . . but the lift didn't stop there. Early shot his friend an anxious look. Jori just smiled. "We are officially off the dial now and going a little deeper. Pun intended."

Jori pushed a sequence of floor numbers on the elevator panel as if punching in a code. Immediately, the rickety lift began to descend faster, free-falling, no longer restricted by cables and machinery. Coincidentally, the air became cool and moist as if they had just entered a vast subterranean cave.

The elevator slowed, then landed gracefully, the gate automatically opening. Leading the way, Jori stepped out into the mouth of a tunnel, the smell of damp soil immediately filling their nostrils.

"Follow me one more time. We're almost there."

Although they walked in pitch-blackness, Early felt at ease, oddly confident of his steps. Twenty yards later, Jori stopped and motioned toward an arched doorway made of old stones, his voice becoming reverential. "Be warned. This will contradict everything you have ever known."

Early's legs quivered and he stumbled. Regaining his balance, he took Jori's arm. "Is this . . .?"

"For now, let's call it a gateway. I leave you to it."

Early was about to protest, but Jori was already walking away. Whatever waited in there was going to change him forever. Then again, wasn't it his desire for change that had started him down this path in the first place?

Stepping over the threshold, he entered a field of vibrant but gentle energy. Instantly, he felt the same eloquent silence of uncluttered space he had experienced with Palden. Impossible but undeniable, he was in the Akashic Realm! Eyes adjusting, Early could make out a sparsely furnished room: a small wooden coffee table, an old wingback chair, and a cot pushed into the corner. All incidental. Rising from the center of the room was a glowing circle of fire.

Early stepped closer. Now it appeared to be a shaft of light, golden-white, streaming from a base on the floor. The beam was about eighteen inches in diameter and pulsed upward to nearly three feet in height—then stopped completely, as if its top had been sheared off. It did not cast its light about the room or illuminate the ceiling but remained a tight gleaming cylinder, contained and flowing back into itself.

As Early began to focus on it, his mind suddenly became quieter and more receptive. Soon an effortless understanding began to form.

You are looking at the Fountain of Light . . . a small reminder left behind by the Ancients before they transmigrated. It has no explanation. It defies all logic and can only exist in a timeless environment. Like a cutting taken from a plant, a piece of the Akashic Realm has been extracted and smuggled through the outer dimensions to arrive here. It will be your connection to the Library of Souls. It is for your eyes only and must be guarded with your life.

Early stood very still, heart pounding, waiting. Soon the words came again.

The Fountain does nothing on its own. It does not cure or heal. It simply "befriends," augmenting one's own existing powers. If motives are pure, it will bond and translate thoughts into functions. If agendas are scrambled and distorted, nothing will happen. It is not something one operates. With those who have been chosen, it will form a living partnership—a relationship forged in honor.

Early continued to stand awkwardly beside the Fountain, trying to fathom. It brimmed with primal intelligence and emitted the faint scent of sage. Mysterious, miraculous. *Now he wanted to know everything.*

As if in response, Jori's voice rang out, "The Fountain will act as a terminal, linking you directly with our mission." A moment later, his Tibetan friend stood beside him. "For now, all you need to know is that at the other end of its arc is a different kind of library with more 'books' than there are drops in the sea. That's why we have chosen this site for your apprenticeship. Right now, I want to introduce you to another phenomenon you may remember from your youth in Tibet."

Early sighed and slowly pulled himself away from the spell of the light. "Go ahead."

"Soulprints," Jori announced, eyes glittering, "the fingerprints of the soul."

Early repeated the word to himself and nodded slowly. The memories were vague, but the name sparked images from the past. "I remember the word—doing exercises, training drills. Palden said I should apply myself. The knowledge would be very important in the future."

Early blinked. Again came the question. *Had Palden predicted this moment a lifetime ago?*

He glanced over at Jori, but his Tibetan friend remained deadpan, continuing his train of thought. "Soulprints are energy patterns—in all the universe, no two are the same."

Early could only smile. Having been a detective, he now appreciated the power of this discovery more than ever.

"Fingerprints are obliterated by death. Soulprints don't perish. They stay with the soul through the birth and death cycle, lifetime after lifetime. That was a monumental discovery for us."

"Didn't Palden bring us all out to the cliff to make that announcement?"

"Your memory serves you well. We had finally found the spiritual DNA that left traces. Now we could track that individual through time."

Early shook his head. "How does all this fit together—the Fountain, the library, soulprints? I'm not connecting the dots here."

"You will. But for now, let's just stay with soulprints."

Jori led Early back to his book cart parked outside in the hallway. "Exercise one. I dragged these books down here to serve as examples. All of them handled and returned today. That's significant because soulprints are fragile. They decay within twenty-four hours. After that, they become distorted and can't be tracked."

Early looked at the stack of books more critically. "These prints. Are they invisible?"

"To normal human tunnel vision, yes, But for someone with a practiced eye, especially one who has had some training, they can be very visible. But to perceive, one must have all his attention in *this* here and now—nowhere else. We call it deep sight."

The phrase hit a nerve, and Early was quiet for a moment. "Jori, what exactly am I looking for?"

Jori's eyes filled with strange light. "When you see it, you will *feel* it . . . here," he said, tapping his heart, "like the fang of a cobra."

Early said nothing.

Jori laughed. "I know, it's a lot. Just don't forget. Deep sight is a state. Once you've mastered it, it's never truly lost. A little coaching, some focused work, and it will find you again."

"I'll try," was all Early could manage.

Preliminaries done, the two old friends began formal practice—Jori holding a book in his hands, Early trying to pierce the solid surface to see the spiritual markings of a person who had recently touched it.

After much trial and error, Early slowly began to detect the ephemeral patterns. Surprisingly, the colors were not uniform and covered a broad spectrum of hues.

Jori explained, "When a soul is new, the original print is a pale gold, like the color of the Fountain. Through time, the colorations change, reflecting the individual's choices. Palden calls them karmic scuff marks. But let's keep going. You're doing splendidly."

At one point, Early detected a soulprint that sent shock waves through his system. "It's red. What the hell is that?!"

Jori leaned forward, eyes widening. "*That* is what you'll be looking for! A red soulprint means active evil is present. All of your suspects will have that. Let's have a look."

Turning the contaminated book over, he examined the dust jacket. "It appears to be a generic mystery story. Nothing special about it," he said thoughtfully. "We don't know if we're dealing with a perpetual criminal or someone who temporarily went out of control."

Early's cop instincts flared. "Shouldn't we find out? I mean . . . this guy's dangerous!"

Jori raised a hand. "Remember, your job is not to chase down every criminal. Your job is to thwart a very specific killer who's stalking an individual with great karmic value. For now, we need to develop your instincts. Everything will follow from that."

On they went into the late afternoon until Jori felt Early's restlessness on the rise. Laying a book quietly on the table, Jori said, "You'll probably refuse, but I say let's take a break, reset, and hit it again on the other side."

"I don't know. I'm willing to go flat-out, if you are."

Jori just smiled.

Before buckling down again, they decided to go out for pizza. Having it delivered would have been a bit out of the question.

*   *   *

For the next few days, the instruction went from dawn to late into the night, with Early only returning to his apartment to check his mail and sleep. Despite frustrations and disappointments, he was now keenly aware of the Fountain of Light, a timeless presence hovering in the background, anchoring his quest for deeper awareness.

As before, questions frequently arose that Jori refused to answer. One such incident occurred when Early wanted to know how a soulprint was lifted from an object. In response, Jori became very solemn even while declining comment.

"Again, when you're ready, you'll know what to do. I *will* tell you, there is one thing you must never forget. When you have secured the red soulprint, you must act immediately. If you don't, the print will bleed into your system and metastasize unless handled in the twenty-four-hour frame. The evil will infect you, become your evil . . . and you may find yourself acting out its madness."

Despite loud protests, that was all Early could wrest from his mentor. Somehow he had to trust.

It was the end of the fourth day. Jori had been testing Early's perception of prints on a can of Coke he had taken from the library trash bin. Mid-sentence, he suddenly stopped talking and rose to his feet slowly. Early knew the signs. Jori had just become aware of something, like a distant storm approaching. After a moment he looked directly at his student.

"I don't know if you're ready, but you'll have to be. There are tensions developing. It's time for you to return to the trenches."

Feeling the pressure himself, Early threw his jacket over his shoulder and simply nodded.

"I'll be in the vicinity," Jori added, "but from here on out, it's up to you."

They shook hands and said goodbye. By now Early was familiar with the idiosyncrasies of his new office and let himself out.

Returning to his apartment that night, he felt changed. He was stronger and bigger as a being, with a whole new arsenal of knowledge. The process had sensitized him. First impressions and outward appearances now surrendered quickly to a lingering double take. Most dramatic of all, he now had a colossal secret—one that would put a marked distance between himself and his fellows. This could make all future relationships uncomfortable, possibly closing the door on anything resembling intimacy. He was very much a man, but no longer *just* a man. He was becoming something else that had no comfortable definition.

THREE

WhiteMan's eyes flew open like twin pale portals. Sleep-crusted and watery, they stared out into the soothing blackness. Subliminally, he could hear the incessant grinding of Manhattan, sodden with machines and men. Slowly, thankfully, the images of his "journey" began to recede. Soon the comfort of his own dark domain would settle back around him like an old cloak.

Turning his head, he checked the time on his bedside clock. He had been "gone" for twenty hours—an unusually long time for one of his research forays. It had been worth it. Not only had he been well paid by Mr. Raines to uncover who was behind this invisible threat, but the information itself was staggering!

Malcolm had called him twice, brimming with frustration. The psychic could feel the pressure mounting in his client, his desire for violence about to hit critical mass. WhiteMan had weighed all options. It was clear he needed more "opposition research." He had done so.

Still recovering, he continued to lie in his bed, digesting his new discoveries. While he pondered, his long fingers unconsciously skittered across the bones of his face and around the thin prongs of his rib cage.

Although he had only been able to scavenge scraps, his suspicions had been confirmed. Off-world eyes *were* upon them! Unbelievable but true, some renegades from the hierarchy of souls were now *physically* involved in the human drama. By containing certain elements, they were trying to orchestrate a shift in the balance. Unprecedented? Impossible? In violation of all previous strictures against meddling in human affairs? Yes! But it was happening! The business of Mr. Raines seemed to be a focal point. The intention toward him, however, seemed to be preventive rather than vindictive. This indicated that Malcolm was under surveillance *only* because one of his business targets was someone they wanted to protect.

Most distressing of all, WhiteMan's findings showed that these outsiders were attempting to take permanent residence on the earth plane. This did not bode well for WhiteMan's practice at all. Most of his celebrity clients wanted their affairs to remain in perpetual shadow: unseen, unheard, and unknown. Any form of light would send them scurrying like cockroaches. The psychic had to do something. His livelihood depended on it.

Tenderly, he convinced his fragile body to sit up, noting once again that his health was deteriorating. Ever since his mistress of long ago had accused him of "criminal activity" and fled with their infant twins, his physical condition had worsened. Her accusations had, of course, been misguided, myopic at best. He had been undeterred. Whether she or anyone else appreciated his work, he *knew* he provided a remarkable service. He earned his substantial paychecks *and* his moral loopholes.

She had never understood and, consequently, had to be eliminated. There had been the messy fire where she had been cremated along with her incendiary knowledge of his practice. The whole episode had been time consuming and crude. Not his style at all. Careerwise, though, it had proved to be a stroke of genius.

Once alone in his ebony kingdom, with no threat of disclosure or need to defend his positions, his nefarious trade had flourished. Nevertheless, since her death, he appeared to be growing weaker, year by year. Droves of well-heeled specialists had come and been dismissed. There had been tentative and incorrect diagnoses with no signs of improvement. He was only marginally worried. He was WhiteMan. When everything was in place, he would take matters into his own hands and heal himself.

Sighing, the Albino turned his attention back to the matters at hand. The game plan had been expanded. The first few moves were obvious. All the signs indicated it was time for boldness. Malcolm could now strike directly. But WhiteMan was already moving sideways. Self–preservation was senior to the petty world of his clients, including Malcolm Raines. Unless this invisible threat was eliminated, WhiteMan himself was in jeopardy. The saving grace was that he had discovered that the "outsiders" had a weak link. A *human* was being employed to do their footwork. WhiteMan had done diligence, now knew name and address. This individual would have his soft spots . . . and his price. A threshold of pain could always be found. This was something Mr. Raines could easily accomplish, even relish. A clever way of dealing with both threats to their dark kingdoms.

Later that evening, he would convince Mr. Raines to unleash his violent talents. The human agent of this intervention *must* be eliminated first, or nothing else could be accomplished. After that, he was free to spew his vitriol anywhere, anytime he chose.

Surprisingly enough, the Albino was not despondent. In fact, for the first time in years, he felt his feathery heartbeat accelerate, the blood that limped through his veins suddenly quicken.

Invigorated, WhiteMan gripped his spindly legs, one at a time, and encouraged them to find purchase on the floor. As he lurched forward to the bathroom, his elongated fingers danced along the satin piping of his robe. The news was scintillating. A worthy opponent had finally arrived!

Early's Apartment

It was that initial rude stretch of the morning where body, mind, and soul are full of complaints yet duty-bound to synchronize. Lit only by a sleeve of sunlight pouring through a slit in his bathroom curtain, Early applied the shaving cream, avoiding eye contact with the craggy face in the mirror. Jori had warned him. The

Fountain of Light had an addictive quality about it. Now Early wanted to spend every waking moment sequestered in his office huddled beside it, trying to warm the frozen places inside himself, trying to fuse with its mystery and power.

Last night he had ventured closer and placed his palm on the surface of the beam. Like the lick of cool flame, he had felt his bones tingle and his blood spark. In his mind, a sensation had begun to crescendo, threatening to unravel his equilibrium. He had withdrawn his hand quickly. He wasn't ready. His mentor had once called the Fountain an outlaw vortex, a shaft of stolen light still connected to the mystery of karma. It was not to be trifled with.

Absently, he blotted a small nick on his chin with the corner of his towel. Bottom line—there was a serial killer loose on the streets of New York. It was his job to stop him. Unfortunately, the only place where the disparate worlds of the Library of Souls and the psychopath intersected was the soulprint. Early was stymied. Until he had Quill's spiritual print, he was grounded, forced to work within the narrow confines of current knowledge.

Resigned to this, Early spent the day in his apartment conducting his own private investigations. Despite a public show of police bravado and "suspects under investigation," the NYPD didn't have a clue as to the identity or whereabouts of Quill. On the QT, he had borrowed Sam's collection of reports and now went through them methodically: Interpol, FBI, CIA, and NYPD. He turned the pages lethargically. Glacier-like, the hours crept by. By the time evening came around, Early was thoroughly disgusted. Another wasted day when everything hinged on speed and timing.

Taking a break, he picked up a newspaper and scanned it until he found what he wanted. The assassination attempt on Billy Burwell had garnered massive press. Nevertheless, despite the pressure, Ellen had remained silent, waiting for her head and heart to clear before speaking. Evidently that moment had arrived. Early folded back the page and read.

Letter to the Editor:

What happened to Billy Burwell during the most recent Old-Timers' Day at Yankee Stadium was the act of a sick human being. But beware! The media have already blown this cowardly incident out of proportion. They are talking once again about the American tradition of violence, the omnipotent danger that is spreading throughout this country. It goes without saying that we all must be very aware of compromising situations. We all must take the necessary steps to safeguard our homes and our families. But I implore you, do not buy into this aggrandizement of fear! Do not add another lock on your door or buy another gun. Above all, do not be fearful of living your lives on your own terms. Otherwise, we'll wind up as more timid, less effective human beings. Then we all lose.

There are some people who profit from fear. They must not be allowed to become richer because of one psychopath with a rifle in Yankee Stadium. Billy will live and continue to do his work. I will continue to do mine. I ask all of you to do the same.

Respectfully, Senator Ellen Burwell

Early slapped the paper down on the table. Good for you, Ellen Burwell! It was the right message at the right time—in complete alignment with the karma mission. As if in concert, the phone rang immediately.

Without thinking, he picked up the receiver. "Hey, Mom!"

There was a long pause. "Well now," Ida said, clucking her tongue, "you're growing like a mystical weed, aren't you? I won't ask how you knew it was me, I'll just ask you if you're happy. That's still more important." She sounded more excited than surprised.

Early flushed. Happy? He hadn't been thinking in those terms for years. Somehow it hadn't seemed relevant. "I'm fine. And thanks for understanding. When am I going to see you again?"

"That's why I called. I have a gift for you."

"What's the occasion?"

"Let's just call it an acknowledgment, son . . . the tough little tree that managed to grow through the concrete. I've been painting your portrait. I want you to come over in a few days and pick it up."

"I'm honored. I'd love to see it."

"Save your applause until you have a look. You might want to hide it in your closet. I haven't done one of you for a long time and, well, it seemed appropriate to do one now."

As she was talking, Early suddenly felt distracted. Following his instincts, he moved to the window, parted the curtains, glanced down at the street below.

Illuminated by yellowish streetlights, a young couple was walking their dog across the street, an elderly woman was dumping her trash in a garbage can. For some reason, he leaned over and looked directly below. A dark, well-dressed man stood alone, partially obscured by the shadow of the building's entrance awning.

Early instantly felt a wave of dirty energy pass through him. The man appeared to glance up, nod imperceptibly, then move away toward Columbus Avenue.

He had an almost dapper, gentlemanly quality about him—nothing that outwardly indicated danger.

Early put the phone back to his ear. "Sorry. Just got sidetracked. You were saying . . . ?"

Ida was quiet for a moment. "Son, whatever you're doing, I won't ask you to be careful. Just be real, real smart, you hear?"

"Yeah . . . yeah, I will. How about I drop by on Wednesday?"

"That'll be fine." Ida cleared her throat. Her voice came back sounding thinner and tired. "This will probably be it for me. Damn arthritis. I can't hold the paintbrush anymore. Bad heart, old legs. It's sad we all go down like that—whimpering and fading away."

"Don't talk like that, Mom." Early fumbled with the cord. "You'll outlive the rest of us!"

"Wouldn't want to," she scoffed. "By the way, do you realize that when I die, they will refer to me as the 'late Early'? I kinda like the sound of that!"

Early grunted.

"All right, son. I'll let you go. Come and take this painting out of my sight. It's in my living room, and I have to look at it every morning, noon, and night. Even for a mother who's crazy about her son, that's asking a lot."

Early grinned. "Sounds like punishment. I'll be there to rescue you within the week."

"Always the joker. I like your face and I love you. Don't ever forget that, okay?"

"I won't. You're the best. Call me if I can do anything for you."

"I will. Goodbye, son."

Early put the phone down gently and got ready for bed. As he undressed, he found himself still agitated by the nameless menace who had intruded while on the phone. Oddly enough, he did not feel personally threatened. It was the sense that something close to him was about to be taken away. Still looking for answers, he fell asleep.

FOUR

Big Daddy's

"Hamburger on a toasted hard roll, fries, and a cup of coffee, black. That'll do it." Early settled back in the corner table of his favorite Midtown dive. He had made himself do it—a day off, a Big Daddy Burger—pure bliss! After a month of spiritual Chutes and Ladders, this kid from Brooklyn wanted to be nothing more than a kid from Brooklyn. Right now, it was time to feast and forget. To hell with karma! To hell with everything other than the smells of sizzling burgers and bacon and the blare of the jukebox. Big Daddy's was here and now and in your face. It was one of the few places where all the American gaps—gender, cultural, racial, generational, and otherwise—closed ranks around a greasy double-double with cheese. At least for today, that was enough.

Twenty years ago, he would have been plotting some improbable adventure with his high school buddy Tony Deluca. Before descending into the netherworld of drugs, Tony D had been Early's sidekick—a firm believer in turning every waking second into maxed-out, high-voltage drama. At twilight, on any given Saturday, they would roar into the West Village on Tony's old Suzuki—prowling the club scene, prospecting for the hip chicks and the unforgettable night.

In those days, it was more about the looking than the finding. The more torqued the fantasy, the better. But their tacit agreement never changed: go for broke—get laid, drunk, whatever—but keep the illusions intact. As teenage kids, they had reached the same conclusion: without the bravado of their dreams, the world was nothing more than a ghost town in drag.

One lusty bite into his meal, Early noticed a dark-haired, light-eyed young woman approaching his table. She wore close-fitting black jeans, an olive-green sweater, and black ankle boots. Even from a distance, he found her striking—far too complex to immediately categorize.

As she moved closer, however, her body spoke volumes—restrained power, seduction—a sensual weapon she fully knew how to operate. In stark contrast, her sensitive face and luminous eyes seemed to plead for something far more refined. Self-conscious and visibly agitated, she came to a standstill a few feet in front of him.

Early glanced away. Inexplicably, he suddenly felt shy, almost afraid. *What the hell was this?* She was beautiful! A month ago, he would have slipped effortlessly into his routine of well-oiled moves. Now all he could manage was confusion and a sudden dip in confidence.

"May I join you?" she asked as she leaned against a vacant chair on the opposite side of his table. Although her hands trembled, her voice remained steady—cigarette-husky and direct. Her blue eyes danced with uncertainty amidst the fine features and pale skin, then held absolutely still as she waited for his response.

After hesitating, he finally motioned with his hand, beckoning her to take a seat. Making little effort to be friendly, he shifted back against the chair and waited, suddenly uncomfortable. There was a nameless threat, a soft-spoken danger about her that should be avoided. And yet . . .

Desda smiled weakly as she sat down, trying to quiet the anarchy of nerves. Once seated, she rested her arm awkwardly on the tabletop, her silver bracelet jangling against the grainy wood. The faint scent of the Orient from her sandalwood perfume hinted at another time and sensibility.

"I'm about to make a fool of myself. I . . . I don't normally do this kind of thing, I mean, throw myself at strangers," she began, frantically trying to stay calm.

Then she stopped. This was not going well at all. But seeing the distant yet genuine curiosity in Early's eyes, she took heart and started again. "My name is Desda Collins. I saw you on TV a while back. The drug bust. This is going to sound lame, like a come-on or something. It's not. I'm not like that at all, but . . . ," she paused.

Suddenly the script she had prepared for this moment crumbled into dust. She was left with nothing but raw emotions and one loaded question. She blinked, then fired her only bullet.

"Do we know each other?"

Early's denial was right there, instinctual and unthinking. "No, I don't . . . " Then he caught himself and reconsidered. *Take your time. Observe. Then answer her question.*

Looking across the table, he tried to scrutinize her from a more expansive viewpoint. The structure of the face and body was not familiar. But the *eyes*, the eyes! Beneath their blueness, down where the blood mingled with the spirit. Something . . .

Early became very still, allowing his focus to be untethered, to drift deeper than the immediate and settle into deep sight. To his amazement, the knowledge came swift and certain. Sitting across from him was Usha! In the center of his heart, he heard a voice. *Yes! Yes, I know you!*

Early clamped down hard on the roar of emotions. At this point, the depths of his feelings would only intimidate her. But inside, behind closed doors, he began to fall apart. *Am I losing my mind? Can this really be happening?* Furtively, he looked at her again.

This time his perception was even clearer. There was no doubt. Blessed? Cursed? Usha had found him.

Pretending to cough, Early covered his face with a napkin, hiding the build-up of tears pressing against his eyes that threatened to spill. Once again, he jammed composure back into place. She obviously did not remember her past . . . or theirs.

That would have to be her awakening, her journey—if she chose to take it.

He blew his nose, then responded. "Could be," he finally said, pushing with his fork at the French fries on his plate. "What makes you think so?"

Watching him tackle the question seriously, Desda felt some dignity restored. Maybe she wasn't crazy? Maybe there was something to this after all? Digging the toes of her boots into the floorboards, she straightened her back.

"I wish I knew. It's driving me crazy," she said, bewildered, "but here's the worst part. Oh, God, forgive me for this! I've been spying on you. I've been obsessed with . . . well, it's not just you. It's the feeling I got when I saw you on TV. You were . . . familiar. There was something about you that . . . Oh, Christ, I don't know!"

Blushing and biting her lip, Desda launched one more attempt. "It's too weird! But, whatever it is, it's not letting up or going away. My last option was to follow you here, sit down face-to-face, ask the damn question, then have you tell me to get lost. I mean, shit! I'm not some crazed stalker. You have no idea how embarrassing this is. I can't even . . . " Desda cut herself off mid-sentence. Her voice had been getting louder and more strident as she groped for explanations.

Early reached over and pressed her arm. Feeling his touch, she tensed.

"Hey, it's okay," he said, trying to keep his excitement under control. "I don't go around looking for mystical connections either. At the same time, I don't believe in sheer coincidences, you know? Things happen for a reason. When I was with the NYPD, I acted on hunches all the time. They usually paid off. So here you are. You took a leap. Maybe there's something to it, maybe not. The least we can do is talk."

Desda held his eyes for a moment. There seemed to be no duplicity about him. No wobble below the surface of his steady gaze. No secretive sticky glances at her lips and breasts.

Early pushed his plate to one side. "Just start somewhere, anywhere."

She nodded and began to fumble through her handbag. "Shit! I keep forgetting I quit!"

"Well, let's both get blasted on caffeine then." Early laughed, signaling for the waitress.

After ordering coffee, he rolled up the sleeves of his blue work shirt and leaned back. Forty-plus years had gone down since Tibet. Reopening their case needed to be handled skillfully. No doubt, Desda's recollections of their Tibetan past were imprisoned beneath brutal memories of rape and murder. Early had no immediate solution for this. He did know that huge amounts of communication would be required. If trust could be established, then a foundation might be laid and a bridge constructed—strong and safe enough to span the lifetimes. Once across, they could truly touch as souls. And perhaps begin again.

For the next few hours, with only occasional sips of his coffee, Early's attention never wavered. Gently prodding and poking, he kept her talking. The time rushed by. He was spellbound! Usha/Desda: one image superimposed upon another. Two utterly divergent expressions of the same extraordinary theme.

Guarded at first, Desda sputtered and frequently hesitated with embarrassment, completely unused to someone being genuinely interested in her. But then, seeing that there was no judgment, no hidden agenda, she gathered momentum. Soon the tales of her jagged past poured forth like long unanswered letters to herself. She wondered out loud, cried, and occasionally broke free into wide-open laughter. Desda was startled to find that, with this man, she could step beyond the cardboard cutout she usually presented to the opposite sex. Surprisingly, the longer she talked to him, the more confident she became. Her experience with other men had been the complete opposite.

Early was also breaking into new turf. His "electric fence" was short-circuiting. For the first time in years, he was free to be with a woman without inner reprimand. And this woman was amazing! One layer down from her streety persona was an extremely perceptive, strong, and kind soul—unusual qualities for someone who had been shuttled between orphanages, living hand to mouth in the urban jungle. Understandably, her self-worth needed some polishing. That would come. And there was no question that the ineffable grace and joy that once filled Usha was still there, a bit bruised but still intact, ready to be summoned.

When Early talked about himself, he was vague about his current activities, simply saying he had quit the NYPD to start a private practice. He also mentioned he had rediscovered spirituality—a path he had forsaken *many* years ago. He stressed, however, that his particular brand of belief system was a very hands-on approach requiring a great deal of worldly action.

The concept of some form of hard-nosed, underlying truths made Desda nod her head vigorously in agreement. She was in the process of collecting them herself. She talked about the mysterious rooms of her self that she was still afraid to enter.

"It's bizarre," she said. "I'm not religious. Not a purist at all. But I do feel . . . unexplored. Like I've been told to stay away, not to trespass—that kind of thing."

Early smiled ruefully to himself.

By the time they finished, it was late afternoon. Early stood up stiffly and reached for the check. Her hand was already there. "On me. Please!" she said. For a brief moment, he let his hand linger on top of hers. Electricity surged between them, warm and intoxicating.

Reluctantly, he let go. "Okay," he said, "but the next one's mine. That is, if you're interested in a next time."

Desda lowered her head, pretending to search for her wallet. "Are you kidding? I've risked my entire reputation as a tough, unsentimental chick just to talk to you."

Then she raised her head. The change in her was remarkable. She looked younger, softer, and less fraught with complications. Her face was flushed, and her eyes had lost the abrasive edge that, three hours before, had steeled her against an unfriendly world.

"Today was a first," she said, shaking her head and smiling. "I never dreamed I could confide like this to a stranger. Sure, I'd really like to get together again."

One heartbeat short of hugging, they agreed to meet in a few days. But before Early could even say goodbye, Desda was off, bounding out of the restaurant and down the sidewalk—hair flying back behind her, her handbag bouncing jauntily against her hip.

Early chose the long way home, a slow savor of what had just transpired. More than anything, he was profoundly moved that the cosmos had befriended them. What were the odds? In the vast expanse of the universe, these two pieces of driftwood had been coughed up from the sea and deposited, side by side, along the same craggy coastline.

FIVE

Around the City

That night, beneath the beacon of a pale full moon, furious wind rose up and raked across the Island of Manhattan. Flags whipped about their poles, and boats in the harbor strained against their moorings as lead-grey waves crashed against the piers. Along the streets, awnings billowed out like sails, and branches arched backward toward the ground. The invisible presence was everywhere—tempting and taunting, railing against all constraints.

Sam Jenkins rescued his kid's mountain bike from the porch and stored it safely in the garage.

Ellen Burwell looked up from her book, put a bookmarker in place, and settled back in her chair—thoughts swirling about her husband, her city, the future.

Trakker flung open his window, leaning out into the gale as it pounded against his face.

Malcolm sipped a glass of wine in a private room in a French restaurant—staring out into the rain-splattered darkness, galvanized by the fury of the elements.

Desda sat on the edge of her bed brushing her hair, strangely soothed by the unseen force that tore through the night all around her.

And James Early went out on his fire escape and stood with his hands gripping the railing—battered by wind and rain but deep in thought about Usha and their sacred home, lost forever in the mountains of Tibet.

Alone in his bungalow, Jori rested his pen on the page and smiled. The storm and Coney Island were making beautiful music. The wind moaned through a crack in the walls, the swollen sea hammered against the rocks. For him, the universe, with all its incorruptible power, was speaking.

As he listened, Jori considered the many lives interwoven with the journey of James Early, how the same wind touched them all in different ways that night. Despite bewitched passions and the pain that seemed to shackle their every step, God's breath was still upon them.

Jori sighed and leaned down again to write. Beside him on the desk, his candle burned steadfast and bright, undaunted by the drafts that swirled about the room.

*   *   *

When New York rolled out of bed the following morning, the aftermath of the storm was everywhere. Things were bent, stretched, torn, and displaced. Now, as if cleaning up after someone else's wild party, fleets of trucks accompanied by droves of grumpy men descended on grass, tarmac, and concrete, picking up, bagging, and hauling the town back to its former self.

"Wild night, huh?" Early said as he walked beside Desda, kicking aside a downed branch that lay across the sidewalk. "Never seen the city get so roughed up without any real damage. Kinda magical."

"Yeah, it was. That kind of raw power always gets me."

They had met on Fifty-Second Street, walked crosstown, and now strolled along the pathway beside the East River. It was a brilliant spring day—blazing sun and blue skies, the air sweetened by rain. In the background, they could hear the cries of gulls above the quiet breathing of the river.

Today's meeting had a very different sheen than their first encounter. Now both had had a few days to absorb the event; time enough for second-guessing, time enough for infatuation to thin with uncertainties. Both knew the flip side of hope was disappointment. Nevertheless, a genuine excitement had been born and the quest for definition already begun. In this, Early had the distinct advantage. He, at least, knew what they *had* been.

As they made their way back along Fifty-First Street, the conversation flowed easily—a natural and comfortable ratio between talk and silence, neither one feeling the need to clog the empty spaces. It reminded him of their long walks in Tibet where neither spoke for hours yet everything was shared. As opposed to the steady jurisdiction of the Himalayas, New York City's urban backdrop was flip and casual, changing its mind and wardrobe every few steps. Pointing things out, discussing and laughing, Early and Desda found themselves in effortless collaboration: differences that didn't grate, similarities that were unexpected.

Both of them took note. If only for the moment, the personas of Desda Collins and James Early seemed to go into remission. Subtle but pervasive, they both experienced the extra elbow room and quiet within themselves to simply enjoy each other. At the same time, the unanswered challenge of their past hovered just outside their conversation. Neither wanted to break the spell of the glorious day. Yet, after coffee and then lunch, the internal pressure was growing—especially for Early, who knew how high the stakes were and what needed to occur.

Feeling the moment had arrived, he began to fumble with the rusty latch of the old gate between them.

"Desda, I'm not sure how to do the segue here, but I keep thinking about your original question... about us."

A shadow shot across her face. "It's a bit like the pebble in the shoe," she said ambivalently. "I was really getting used to walking on it, feeling great, in fact. Then again, it *is* the thing that brought us together, isn't it?"

"I think so. When I worked for the NYPD, I was into pulling strings, seizing on some little detail that seemed out of place and following it down to the end. Worked pretty well."

Desda stopped walking. "All I can say is, right from the start, you took me seriously. You're not playing games. That's really important to me."

"Me too," Early said. "Truthfully, I haven't done that well at . . . well, relationships. But I've gone through a lot of changes recently. Big ones, that don't have easy answers."

Desda shielded her eyes from the sunlight. For some reason, she wanted to cry.

Early squinted down at her, speaking gently, "Look, whatever goes down, I don't want to just go through the motions with you. That'd be unforgivable." Feeling now that he'd overreached, he started walking again.

They waited at the corner of Third Avenue for the light to change. Early couldn't help but notice that Desda had shifted her purse to the other shoulder where it wouldn't be banging between them. A good sign.

Having crossed the street, Desda looked down at the ground, perplexed. "It's not the boy-girl thing we're doing here, is it?"

"Well, I suppose I'd have to give you a yes and no on that. I mean, you're beautiful and we're both unattached. But I agree. There's something else going on here."

Desda once again felt tongue-tied, inexplicably besieged by emotions. "You scare me . . . in a good way."

Early began to put his arm around her shoulder. Catching himself, he let it fall back down to his side. He was on a mission. At least for now, he couldn't be sidetracked—not after last time.

For a while they continued on without speaking, both lost in thought. As they approached the subway entrance, Early fixated on his tactical quandary: how to open up the past. He had been helped by Palden and Jori. How could he do the same for her?

Passing by Bloomingdale's opulent windows, he decided to test the waters. "What's your take on reincarnation. I mean, the idea of it?"

But Desda was not listening. She had suddenly stopped short and was standing with her mouth open, staring incredulously at the storefront window.

Early turned his head and glanced at the lavish array of summer clothes stylishly draped on mannequins.

"Don't you see it?" she whispered hoarsely. "Not the display! Our reflection!"

Early shifted his focus. Slowly, like a photograph taking form in developer, their images began to morph in the glass. Staring back at him were a boy and girl no more than fourteen years old. Both were of Asian descent: high cheekbones, olive skin, and almond-shaped eyes. The girl was dark-eyed, with long raven hair—wearing a handmade dress of coarse, natural fabric. The boy was taller and lean, his shaved head poking out from beneath the cowl of a grey robe. Without a doubt, Early knew he was looking at Tashi and Usha! With smooth young faces, they peered back through the window at their future selves. An instant later, the mirage dissolved.

Desda didn't move. "What the hell was that?" she demanded under her breath. "Did you see it?"

Early was absolutely stunned—then secretly thrilled. Help had found them! Trying to hide his enormous relief, he rubbed his face. "Yeah, I saw it. That was *no* hallucination either."

Desda's features twisted with confusion and fear as if she had unwittingly been found out and cornered. On another level, Early felt her begin to brace herself internally, getting ready for a dogfight. Something had, indeed, been jogged loose. It might take a day, it might take a year, but now it was inevitable: Pandora's box was not going to stay shut.

Although she hadn't fallen down, Desda unconsciously brushed herself off. "I'm over my head here. I mean it," she said tersely. "If it were just me, I'd sit down with a bottle of Bourbon and numb it out. But you saw it too. That's a problem. I . . . I . . . "

"That boy and girl," Early interjected, "they looked like they were from the East. Japan, China, Tibet—someplace like that."

Then he turned to face her, trying to steer her without being obvious. "As I said, I don't believe in coincidences. Both of us saw the same thing. It's got to mean something."

Desda cringed and looked away, still disturbed. While they walked the final hundred yards, she wrestled with the experience. The glow from her new relationship with Early felt sabotaged, the faces in the window now tattooed on the inside of her mind. In particular, it was the image of the girl that unsettled her the most—the dark, calm penetration of the eyes.

Upon reaching the downtown IRT, she turned slowly. "I'm sorry, James. I was having such a great time and then . . . "

She brushed back hair that fell across her eyes. "I'm not upset with you, God knows. But ever since we met, it's been like a rabbit hole. I'm not complaining. I just can't quite get my head around it."

Early bent closer to her. "This is gonna sound like real fluff, so forgive me. I just can't help thinking. All this stuff . . . I mean, you tracking me down, this reflection thing, whatever else—it all has to do with . . . with the question. You know, about us. That's what's pushing things up, prying things loose. I know it's bizarre as hell. But I also really think it's positive."

He glanced sideways at her. "Am I sounding crazy?"

"Yeah, as a matter of fact, you are." A small involuntary smile spread across her face.

"Don't worry, I'm not. Not even close." Early squeezed her hand. "Whatever this is, we're in it together. I say we roll with it."

She gave him a questioning look, then nodded. "If you're not backing off, neither am I."

For a moment, grey eyes spilled into blue. Amidst the storm of doubt and fear, the quiet line of connection between them held still. Simultaneously, they both looked away, and Desda retreated down the staircase into the shadows of the Lexington Avenue subway station.

Early remained on the corner for a moment staring after her, knowing from his own experience what she was about to go through. Like a splinter, the memories would fester and demand to be extracted, and then the whole painful ordeal would erupt inside her. Early could only stand to one side, tangential to the process, wishing her courage and strength.

He turned around and began his long trek homeward. On one level, what appeared to be happening was mind-boggling. His "second chance" was gaining momentum. Even in the arena of the heart, despite all the challenges that lay ahead, he was being given an opportunity to get it right.

Now as he strolled uptown, he couldn't help but notice there was a little spring in his stride where winter used to walk.

SIX

Starting at daybreak, the reckless, supercharged figure of Trakker lay siege to the street corner at the end of Early's block. Dramatically out of context with the soft sunny day and mild pedestrian traffic, he coiled sinuously in torn jeans, slamming the guitar strings with his flat pick, angry at the world––strutting and shouting out the tunes to anyone brave enough to withstand his assault.

Today his scuffed black boots carried him back and forth relentlessly in front of a tattered green blanket strewn with heaps of artifacts from his "private collection." Here, books, records, and almost unrecognizable memorabilia from his travels were being offered for a "mere fraction of their worth."

After three nasty notices from his landlord and two days without food, Trakker had finally allowed the reality of his financial woes to register. He needed cash. Like any other veteran of the edge, he took it in stride. There was no moral chastisement, no desire to change his priorities. This interruption amounted to nothing more than a rude reminder that it was the grease upon men's palms that kept the world spinning, not the poetry in their veins.

One hour into his stakeout, however, the musician could feel his insouciance descending into downright belligerence. Contemptuous of his own needs, abandoning any attempt at artistry, he hurled his next few songs at the passersby like unfriendly heat-seeking missiles. If he couldn't sell, at least he could do his part in making the world a little more hostile for all the sleepwalkers.

But Trakker had another reason for being in the neighborhood that morning. Last night he had caught a dispatch on his internal "radio." Jori had channeled in. He had one more request. This one bristled with consequence and got the musician juiced.

In the nearby apartment, a somewhat deflated James Early sat glowering into the black of his first cup of coffee. Despite the resurgence of Desda in his life, Early was frustrated with his limbo status. Desda at least had her marching orders. But what about *him*? What about *his* assignment? Quill was still out there roaming the streets as death's minion, free to sip his wine, contemplate his victim, and kill. And there was nothing Early could do until he got the elusive assassin's soulprint.

Two ineffectual cups later, Early finally stood up. *The Fountain of Light. Maybe that would change my luck.* After collecting his things, he bounded down the stairs and set out for his subterranean office. Turning the corner on Columbus Avenue, he tripped over an object he hadn't noticed on the sidewalk. Recovering his balance, he looked down and saw the open guitar case, sparsely sprinkled with coins.

"Jesus, man! Enlighten your feet, would you!" Trakker of wild hair, thin arms, and three-day-old growth stood before him. An instant later, a half-grin full of barbed mischief creased the corners of the large mouth. "Testing your chops as a crash test dummy or just into kicking guitar cases to start your day off right?"

Early brightened. He was actually very glad to see him. "Well, well, we meet again. The bad boy poet of the astral plane." Then adjusting to the parlance of the man, he added dryly, "Come to do us a specific disservice or just into disrupting the peace in general?"

So saying, he offered his hand. "Hello, Trakker."

The poet grunted and pushed Early's outstretched arm away. "You can put that thing away unless it's wallet-bound."

Holding Early's gaze, he gestured behind as though inviting a visiting nobleman into his castle. "Behold! I have expanded my repertoire. As always, I give you music that cauterizes the spirit, lyrics that unlace the heart. Today, however, there is more. Much more. Examine for yourself!"

Early eyed the piles of junk that gasped for worth—even identity—littering the ground on top of the raunchy green blanket.

"Deeply unimpressive," Early said.

"Don't go shallow on me here, dude!" Trakker said brusquely. "Perceive the feast beneath the bread and water!"

Early gave him a compressed smile. "Not today."

Truly needing the money, Trakker persisted. "A small tour of items," he announced.

Eager to be on his way, Early fidgeted impatiently as Tracker proceeded to point to various objects, speaking reverentially about each one, as if reading off rare entrees on a gourmet menu.

"Today, we have incense—the smoke'll prowl around your room and turn into the faces of Egyptian Pharaohs. Over here, this bicycle wheel . . . from a bike once ridden by two lovers over the edge of the Brooklyn Bridge. Spin it—you hear their final words. This old boot belonged to the last Gypsy in Hoboken. Look closely and you can still see the stains of wine and fire on the heel. I got a fan belt from a fifty-eight Edsel Corsair, a typewriter with the letter K on strike . . . pots, postcards, rock 'n roll, and hats . . . all yours, today, dirt cheap."

Early shook his head. "Great performance, but I'm not in the market."

Trakker turned fierce eyes upon his hopeful prey and raised his eyebrows. "Then look again, tarnished Tibetan. I offer you a trade."

Beneath the glittering mantle of talk, Early suddenly noticed how thin and besieged the musician appeared.

"Look, we both know you're dazzling," Early said with more compassion, "but if you're trying to make a point here, it's not getting through. Just tell me what you need!"

Trakker liked this directness. "Finally! Step closer!"

Early didn't move. "Talk!"

Trakker shrugged, then leaned forward and whispered, "A dark one grinds his teeth. He's finding loopholes, his ghost ship moored in the harbor!"

"Trakker, I don't have time for this! Conversational English, please!"

The poet muttered to himself and sighed. "Here, I'll slice it thin for you. Subject and verb. You need information about targets and victims. Who's being stalked, who stands in line. I'll find out. Maybe just one squiggly piece, but I'll drag it back to you."

He paused, a mysterious current in his dark eyes. "Perhaps even a net fine enough to catch the print of a soul."

Early felt a chill pass through him. "You can do this?"

Trakker tossed back his tangled black mane. "I go where I choose. Take what I want." Fixing Early in a beady glare, he added, "Sometimes I get a token for my efforts."

Early nodded slowly in comprehension—the deal. Gazing around at the shipwreck of merchandise on the ground, he bent over and picked up an old wrench. "This is going to make the Smithsonian jealous as hell, but if this is still available, I'll take it."

Trakker hid his relief. "Jaws that tighten around its prey." Then he rocked back on his heels. "My price is set by the cash register of your conscience. Think karmically."

Early quickly pulled out three twenties from his wallet and tossed them into the guitar case. "If you can do what you say, I'll empty my bank account in there. These leads—where do you find them?"

"Ahhhh," Trakker wagged his finger, "I go to a spiritual junkyard. Bardo Town. Home of the twilight folks."

Early shoved the tool into his back pocket. "Sounds out of my range. Be careful."

"Not a chance. Careful and I go together like a hatpin and a horse. I like danger. I like against the wind. And that is why you, Mister Detective, have a nest egg, while I, Mister Verbal Spasm, am looking over my shoulder."

Early reached over to shake Trakker's hand. This time the man gripped it, surprisingly warm and sincere. "I'll take anything you can get. Good luck."

Realizing he was now behind his self-appointed schedule, Early nodded goodbye and rushed off to catch the bus. Just before he was out of earshot, however, he heard Trakker yell, "The quill still writes! The poison spreads!"

Early stopped abruptly and whirled around. But to his surprise, the musician had already packed up his belongings and disappeared.

SEVEN

Spanish Harlem

It was after midnight and Trakker was in his personal sanctuary—blinds closed, lights off. The only illumination came from the dancing flame of a black candle and the orange tip of a burning stick of incense. His naked body lay stretched out on a woven straw mat as if lying in state, guitar balanced on his chest, rising and falling with each slow breath.

Outside this one protected space, the poet's other rooms reflected the casualties of neglect: piles of unwashed dishes, discarded clothing, and miscellaneous junk. Disheveled stacks of books rose up like rickety skyscrapers. All of this, however, was part of Trakker's camouflage—a fortress of disorder safeguarding his solitude and sacred turf.

But the room where he lay was as precise and austere as a Japanese tearoom. There was not a particle of dust or dirt on the hardwood floor. There were no pictures, photographs, or posters on the walls to define or limit him; nothing to distract him from his true focus. On the floor beside the mat was a folder of his poems, a bronze statue of *Buddha Touching Earth,* and a worn leather-bound copy of *Songs of Innocence* by William Blake. Other than his guitar, these were the only possessions he truly cared about.

As the tendrils of smoke from his candle drifted upward, Trakker stared beyond the ceiling. Gradually his heartbeat slowed, and his mind became clear and open. Now he could become a drifter in the less-charted realms of existence.

Striking a chord on his guitar, he breathed deeply and let go. Like mist rising from a morning lake, he lifted out of his body. Trakker was going to the land of perpetual shadows. For him, it was like a second home.

Bardo Town

In a landscape of chronic dusk, Trakker touched down. Soon he was crunching along the unpaved roads on the outskirts of Bardo Town. Compared to Earth, the "fiber" of this realm was lazy and tacky—so thin it had the look of peeling wallpa-per, barely disguising the void beneath. The lack of animation was stifling. Dust kicked up by his boots swirled aimlessly, then hung suspended in midair with minimal intention of ever settling down. The trees seemed only marginally rooted. The river he crossed over was sluggish and without music, sliding thickly beneath him like olive-brown putty.

As a seasoned visitor, he was not surprised. In Bardo Town, the motto never changed: If you have to do anything at all, do it half-heartedly. And because of this commitment to noncommitment, it was also a place where secrets were left unguarded and could be made to drift in any direction.

Trakker's journey through the space-time continuum had occurred without incident—an accomplishment in itself. Interdimensional jumping was tricky business, and only a few understood the grid well enough to even try. Ever since he became aware of his "gift" as a young boy, he had one goal: to master the torque, focus, and outrageous intuition necessary to get him to his destination in one piece. Years later, Trakker was an ace—always happy to test his mettle against impossible, ancient odds.

Amidst the infinite folds, there were a few five-star destinations full of maj-esty and grace but restricted to souls whose karma was above reproach. Palden and his entourage resided in one of those. Trakker did not have the grades, nor the power, to qualify for entrance.

But he did frequent the lower range of "landing strips," which went from reputable to utterly bizarre to downright nasty. Bardo Town was somewhere in the middle. What made these travels perilous were the eddies of menace embedded in the Nightmare Zone: strange creatures with distorted cravings that even an intrepid wordsmith like Trakker found difficult to describe. Worst of all, Amnesia Webs were everywhere, seductive and soft-spoken—offering peace and eternal amnesty for weary travelers. These pitfalls lay in ambush, awaiting those voyagers who didn't know the ropes or weren't strong enough to hold them.

As in all matters, Trakker carried his brashness with him like a comb in his hip pocket. These dimension jumps were simply a chance to strut his stuff and do a little surfing along the edges of time and space. Today, however, he had some business to take care of. Dressed in his current favorites—jeans, Rolling Stones T-shirt, black vest, and boots—he moved leisurely along the trail, peering out ahead at the wobbly outline of the Kingdom of Doubt.

Bardo Town was a between-life area for those who had lost their alliances and could not make up their minds. All who lived here had come to the same spiritual nonconclusion: *Right? Wrong? I don't know, and I really don't care anymore!* For them, the promise of goodness had become a sham—impossible to achieve and not worth the effort. On the other hand, outright evil still seemed a bit too excessive to be attractive. What appeared to be apathy was, in fact, an exact equilibrium of these two opposing forces. Caught in the middle, Bardo souls had decided *not* to decide.

And so, before being reincarnated and entering the ring again, they came to Bardo Town for a "time-out." This inertia kept them on the sidelines . . . and waiting. What they waited for was anybody's guess. Sometimes they were there for centuries.

Visually, Bardo Town was a faded costume party. Each inhabitant tended to wear the garb of his or her last lifetime, turning the streets into a haunted parade of history and fashion. The possibilities for unlikely juxtapositions were endless. For Trakker, it was a poetic feast! Where else could one find a Zulu warrior strolling with a flapper from the Roaring Twenties? A Viking prince rolling dice with a proper English butler . . . or, for that matter, an Egyptian scribe flirting with a cowgirl? The list was long and irreverent.

Except for its extremely porous fabric, it could have passed for Tijuana: pawnshops, seedy hotels, pool halls, and bars pitched in garish colors. Like the residents, the facade had become bleached and worn. In the end, Bardo Town was, literally, a ghost town.

It was, nevertheless, a city well-known for its wagging tongues. Since gossip was its only real form of currency, it tended to double as a smoky backroom for the outpost dimensions where rumors could be bought and sold, fabricated or silenced . . . with nothing considered sacred. At the southern edge of the town was Dead Man's Whistle, a cloak-and-dagger watering hole, where the exchange of secrets was particularly hard-core. This was Trakker's final destination.

Sooner than anticipated, he reached the main street and found himself walking through a cluster of tawdry shops gathered along a thin sidewalk. Trakker scowled. Bardo Town used to be a sleepy place for a few souls with spiritual hangovers. Now it was looking like a boomtown. Sad but true, the ranks of the lost had swelled considerably since the last time he was here.

While turning his head to study the curious relics on display in a trading post called Take it or Leave it, Trakker was pricked by something sharp and jumped back. Blocking his way was a pasty-faced woman in a faded blue bonnet and billowy white dress, brandishing an open brooch like a weapon.

"We don't like your type here no more," she mumbled. "Get thee gone."

Trakker was startled but quickly recovered. The residents had always greeted "non-res" visitors with distrust, but this was overt hostility. Something had changed.

Guiding her hand so that the pin was safely fastened to her blouse again, he nodded quietly and continued down the block, this time walking lethargically, emptying his face of any sign of emotion. He needed to conceal that he had the one thing the Res resented most—a life. Wondering again about this new aggression, he turned the last corner. Dead Man's Whistle was now in sight.

While the general texture of Bardo Town could be described as silent and brooding, the saloon itself descended into something closer to sinister—always cluttered with rough-cut souls, mostly outsiders looking for an "in" or an "out." Here, information was the coin of power, and Dead Man's Whistle had become the pipeline for gossip. Tucked away in an unlikely corner of the universe, no one would suspect that a sleepwalking, indecisive place like Bardo would become a hotbed for nefarious trade. But the cover had persisted through the centuries, offering a landing strip for astral-plane hustlers and voyeurs like Trakker, who somehow managed to break the code.

Before entering, Trakker paused at the door. The place had been dangerous before. Right now, it felt as edgy as a blade—complicating his promise to bring back information about Quill. His best hope was the bartender who owed him a favor for services rendered in the past. If he were still there, he might have heard a thing or two and be willing to talk. It was a long shot but the only bullet Trakker had in his arsenal.

Wiping his hands on his jeans, the poet pushed through the swinging saloon doors, picked his way through the freezing darkness, and sat down on a stool at the bar. The only trickle of light came from the dripping candles of a cobwebbed chandelier that swayed and groaned above the bar despite the stagnant air. From around the room, he could hear whispers and joyless laughter. Thankfully, no one seemed to notice him. So far, so good.

Eyes adjusting to the dimness of the room, Trakker surveyed the scene. In scattered vignettes around the room, shadowy figures huddled, buying and selling their clandestine wares—information stolen from the spiritually well-heeled or cesspools of dark karma, whatever commanded a price. Three-quarters of the tables were occupied—another bad sign. Last time, it had been half.

A moment later, Scully, the bartender, approached. In his last lifetime, he had been a sailor and victim of scurvy during the early 1800s. Huge and ugly, his pock-marked features jutted out beneath a red bandanna. Although his eyes were hooded and red-rimmed, they were still uncommonly alive for Bardo Town.

Scully had worked in Bardo Town for the last century. He was a soul without country or loyalties, a traveler who hated anything remotely resembling authority. For countless lifetimes—as sailor, soldier, and degenerate—saloons had been his mistress. In the end, Dead Man's Whistle was just another place to hang his hat until temperatures rose and he packed his bags again.

During the course of Trakker's last few visits, a rough bonding had been forged between the two men based on a mutual love for the reckless spirit and open road.

Scully brought out a bottle of Bushmills Irish Whiskey, poured a drink, and slid it across the bar. "The stink of the poet!"

"The rot of the hull!" Trakker responded, raising his glass to clink. This was their standard greeting. Warmth was not a Bardo feature, but Scully had his own guarded stash that he brought out on the rare occasion when he liked the company.

Tossing down his own drink, he smiled sourly. "Jesus, lad. Only damn Lifer I know who gets a kick outta slummin' with the bottom-feeders."

"I make the rounds," Trakker snapped. "You?"

"Just where I want it," Scully growled. "I'm an iceberg in cold waters. Nothing changes."

Then he scrutinized Trakker more carefully and lowered his voice. "Yer up to somethin.' What's on yer mind?"

Trakker leaned in. "Information . . . A viper known as Quill. There's some high folks who want him shut down. I'm doing a little reconnaissance."

Scully glanced around furtively. "Watch what ya say! There're big ears in this room right now, and things have tightened up. We had some scum in here, and folks ain't feeling too generous."

While speaking, he had quietly unbuttoned the cuff of his shirt, allowing a four-inch switchblade to slide unseen beside Trakker's elbow. "If yer planning to stay awhile, ya may need a friend with some teeth."

Trakker nodded with silent appreciation and covered the knife with his hand. "I'll bear that in mind."

Scully glanced around the room. "Traders don't give a damn. Come for the deal . . . strictly hit and run. But some Res folks are here too. They got a score to settle with Lifers who break and enter, and you're red meat."

Looking sideways over his shoulder, Trakker could pick out some residents, heads turning, haunted eyes staring in his direction. Trakker didn't care. He had given Jori his word to help and taken Early's money. Now he had to deliver.

He bent forward and whispered fiercely, "C'mon, Scully, give! What happened?"

The bartender shifted his weight uneasily behind the counter. Trakker pressed on. "Unzip, man! I did you some solids. Now it's your turn."

Scully pursed his lips, scowled, then nodded imperceptibly. "A few days back, a tall, pointy guy was here. Albino, by the looks of 'im," the bartender said, barely moving his lips. "He said the demon gods was interferin.' Wanted to know who was behind it. How to change the odds."

Scully took a swig from the bottle and shook his head. "The bloke was filth . . . white skin, black heart, that I can tell ya. Raped with his mind, he did. Bent a few souls, got what he wanted, then left. Sent a squall through the whole bloody town."

"Names, Pirate! I need *names*," Trakker hissed under his breath.

But Scully didn't have time to answer. Three large men, faces hard and ghoulish, had detached themselves from the shadows and now surrounded Trakker. Alone, Bardo Town residents were vague and easy to control. In a pack, however, vicious intentions amplified, and they could be dangerous. Trakker could feel their frosty exhale on the back of his neck and groping hands along his arms.

"Fucking zombies!" Trakker cursed and spun around. In his right hand, the blade flashed out from its ivory handle. Easing himself off the stool, he waved the knife and glared into the ring of gnarled faces. "Okay, brain-deads, who's first?"

By now the entire cast of residents was on alert, and the vigilante crew around him was swelling. Scully had suddenly distanced himself. Seemingly indifferent, the bartender was now bending over behind the bar, busying himself with something else.

Trakker backed his way toward the door, slashing at the jungle of reaching arms. Five feet from the door, he stopped. Two men now loomed behind him, blocking his exit.

In the sputtering light, hoarse, lifeless cries began to echo around the room, chanting for revenge, thirsting for a chance to destroy a Lifer.

"He's bloody mine!" Scully's rumbling voice pierced the fracas as he brawled his way toward Trakker, knocking over tables and chairs in his path. Seizing the poet under the arms, he lifted him off his feet and carried him through the doors. "Out, damn ya!"

Hoisting the body over his head, he tossed Trakker into the dusty street. Leaping on top, he pressed down violently against the poet's chest with a massive hand. "Friggin' Lifer!" he yelled. "If I ever see ya again, I'll rip yer heart out!"

At the same time, Trakker felt thick fingers secretly force something inside his vest pocket. Quiet as a breeze, and only heard by Trakker, Scully whispered his apologies, "Read it later, laddie. Best I can do. Now get the hell out of here."

The bartender stood up, wiped his hands together, and spat at the sprawled figure. His reputation intact, he strode back into the bar.

Trakker got to his feet gingerly and brushed the dirt from his face. But the crowd still tasted blood. Armed with pool cues, splintered chairs, and broken bottles, they edged closer. Time for the kill.

"Stop! He's with me!" With feline grace, a young woman sprang forward and stood facing the mob. "Back off!"

An uproar swept through the angry throng. One of their own kind was betraying them! They shrieked at her, rattling their weapons. But the woman held her ground.

"*I'll* make sure he goes. Now stand back. All of you!"

A restless silence followed. Then, as if a blister had been lanced, the blankness returned to the faces. One by one, they turned and drifted away.

Trakker drew a shaky hand through his hair. Why would this resident and stranger act on his behalf . . . or had she? He had no idea what she planned to do.

With one hand on her hip, the woman stood motionless, watching the crowd dissipate. Once the street had emptied, she slowly turned around, revealing her face.

Two huge condemned eyes stared out at him. They were opaque, bleak, and tinged with hurt, completely dominating her face.

Overshadowed was a graceful symmetry of full lips, straight nose, and alabaster skin. Partially hidden behind ringlets of black hair, a broad scar covered the left side of her head, like the map of a dark continent. Dressed in nondescript clothing, of medium height and build, she managed a tiny crescent of a smile, then glanced away. Except for the scar and obvious emotional pain, she would have been astonishingly beautiful.

Trakker was utterly taken aback. The face was harrowing—dark, tormented, and utterly fragile. And yet, this woman had just fought off a hostile crowd, seemingly to save his life! Humbled and confused, the rebel poet's brazen facade began to break apart. Now he struggled for words.

"There's nothing I can say that's gonna do this justice . . . but thank you! They would have torn me to pieces."

She didn't say anything, just stood motionless in the dust.

"I don't get it. I'm a Lifer—you're a Res. You're not supposed to help me, but you did—and now they're gonna treat you like a Judas."

"I won't even notice." She kept her head lowered, her voice dry and mono-tone as if unused to speaking. "They're just frightened homeless children. Like me."

Then, with a slight gesture toward the end of the street, she started walking. "First we get you away from here. Then I have something to say."

Trakker shrugged and strode silently beside her, still unsure of her intentions. Twenty minutes later, they began an arduous climb to the top of a bluff overlooking Bardo Town. Halfway up the incline, she lost her balance and began to slide back-ward. As stones and gravel rattled past him, Trakker reached out and grabbed her hand. It felt cold and lifeless. Yet when he glanced down, he had the odd sensation that he was holding his own hand. In shape and contour, they were almost identical. With a noticeable quiver, she righted herself and pulled her arm back, forcing him to let go.

Once at the crest, she stopped walking and turned sideways, shielding her scar from view. With obvious effort, she began to speak.

"Look, like everyone else in this dead zone, I'm a broken piece that doesn't want to be fixed. Don't try. The only reason we're even talking is because I came here with unanswered questions. Bardo is supposed to make you forget. It didn't."

"What are you talking about?"

"Last week a man came in. He was pale—a lot paler than any of us. Usually drifters are slime but just go about their business. Not this one. He was a high roll-er, looking for elite stuff. He used his mind, I don't know how. He held everyone hostage, had them strung out around the bar 'til someone gave him what he was looking for. Then he split. I learned something, though. Something that hooks you and me together."

"What?" Trakker demanded, beginning to wonder if this broken woman was also crazy.

"He was my father." Her eyes danced toward Trakker, then shot away. With her voice swollen by tenderness and horror, she spoke again, "You're part of this. He's your father too."

Trakker felt the blood freeze in his veins. "Hold on!" he protested. "A long time ago, I had a mother and a sister who got killed. I never even knew my father! How can you say these things?"

As if she had decided to remove the bandage from an infected sore, she turned her head into full view and raised her chin. "Look at me! For God's sake," she cried, "look at this face, this hair, these hands!"

Then, with a fierce appeal in her eyes, she pleaded, "Recognize me! I'm your *sister, your twin*!"

Trakker reeled away—then steadied himself, refocused. Irrefutably, lines and proportions, the bone structure and meld of features were almost identical to his. In a wave of emotion, the truth of her words found his heart.

"Forgive me, Tess. Forgive me," he said quietly.

A pronounced silence followed—he, looking out with unseeing eyes at the distant town, his sister, staring down at the ground.

She spoke first. "When we were three years old, our house caught fire. The roof caved in, Mother got trapped and burned to death. I don't know how we got out alive, but we did. Then we were separated and completely lost touch."

Trakker felt the whiplash of the old memories. He vividly remembered the fire, flames engulfing his dark-eyed mother, his sister suddenly ripped from his life.

Finally, he shook his head. "I never forgot you. You were part of me. Up 'til about five years ago, I kept going back to our old neighborhood, trying to find out what happened to you. No one seemed to know. After a while, I numbed it out, decided you must have died too."

"Part of me did," she admitted ruefully, tracing her hand across the discoloration on her cheek. "I got branded for the rest of my pathetic life. After the fire, I was never right. I became a ward of the state, then abandoned, then picked up, then kicked out . . . back and forth. There were medical nightmares, detention homes, abuses. I began to feel like I was a curse or a disease or something worse. Finally I dove into drugs. When I was sixteen, I got into a hot bath with a razor blade."

A lump filled Trakker's throat. "Why stay here? Why this graveyard?"

"Where else?" She shrugged with annoyance. "Can't you tell? I'm not even a shell anymore. There's nothing that beats inside me. I don't want to laugh or cry or do anything anymore . . . and I don't care."

"But you're my damn sister, I—"

"I *am* damned! That's the point! You aren't. Please, just listen!"

Trakker bowed his head and let her talk.

"It's about our father."

"I don't remember him at all. Not even fragments."

"He *killed* our mother," Tess said angrily. "He torched our home and disappeared. When I was . . . alive . . . I tried to track him down. Got a little info, then nothing. They were never married. His name wasn't on our birth certificates. So he did his evil shit and walked away, free and clear. But that's not the worst part."

Trakker bit his lip. "Go on."

"He's clairvoyant and pimps himself out to the shit of the earth—the real bad ones. Wherever he goes, whatever he does, he's destroying lots of lives."

She raised her voice, almost commanding, "We're his seeds! I can't do anything. But *you* can. Find him! Stop him!"

Trakker held this for a long moment. "Consider it done." He put his hand on her arm.

Tess cringed, recoiling from his touch as if afraid of contamination. "Leave me alone! If you care about me, honor my request. Now go! And don't come back!"

Finished, she turned on her heel and began to stumble back down the hill—a desolate figure, clasping her arms around her wan body, descending into the engulfing shadows of purgatory.

Trakker helplessly watched her go. Heavy-hearted, he trudged back to the hidden location of his exit port. Somehow, he would fulfill his promise to her. Someday, he would come back and drag her away from this self-made hell.

When Trakker finally returned to his room in Spanish Harlem, the earth plane greeted him like a slab of cement. As always, the interdimensional jump was an energy drain. But this one had huge, twisting content that made his body feel like rusty iron, his mind like dirty water. Despite the clawing demand for sleep, he tried to resist. Obsessed with images of his sister and the devastating knowledge of his father, he knew something had slipped through the cracks—something very important.

Struggling to remember, he dimly registered that one of his hands rested on something in his breast pocket. *Scully's note. That was it!*

Using all of his available strength, he tore himself away from the grip of blackout and sat up. With shaky hands, he read the message and cursed. He had to get to a phone. He had to warn Early immediately!

Desperately, he tried to push himself up to his feet. But muscles would not respond, and his arm collapsed, sending him crashing back to his mat. Soon the abyss was upon him, pressing down until he passed out. He would lie motionless for many hours, and his urgent message would remain undelivered until the next day. By then . . .

EIGHT

The Garden Apartments

Ida Early leaned across her walker and put the finishing touches on her painting. The whitish tinge behind her son's face, nothing overstated or corny. Just a hint. Something to suggest . . .

She stood in her living room, her back to the large window where morning light washed across the canvas. Her muscles ached, and the fingers that gripped the brush felt like brittle sticks. Looking sideways at her hand, she accused out loud, "You want to be stiff? Then be stiff. But let me finish the damn portrait!"

With a sigh, she finally laid the paintbrush across the palette. "All right, let's have a look at you." Dragging her walker backward, she settled three feet away from her work. A reproachful twinkle came into her eyes as she scrutinized the portrait.

"You always ask for more, and I usually give it to you," she chastised, "but I swear, if I keep going, the soul in the boy'll get tarted up, start looking like something out of Madison Avenue. Nope, I'm done!"

Making this pronouncement, she was about to start her brush-cleaning routine when she heard a noise. It sounded like the click of her front door being quietly closed. Curious, she pushed her walker to one side of the portrait so she could see.

He was a nicely dressed man wearing a dark suit and black gloves. He stood quietly about ten feet in front of her with the coldest smile on the thinnest pair of lips she had ever seen. In his right hand he held a snub-nosed revolver with a silencer, pointed directly at her heart.

Ida gasped, blood rushing, legs trembling. But Ida was a woman who never allowed anything in life to go unchallenged, and she recovered quickly.

"My, my," she said acidly, "suit and tie. A little overdressed for the occasion, aren't you?"

Still getting his bearings, Malcolm did not respond.

"Look," she said, continuing to glare at him, "I don't have time for this. If you're robbing, then rob. There's a few keepsakes in my bureau that might get you cab fare. If you're raping, well then, I feel sorry for you. Real sorry. Whatever you gotta do, just do it and leave me in peace."

"I have something else in mind for you. You'll become acquainted with that soon enough," Malcolm said coldly.

Ida hesitated, then began to rattle her walker in his direction. "Enough. I need you to look me in the eyes and talk some sense, or I'm throwing you out."

Malcolm cocked his gun. She stopped, her heart beating faster.

"Let's be civil," Malcolm intoned with quiet menace. "And if I were you, I would refrain from disturbing the neighbors. Any cries for help may be injurious to them as well."

"I wouldn't waste my breath. Not on the likes of you. What the hell do you want?"

"You are incidental. Frail, worthless. I take little pleasure in doing this."

"Then don't do it," she wheezed. A pain was knotting inside her compressed chest. The air was not finding the lungs.

Malcolm ignored her and studied the room. The corpse would look dramatic sprawled in front of her son's portrait right here in the living room. In fact, the impact would be exceptional.

With his free hand, he reached out and took hold of the upper bar of the walker. "You need to be positioned over there," he said, nodding toward the painting.

"I'm not going anywhere until you tell me what this is all about!" Ida announced, trying to stay forceful but beginning to feel faint.

"You've created a little monster," he said absently, noting the area of faded carpet below the picture. "He's become a problem. I'm about to teach him a lesson."

Ida began to tremble. This was about her son.

An icy fury coiled inside her as she looked directly into his black eyes. "I pity you. You're weak and you're evil. Whatever you do, wherever you go, my son will find you and send you back to hell!"

Now that she knew James was involved, she was prepared to fight. Using every muscle in her withered body, she wrenched the walker unexpectedly away from the assassin and hobbled into the kitchen, distancing herself from the portrait. The air was thinning and her pulse was banging in her ears.

Malcolm watched her spastic efforts with frostbitten amusement. Lowering his gun, he followed her and mocked her from the doorway. "Where will you go, old woman? You can't escape. Your time is up."

Ida didn't hear him. Now *he* was incidental. Collapsing against the kitchen window, she looked outside, tried to catch her breath. For an instant, time appeared to slow down . . . then suspend. As though from far away, she could hear her breath come and go like distant tides, ebbing and flowing. For the last time, she squinted out at the world. All around, brilliant colors lapped against her tired soul.

It was morning in Brooklyn. In the yard next door, a child was watering the garden. Holding a green watering can in her tiny hand, she pranced on the lawn in front of the rows of tall flowers. She wore blue overalls, her silky curls bouncing beneath a large straw hat. Two golden-winged butterflies fluttered about her round little arms, and bees buzzed in the warm sunlight. As Ida watched, her eyes began to tear and mist over. *It's all so young! So very, very young . . .*

It was then that the old woman's heart began to thrash and misfire, demanding far more than she could give. Ida was a practical woman. It was time for her to say goodbye.

With a small sense of victory, she completely ignored the presence of the killer behind her and straightened the collar of her blouse. This was *her* decision.

She wouldn't resist any longer. In fact, she would meet her invisible suitor halfway. Taking matters into her own hands had been her style for an entire lifetime. Why change now?

When the first brutal wave of the heart attack crushed through her body, she staggered forward but remained upright. With great effort, she eased herself slowly down to the floor and lay back.

Using every gasp of strength available, she raised her trembling hands, folding them neatly above her heart. This was the way she liked to sleep. This was the way she wanted to die. With a silent prayer for her son, she closed her eyes. Now she would wait for God's finishing touch.

It came like a rush of the wind and struck with the sharpness of a dagger. She gritted her teeth and moaned softly. With a fleeting smile on her weathered lips, she consciously stopped breathing.

Malcolm shoved his gun back into his belt. He had intended to leave his mark by planting a bullet in the middle of her heart. Now he was forced to be more creative. Looking from corpse to portrait, an idea slowly emerged that made him smile.

A moment later, he stood in front of Early's image, a paintbrush in his hand. Using crimson, he placed a small dot on his adversary's heart and stepped back. The red mark was in contrast to the rest of the painting, but only to the discerning eye. This would do the trick. If this James Early was half as smart as WhiteMan had cautioned, he would eventually discover the incongruity and know that his mother's death was not an accident. The assassin's message would be clear: Any further involvement would cost the bereaving son and his "outside" cohorts dearly.

Satisfied, Malcolm picked up the painting and easel with his gloved hands, carried them into the kitchen, and set them down next to Ida's body. Just as he was about to leave, the phone rang, jarring and surreal in the deathly quiet room. He hesitated for a moment, deeply tempted to pick it up. It might even be her son.

Speaking to him at this very instant would be thoroughly delicious. Nevertheless, Malcolm ruled against it and prepared for his exit.

As before, the hallway was deserted when he quietly let himself out. No one had seen him enter; no one saw him leave. Cutting through the backyard, he passed unnoticed behind a young girl playing in the garden, eventually finding his way back to the street. There, he flagged down a cab and settled into the backseat for the long return ride to his Manhattan hotel.

Malcolm was pleased. Artistically, it had gone better than planned. His "message" was subtle, yet full of latent power. In addition, he had been able to accomplish his goal in a bustling town in broad daylight without wasting a single bullet.

Smoothing back his hair, he looked out at the passing traffic. At last! Now he could do what he came here to do. Even the prickly albino had given his blessing.

NINE

New York Public Library

It felt like the sharp tentacles of a tarantula were clawing his face, invading his sleep. Early's eyes flew open, head shooting up from his cushion of folded arms—ready to fight. A quick scan told him nothing. He was in his "office." He had fallen asleep in front of the Fountain, drifted into fractured imagery, a mosaic of Trakker, Desda, and his mother. Now awake, he couldn't shake the knot in his stomach. Something terrible had just happened. Someone needing his help was trying to reach him.

Early stood up on wobbly legs. Whose cry had he heard? Of the three suspects, Trakker was the most unlikely candidate. Desda was a possibility. She may have run into a snag trying to unsnarl her traumatic past. It was also logical to assume that his mother might want to talk to him. He was scheduled to visit her tomorrow to pick up his portrait. Had something come up?

Thoroughly frustrated with his inability to decipher, Early paced the room. The only thing left to do was contact these people directly, find out if any of them were in real danger. He had to move quickly. He sensed the plea getting more and more frantic.

Once outside the library, he sprinted to the bank of phone booths. Ten minutes later, full of misgivings, Early stood awkwardly in the middle of the sidewalk—was his perception off? His calls had neither verified nor eliminated anything. Trakker didn't have a phone, so he had immediately tried Desda. He'd left a message, then dialed his mother. After ten unanswered rings, he dejectedly hung up. Ida occasionally liked to take walks with her walker around the block. It was possible she was out on one of her rickety forays. By now, the appeals seemed less urgent, more like fading echoes. All strange and unsettling.

Early smiled grimly to himself. Maybe this episode had simply been a product of his overzealous imagination—a boots-on-the-ground, reality check about the foibles of his so-called psychic perceptions.

Deciding that his skills needed an overhaul, he trudged back to his office.

Early's Apartment

When Early entered his apartment that evening, the light of his answer machine greeted him, pulsing like a beacon in the darkness. Rushing over, he crouched down, hit replay.

There had been three calls. While he waited for the tape to rewind, he found himself praying he had been mistaken, that no news would be the good news.

"Hey, James. Desda, here." There was a long pause, then, "Okay, you're not there. I'm . . . well, I'm . . . interesting. Call me."

Early sighed with relief. Desda was *not* the one in trouble. He waited for the next message.

"Early, this is Sam." There was a long pause. "Give me a call at the precinct when you get this. I need to talk to you."

Three seconds of silence, then the next message. "Bro. Sam again. . . . Okay, I'm at home now. I really need to talk to you. It's about your mother."

By the time the message finished, Early was already punching in Sam's number. His first message had sounded somewhat formal. The second one sounded sad. Sinking into his armchair, he prepared himself. Sam's deadened voice told him everything he had feared.

With deep compassion, Sam told him about his mother's heart attack. Her body had been discovered by a neighbor, who had dropped by to say hello. The friend knew James, had called the Thirteenth Precinct trying to locate him, and she had informed Sam. The coroner had been summoned and the body taken away. According to preliminary reports, she had died of natural causes at around nine o'clock that morning.

Early fought back tears. "Foul play? Anything?"

"Nothing. I knew you'd ask, so we checked the initial report. No bruises, no signs of struggle. As a matter of fact, they found her lying on the kitchen floor with her hands folded neatly across her chest. Coroner said she had a little smile on her face—like she was happy to go."

Sam paused, dealing with his own emotions. "I'm real sorry, man. I knew your mama. She was special. Tough as nails, but real thoughtful and kind. All I can say is that she went peacefully. Did her thing, then let herself out. That's about as good as it gets."

Through smarting eyes, Early smiled, remembering. Ida was the best—one of the most thoroughly decent and wise souls he had ever known.

Sam's quiet voice came down the line again. "Take a moment, James. I got nothing but time for you."

Early cradled the phone on his shoulder, suddenly flooded with memories of her.

His mother personified the quiet, rich details of ordinary life: her hands that wore the faint smell of leather and oil from polishing his shoes for school; the creak of her rocking chair on the porch during a summer afternoon; the comforting hiss of steam from the iron when she touched up a blouse or creased his pants before going to work. Ida found beauty in the honest stitchwork of things, never fooled by the razzle-dazzle of outward appearances. With society hell-bent on embracing gadgets, glitz, and mediocrity, she had simply stepped to one side, allowing it to pass by without her, quietly continuing along in her own fashion. For Ida, there was no substitute for substance. End of discussion. And through all of life's hairpin turns, sudden and often painful patches, she had been Early's touchstone. Now she was gone. He would miss her incredibly.

Wiping his eyes, Early put the receiver back to his ear. "Sam, I think I'll go take a look at her apartment," he said sadly, "just to satisfy myself."

"Up to you, my man," Sam said, "but when I heard the news, I busted up my schedule to drive over there, just to make sure. It was the least I could do. Believe me, there was nothing to see. No scratch marks on the locks, nothing turned over, no things tossed around. But I did see the portrait she painted of you. It's totally amazing. If it's any consolation, she really loved you. It shows in the painting. She died next to it."

"In the kitchen?" Early knew his mother liked to paint in the living room next to the big picture window.

"Yeah."

In the face of the detective's overwhelming sorrow, this small discrepancy registered, then fell from view. "Thanks for your help," Early said, trying to pull himself together. "I'll be okay—just need a little time."

"'Course you do. I lost my mother coupla years ago. I know what it feels like. Look, when you go to do the formal ID thing, give me a heads-up. Maybe we jump for a cup of coffee? I mean, if you want to talk or anything."

"You're a good one, Sam, but . . . well, I think I just want to sit with this for a while. I appreciate the offer, though."

"Okay, James. I'm here if you need me." Sam offered his condolences once more, then hung up.

*　　*　　*

Two hours later, Early returned to his apartment after a sobering trip to the morgue. The spectacle of her ashen, unanimated features had shaken him deeply. But Sam was right. Early's suspicions of anything irregular had been a figment of his own paranoia. Ida had died of natural causes after a long, productive stint on Earth. Who, indeed, could ask for more?

Because of this, Early hadn't gone to Ida's home. In addition, seeing his portrait right now, in those empty, abandoned rooms, would be devastating. He would delay that for a later date. All he wanted to do now was give it time to heal, find a way to bring this final chapter to a graceful close. It wasn't an easy assignment.

He sat on the edge of the bed for several hours, sifting through his thoughts and feelings. In the distance, there was the knowledge that souls lived to be born again. This did not help Early dispel the immediate, visceral loss of his mother. In the end, he was here, and she was not.

That night, he bitterly questioned the nature of things. Even if beings *were* deathless, in his unhappy opinion, the whole setup stunk. *Why should we all work so hard to become kinder and wiser, struggle with the impossible challenges of being alive—then have it ripped away, forget everything, and have to start all over again from square one? What a brutal arrangement!*

But no question and no answer could lessen his pain. When morning sun finally bled through the curtains, Early lay back against the coolness of his pillow. By the time he fell asleep, he had come to one reluctant conclusion. Birth and death were the twin gatekeepers of karma. That was their function. Despite all the obstacles, he wanted to remain focused on the light—no matter how faded—that still flickered from the end of the tunnel.

An hour later, the strident ring of the phone ripped him awake. The whoosh of traffic in the background seeped through the line. Somehow he instantly knew it was Trakker calling from the street.

After a slight pause, the poet's groggy voice came through the wires. "I'm trashed and I'm late," he muttered apologetically, "and what I got for you ain't real rosy."

Early remembered their "deal" and tensed. "Give it to me straight."

"You're being watched, dude. Crosshairs probably not on you but someone close by—a chink in your armor."

Early's mind raced. "Give me the exact information!"

Trakker smoothed out Scully's note and haltingly read it over the phone.

"A bloke named Early bars the way. The viper will find a weak spot and attack. You got twenty-four hours."

Shivers exploded through Early's body. *Weak spot?* Two immediately came to mind. Desda, who seemed to be okay, and—

"Oh, Christ!" Early howled in anguish. He glanced at his watch and slammed the phone down.

Trakker understood. He *was* too late. Something had already happened. Now the guilt for his delay tore away at his conscience. As he angrily walked back to his apartment, he silently condemned his father. Although he couldn't prove it, he knew James Early's sorrow could be traced back to the Albino. Now more than ever, it was time for payback.

Early frantically threw on his clothes. The coroner had estimated Ida's time of death as approximately nine o'clock yesterday morning. It was now 8:20 a.m. Soulprints had a twenty-four-hour window. If this was the work of Quill and there was a soulprint, Early only had forty minutes left before the print decayed beyond recognition. There would be morning traffic, and Brooklyn was a long way away.

Hitting the street at full stride, he stepped in front of a yellow cab on Columbus Avenue. Breaks squealed, cab fishtailed, Early flung himself into the backseat.

"Brooklyn!" he yelled, yanking the door closed behind him. "Drive like your life depends on it!"

Whipping two twenties from his billfold, he waved them at the driver. "All yours if you're fast. Now, move!"

Gears shifted, tires screeched, and the car surged forward, darting through traffic.

Cursing every delay, Early watched in horror as each precious second slipped away. There was a morbid silver lining. If he could get there in time, salvage the soulprint, his mother might not have died in vain. It would have been classic Ida. Even from beyond the grave, she had found a way to help her son.

Two elderly residents of the Garden Apartments watched in dismay as a crazy, rude man kicked in Ida's front door. Early didn't care. The ticking clock allowed no time to do it politely.

Charging into the apartment, he was immediately struck by the lingering presence of his mother. The rich smells of oil paint still mingled with her vase full of fading flowers and the clock in the hallway still tapped quietly onward. The air still retained the same invisible silt, the dusk-like feel of an old woman maintaining dignity in the final chapter of her life.

Early shook himself and pushed ahead. Noticing that everything in the living room was in order, he raced into the kitchen. There he found himself staring into his own eyes—his portrait looking back—Ida's last communication to her only son.

Early ripped himself away to look for clues, then jerked his head back to the painting. Something had caught his eye, something out of context. Then he froze. Glaring back at him, with the fierceness of a raw scar, an incongruous red splotch seemingly punctured the blue shirt over his heart. It mimicked a bullet hole. *What was this? A mistake?* It couldn't be! His mother's work had always been meticulous and understated. In her own words, primary colors were garish and in bad taste. No, this was not . . .

As Early studied his portrait, the dark truth began to take hold. This splash of red was a message for him from Quill. He had left his calling card. Somehow, without the use of force, the killer had pushed his mother over the edge to a premature death and wanted Early to know.

Steadying himself, he let the gale blow through him. Quill had done this as a show of power to rattle him. He mustn't succeed. More than ever, Early needed to stay cool and efficient. The cat-and-mouse game had begun in earnest.

Soon he was thinking rationally again and went to work. Time to slow down, lean in . . . open the threshold to deep sight.

Everything hinged on finding the soulprint quickly. No form of clothing or glove could block the ultrafine wavelengths of an immortal print. The assassin had used crimson paint and, therefore, must have touched the handle of a brush. Fortunately, Ida had been cut down before cleaning her brushes. Early immediately found the culprit with the dried red tip.

Placing the brush on top of the coffee table, Early took a deep breath, let go, and began following a path into the realm of deep sight.

Soon he had penetrated the thin veneer of the physical plane, entering the quiet world where spirit ruled. As he scanned below the surface, he came across the golden glow of normal soulprints. They belonged to Ida. Systematically, he swept along the inner core of the brush. Moments later, he felt the telltale pang in his heart. Down where the assassin had gripped the handle, a red blemish pulsed.

As if drawn by a magnet, Early instinctively placed his palm over the mark and pressed down—his lifeline fusing with red soulprint—a tingle as it locked into place, instantly followed by a spike of hysteria, rising shrilly, then fading. Early listened carefully to the spasm of urges and understood. The soulprint needed to be scanned by the Fountain, processed by the Library of Souls. He had twenty minutes before the print decayed and became meaningless. The thought of Quill getting away with murder again made him want to scream.

Hailing a cab, Early leapt inside and collapsed on the backseat. He looked out the window as the cab pitched and jostled its way to the public library. Either he would arrive in time—or not. There was no middle ground.

Twenty-five minutes later, Early stood before the Fountain, gazing into its whitish aura of light. His hand carrying the imprint now throbbed, seemingly paralyzing the nerves, threatening madness.

Early straightened his palm over the surface of the shaft, forced it to hold still. The light licked against his skin—it seemed to pull at his mind and inside his heart. Then something lifted, and suddenly Early felt released. The print had been scanned and stripped. All around the room, the Akashic Realm appeared to be reformatting—about to deliver a new setting. If the print was intact, Early would find himself in the Library of Souls, ready to reveal the Akashic Record of the spirit named Quill. If not . . .

Pacing on a tight, nervous leash, Early prayed for a positive result. The judgment was handed down shortly. As before, he did not hear a voice. He simply knew. The print had already decayed beyond specific recognition. With only this partial information to go on, millions of souls fit this incomplete profile.

Early shuddered. His mother was gone, and Quill had, once again, slipped through the nets and was free to kill again. Early felt his old nemesis taunting him: *Early was out of his depth. He could never make up for the damage he'd done.*

A moment later he rose to his feet. That was the trap! That was exactly what Quill wanted him to believe. The more he went south on the case, the more the assassin had the upper hand.

Pissed at himself and a world riddled with injustice, Early bolted out of the library and hit the streets. He had a maxim that he had carried over from his cop days: *When in doubt, take a good long walk.* The city, with all its spit and polish, had a habit of straightening out thoughts and clearing his head.

After that, he would return . . . and begin again.

Nearby, in one of the more traveled underground corridors of the library, Jori looked up from his work among the stacks. He had been listening to the plaintive "music" of James Early, acutely aware of his friend's turmoil.

Such a test of fire! Jori thought, remembering his own past. And his pupil was having to deal with all of it at the same time—a tragic loss, a killer who seemed to be unbeatable, the karma at stake. And yet, Early was holding his own. No one could have possibly hoped for more!

Wondering how to acknowledge him for his fortitude, Jori realized he could, at the very least, relay a bit of good news. With long strides, he made his way to the gutted elevator, then down to Early's hidden office. Writing quickly, he penned a note on a piece of paper, rolled it into a neat little scroll, and placed it on his friend's desk, then returned to his earthly job. The message had actually come from Palden. Jori was simply passing it on.

At dusk, when Early returned from his walk, he immediately spotted the curled note on his desk. He read it quickly. Then read it again, and again, until tears of joy and relief filled his eyes.

> *Your mother is with us now. She is young again and at peace. In due time she will be returning to her beloved Brooklyn for her next lifetime. Her karma shines!*

Still holding the letter, Early sensed something behind him and turned. For a brief moment, a white Bengal tiger appeared in the doorway . . . then faded away.

TEN

Early's portrait now hung in the bedroom, stationed like a sentry above the place where, every night, he came to dream. Sometimes the painting seemed overly dramatic, sometimes inspiring. Regardless, Early had made a pact with himself. Quill's insidious drop of blood would remain above the heart until the case was solved. Then, and only then, would Early have it removed.

Ida's instructions for her funeral service were very much in keeping with her character: brief and without emotional fat. Her God didn't ride through the universe in a Cadillac. He wouldn't have dared. Instead, she honored the supreme pedestrian spirit who walked along the cracked sidewalks of the world, who waited at bus stops and tipped his hat warmly to all passing strangers, no matter what religious persuasion they held.

Her final request had brought an involuntary smile to Early's face. She had wanted to be cremated, her ashes scattered around the four blocks in Brooklyn where she had been born, lived, and died. According to her will, she had wanted her son to perform this task. She had written:

Wear something comfortable and take a little stroll around the neighborhood. When you're through, have an egg cream on me at Lilly's. Then get on with your life.

That week, feeling very much as though his mother's frail arm were linked in his, Early ambled around Ida's old stomping grounds and distributed her final goodbye—a little here, a little there. The fine smoky particles momentarily caught up in the mild breeze, then settled gently on the places she had loved: a few ashes by the newsstand where she had bought her morning paper, a few by the dress shop where she had toiled, a handful placed in the sidewalk planter by the art store where she had purchased her paints and brushes.

In final tribute, two fistfuls were thrown through the mesh of a chain-link fence that surrounded a vacant lot. Many years ago, it had been the site of an Irish pub where Thomas Early had fumbled with the shiny buttons of his new NYPD uniform, wiped his brow with a napkin, and asked Ida for her hand.

Sitting at the counter on one of Lilly's stools, Early stood up slowly and raised his glass with the last few drops of chocolate egg cream toward the sky. "Okay, Mom. We're done. Come back home to Brooklyn soon. It's a lonely place without you."

Downing the drink, he placed the two dollars in change Ida had designated for this occasion on the counter and left the shop.

Out on the street, he headed back to his office. For the first time in three days, he had some room in his head to think again. It was time to go back to work. Square one of the Quill case was a bad place to hang out.

And then there was Desda . . .

The Cloisters

Only a few miles away, the woman in question clung to a chrome pole in the middle of a subway car, jockeying for balance as the train thundered through the burrows beneath the city. At that exact moment, she had no idea what train she was riding or where it was headed. For her, this was just what the doctor ordered.

She was tired of the "James Early factor," tired of the ponderous riddle, sick and tired of being so damn confused! After X number of sleepless nights and long inner debates, she had finally had enough. Whatever forces were out there, whoever was behind the faces in the Bloomingdale's window, it was time for *them* to put up or shut up. If she couldn't find the answers, the answers would have to find her.

True to her word, she had started out early that morning and cast herself upon the day. Consulting nothing but whim and fancy, she opened her arms to her city and herself: stopping for coffee here, going into a bookstore there, talking to a stranger, avoiding an old acquaintance, turning left or right on any given street at any given moment. Eventually she had climbed aboard a random subway bound for an unknown destination, fully enjoying her newfound freedom.

After the train jarred to a halt at its last stop, Desda climbed the subway stairs up into the hazy light of an overcast day. She found herself standing amidst trees and lawns. With no objective in mind, she followed a winding road, mingling with a crowd of late-spring tourists. Coming around a bend in the path, she was unprepared for what she encountered.

Nestled in among trees and rocks at the top of a hill loomed a sprawling estate. Austere yet inviting, it commanded a breathtaking view of the Hudson River below.

Desda shook her head in wonder. *How auspicious! How magical!* The currents of the day had deposited her at the doors of the Cloisters—a collection of medieval architecture and artifacts, relocated from Europe, now a museum dedicated to monastic life.

Yet, in feel and texture, it was a living, breathing retreat only a heartbeat away from the urban madness. As Desda approached the entrance, she experienced an odd sense of returning home.

After paying the donation fee, she began to explore, soaking in the rarefied ambiance. Almost palpable, a stillness pervaded the corridors as if the old stones themselves were saturated with centuries of prayer and meditation. Taking her time, she wandered through the chambers, pausing before tapestries, frescoes, and artifacts.

Surrounded by the gentle themes of peace and humility, Desda felt herself soften. Even the sounds were comforting: the hushed voices, the quiet shuffle of footsteps.

For a moment, Desda stopped before a portrait of the Virgin and considered: *Why did it now seem so benevolent and forgiving?* Desda had spent her youth in convents and churches, resenting every moment. There, she had somehow been made to feel that, whatever she did or tried to do, a stern God stood in judgment, always eager to punish. Yet here, bathed by the stream of light from high windows, she felt emancipated.

Basking in the sense of grace, she was completely caught off guard when something sharp and old began to turn inside her like a rusty nail. Halfway through the tour, she became inexplicably queasy, a nameless dread gnawing at her insides.

Trying to suppress her panic, she pushed her way through a group of spectators until she slumped beside an open window in the passageway. Catching her breath, she attempted to organize her thoughts. *What was this?* She had felt utterly swaddled when she first arrived. One hour later, she was suffocating, as if the monastery had turned against her.

Dismissing it all as paranoid nonsense, she shook it off and resumed her tour. Yet as she moved from room to room, the sensation thickened. Everywhere she went, a crowd seemed to press against her, even when no one was present. Completely unnerved, she looked for a way out.

An eternity later, she staggered into an open courtyard. Her lungs gasped for air; sweat poured from her brow. Haltingly, she walked around, trying to reclaim her equilibrium. *This is absurd! What the hell's wrong with me?*

Exhausted, she sat down on a granite bench that faced the garden. Before her, a fountain splashed amid blooming flowers. Leaning forward, she rested her hands on the slab of cool stone. As soon as her flesh made contact with the worn surface, she felt an infusion of energy. It poured through her skin and flooded her heart, flushing and cleaning until her mind opened. *This is not about James Early or mysterious forces or anything else. This is all about Desda Collins!*

Melded with the ancient stone, Desda closed her eyes. *Let it come. Whatever it is, let it come now.* As if released from bondage, images of stone began to flash through her consciousness . . .

Starlight glinting off a mountainside
The mouth of a cave looking out across a ravine
A courtyard slick with blood

As the pictures in her mind grew more and more vivid, the lines between the present and past became arbitrary, wavering and blurring in the afternoon light. With a deep breath, she summoned all her willpower. A split-second later, she crossed over and stepped inside the vaulted memories of another monastery . . . *soldiers, carnage* . . . Tibet.

While the mottled sun slid toward the western horizon, groups of sight-seers came and went. As they left the Cloisters and walked back along the path toward the bus bay, many commented about the peculiar, motionless woman who sat transfixed in the courtyard. Although she had seemed troubled, no one had dared to disturb her.

At six o'clock, an attendant tapped Desda lightly on the shoulder. It was closing time. She would have to leave. But Desda was still straddling the gaping fissures in her mind. Wide-eyed and vulnerable, she stared back at the curator without comprehension.

Then, looking around glassily, she slowly rose to her feet. She wasn't done.

The vein was still open and bleeding. Now she was committed to knowing every detail about her Tibetan past. She needed more time.

With a far-off expression and the unsteady gait of a sleepwalker, she navigated the winding stairway down to the exit, only vaguely aware that her eyes were wet with tears.

Once outside the buildings, she found a tree in the surrounding grounds that overlooked the river and slumped down beside it. Here she could continue her dialogue uninterrupted. Cradling her legs in her arms, she rocked slowly back and forth. The sun was going down, and the pain in her heart was almost unbearable.

Sunset came and went. The hours passed by and the temperature dropped. Desda remained oblivious to it all.

It was midnight. The wind rustled leaves in branches overhead. Slowly she pushed herself away from the damp grass and stiffly rose to her feet. She had taken it as far as she could go. Without knowledge or experience, she had had to use a machete to hack her way through the Tibetan lifetime. Some things she knew for certain, some areas were still grey. Nevertheless, she had done the best she could.

For better or for worse, she now understood her excruciating role in the demise of the Tibetan monastery and the death of Palden, her uncle. Now she understood who James Early was and why he had entered her life.

With tears still glistening in her eyes, she started back to the subway.

Early's Apartment

Another cup of coffee. Another game of solitaire, Early hunched over his kitchen table, looking for distraction. All in vain. His attention remained riveted on Desda. He wanted to hear from her, to know she was okay. Right then, nothing else mattered.

He slipped another CD into the player, this time Springsteen's *Darkness on the Edge of Town*. Shuffling the deck, he dealt himself another round.

It had started earlier that afternoon. After completing his mother's final requests, he had gone directly to his office. As the day progressed, however, he found himself thinking more and more about Desda. Finally he stopped batting it away. His obsession was *not* happenstance. She was up to something. And whatever that was, it was stirring up a hornet's nest. He could feel it viscerally.

Placing a black ten on top of a red jack, he played on. Midway through the game, the buzzer rang. Cards flying, chair skidding backward, Early leapt to his feet and rushed to the intercom.

"Desda, is that you?"

There was a long pause, the line between them crackling with static, then her voice—recognizable but strained. It wasn't until he heard her feet on the stairs below that he fully registered the impact of her words.

She had said, "Yes . . . I'm here with Usha."

A minute later, backlit by the yellowish glow of the hallway light, Desda stood framed in his doorway. Her clothes were grass-stained and creased. Dark tresses of hair tumbled over pale skin, features carrying the imprint of a long traumatic night.

Jolted hard by the first impression, Early stood without speaking. She looked thin and haggard, but her eyes told a different story. From deep-set hollows accented by smudged mascara, they gazed out with new depth and no excuses. For a profound moment, they just looked at each other.

Early finally broke the spell. "Come in. Please."

Desda hesitated, then took a step forward. "I . . . I need to warn you. I'm raw . . . ripped open right now. I don't quite know where I am."

Early simply nodded, gesturing her to enter. He didn't want to crowd her with words or emotions. Right then, she needed to find her way back. The rest would come.

She filed in wearily. Once inside, she gazed around his apartment—uncertain and questioning. In this highly sensitized state, she moved in slow-motion around the living room. Stopping to inspect, gingerly handling objects, she drank in the details of Early's life.

Wanting to be unobtrusive, Early stood to one side, watching her intently. Soon he was completely inside her mind. *Usha was, indeed, present*, trying to reconcile his current home with a faraway cave, still preserved in the mountains of Tibet. There, each rock, feather, or prayer wheel had been a token of their love. In comparison, his apartment would seem cold, distant, and without intimacy. The shock of this alone would be painful for her.

When Desda came to the blue bowl, now resting on the mantelpiece, she stopped and stared at it incredulously. Turning to Early, she shook her head in disbelief. "This . . . ? No! It can't be!"

Early met her eyes. "Yes, it's the same one. It's not a copy."

Desda squinted back, then looked away, her mind unable to assimilate, her nerves about to overload. Fully attuned, Early saw her falter. In two quick strides, he was standing beside her. All the signs were there. She was about to break.

"I'm right here," he whispered, putting his hands on her shoulders.

She immediately stiffened. "Oh, Christ," she moaned, "I'm afraid . . . I'm so damn afraid!"

Then it came. Erupting with the force of a cloudburst, huge wracking sobs shook through her as tears streamed from her eyes.

Early put both arms around her. Picking her up gently, he carried her to the sofa. Seated with her head cradled in his arms, he stroked her hair as she continued to cry.

As he held her, the heat of their bodies, the scent and warmth of her skin began to stir something inside him. On that fateful night, surrounded by snowfall, they had laced themselves together, soul to innocent soul—oblivious to past or future. He would never forget.

Now, as his lips helplessly brushed against her cheek, the physical longing for her began. Fighting the urge, he leaned back.

Sensing his struggle, Desda stopped crying and opened her eyes. Thoughts passed between them—a tender question, a reluctant answer. *No. They weren't ready. Maybe later, maybe never. For now, there was only their karma and the work that lay ahead.*

As if released, they uncoupled their bodies, and Desda moved off his lap.

Early stood up and shook his head in wonder. "We'll get through this. I mean you and me and all the stuff around. But how strange. How very, very strange."

Desda smiled wanly. After the deluge of tears, she now seemed more like herself, her pallor beginning to show a hint of color.

"Thanks for letting me cry," she said sheepishly. "I really needed that. I spent the whole day looking at myself in the mirror. Some things were beautiful—states of mind that I had totally lost sight of. But the other stuff . . ." She shuddered, then reached out and took his hand. "I tell myself to keep going. There's gotta be strength on the other side of this. Maybe some amazing truths. But right now, James, I'm burnt out. I want it all to go away."

Early squeezed her hand. "Look, you need sleep. Why don't you just stay here tonight? Take the bedroom. We can pick it up tomorrow."

"That sounds great. Truth is, the thought of being alone is a bit terrifying right now. Just set me up on the couch. Please, that's more comfortable for me."

He brought her the bedding, then disappeared into the bathroom. Desda took off her jacket, untied her boots, and slid in beneath his plaid quilt.

When Early returned, she propped herself back up on one elbow. "I know we can't undo, but can we fix it?"

"Not sure," Early said thoughtfully. "The fact is, we found each other again. That's unbelievably positive. I mean, you and I could have—"

He caught himself and smiled. "You've had enough. Let's talk about it all tomorrow. Sleep well."

With that said, he turned off the overhead light and headed into his bedroom.

Desda dropped her head back on the pillow, surrendering to the exhaustion. A "goodnight" escaped her lips. Then she was asleep.

A soft breeze wafted through his open window, stirring the nearby curtains. Early lay in bed thinking, replaying the twists and the turns of the day. How utterly bizarre! Layer upon layer of karma. The problem and the solution, always and forever walking side by side.

Turning toward sleep, he listened to the night. From out of the darkness came the soft rhythm of Desda's breathing, of Usha's living presence. It filled the night with a fragile sense of wholeness.

ELEVEN

Riverside Park

Armed with hot coffee and a bag of fresh bagels, Desda and Early sat on an old park bench at the river's edge. To the left, boats bobbed in the 79th Street Boat Basin marina. Behind, a fountain flowed beneath a stone archway marking the entrance to Riverside Park.

Desda raised her cup to Early's, a slight narrowing of eyes. "I hope you can walk me through this, James, because I'm still short-circuiting. I mean—Tibet? New York? Where the hell are we?"

Early laughed. "I could go Zen here, say something like 'neither . . . both.' But truthfully, I'm still finding my way too."

"Well, talking it through can only help. I need to get it out, make some sense of it. Then, for both of our sakes, I think we should put it way behind us."

Early settled back, took a long sip of coffee. Then they began.

Starting with their earliest childhood memories of Tibet, they proceeded to reassemble their past. Anxious at first, they became increasingly excited. Outside of an occasional blank spot or minor discrepancy, their stories were completely compatible.

Early's association with Palden had started humbly just a few days after his birth. Wrapped in a yak wool shawl, the baby boy had been left for adoption on the doorstep of the guru's Nepal monastery—parents unknown. The sage had immediately taken the child under his wing, adopting him, naming him Tashi. When the boy was five, he accompanied his father through the Himalayas, eventually ending in southwestern Tibet, where the mission was established. Soon thereafter, Palden's widowed sister followed, settling in a nearby village with her only child, a girl named Usha.

With Palden utterly engaged in the karma project, Tashi was largely raised by his aunt. Both Desda and Early vividly recalled their initial meeting—the young boy standing awkwardly on the front step, Usha catching his little face peering in. Leaping from her mother's lap, both children had hugged, laughing with delight—instantly best friends.

When Tashi was nine, Palden had shown him around the research facilities, inviting him to consider becoming an apprentice and participating in the karma project. "Observe our practice. Spend time with the members. Listen to your heart. The decision is yours and yours alone to make."

The decision was already made in his mind. A few days later, he said goodbye to his surrogate family and took his pledge as a member of the team. Regretting he would have less time with Usha, the young boy set out on his own journey, this time out along the borders where science touched spirit. Although Usha's mother had forbidden her to join the mission, Palden invited his sister and niece to visit the monastery whenever they wished.

Desda smiled at the memories. While the rooms and equipment were still under construction, she and Early had played hide-and-seek amidst the odd machinery and crude scaffolding. They had also helped out by occasionally running errands to the neighboring village, telling the shopkeeper little "untruths" to avoid suspicion.

Planted side by side, they continued to grow together like two flowering vines on a trellis, entwining closer and closer as they climbed through the years. With adolescence came the yearning for privacy. Their needs were changing. They sought a different kind of sanctuary—one slightly distanced from the sterner disciplines of the mission. It was then that they found the cave in the side of the mountain, carving out a world of their own design—a place where God and dreams and beauty could be articulated with a look or a smile. For both of them, this little alcove would forever represent their one true spiritual home on the face of the earth.

Pausing for a moment before continuing their stories, Early and Desda exchanged a painful look. In retrospect, they could now see themselves through the members' eyes. Without question, they had been the darlings of the monastery, deeply loved by the brilliant and noble members of the Tibetan crusade. In this light, their subsequent betrayal was even more harrowing.

Soon the narration led them to the nightmare of their last night in Tibet. Here again, their accounts coincided: Early's race through the snow, their night of farewell, the devastating aftermath.

In Desda's moist eyes, the salient question formed again and again. *How could anything as pure as their relationship have created such monstrous consequences?*

Early could only bow his head and hold on tightly to his one piece of truth. *There had to be a reason for all of this. Somehow if they just kept going, things would become clearer.*

Before closing the book on this gruesome chapter, Early had a final question. It was a hard one to ask.

"I remember the night I was killed. Just before I passed, I caught your eye. You had soldiers all around you. The next thing I can recall is, well, Brooklyn. You weren't reborn 'til eight years later. Do you know what happened?"

Early felt her instantly contract, her eyes becoming opaque. "Don't push me on that," she said coolly. "Leave it alone, okay?"

Early waited a beat. "All right," he said without letting go of her eyes. "Just for the record, though, I think it's important to put *everything* on the table. If we don't confront it now, it's not really over, you know?"

Desda shivered, turning away to hide her face. Eventually she spoke, her voice hollow and dead.

"I remember the soldiers . . . what they did to me after you went down. Sexual abuse wouldn't even begin to describe it. To them, I wasn't human—just a dumping ground for their hate. After days of that, I think my heart just stopped beating."

She shrugged her shoulders. "From there, all I can remember is drifting, feeling filthy . . . contaminated. If I could have, I would have killed myself over and over again. Maybe that's where the time went. I don't know. At some point, I became a kid again—living in New York, all set up to hate myself, feeling like I belonged in the gutter. The blueprint was right there."

She drained the last drops of coffee and looked darkly at Early. "We messed up. Talking about it *does* help. But Christ, can't we make amends, do something to atone for what we did? I mean…"

With growing admiration, Early listened to the tenacity behind her words. Against staggering odds, odds that usually led to needle tracks and body bags, she had played her hand with courage and dignity.

"I agree," he said, "and two more people banging around with bad karma is not quite getting it done."

Crushing his empty cup, he stood up. "I have some ideas. Feel like walking?"

Together they meandered uptown along the pathway beside the river. As they walked, Early thought about his next move: how to frame his disclosure. Some things couldn't be revealed. The Library of Souls, the Fountain, the location of his office were all bound up in his vow of secrecy. Other areas were less defined. For them to work together as a team, Desda would have to know enough to function.

"I'm working on something," he began. "It's big. It has a lot to do with karma."

Searching for words, he slowed his pace. "It wasn't relevant until you knew about us, what happened in Tibet. You would have thought I was crazy. We're past that now."

Desda nodded, waiting to hear more.

"Okay," Early began, "but we're talking absolutely confidential here, I mean, truly. And it's gonna be devoid of details. That's part of the bargain."

Desda began to get edgy. "Lips sealed, whatever. Just tell me what the hell it is!"

Taking a deep breath, Early dropped his bomb. "I'm currently in touch with Palden."

At the sound of the sage's name, she bent over as if she'd just been punched in the stomach. "Oh no! Oh my God, no!"

With a face gone deathly pale, she slowly straightened up. "Of all the souls in this damn universe, he's the one person I can *never* face. Never. Don't you see? He was my uncle. I completely betrayed him!"

"I realize that. But first and foremost, you need to know I'm working with him now."

She stared at him mistrustfully. "For Christ's sake! Doing what?"

Bobbing and weaving between confidential areas and acceptable truths, Early gave her a rough sketch of his new job. When he finished, Desda remained quiet, pondering the wider implications. Finally she folded her arms and gave him a slow nod.

"Sherlock Holmes meets Siddhartha. The funny part is that it makes total sense. It doesn't mess around with the symptoms. It goes right to the heart. How do you—?"

Early raised his hand to interrupt her. "I can't tell you the hows and whys right now. Maybe never. Just know that I have some unique tools at my disposal. If you can live with *that*, then we're on."

Desda kicked at a stone. "Just give me what you can."

For the next half hour, Early gave her a brief synopsis of the Quill case: the seven dead bodies in Europe, the lack of evidence, the recent attempt on Billy's life. When he talked to her about soulprints, Desda had looked at him quizzically. Once she was reminded of what they were, vague memories began returning, and she immediately saw their application to the case.

Early underscored the point. "Getting Quill's soulprint is critical. We're *no-where* without it."

While dark clouds began to pile up above them, they continued their way uptown—talking, pausing to consider, talking some more. Eventually they came to the same conclusion. Since Quill had only wounded Billy, he was probably not finished with the Burwells. That was the obvious place to start.

They decided on a course of action: First, Desda would join Early in his detective work. Then, Early would use his connections inside the NYPD to help her obtain employment with the Burwells, even if it meant volunteering her time to work on Ellen's campaign. And then, once situated, she would keep a watchful eye on the premises, reporting back to Early on anything that might be relevant to the case. This would put her in a position to alert him instantly if anything possibly bearing a soulprint came into view.

Desda was thrilled. It gave her something tangible to do. It also put her in the company of Ellen and Billy Burwell, two people she admired enormously.

"There's one last thing I need to tell you." Early turned to face her. "I have an opinion completely unsubstantiated by *physical* proof, which leaves me out in the cold as far as the NYPD is concerned."

"What's that?"

"They're protecting the wrong person."

Desda looked shocked. "How so? Death threat, attempted murder. Seems pretty clear."

"That's the intention. But it's one big smoke screen. I don't know why. All I can say is that, in the big picture, Billy is small potatoes. He doesn't match the profile we're looking for. Ellen does."

Desda stopped to consider this. "I'm a little new at this, so I'm not really in a position to judge. Billy's a blue-chip hero and all that. But you're right. Ellen's in a whole other league. I mean, she's got a vision, basically said to hell with the status quo. That's gotta be making some of the big boys *very* nervous."

"She's for real—something we haven't seen for a long time. Can you imagine what would happen in this country if she got elected?"

Desda sighed. "I'm almost afraid to hope. I haven't quite given up, but I also haven't voted in years."

"That's the point. Despite all the bullshit, we all still want to believe."

"Well, I'll agree with you on one thing— Ellen's the best I've seen. Period. If anyone can turn this thing around, she's the one."

Early took her arm. "Well, that's the long and the short of it. We stop the killer, America gets the chance to see her in action. Are you in?"

"Totally."

After all was said and done, their departure was oddly anticlimactic. Early said goodbye at the bus stop, kissed her on the cheek, then headed home. Much had been accomplished: the bridge between them had been rebuilt, the past reunited with the present. What lay ahead in the future was anyone's guess.

TWELVE

Early's Apartment

Early slammed the phone down, threw a karate chop at an invisible foe. Done! Desda was now officially part of the team. The timing of events couldn't have been better. Responding to Ellen Burwell's timely request for part-time help with her campaign, Desda had applied, aced the interview, and just needed to clear security hurdles. Only a few days before, the chief had spoken to Early about Desda's prospects, and Ripley was not a subtle man. He had immediately started in on his former officer—wanting to know what Early had recently been sniffing and if he and this ex-stripper chick were, "you know, getting it on."

The chief was not prepared for the rush of expletives that exploded from Early's mouth. And Early was equally surprised when his show of force actually impinged. Seemingly, despite all obstacles, the Burwells had loved Desda's interview and wanted her to start immediately. Listening to Ripley's awkward backpedaling about this "fine young woman" had made Early's day.

Since their marathon talk beside the 79th Street Boat Basin, Desda and Early had been in frequent contact, excited by the deepening groove of their relationship, worried about the uncertain future. They knew the killer would strike again—probably soon and definitely without warning.

Early repeatedly voiced his concerns about her safety. Somewhere, somehow, there was a leak. Trakker's note and Ida's subsequent death had proven that. Desda could easily be next.

Because of this, they had agreed to stay attuned to the sensitive channel between them. In Tibet, they had perfected that ability to a fine art. In New York, it might prove to be a matter of survival.

The following day, Early met Sam in an ambulatory chat around Washington Square; an off-the-record update. For the sake of their friendship, they attempted to sidestep their unresolved issues. But after firing opening salvos of genuine warmth, the conversation had nowhere concrete to go and cooled off considerably.

For Early, this was not a cause for major concern. Someday he and Sam would rediscover the right pitch between them. Until then, all Early wanted to do was find out what the police were doing regarding Quill.

According to Sam, the basic line of investigation hadn't changed since the day Billy got his death threat. Every international terrorist who had a known grudge against America was still being checked out, particularly those groups and individuals based in England. As Sam had put it, "It's a joke. Everybody has the same long list of potential suspects, zero evidence, and big-time pressure."

The prevailing opinion was that Billy was far from safe. Sam concurred. There was no indication Quill would leave an "almost hit" on his previously perfect scorecard. All in all, things were not so cheery down at the station.

There was, however, one new piece of information that grabbed Early's attention. In a matter of days, Ellen would be speaking at a fundraiser at the Metropolitan Museum of Art. Billy would accompany her in his wheelchair. This would mark the ballplayer's first public appearance since the attempt on his life. For hard-core news buffs, gossip racketeers, and fans, this loomed as an event of legendary proportions. It also meant massive security and headaches all around. Despite the fact Early's angle was different from that of the police, he had to agree with their equation: Media + Art + Billy Burwell = Quill. Whether the assassin chose to strike or not, this superstar event would certainly tempt him.

Sam had then been called away to duty, and Early had headed home. He didn't need any more information. His inner barometer told him that pressure was building and something was about to break.

*   *   *

That night, the Burwell show hit the Metropolitan Museum of Art with all the fanfare of a three-ring circus. Billy was now close to deification. He had risen from the dead to risk his life again by coming to stand beside his wife. Ellen was equally lionized.

Although not yet running for public office, recent polls showed Ellen's favorability numbers near seventy-five percent. According to some, barring disaster, she was on the fast track to becoming one of the most powerful people in America—perhaps the world.

Now with both members of the celebrity couple in attendance, the atmosphere literally crackled. From around the hall, animated talk alternated between the pennant race, tax reform, and Matisse. Clustered about the stage, the media primed their engines: testing microphones, checking lighting, huddling for last-minute assignments. Sprinkled throughout the auditorium, plainclothesmen circulated through the crowd—armed and alert—eyes sweeping around the hall, back to Billy, then around the hall again. As the MC stepped forward to announce the evening's illustrious speaker, a hush descended, and the overflow crowd scampered to find their seats.

Dressed in sports coat and tie, Early scanned the crowd from his perch near the entrance. The team was in place: Sam behind the stage directing traffic with his portable radio, Desda stationed just outside the circle of security men who ringed Billy's wheelchair. When she felt Early's attention on her, she immediately glanced in his direction, nodded imperceptibly, then returned to her vigil.

Early closed his eyes for a second, trying to get a deeper fix on the room. It was an unlikely confluence of energies—rowdy ballpark enthusiasm mingling with restrained artistic sensibilities. Yet, seemingly unrelated, a tension was evident. Perception? Imagination? Time was about to tell.

Early opened his eyes and looked around the auditorium. Whatever this sense of threat was, it was not attaching itself to a location or face. A moment later the prickly sensation came again. Stronger this time. Early slid his hand across the handle of his concealed revolver. *Quill was definitely here.*

The hall lights dimmed. The audience rose to its feet and applauded. Ellen walked up the steps, crossed to the center of the stage, and stood before the podium. Wearing a simple black dress and only a touch of makeup, she greeted the crowd warmly. After her preliminary hellos and thank-yous, the audience settled down, and she began her unscripted talk.

"Some people speak about art as if it were the sprig of parsley beside the meat and potatoes of real life. I beg to differ. I'm here to say that art is the plate upon which it all rests."

She paused as a round of applause echoed through the hall. "Tonight, I join forces with The New York Council of the Arts to solicit your help. As you know, the funding for the arts is being cut in schools and . . . "

From his seat near the back of the hall, Malcolm unthinkingly massaged his painful thigh. The cadence of her voice was oddly familiar and making him ill. She was now only a stone's throw away. Close enough to . . .

Relegating her words to background noise, he let himself indulge. Pure titillation! At that instant, he was deep inside the enemy camp—unobserved, undetected. His magic was holding and would continue to hold. Rape, murder, anything he wanted—right beneath their noses.

Now his eyes slid across the faces of his opponents.

The chunky Black cop—harmless, of no consequence. Billy Burwell—still alive, still being the good little pawn in the game. James Early—damn him! A thorn. Despite the Brooklyn warning, he was still in the hunt. Then there was Ellen Burwell . . .

An hour later her speech concluded with a call to arms for the arts. After a standing ovation, the crowd circulated noisily about the room. As anticipated, Billy's presence was a magnet for many in the audience. The Burwells had discussed this likelihood and agreed on a plan. He would greet, wave, and thank, then encourage his admirers to visit the tables where the museum was soliciting donations for its "Keep Art Alive in Our Schools" project.

Despite this arrangement, throngs of well-wishers and press continued to gather around the ballplayer, keeping Sam and staff very busy in that corner of the auditorium.

Through the sea of waving arms, equipment, and people straining to see, Early and Desda maintained frequent eye contact as they moved about the room. Early had alerted her. *He's here. Find him!*

In the back of the hall, Malcolm was biding his time. Leisurely, he moved between a series of paintings on the far wall, pretending to admire. Ellen's talk had galvanized the spectators, and twenty minutes later, many still lingered, replaying her words. Hearing this, Malcolm smoldered. *Bloody fools. Wherever Americans go, even in the midst of high culture, they bring along crude behavior—destroying beauty, contaminating sensibilities. Americans aren't only ugly; they're a disease. And **she** is a pathological carrier!*

Taking a breather, Ellen Burwell stood beside one of the contribution tables. A seated volunteer flashed a smile at her and opened the donation box. It was stuffed with checks and paper currency. "Mrs. Burwell, look! We're doing great!"

Ellen looked down, beamed, and patted her assistant on the shoulder. "You see? I told you. Underneath it all, everyone's really an artist. We're just encouraging them to step out of the closet *and* bring along their wallets!"

They both laughed. Then Ellen went back to her official mingling. A well-dressed man with a military posture was suddenly standing next to her.

"Thanks for coming," she said graciously.

"I wanted to meet you. You are impressive. A worthy candidate," Malcolm said dryly, his eyes glittering like two hard pieces of coal.

He extended his hand.

Her fingers anticipated the warm flesh of a handshake. Instead, she found her skin pressed against the sharp corners of a folded piece of paper. Instinctively she stiffened and pulled away.

His gloved hand now dangled awkwardly in the space between them, revealing the creased edges of a new one-hundred-dollar bill.

Ellen felt her guard go up. This had the innuendo of a gangster tipping a call girl.

Malcolm continued to stare at her. "This is my first contribution. More will follow, I assure you."

"I'm not sure I like your money," Ellen said coolly, then nodded toward the volunteer. "Cindy here will help you . . . if she wants to."

Turning her back on him, she engaged with a young couple waiting to talk to her.

Without taking his eyes off Ellen, Malcolm tossed the bill like a piece of litter toward the table. It floated in the air and landed beside the cash box.

The volunteer looked up uncertainly. "Thanks. Now we just need your name and address. For tax purposes. That also gets you on our mailing list."

"Anonymous," he said without taking his eyes off Ellen's profile.

"Sir, we—"

On the other side of the auditorium, Desda stood next to the stage, and was surveying the room. When she finally spotted Early, he was gesturing franticly. Trapped behind a knot of reporters, he looked desperate, waving his finger toward the donation tables. *GO!*

Desda nodded and began to run.

As she wrestled her way through the crowd, she caught glimpses of a man in an immaculate suit standing by the cashier. Her heart began to pound.

He was mysterious and handsome and charismatic. His body rippled with a dark and dangerous sensuality thinly concealed beneath his perfect grooming. As his image seeped inside her, a cross fire of urges erupted: attraction . . . revulsion . . . attraction.

Drawing closer, Desda slowed and absorbed the full impact of his face. Her inner war of impulses instantly subsided. The mouth was cruel and arrogant. Everyone else in the hall was smiling. This man was not. In fact, he seemed to emanate a coldness, veiled and malicious.

Sensing Desda's presence, Malcolm slowly turned his head toward her advancing figure. Their eyes locked. Neither backed down.

Anxious and breathing hard, Desda arrived at the display and stood behind Cindy.

"Problem?"

Cindy looked up with a troubled expression. "Hey, I'm just doing my job. We need his name and address. What's the big deal?"

"Forget the name," Desda said sharply as she placed her hand over the hundred-dollar bill.

Scowling, Malcolm tried to snatch it away from Desda's tightening grip. She didn't let go.

"Damn you!" he snarled under his breath.

For a moment they strained in opposite directions, glowering across the table at each other. Terrified but tenacious, Desda held on.

Smiling icily, he twisted his wrist and the bill tore in half.

"Satisfied now?" Malcolm spat, his contemptuous eyes burning into her.

Desda didn't speak. All she wanted to do was rake her nails across his face.

Malcolm stepped back slowly. "Pity, it's worthless now. One half won't buy you a thing." Smoothly, he pocketed the other half in his trouser pocket and walked away.

Desda watched him go, her nerves jangling, her hand shaking. Without question, she had just looked into the face of evil. *He was Quill. He had to be!* Now all she could do was pray that the soulprint was on the half of the bill she held—not the half that was escaping out the door.

Nodding at the confused cashier, she turned and rushed out to find her partner. She didn't have to go far. Early was already racing toward her.

Desda grabbed his arm. "You were right! That was him! I know it!"

Without letting go, she turned to follow the dark figure disappearing out the side door. "He's right fucking here! We can't just stand around and let him walk away!"

But Early's eyes were fixed on the torn bill in her hand. "We'll have to." He tried to still his own thundering heart. "You got what we needed. You were incredible!"

"But . . ."

"Premature. We can't move until we know more about him. Believe me, I'm talking to myself real loud here. We're in the business of changing karma, not taking out hoods."

Desda stepped back, her adrenalin still coursing. "Yeah, well, I'd like to cut his balls off. He's definitely after Ellen. The way he was looking at her. Total slime!"

With obvious reluctance, she handed the ripped hundred-dollar bill over to Early. "Let's just hope we got the print. I'll scream if we didn't."

"Nice work," he said, carefully taking the C-note from her. Holding the bill for a moment, he gathered his attention into a focused beam . . . and slipped into deep sight. A rush of adrenaline filled him. *They had it! The soulprint was there, distinct . . .* as red as fire.

Desda watched him curiously. "Your eyes just changed. You're doing something. And you can't tell me, right?"

Early nodded.

Desda grimaced. "I don't know where this goes from here, but it better include me. It's personal now."

"I can't," Early said. "My hands are tied. For the time being, you're gonna have to be patient. Let me disappear from time to time and do my work. I'll share everything I can with you. I know it stinks, but that's the way it has to be for now."

Desda's expression hardened. "I got the damn print, didn't I? What the hell am I supposed to do? Sit on my butt and wait for little girly assignments?"

"Hopefully someday I'll be able to involve you in *everything*. But yeah, if you hadn't fought him off, gotten the print, we'd be back to nowhere. You did your part. Now I've got to do mine."

Placing the torn bill in his pocket, he began to usher her out of the hall. "There's another issue we need to discuss. Let's get some privacy."

Once outside the museum, he steered her to the side of the building, away from the foot traffic.

"We've got a new problem now," he said evenly, "and please don't get your hackles up on this one. It's about *your* life. I don't want to take any more risks than we have to. If this man *is* Quill, and I'm ninety percent sure he is, you're in trouble. I couldn't get over to him, so you had to do the dirty work tonight. Problem is, now he's seen you. Worse, you've humiliated him in public with that little tug-of-war. He may come after you."

"I thought of that too," Desda agreed. "The only thing is, he's after the big game. I'm just a mosquito."

"Let me ask—do you own a gun?"

"I've got mace in my handbag. I can handle a knife. But, no, I've never owned a gun."

"Well, I think we better set you up with a little more firepower," Early said thoughtfully. "In any case, do me a favor. Stay at my place tonight. You'll be safer there. I'll need to go out for a while, but I'll leave you my gun . . . just in case. Also, when I get back, I may have some interesting news."

Desda considered, then reluctantly agreed. "Okay, deal. Just for tonight. If you *do* have a breakthrough, I want to be right there to move on it. This psychopath has got to be stopped!"

Early nodded grimly, then hurried down the stairs to hail a cab, the killer's soulprint ticking in his pocket like a time bomb.

He had twenty-three hours.

THIRTEEN

New York Public Library

The torn face of Benjamin Franklin lay before him, the one remaining eye staring back with mild disapproval. Backlit by the eerie glow of the Fountain, Early leaned over his desk, studying Quill's hundred-dollar bill. The irony of the moment was not lost upon him. After murder, rape, God knows what else, this torn piece of paper was the prosecution's only witness. Now it was up to Early to make it testify.

Early consulted his watch. It was just after midnight. Still plenty of time. Only an hour ago, he had dropped Desda off at his apartment. With unspoken misgivings, she had accepted his gun, nodding mechanically as he instructed her on how to use it. From there he had gone directly to his Akashic office in the New York Public Library. Thanks to Jori's ingenuity, he was now able to bypass the security system and let himself in.

Delaying the moment a little longer, Early smoothed out the wrinkles on the bill, wondering about the strange karma that had brought this piece of currency through countless hands and situations to end up here as the carrier of this malignant cargo.

Double-checking his earlier perception, he altered his vision and slipped down past the image of Franklin into the molecular frenzy below the surface. Two spiritual impressions were visible. One shone like burnished gold. Desda's print. There was no guesswork about the other. Screaming back at him was Quill's blight of crimson.

Early pressed his palm over it, holding it still. Now it was his hostage. He would need to transfer it quickly from this world to the next. Per Jori's warning, if he allowed the red soulprint to fester on his lifeline longer than twenty-four hours, the killer's evil would infect him, become his own, and begin its deadly crawl to the center of Early's soul.

Holding his "infected" hand with the other, he stood directly in front of the Fountain, then rested his palm on the surface of the light. Immediately he felt a slight tug—an invisible force coaxing the soulprint away from his hand—followed by a sense of relief as the print was released into the Akashic system.

Now Early had to wait. Somewhere outside this world in the Library of Souls, the history of the universe was being scanned until one troubled soul was isolated for questioning.

A moment later, a seismic shift erupted, restructuring the room. The print had found its match! Now the small outpost of the Akashic realm in New York City was morphing into its full and spectacular proportions. Early watched in awe. The Library of Souls, the mythic gatekeeper of all storylines, was revealing itself.

Rising up majestically around him, rows and rows of bookcases surged into view, stretching out beyond sight in all directions. Every shelf was jammed with books, seemingly made of light—each volume emanating a quiet brilliance as if alive and humming at varying wavelengths. Early remained speechless, humbled by the Ancients who had created this miracle, humbled by the fact that he was the first living soul to ever witness this realm of the dead and their never-ending story.

Adjusting to his surroundings, Early became aware of a quiet murmuring—a sibilance that swept through the library like wind through tall grass. Somewhere unseen, the recently dead were retelling their life story to attendant scribes, adding one more chapter to their Akashic Records; trying to defend, trying to glorify. Nevertheless, after dodging and pleading, each soul would end up desirous of the truth, attempting to reveal the naked goodness beneath the dishonest personalities that cluster around the soul.

By now, the surface of the Fountain was beginning to swirl, the flow of energy moving like liquid muscles. Then, like the Arthurian sword rising from the misty lake, a form rippled upward. Bathed in a whitish aura, a book took shape. Quill's long strange story, with its thousands of deeds and denials, was giving itself up.

Early heard the voice in his head. Instead of turning pages, he was to merge with Quill's journey, then direct it. Once engaged with the narrative, Early would become part of the interdimensional linkage—and at risk. If too much time elapsed while connected, he would overload, jettisoning him out of this lifetime into the sea of karma.

He had one purpose and one purpose only—to fully understand this man. There could be no other agenda, no desire for revenge or punishment.

Placing his full attention on the tome, he projected his first command:

An overview. Start where it began.

Instantly his mind flooded with images, enveloping the entire room as a storm of lifetimes rolled by. When the motion stopped, there was no library, no Fountain—only a pastoral setting of rolling hills above a body of water where a shepherd boy tended his sheep. This was Quill's initial lifetime, somewhere in Mesopotamia near the Euphrates River, circa 6000 BC. Tempted to stay and peruse, Early heard the voice of the library in his mind:

Keep moving until you find the keys that unlock.

Early refocused. His job was to find the turning points, *pivotal* incidents that turned the innocent soul into the walking demon he was today. That meant uncovering the specific deed that created the karma Quill was now replaying. It would repeat itself over and over, like a scratched old record. If Early were to be successful, he would have to lift the needle from the groove so the deadly song would never play again.

Bending to the task, Early followed the soul through time: the rises and falls of his fortunes, the major karmic fluctuations, both good and bad. The chapters concluded in 1951 when the suspect had been burned to death in a fire in Scotland. There would be no Akashic Record of his current lifetime—that would be downloaded after Quill's death. Where he was today, his actual name, why he had become a serial killer was anyone's guess—and Early's challenge.

Still invigorated, Early sat back and studied the patterns. It was time to start gathering specifics. Deciding to work backward, he instructed the Fountain of Light to show him Quill's silver linings:

Give me the brighter side, the times of good karma.

Images of the assassin's more positive lifetimes flew by. Early looked for threads of behavior that might still be part of his current makeup. As he digested the information, he grimaced. The utter waste of potential was staggering. Quill could have been a powerful leader—courageous, smart, and compassionate. At his apex, especially in a handful of English lifetimes, he had worked diligently to forward humane causes. But noble purposes had become inextricably confused with selfish intent, allowing negative karma to kick back in, eventually gaining the upper hand.

Just before concluding his initial probe, Early became aware of an unlikely footnote. Whether as soldier, shepherd, or criminal, the soul was extremely capable with animals—particularly horses.

Early noted this and directed again:

Those were his spiritual peaks. Now let's go for a walk in his valleys.

After viewing some of these, Early wiped his face with disgust. The assassin was a disease among the living. Inevitably, he had sided with oppressors and tyrants, squashing humanity's fragile struggle for freedom at every turn. From African jungles to the courts of Spain, he had robbed, raped, and killed his way through time—plunged so deep in darkness that the quest for redemption had been abandoned.

"Got the picture," Early mumbled, pulling himself away from the horror stories.

Aware of the shortage of time, he worked feverishly, checking the karmic balances in major categories: love, money, careers, et cetera.

Surprisingly, some transgressions hadn't yet caught up to Quill in a few areas, particularly the arts and finances. His relationships with the opposite sex, however, were deeply entrenched in the gutter.

Rapidly sorting the data backward and forward, collecting tendencies and patterns, Early completed his profile. Later, when there was time, he would sift through his findings with a fine-tooth comb.

But the clock was ticking. He had to forge ahead. Early made his first general conclusions—past to present. The man at the Metropolitan Museum still embodied the persona of an English loyalist. His bearing had reeked of old money, landed gentry, and aristocracy.

Using this as a possible lead, he gave his next command:

Show me British lifetimes—violent ones when he was rich or powerful.

Six episodes were revealed. Hoping to narrow the field down to one, he took his best shot. First, he rattled off three negative and two positive karmic attributes that repeated from lifetime to lifetime:

Cross-reference the above with any lifetime where he tangled with America and had reason to seek revenge.

The pictures flowed before him. Three lifetimes emerged as possibilities. As fur trader, ship captain, and colonial lackey, the suspect had been embroiled in corruption and treachery, dying in utter humiliation. Each gruesome story was capable of motivating a deep-seated hatred for the States. Early felt a wash of disappointment. He was closer, but still light-years away. He didn't have the exact information he needed. And he didn't have time to research all three.

Drenched in perspiration, he sagged backward, cursing the fact that he was so uncertain of his trade. The odds were down to one out of three. If forced to choose, however, he would be playing Russian roulette.

Frantically he ransacked his mind for a small detail, a little dirty string he could pull. Anything to open that final door. Tearing through the raw data of the case, Early collided with the obvious. *THE QUILL!*

With a hoarse whisper, he commanded the Fountain:

Keeping everything in play, add in a quill pen or some similar form of writing tool.

Instantaneously the tension between question and answer dissipated. Before his eyes, the Fountain Light began to undulate, the book losing form as the environment began reformatting itself to a point in the past. The pivotal lifetime had been isolated, the karmic turning point located. With the portal now open, Early would have to climb through it.

Mentally preparing himself, he gave his final order:

I need to know everything. Merge me with the incident!

Instantly, everything around him—his body, his office—became translucent, then faded to empty space. Stripped down to an invisible essence, Early watched as a scene from history began to unfold . . . .

FOURTEEN

It was Philadelphia 1776, the summer of discontent for colonial America. A time when the settlers' dissatisfaction with their English landlords was hardening into outright rebellion. It was also a time when the Declaration of Independence was on the tip of the tongue of a certain American patriot.

Early viewed an urban setting: a cluster of stone and wooden houses parted by a narrow cobbled road called Market Street. From sidewalk and alley, the hot, stagnant air was heavy with the odors of manure and garbage. In the distance, he could hear the rattle of carriage wheels mingling with the clatter of hooves striking hard ground.

At the end of the road, Early saw the lone figure of a man approaching, seemingly deep in thought, barely aware of his surroundings. As Early drew nearer, he recognized the face and felt his emotions stir. Taking a leisurely evening stroll, perhaps pondering the fate of a nation, the bookish Thomas Jefferson came walking toward him.

Early heard a rustle to his left and fastened his attention on an open window in a nearby darkened residence. Someone, presumably Quill, was lying there in wait. Protruding coldly through the curtains was the tip of the long barrel of a Brown Bess.

Pieces of the assassin's storyline slammed into place. *A different lifetime, the same motivation: murder a visionary leader. Suppress hope. Keep the old status quo in place and in control.* This was the exact description of Palden's antihero whose sickness pervaded society.

Galvanized by what he was seeing, Early moved in for a closer look.

The killer crouched in the pitch-black room, his weapon propped up on the windowsill, waiting for the perfect shot. It would be hard to miss. In less than a minute, Jefferson would pass within a few feet of the ambush.

Early heard the sound of footsteps near the entrance of the house. In the shadows, he could see a woman shaking her head and hurriedly opening the front door, and somehow he understood. The woman had forgotten something and was returning home to pick it up. Early held his breath. But Quill was completely focused on his prey and didn't hear her come in. Pulling back the hammer of his rifle, he steadied his arm, preparing to fire.

When the woman stepped into the living room, she spied the man with the gun and covered her mouth, stifling a cry of alarm.

Recovering quickly, she cast about, then crossed silently to her desk. Groping in the darkness, she managed to grab a handful of sharp objects, then moved stealthily toward the killer in the shadows. Early could read her thoughts. She had put the pieces together. She knew the man and what he intended to do. If it cost her life, she would stop him!

Jefferson was now only ten yards away. The assassin steadied the musket in the crook of his shoulder and fingered the trigger. As if subliminally aware of movement behind him, he turned slightly.

Eyes pitted with hatred and fear, she loomed above him, clutching a handful of needle-sharp writing quills. With all her strength, she plunged them deep into his thigh. The assassin howled and spun toward her. Hurling her body on top of his, she jerked the quills free and stabbed again. The gun fired into the air, sending a shower of rubble down from the ceiling. Bleeding and furious, the killer wrestled her to the floor.

But the gunshot had been heard by others. From around the neighborhood came the sounds of men yelling, the crunch of flying footsteps. Help was on its way.

Early absorbed every detail. By permeating Quill's mind, he found he could get his full story—before and after the incident.

Spellbound by what he was learning, he was only dimly aware that other forces were at work. The bubble around him was beginning to distort, about to have a seizure. Moments later, the cobblestones started to shake and buckle.

As the wind began to whip about his face, Early realized his error. *He had overstayed his time in the loop. Soon the time capsule that protected him would break apart. Soon his consciousness would fracture into shards and be scattered along the void.*

Early shielded his eyes and fought his way through the growing holocaust. All around, walls collapsed and buildings torqued, sending stones rattling down. Using every drop of willpower, he tossed a mental lifeline back to the twentieth century. Visualizing the Fountain, he reached out with one last command:

Bring me back! Now!

To his horror, the upheaval intensified. Lightheaded and disassociated, Early felt the core of his identity beginning to melt away, dissolving like snow beneath a blazing sun. He couldn't move. He couldn't think.

Suddenly all motion ceased. The noise stopped. The furious whirlwinds subsided. In the background, he heard the comforting hum of the Fountain. Beneath his chest, he felt the steady, solid presence of hardwood floors. Gasping, he felt the cool rush of air fill his lungs. A quick inventory told him his body was battered but all there and functioning.

Before passing out, he gave thanks. He had managed to siphon off some karmic truths from the vaults of history and still make it back in one piece.

FIFTEEN

Prelude to sunrise. The opaque sky, streaked with pale gashes like scar tissue along the skyline of the city. In the vague light, Early stood by the window in the hallway outside his apartment door. Straining to muffle the sound, he turned the key in the lock and slowly entered. Shoes in hand, his attempt at stealth only got as far as the edge of the carpet when a husky voice called out from the darkness.

"Forget the tiptoes, James. I'm awake." Desda pushed away the covers and sat up abruptly. "Sooo, . . . what happened?"

"You're supposed to be asleep."

"Jesus, man! Tell me!"

Gradually a smile spread across Early's ravished face as his hand formed the thumbs-up sign. "The soulprint worked. We're in!"

Desda leapt off the sofa.

"Whoa! Hold on!" Early raised his hands in mock protest. "We're just getting started. All we know is who Quill *was*. That's it."

"Well, *I* think it's great!" she said, still beaming. After a closer look at his face, her eyes narrowed. "You all right?"

"Still standing. Let me put up some coffee and I'll download. I'm giving you the edited version. No hassles about that, right?"

"Hey, what do I have to complain about? *You* go out and chase psychopaths around the universe. *I* get to stay home and do my nails. Excitement is pretty evenly distributed, I'd say." Then she laughed. "Not to worry. Just give me what you can."

While the coffee dripped down and hissed into the Pyrex pot, Early went into the bathroom and splashed cold water on his face. When he returned, Desda was sitting alert and cross-legged on the couch, looking diminutive in his bathrobe. Beneath the dark, disheveled hair, her blue eyes seemed huge, watching him intently, trying to absorb every detail.

Early handed her a mug but remained standing. After the long night immersed in the karma files, after barely avoiding spiritual meltdown, he took a moment to gather his thoughts.

"Yeah? . . . So?" Desda said, growing impatient. "You're going to drive me crazy."

"Sorry," Early mumbled. Then he began, trying to distill the information down to bite-size portions. "First the disclaimer. Even after I give you all this information about Quill, we still will not know his current name or whereabouts. That's what we have to piece together. What we *do* have, though, are his *probable* flight patterns. Things he's *likely* to do. Some of them have been in place, gaining momentum, for hundreds of years. He's got serious internal pressure to act them out."

"Karma 101."

"Yeah. In any case, the only thing strong enough to break the mold is free will, the power of choice. Quill isn't up to that. He's not a free agent anymore because he's run by his old, nasty tapes. And *that* is why we have a chance to catch him."

Desda looked skeptical. "So . . . if we understand Quill's machinery, we can anticipate his actions. But that means we've got *no* margin of error. Christ, James, is this really possible?"

"We have to hope so. But at least we have the blueprint of his internal wiring now. That's what I want to get into."

Desda raised her coffee cup in salute.

Early told her everything he had retained from his frenzied night with the karma files, from Quill's personality traits and karmic patterns to a recounting of the foiled assassination attempt on the life of Thomas Jefferson.

"It doesn't sound like much, but a handful of quills could actually do a lot of damage."

"And now he's using them to write death threats," Desda said, mulling over Early's words. "This whole thing is so convoluted."

"Yeah. It's all about staying one step ahead. That's the only way we can win."

"Anything else?"

Early paused, trying to reassemble the historical bits and pieces the Akashic Records had revealed about the assassin. "My memory's sketchy, but there were a few plums along the way. Quill's name at the time was Patrick Wellington, born to well-to-do parents in Virginia. He's bad news right from the start. So when he's old enough, his family packs him off to England. They're probably thinking an Oxford education will give the kid some manners. It doesn't, but this is where Quill formally switches loyalties. He's picked up this upper-crust thing, airs, big-time snob, loves the whole thing. He's turned against his parents and despises the filthy colonists.

"When he gets back to Virginia, he poisons his parents, gets the inheritance. The law can't prove a thing. Suddenly he's young and rich, free to indulge his passions. Predictably, he squanders it immediately—gambling, horses, women—the usual stuff. He, of course, blames Americans for conspiring against him. So when Jefferson's star begins to rise, Quill takes it upon himself to save the British aristocracy. He's gonna kill this rebel upstart and be the savior of the old guard.

"Now understand, Wellington's a charmer, just like Quill. Knows how to work the room. Pretty soon he's maneuvered his way right beside Jefferson, hired as his lackey at Monticello. That follows one of his current patterns. He likes to get close to his enemies. Rub up against them—just the way he did with Ellen. Anyway, he's taking care of the horses and doing odd jobs. From what I can gather, he also works as a scribe, copies some of Jefferson's manuscripts, maybe to get a sneak preview of what the man's thinking. Here's another obvious parallel. He had impeccable penmanship back then. If I could show you the letter he sent Billy, you'd see he's doing it again. It's creepy."

Early paused to massage his tired eyes, then went on with his story. "Around this time, Quill gets caught raping one of the servant girls and is fired. This doesn't stop him in the slightest. As a matter of fact, he's even more stoked. He's got a plan and practices his shooting. Apparently he was good before. Now he's a top marksman."

"Another carryover," Desda chimed in. "As a sniper, he's been deadly."

Early nodded. "Some months later, he secretly follows Jefferson to Philadelphia. He's armed with information about his former employer. He knows his habits. He knows Jefferson likes to take his evening stroll at a predictable time. So Quill puts his plan in motion and finds a vulnerable woman who lives in that neighborhood. He lands a middle-aged spinster who dabbles in arts and crafts—easy picking for a smooth operator like Quill. He plays his cards just right with her; comes across as a well-educated man who's a little down on his luck. He can also drop a few names, like Jefferson, talk political talk, the whole nine yards. She's putty in his hands. Soon she's allowing him to court her. After a few get-togethers, he's invited into her parlor. Now he knows exactly where he wants to position his little ambush.

"Then the big night arrives. He knows she's going out to visit friends, knows when Jefferson will be passing by. When she leaves, he sets himself up. What he *doesn't* know is that she's going to a birthday party and has forgotten to bring the gift. She turns around, walks back through her door, sees him with a rifle, ready to kill. She understands his real motives . . . and gets her revenge."

"Do you know what happened after she stabbed him?" Desda asked.

"Some. Quill gets hauled away by a neighborhood vigilante crew. Colonists. They don't have their own jails yet, so they chain him up in somebody's cellar. Quill, of course, is pleading it was all a big misunderstanding. He was just cleaning his gun, and it went off by accident. The colonists don't buy it. They know he's scum and have some perverted fun at his expense. Pretty gross stuff—crawling on his belly for food, torture—anything to humiliate him.

"So they keep him locked away and taunt him every time the rebels make progress. It drives Quill mad. Finally, when he hears that the Declaration gets ratified, he tries to escape. Gets himself shot. He never made the history books because there was no murder. Didn't stop Jefferson or the movement. Two hundred years later, he's trying again."

Desda sat up straight. "The timing makes a lot more sense now. Since I've been working at the Burwells', I've had a chance to see some of Ellen's press clippings. She's getting coverage all over the world. I mean, even the British media are rallying behind her! Quill hears all this, is already knee-deep in American blood, sees a big opportunity."

"Exactly, and even worse for him, Ellen's dusting off the Constitution, talking about a true democracy. He can't just stay in England and protect his home turf. He's got to come here and take her out."

An uncomfortable silence followed, each reminded of the immediate danger. Ellen aside, they were both at risk.

"Look," Early said with effort, his bloodshot eyes beginning to burn, "I'm starting to fade. Before I become completely useless on my feet, I want to go over a few things . . . things to be aware of."

"That would really help."

"So, here's what we've got. First, all of this karma stuff is unconscious. He has no idea why he's a tortured soul obsessed with revenge. But he's stuck in time, not indigenous to our culture at all. His body is walking around in the twentieth century, but his mind is in the eighteenth. He'll be drawn to things that were around in the seventeen-hundreds. I'm talking about artifacts, furniture, art, music, et cetera. Also, he'll consider himself an aristocrat. Since money doesn't seem to be a problem for him, he'll be holed up in plush quarters, buying expensive wines. That kind of thing. Even from that brief encounter at Ellen's talk, I got the feeling he was looking down his nose at all of us."

Desda shivered, recalling his image. "Cold . . ."

"Right. There are some other things to consider. Because of the stabbing in the incident—the quill aspect—the old pain in his thigh might have moved back in. It can happen that way. He may even walk with a limp. I didn't notice it in the museum, but he might be on medication or drugs, so it wouldn't necessarily show. Also, sexually, he's probably perverted—possibly feeding off hookers and helpless types."

"He oozes sex," Desda added disgustedly. "On first hit, he gets into your hormones. Get a little closer, and you start to realize where he's at. Scary."

"I know. One of his many charms. But maybe that will be his Achilles' heel. We're going to need something."

There were other things Early was still mentally working on that he refrained from mentioning. One of them was Quill's tendency in the past to grandstand. He liked theater, he liked celebrities, Thomas Jefferson certainly fit that description. This time around, his European assassinations reflected this tendency, as did his choice of Yankee Stadium for Billy Burwell. What would he choose for Ellen? Early didn't know and didn't want to cloud the picture with more conjecture.

"Okay," he concluded, "that's my list for now."

Desda looked down at the floor. "That's a lot of ground to cover. Can we get Sam to pull some strings, help out on the research?"

"I don't think so," Early said with a touch of sadness. "Sam doesn't know what to do with me anymore. He's polite and all, but he gives me that little second look when we talk, like, *are you all there?* I don't blame him. Right now, all I have for him is a description of a man who tried to give money to help fund the arts. That's not what you'd call a hot lead."

"Well, should I start checking around? Stores that might sell quills or antique furniture, . . . anything?"

Early thought this through. "No, I'll cover that. Stay with the Burwells and add these things we've discussed to your alarm system. You know what the killer looks like. That's our best defense."

Early walked back to his desk, picked up his revolver where he had left it for her, then placed it in her hand. "Don't argue. I want you to carry this in your purse. I won't be able to sleep if you don't take it with you."

Desda didn't protest. With a quiet "Thanks," she stuffed it in her handbag.

By now the morning was in full swing, bright sunlight washing through the apartment windows. A blaring horn seemed to snap the spell. Suddenly the surreal world of Quill and karma files and 1700s America dissipated, depositing them back into a small apartment on Seventy-Eighth Street. A man and a woman—emotionally drained—and a relationship, with one foot in Manhattan and one planted in the Himalayas. They posed the question with their eyes, then looked away.

Desda took the lead. "Time for you to get some rest. You've earned it."

Early was literally weaving on his feet. "Well, we both have. But yeah, I'm wiped."

They stood for an awkward moment, then Desda leaned over, cupped Early's face in her hands. "We're doing it. When I think about us in Tibet now, we seemed so . . . so innocent. Living in a cocoon while the rest of the world was going to hell. Now we're back out in the war zone. I'm just glad we're together."

Early couldn't begin to find the words and simply put his arms around her.

With Desda settled on the couch, Early retired to his bedroom. He sat on his bed for a moment in the darkness before laying his tired body against cool sheets. His thoughts, however, did not lie down beside him. Instead, they wandered between the asphalt streets of New York and the cobbled roads of Philadelphia. He finally passed out with his fist softly clenched beside his forehead. The work was progressing. The specter that walked ahead was beginning to turn and show its face.

SIXTEEN

Desda propped the "I'll be in touch" note against the old blue bowl on the mantelpiece, then looked at her watch. It was almost five o'clock. Time for her to go back to her apartment, clean up, then head over to the Burwells'. Early lay with one arm slung over his eyes, still crashed out. Desda hesitated, then leaned down, kissed him lightly on the lips, and quietly left the apartment.

Outside, the once generous morning had given way to a sullen grey afternoon. As she walked along the street, the stark reality of her situation suddenly hit home. She was alone and out in the open—fully exposed. It felt like a hundred years ago, but it had been less than twenty-four hours since she had come face-to-face with the assassin. Now it was visceral. Her life *was* in danger.

Thankful for the extra bulk of the gun in her handbag, she decided against taking the subway and flagged down a cab. Nevertheless, as she jostled in the backseat, her purse lay open in her lap, her hand poised beside it.

Over the last few weeks, her Eastside apartment had seemed less like a sanctuary and more like a stage set for someone else; someone whose life had many interesting forays but no single through line. Hidden away, even from herself, was one reluctant confession. Her only real home in this crazy world was tucked away in another time and place, alongside James Early. Maybe, when all of this was over, they could finally . . .

Catching herself, she tensed and leaned forward. She couldn't afford to drift. For the rest of the ride, she looked warily out the window, her thumb tracing the hard edge of the revolver's barrel.

Following her normal routine, she stood in the lobby of her building, sorting through her mail. Disgustedly, she crammed a handful of flyers and catalogs into a trash bin. But something else was bothering her. And she didn't understand the growing tightness in her stomach.

Finding the elevator not working, she climbed the stairs to her third-floor apartment, then paused before inserting the key. It was nothing tangible. Lowering her eyes, she noticed an almost imperceptible bit of paint had been chipped from around the lock.

Her first instinct was to run, to get the hell out of there. Turning, she took a step toward the stairs, then stopped. *No. If this is Quill, bring him on!* With a trembling hand, she pulled the revolver out of her handbag. A slight push and the door creaked open. Raising her gun, she stepped inside.

Nothing moved . . . darkness . . . an eerie silence. She flicked the light switch on, but the room remained cloaked in darkness. With shallow breaths and a racing pulse, she felt her way down the hallway of her railroad-style apartment, gun swinging left, then right. Ten feet later, she stood stock-still. It was subtle—a faint smell of citrus, like lime cologne. Soon the scent was joined by another—paraffin, smoke.

It became stronger as she approached the kitchen. The hairs on the back of her neck prickled. From inside the doorway came a flickering light. Finger on the trigger, heart in her throat, she sprang around the corner . . . saw no one . . . and stifled a scream.

It was a romantic vignette. A table set for two—a pair of thin white tapers glowing warmly. Glinting in the tawny light stood an open bottle of cabernet. On either side, two half-filled glasses with delicate stems blushed with burgundy. Completing the picture, a baguette rested on top of a platter surrounded by assorted cheeses.

But it was the centerpiece that sent a spasm of horror through her body. Terrified, she took a step closer.

A pair of her black silk panties was spread out on a place mat as though it was being served as the main course. Pinning it to the table, and driven through the middle of the crotch, was a long feathered quill pen.

Dumbfounded, she continued to stare at Quill's grotesque display of power. His obscene coupling of intimacy and depravity filled her with fury. He had invaded her home, her possessions, her thoughts . . . her body his for the taking, if and when he desired.

Just then, she heard the click of her front door closing quietly. She whirled around. With a cry, raising her gun, she burst through her apartment and out into the hallway . . . no one. The corridor was empty. But a motion to the left caught her eye. The creaky old elevator was slowly moving downward. Cursing, she ran to the stairwell and bolted down the three flights to the lobby. The elevator dial showed it had reached the ground floor. But it didn't stop there. Instead, it continued down toward the basement.

Desda hesitated, gasping for breath, trying to make a rational decision. Take on Quill alone? Total madness! But by now her outrage had gone past the point of retrieval. Karma be damned—Quill had to be stopped.

Trying to steady her nerves, she began her deliberate descent down into the musty cellar.

Three floors up, Malcolm stepped out from behind the shower curtain and shook his head, almost embarrassed. It had been a little too easy. There had, however, been some side benefits. Alone with Desda's femininity, he found himself becoming aroused: her soaps, her scented bath oils, her lacy bra draped casually over the towel rack. He entertained the prospect, then rejected it. Not now. Maybe later.

Calmly, Malcolm walked out the front door into the hallway. She had taken his bait, following the empty elevator down into the basement. Even now, she was probably halfway out of her mind with fear, pointing her gun at every shadow, every creak in the large cluttered storage rooms. If his assessment of her character were correct, she would probably remain down there for another minute or two before realizing she'd been had. Then she would race to a phone. By then he would be long gone.

Malcolm strolled down the stairs to the lobby. Time to savor.

Two hours before, he had broken into her apartment, disconnected the lights, set up his little tableau. After blocking the elevator so that it remained on her floor, he had gone back into her apartment and waited by the front window. Seeing her get out of a cab, he then lit the candles and concealed himself in the bedroom. A few minutes later, she had entered. He had been standing no more than two feet behind her as she crept toward the kitchen. He could have reached out and touched her. Then she discovered his masterpiece.

Titillated, he had watched her profile: the trembling lips, the contorting face. Confident she would become immobilized by the shock, he had soundlessly stepped into the hallway, pushed the button, and sent the empty elevator down to the basement. Slipping back into the apartment, he had closed the door loudly enough to be heard. From there, it was only a few strides to the bathroom. He had just stepped within its shadows when she came flying by.

Now at ground floor, he glanced approvingly at his image in the foyer mirror, pleased with the style and power of his work. Now his quill was lodged somewhere between her head and her groin, never to be forgotten. With a small salute to his reflection in the glass, he stepped through the lobby door out into the gloaming.

Early's Apartment

Early laced up his boots. He was groggy. He was pissed. All he wanted to do now was lash out blindly. He had just gotten off the phone with Desda. Her tearful, frantic call had punctured his thick sleep and thrust him into gear. Quill, damn him! A rape without lifting a finger. The murder of his mother without shedding blood. Goading them on, laughing at their expense. *Enough!*

After much consoling, he had finally managed to calm her down. Possibilities had been discussed. Early had pleaded with her to move in with him. Stubbornly, she declined. Two days ago, the Burwells had offered her a position as their live-in personal assistant. Early liked this for numerous reasons, one of which was Desda's safety. The Gramercy Park townhouse was under constant armed surveillance. Also, from there, she'd be able to monitor the case full-time. Despite droves of agents, she had a distinct advantage: she and Early were the only people in the world who knew what the English killer actually looked like.

Desda had agreed. She would accept the Burwells' offer and move in the following day. Tonight she would stay with Early. Her apartment was no longer a friend, forever contaminated by Quill's evil touch. It would be impossible to live there ever again.

Early stood up, trying to tame his anger into steady resolve. Throwing on a denim jacket, he rushed downstairs to the street. If he hurried, he could get to the store just before closing time. Metaphysical truths were fine, but things were getting out of control. With silent apologies to Palden, Early ran toward Broadway near Eighty-Third Street. It was time to buy another handgun.

*   *   *

Jori stood on the corner of Forty-Second Street and Fifth Avenue, waiting for the light to change. His charade of "lunch break" over, it was time for him to return to his duties. As much as he tried to resist, his thoughts surrounded the pensive figure slouched against the base of the lion statue in front of the library across the street. *James Early. James Early trampled by thoughts, struggling with . . . well, so many things*. Jori could walk inside his pupil's mind, resonate with every thought and emotion. And yet he could not force-feed his growth.

Opting not to disturb him, Jori fell into step with a group of tourists entering the public library. Offering up a silent prayer of encouragement, he glanced back at his friend, then disappeared into the building.

Early looked up at the afternoon sun moving restlessly between the clouds overhead. After long hours, his subterranean office, his work, even the Fountain itself, had felt suffocating, and he'd stepped outside for a change of scenery—anything to inspire new thoughts from his overworked brain. Inexplicably, pictures of Jori had briefly touched his mind, then melted away.

Feeling slightly brighter, he took a sip from his coffee, then returned to the harsh grids of the soul named Quill. Understanding him was one thing. Finding his whereabouts in *this* century, in *this* city, was another. Even with karmic assistance, New York was a vast arena, and Early was, primarily, a one-man band.

Possessed with the need to complete this mission, Early began again to mull over the specifics of the man—the themes and variations of his character. Eventually, he leaned back against the cool stone and closed his eyes. Too much and too little! With Quill about to strike again, Early would need an army to explore the possibilities. The categories were either far too general or completely impractical to investigate. Whatever optimism he could muster seemed fleeting and unfounded.

Early rose slowly to his feet. Now what? Knee-deep in uncertainty, a small internal voice interceded.

The problem is not with your data. The problem is your approach.

Once again, his tendency to force an issue was prohibiting perception. Trying to lighten his pitch, he decided to take a slow walk around the block, this time allowing enough space for his thoughts to breathe and insights to be born.

Half a block later, Early sat down on a bench along Fifth Avenue. What had started as a small ironic thought had mushroomed into a serious tactical possibility.

Rather than follow the vast outpouring of the man's hate and evil, follow the thin trickle of his goodness! The man loved horses! This had been Quill's one consistent area of strength down through the ages, even during his most diabolical lifetimes. Early got excited. *This might be the thread he needed!*

After some mental cross-checking, he found that if he used this new approach and mixed it with karmic themes, he might have an interesting lead. Energized again, he returned to the library and headed to the reference room, immediately digging into information about local stables—places where pedigreed racehorses might be groomed and bred.

Somewhere listed in the directories might be a livery with a particularly European bent. If Early's hunch was correct, he would find a horse boarded there with a name summoned from the eighteenth century.

SEVENTEEN

The Hensley Stables

No Unauthorized Vehicles Allowed.
Violators Will Be Towed At Owner's Expense!

The large sign meant to intimidate, even beyond its words. Early shook his head with disgust as he navigated his rented car alongside the high brick wall that surrounded the estate. He parked behind a black Mercedes, then turned off the engine. For a moment, he leaned back against the seat, resting his eyes.

The sixty-mile drive to the Hensley Stables in rural Upstate New York had been meditative. Commuter mug in hand, he had watched the stark lines of the urban landscape soften and warm into the rolling greens of the countryside. Now that he was here, his anticipation grew. It was showtime. His karmic theory was about to be tested.

Early climbed out of the car, readjusted his shoulder holster, and pushed the intercom on the side of the main gate to identify himself. Soon the pedestrian door clicked open, and he crunched up the gravel driveway toward the house. As he walked, he absorbed the details of the grounds.

The small picture in the library reference book had portrayed the estate as picturesque. Up close, however, it had about as much soul as a wax museum. The lawns were manicured to a point where the grass seemed artificial, the hedges so severely pruned and uniform they appeared disassociated from nature. Even the rows of flowers stood stiffly at attention, as if too frightened to relax. Early scoffed to himself. *This isn't beauty. This is life beaten into submission.*

The proprietor, a Mr. Arlo Hensley, had taken his phone call yesterday evening with the same starched formality: clipped sentences bracketed by guarded spaces. He had "permitted" the visit only after Early snarled the word investigation, threatening to pursue him with a little extra heat a day later, bringing in the law, warrant in hand.

In equestrian circles, Hensley was a big name. Not only had he bred his own winners in the Kentucky Derby, but he also reared and boarded horses for an elite clientele. He was very old-school, very expensive, and very upper-crust—which made him *very* interesting. Most compelling of all was the fact that Hensley was the trainer of a horse named King George.

This piece of news had caused Early to smile, silently acknowledging the karma files. Rising out of the mists of time, a bridge between lifetimes might have finally been found.

Up ahead, the front door of the Tudor-style dwelling opened briskly, and Hensley appeared on the steps, dressed in a tweed Norfolk jacket, white button-down shirt, brown jodhpurs, and English riding boots. He was in his sixties and a full-blown caricature of censorious propriety—sharp nose, trim mustache, and a down-at-the-corners mouth.

Scowling slightly, he watched with cold blue eyes as Early approached.

From fifty yards away, Early could viscerally feel the man's judgmental mindset spewing out critical thoughts in his direction. Early mentally batted them away, his mood growing more foul with each stride.

The initial interchange was terse and brittle—Hensley bearing down with thinly veiled hostility, Early staying right in his face. After Early's PI license was inspected and tossed back disdainfully, the owner led him inside to a small office that smelled of lemon wax, leather, and polish. The walls were decorated with photographs of horses and jockeys. A glass case protected numerous trophies. In Hensley's environment, everything was locked up and tidy, everything held captive under relentless supervision.

Early sat on the edge of a beige couch while Hensley laid down his rules of procedure. "I'm extremely busy—something you might not understand. I won't allow you to wander aimlessly around the grounds, nor can you enter the stables and disturb the horses. My information about my clientele is limited and confidential. You have five minutes to ask your questions."

"That's your agenda. Here's mine," Early shot back. "You have a horse here named King George. I want to know about its owner."

"I am not at liberty to divulge that. The bills are paid, and the horse has been extremely productive. Next question."

"I need a name."

"Your need is not my concern," Hensley said curtly. "If that is the extent of your curiosity, our conversation is concluded."

Early stood up, grabbed the man by the lapels, and was about to hoist him off his feet when he paused abruptly, then relaxed his grip.

Look again! Hensley's playing you like a stacked deck. He wants to get under your skin so you'll do something stupid. Then he can throw you out. Just perceive what's going on with him and work from there.

Taking a slow step backward, Early scrutinized the man in front of him. Now it was obvious. Hensley was absolutely terrified. With a thin smile, Early began again.

"Listen, Arlo. We're off to a bad start. Let's take this whole thing over again from the top, okay?"

Hensley continued to glare, so Early proceeded. "I'm here because I need your help. There's reason to believe King George belongs to someone you don't want to mess around with. He's dangerous. Maybe you already know this?"

Hensley did. A twitch along his left cheek was beginning to fire, and his skin seemed to grow instantly paler. "I think you better leave," he said tightly.

By now Early was inside the man's head, listening carefully for what was hidden behind the words. Hensley didn't like that client at all. Something other than confidentiality was keeping him quiet. Had he been threatened? Was it Quill?

Early took a leap. "Let me give you a likely scenario. Within the last few days, the owner of this horse comes by to pay you a visit. Maybe he puts a gun to your head. Maybe he just talks tough. He tells you if you ever mention his name to another living soul, he'll put a bullet between your eyes. Then he leaves you, and you're pretty sure he's not kidding. Then I come by and start—"

Early stopped talking. One foot away, Arlo's face was transforming. The mask of composure was peeling away like strips of varnish. Poking into view was the countenance of a rickety old man. His mouth had suddenly begun to tremble, and his shoulders seemed to shrink inward.

Hensley shot a nervous look toward Early's shoes. "He was just here. Right where you're standing," he whispered. "He burned his records. Then he . . . he threatened me."

Early glanced down. Now discernible on the worn carpet were bits of charred paper and ash. Bending down, he fingered a blackened scrap, still warm to the touch. *The Mercedes out front!*

"He probably just drove away. What are you doing?"

Early had placed a firm hand on Hensley's back and was pushing him away from the window and down behind the couch. "No, he's still here. He may be watching us."

Arlo tried to wrench away. "Take your hands off—"

Early shoved him to the floor. "Stay put, damn it! He knows who I am and why I'm here. If you want to live, do what I tell you!"

For the moment, Arlo stopped resisting. Rippling with indignation, he glowered back at Early. "This is pure madness! No one tells me what to do. No one!"

"You're missing the point," Early snapped, as he ripped his revolver from its holster and made a quick scan of the front yard through the parted curtains, then back at Hensley. "Look, I'm sorry about the rough treatment. But we have a moment here, so I want you to listen. First, you're going to stay down, out of sight, and not get killed. Second, you're going to tell me everything you know about this guy. Then, after he leaves us alone, you're going to get out of town for a while and let the dust settle. I mean today. You understand?"

Arlo didn't respond immediately. He was beginning to regroup, the hard gleam returning to his eyes. Finally he nodded stiffly. "I'll cooperate with you only because the man in question just terminated his contract with me. But I will *not* forget this. Believe me, the police will hear about your conduct."

"You don't understand," Early tried, then backed off. "Okay, whatever . . . just talk."

Arlo spoke without emotion. "I had never met the owner until today. Five years ago, when King George was first put under my charge, I was paid a large sum of money up front . . . cash, delivered by a courier. The owner lived in England and desired to remain anonymous. When his horse won, the same courier would show up and collect the prize money. The only document I ever demanded was the original client agreement form, which is protocol for all my clients to sign. That piece of paper has just been reduced to ashes."

"The name on the contract!" Early demanded.

"The signature was M. Raines. That's all I know."

Early exhaled and relaxed slightly. *At last!*

Hensley seized the moment. Sensing Early's momentary lapse, he suddenly bolted, crawling on his knees outside of Early's reach.

"I'm through with both of you! You will leave immediately and I—"

"Don't!" Early yelled as Hensley stood up. Frantically, he dove at the man's legs to knock him down. He was too late.

The instant Hensley rose above the couch, a bullet tore through the window and exploded against the top of his head, sending a plume of blood into the air and a chunk of grey matter splattering against the back wall.

Early felt his stomach sink and whirled around. The force of the impact had propelled the body three feet behind him. What was once Arlo Hensley was now a contorted mass encircled by a thickening puddle of crimson.

Early spun back around, gun raised. Instinctively, he went into a roll across the floor littered with broken glass and came up standing by the side of the window that looked out across the empty gardens.

"You coward!" he yelled. "You kill old men and women. Come on, damn you. Try me!"

Nothing moved. No one answered. Early scrambled through the deserted house to the front door, cracked it open, and looked anxiously around the grounds. Then he spotted him.

Two hundred yards away at the end of the long driveway, Malcolm stood with casual insouciance, his rifle held lightly in one hand. Faint but clear, Early heard the icy voice carry over the immaculate lawns.

"You're doomed, James Early. Just like your mother!"

The words tore into Early's heart, and his old instincts kicked back. Blinded by rage, he rushed out into the open and began firing wildly at the distant figure. Unruffled, Malcolm turned slowly and disappeared through the gate. An instant later, two shots could be heard, followed by the sound of an engine starting up and tires spitting through gravel.

Early stopped racing and slowed to a walk, letting his gun drop limply to his side. When he finally pushed through the outside gate, his suspicions were confirmed.

There would be no chase scene. The two gunshots had flattened the front tires of his car. Out along the horizon, the assassin's Mercedes was now a distant speck speeding along the winding highway that clung to the edge of the hills.

Early stood for a moment watching Quill vanish. He had just witnessed a murder. He had been taunted by the man who killed his mother. And now he was helpless to prevent his escape. Early had every reason in the human book to be wracked by violent emotions. But now he couldn't indulge, couldn't think in terms of getting even. The emphasis of his work *had* to remain in the realm of karma. Otherwise he should return to the NYPD.

Frustrated and discouraged, he thrust his gun into the holster and turned back toward the house. A murder needed to be reported. Two tires had to be replaced. But there was one consolation:

Quill wasn't one step ahead anymore. The race was now neck and neck.

EIGHTEEN

Gramercy Park

The day after Quill's insidious violation, Desda arrived at the Burwells' front door, suitcases in hand. They welcomed her with open arms and gave her their son's room, who was now away at college. Desda placed her suitcases beside the dresser, sat on the bed, and digested her surroundings. Sensing the room was missing something, she left and went to a nearby florist. She returned with a small bouquet of spring flowers, placed them in a vase on the nightstand, and now felt ready to start her new life.

With two large lives perpetually in motion, she found herself constantly busy, doing everything from polishing silverware to taking part in political strategy discussions. She established an immediate rapport with Ellen. Now, with Desda as a full-time fixture in the household, their relationship took on the feel of sisters. Within a few days, they adopted an after-dinner ritual. Together, side by side, they attacked the dishes—washing, drying, and chatting. It was a chance to let their hair down and have some girl talk, something they both enjoyed.

Tonight, however, Desda was preoccupied. She heard from Early about his run-in with Quill and the murder of Hensley. They agreed. The Burwells needed to be apprised of the *real* situation. The sooner, the better. While the conversation flowed between the two women, Desda waited for the right moment. It came sooner than expected.

"By the way," Desda said, drying a plate, "I really enjoyed your speech about the arts the other night."

Ellen placed a rinsed wineglass in the dish drainer. "Thanks. It was a special evening for me too. Which reminds me, do you remember that very insulting man, the one in the suit, who was so . . . so peculiar with his donation?"

Desda stopped drying. "Yeah, I certainly do."

"Well, I saw him last night. He was on the corner of our block, right under the streetlight, looking up at my window. I felt like he wanted me to see him. I don't quite know what to think. I find him ghoulish."

Desda's hand shook slightly as she took hold of Ellen's arm. "Don't bother to think. He's the man we're looking for. I was going to talk to you about it after we finished the dishes."

"He's *Quill*? For Christ's sake! Why hasn't anybody told us?"

"It's complicated. Basically, it's just Early and me. The police don't agree with our premise. But I'm telling you, he's the one."

Ellen stepped back in shock. "How could you withhold this from me?! I don't care if it's rumor, speculation, or gossip. You must always tell me *everything*!"

Desda hung her head. "I'm afraid there's more."

"For God's sake, tell me! My husband's life is at stake!"

"No, that's just it. Billy's probably safe. But if you ever see that man again—run! *You're* the real target."

Ellen sat down heavily at the table, her mind churning with this revelation. Eventually she took a deep breath and talked slowly, almost to herself, without raising her eyes. "In an odd way, I'm relieved to hear this."

She remained seated quietly for a while, as if shouldering the weight of this new revelation. Then she stood up resolutely. "I don't understand why we have divided camps here about Quill. At this point, I don't care. We have to do everything we can to protect ourselves."

Ellen hung up her apron and turned back to Desda. "In any case, the dishes can wait. I want you to brief everyone in the household about this—what he looks like, what to expect—anything that will help us. Will you do that?"

Desda agreed, and Ellen summoned family and staff for an urgent meeting in the living room. When assembled with no law enforcement agents to contend with, Desda shot from the hip. Incorporating most of Early's notes, she gave them the hard-won details of the assassin—omitting the karma factor.

At the end of the briefing, Billy limped across the room and took Ellen's hands. They both understood. Their roles had just been reversed.

NINETEEN

Early's Apartment

On the day before summer became official, the sun bore down on New York and spread through the grimy streets like a vendor peddling fire. Stubborn and intractable, it chose to hang low and stifle rather than rise. In its honor, every cabby honked louder and longer; as pavements grew hotter, every swear word known to man proliferated.

In the middle of the scorching city, Early sat by a fan in the open kitchen window and glared down at his scribbles on a piece of paper. At the top of the first page was the name M. Raines, the name on Hensley's contract—the first known a.k.a. for Quill.

Early scratched his ear absently with his pen. Scattered around the table were lists of posh hotels in the five-borough area. *He had to be staying somewhere!* But after days of work, all of the possibilities had a line drawn through them. In the course of the investigation, three dark, well-dressed people with the name "M. Raines" had been discovered and tracked down—a computer programmer named Michael and a shoe store owner called Mel—both leading to dead ends and wasted time. The third suspect had been a woman named Mandy. Although it didn't seem to be his style, it was increasingly likely that Quill was now operating under an assumed name.

Early sat back and wiped the perspiration from his brow. Again, he didn't like his approach. It seemed too mechanical, too much like his NYPD days. As Jori had said, this case would require a *spiritual* detective, not an earthly one.

Crumpling his paperwork into a ball, Early tossed it in the general direction of the wastebasket. He had one option left, one that he dreaded. But there it was. He needed to leap outside the straight lines of logic.

Reluctantly, he pulled an old link chain from his toolbox and a pair of hand-cuffs from his desk—a holdover from his cop days. Intellectually, he knew the killer. But that wouldn't get it done. To outfox him, Early needed "insider" information. This meant he would have to *experience* what it was like to be Quill, to walk in his shoes . . . and *become* the psychopath.

*   *   *

One hour later, seated in a chair in the sanctity of his Akashic office, Early inspected his makeshift restraints. If, in fact, he could achieve a merging with Quill's consciousness, serious precautions were warranted. He had succeeded in wrapping his six-foot chain around his body, pinned together by handcuffs at his wrist, binding him to the chair. The keys had been kicked beyond his reach. This was the only line of defense between himself and unthinkable disaster. He had no idea what to expect, what he might become. As desperate and risky as this seemed, time was running out, the stakes were too high to please caution.

Next he put his attention on the Fountain, which gleamed a few feet away. Hopefully the Akashic Light would serve as his anchor, possibly amplify his own powers of perception. Early was about to recreate his adversary. Past lives, recent encounters—all the explosive pieces waiting to be reassembled and animated.

Bracing for battle, he focused on the Fountain until he sensed the connection. Feeling his mind open, he plunged through the portal, deeper and deeper, letting go of the James Early identity . . . hunting, searching until he finally locked on to the bandwidth of the nightmare called Quill.

While putting a volume on a shelf, Jori felt something sharp prick inside his mind. Closing his eyes, he studied the source of the disturbance. The emanation had been blurred and almost unrecognizable. A second later, he realized what was happening and went into full damage control. Leaving his cart unattended, he hurried down the corridor toward the underground elevator, then broke into a run. Early had apparently played the most dangerous card of all. It could easily backfire. Like the red soulprint, if Early spent too much time with the killer's evil, he might lose control and begin to adopt the assassin's depraved personality. Then there would be two Quills loose in the world!

In the middle of the labyrinth, down in the bowels of the library, an embattled James Early stopped wrestling for a moment and surveyed his entrapment. He felt feverish, sweat rolling down his face, yet something deadly cold and dark and alien was coiling inside him, threatening to occupy—its menacing presence spreading out, eating away at Early's mind. He could feel his face distorting as another set of features—dark and cruel—reared up from below the surface, fighting for supremacy.

Moments later, the semblance of Quill won control—leering out through the grey eyes, the mouth sharpening into a tight gash. Looking about, his gaze locked on to the handcuff keys on the floor, just out of reach.

Gritting his teeth, the mutant began jerking his chair toward them. Once free, he would find those who had thwarted him, those who had butchered his dignity. Then the blood would flow.

As if huddled in a tiny pit, impaled by the dark creature, the true consciousness of James Early became aware of a feeble sound. It seemed to emanate from somewhere buried deep inside. Vaguely, he recognized it to be his own voice, crying out. Something terribly wrong was happening. He had empowered the creation too much and was going under.

Calling on every instinct, Early tried to collect himself and grab on to the faint resolve to regain control.

One breath away from obliteration, he made a desperate call. The psychopath was still gaining momentum, had grown too strong. Early could not win the fight. Instead, he would have to dive deeper, *down through the murky waters of time to the days long before the soul had descended into the horror of Quill.*

As Jori flew through the corridors, he prayed. This "mutation" must be prevented! If not, everything would be lost! A hundred yards away, he registered a shift in the vibration. The cold, deadly fury at the other end was abating, gradually being replaced by a sense of calm . . . then profound sorrow.

Jori immediately understood and slowed to a walk. Thank God for Early's courage and tenacity!

Upon reaching the office, Jori found his pupil shackled in metal chains, the signs of battle everywhere. His clothes were torn, his hair matted and drenched with sweat. His wrists were bleeding. With hunched shoulders, head bowed, Early wept.

Jori felt his own eyes begin to tear. In the end, Early had not given in to Quill's depraved urges. Instead, he had gone back in time—prior to the decisions and deeds that had locked the assassin's dark karma in place, all the way back to when that spirit was still pure.

Unlocking chains and handcuffs, Jori wrapped his coat around his friend, then left. His walk back to work was slow and meditative. He completely empathized with what Early was feeling. It had nothing to do with condoning the assassin for his atrocities. It had everything to do with compassion—the inevitable loss of innocence of every soul who walks the face of the earth.

Tales of the Tigers

ONE

Gramercy Park

On this mulish, humid day, the eddies of tension surrounding the Burwell household seemed to thicken. Ellen stood on her second-floor balcony, absently watering the geraniums in the planter box. She had been working on her opening remarks as keynote speaker for the massive Independence Day celebration in Central Park, now less than two weeks away. This was to be her seminal speech, a detailed outline of her vision for America in the new millennium. But today she felt preoccupied, and her face looked haggard in the afternoon sunlight. It wasn't simply that the writing wasn't progressing smoothly or even the fact that her life was now in danger. It was the sense that powerful forces were in motion, far beyond her ability to control.

Desda stood uneasily in front of her in an awkward attempt to shield this valuable life from a bullet that might come from any direction at any time.

"Bored, isn't he?" Ellen observed, looking down over the railing at the security guard who stood in front of the small greenhouse in the backyard. Unaware of their presence, the policeman had been caught in the middle of a prodigious stretch and gaping yawn.

"All that standing around in this heat," she muttered. "It's a thankless job."

"Let it stay thankless," Desda said dryly.

Ellen sighed and returned to her watering.

As Desda waited, she contemplated the thin line of defense that stood between the candidate and the man who stalked her. By now, Desda knew all the bodyguards. Tim Edwards was a fixture in the backyard—a beefy man, dedicated but oafish. In contrast, the front area cop, Chuck Fisher, was pressurized and over-heated. The park itself was handled by a mobile, rotating crew. In Desda's estimation, none of them had a clue about what they were up against. If Quill ever decided to penetrate the Burwells' home, these men would be out-thought, out-shot—and dead meat.

As if on cue, Ellen rested her watering can on the table beside the two deck chairs. "It's strange. Ever since the death threat, everything seems attached to associations."

She gestured to include the balcony. "Billy and I have sat and talked out here a million times—when he was going gangbusters with the Yankees or when he couldn't buy a hit and needed to pour out his heart. Two years ago, sitting in *that* chair, I made my decision to quit the Senate."

Ellen pointed down to the yard. "See the big elm? Underneath all those leaves is a tree house. Michael and his father slaved over it. They used to spend weekends sleeping in it, scaring themselves half to death with ghost stories."

They both managed to laugh.

"Please forgive my nostalgia. How about we go inside and get something cold to drink? I want to talk to you about the household."

"Something happen?"

"Our maid has disappeared," Ellen replied as she led the way into the safety of the living room.

Desda froze. "Are you talking about Joanne?"

"Yes," Ellen said as she poured them both a glass of iced tea. "She's always been a little wild. But we have a daughter who's also around twenty. It's clothes and boys, boys and clothes, with a little education on the side. To her credit, though, Joanne's had a good track record with us—punctual, does her job reasonably well, polite. Last week I found her going through my calendar. She actually got hostile. Then two days ago, she didn't show up for work. I've tried calling her a few times, left messages, but she hasn't responded. It may be nothing, but I thought I should tell you."

"I'm glad you did," Desda murmured, her mind instantly racing toward the implications. The likely conclusion was logical and grim. Following his pattern, Quill had gotten to her—probably parting her legs and then her loyalties. By now, the young girl was either on a Greyhound to another town—innocently expecting him to join her later—or she was dead. And now the assassin knew Ellen's agenda and the inside layout of her home.

"Do you think this is connected to the case?" Ellen asked.

"Maybe," Desda said, trying to mask the queasy feeling in her stomach. "She was pretty impressionable, as I recall . . . lotta things could account for her absence. But, yeah, Quill's been known to feed off young girls, and we should be prepared for worst-case scenario. The question is, how does it affect our strategy?"

Ellen slumped back into an armchair. "I'm not sure. We've been over the schedule. As you know, Billy is supposed to be out of town for five days at a baseball conference in LA. Back on the third. For me, it's business as usual except for the talk I'm giving in Central Park on the Fourth. The police, of course, would love me to cancel since Billy will be there too. I can't do that. I made a commitment six months ago and can't back out now—nor do I want to."

Desda didn't respond, her mind still sorting and sifting the ramifications of the missing maid. Both Early and she had agreed on the obvious. For historical and karmic reasons, Quill would seize the opportunity to showboat, to send his diabolical message to all of America. Independence Day was a perfect medium. There would be chaos that night. Thousands of spectators interspersed with fireworks and trigger-happy cops. Hard to defend, hard to maneuver, hard to control.

But Desda was not convinced it would be Central Park. *Suppose the assassin did plan to murder Ellen in her own home? It didn't follow his normal tendencies. Or did it?* She decided to pursue this remote possibility and chose her words carefully.

"I'm going to ask you a hypothetical question that might sound a bit odd. It may or may not be pertinent. Okay?"

"Of course," Ellen said. She placed her tea on a coaster.

"Let's say you were going to hire a photographer," Desda began. "You wanted him to take a picture of you in a setting that would best represent you—show what you're really about. What would the setting be?"

"Political or personal?"

"Both, I guess. Take your time."

Ellen pondered this for a moment, then lowered her eyes. "I see where you're headed with this. That first night, right after we received the death threat, your friend and another detective came by. They mentioned that Quill thinks of himself as an artist. Each victim died in some kind of significant setting. Thank God my husband lived, but look where he was shot! Sliding into second base at Yankee Stadium! That's Billy to a T!"

"Quill does his homework."

Ellen mulled this over and rubbed her hands along the arms of her chair. "Thanks to Joanne, he probably has a complete description of my retreat."

"Retreat?"

Ellen smiled softly. "Well, that's how I think of it. But if I were going to have this photograph taken, it wouldn't be with crowds of people or fireworks or any of the fanfare."

"Then where?"

"I'll show you."

Ellen took Desda's hand and led her up to her private study on the third floor. Desda had never been invited inside or even considered entering. There was an imposing air of "off-limits" around the space.

"Sometimes one needs to take a break from public life—even from family. My kids had a tree house. I have my study."

Desda felt an immediate elevation when she walked through the doorway—the milieu entirely dedicated to scholarship and intellectual reflection. Wooden bookcases lined the room, presenting rows of books, weathered titles on faded bindings. A Windsor rocking chair with a blue and white needlepoint cushion in the seat angled toward a Franklin stove. In the corner beside the long damask curtains that framed the window was an old Chippendale desk. On its drop-leaf surface rested embossed stationery and a brass letter opener.

"This is where I would pose for your photographer. For me, this is home."

It occurred to Desda that she had just stepped inside a slice of one of Ellen's previous lifetimes, uncannily similar to Quill's sticking point—begging many questions. Pushing them away, she turned to examine the collection of antiques. "It's really wonderful!"

Ellen was visibly pleased. "All the furniture has been restored but are original pieces. As I mentioned, I'm a bit of a fanatic. Even when I was a kid, I was interested in colonial this and that—clothes, heroes, literature. Historically speaking, it was a pivotal time to be alive."

Then Ellen pointed to the wall beside the window. "Take a look at this." Protected in a mounted display case was an antique American flag, red and white stripes with its circle of thirteen white stars in a blue field.

"This is what our first flag looked like," she said proudly. "Obviously, it's not authentic, but it's an excellent replica of the one attributed to Betsy Ross. Whenever I spend time in here, I always feel revitalized."

The candidate waited for a moment to allow Desda to finish her perusal, then ushered her out of the room. "I really have to get back to work," Ellen said apologetically. "Now you know my secret. I hope it helps."

"Everything helps, Ellen. Thanks for sharing that with me."

Before retiring, Ellen glanced back. "You know . . . for me, the Independence Day date is not entirely accurate."

"How so?"

"Jefferson's Declaration was ratified by the states and adopted by the Second Continental Congress on the Fourth of July, 1776. By then it was a mere formality. The actual agreement between members was reached on July second. That's the date I personally choose to celebrate."

Desda stood still. "Is that a generally known fact?"

"Maybe not, but anyone who was around at the time would definitely have known."

Smiling ambiguously, Ellen vanished down the hall.

Desda waited until she was gone, then rushed to call Early.

TWO

It was dusk in Central Park. Early crouched in a little nook surrounded by rocks, waiting for Quill. It was the perfect setting for his ambush—close to the path-way, yet obscured enough to avoid detection. It would be here, in this patch of twilight, that the karmic hand-to-hand combat would truly begin.

After "wearing Quill's shoes" back and forth through time, Early had followed the assassin's footprints to this exact spot. Once again, the "goodness" string had been pulled. Aesthetics and horses had led the detective to uncover Quill's whereabouts. Only a few hundred yards away on Fifty-Ninth Street, horse-drawn carriages were in abundance, offering tourists an expensive half-hour ride around the park. Brief discussions with local doormen had confirmed his suspicions. A day after the Hensley incident, a taciturn, well-groomed Englishman had registered at The Sherry Netherlands, a posh hotel across the street from the Plaza. He was memorable by his unvarying timetable. Every night at approximately 7:15, he summoned his private carriage and went for a ride around Central Park.

A twenty-dollar tip from Early resulted in a description of the carriage and a side comment that the Englishman's mental state seemed "slightly altered" after his evening jaunts.

Early checked his watch. Soon. All he planned to do was rattle Quill's cage—agitate him, plant certain seeds that would predispose him to error. If Early could accomplish this, Ellen stood a slightly better chance of living.

Malcolm Raines strode through the hotel doors into the fading evening light. Spotting his ride, he tipped the doorman and sauntered leisurely across the side-walk. He owned many horses all over the world. Some of them were raced, some were bred. One recent acquisition had just trotted up to the curb outside the hotel.

The driver was also one of Malcolm's new purchases. As always, the assassin had made certain he owned his employees' loyalties. If the coachman did well, his fantasies and addictions would be more than satisfied. If not, his body would be used as horse meat. Either way, the man's mouth would remain hermetically sealed.

The assassin handed the driver his customary envelope—something for his wallet, something for his nose—and climbed into the enclosed cab. Tonight Malcolm was particularly unsettled. Part of this was the unrelenting presence of James Early. The Albino had called him an agent of unseen forces. Malcolm was not impressed. The man was challenging his art, cramping his style. It was time for him to disappear.

But for now, all Malcolm wanted to do was relax and enjoy. With this in mind, he laced his normal lines of cocaine with a potent hallucinogenic. Soon he would be completely walled off from the colossal error of America—nation of thugs devoid of taste or artistry.

Before he signaled to the coachman, he slipped on the headset for the cassette player he kept in the backseat. He chose the music of Purcell. Settling into the soft embrace of pillows and cushions, he rapped with his knuckles against the side of the hansom cab. The carriage lurched forward. As the horse fell into its soothing rhythm, the classical music soared inside his head, and the night spread out into its vast network of stars and illusions.

A short time later, Early heard the clatter of horseshoes in the distance. Remaining hidden, he stood up quietly and removed his revolver from its holster. Moments later, he could see the jerky outline of Quill's carriage emerge from behind a bend in the road. When it rolled within striking distance, Early went into action.

Dressed in the requisite uniform of top hat and tails, the coachman stared glumly at the road up ahead, the reins held loosely in his left hand. Pug-faced and dull-eyed, he counted the moments until he was out from under the tyranny of employment. His new foreign boss had the personality of a cobra. On the other hand, the "benefits" were unbelievably generous. Within an hour, he would be free to spend them.

As the coachman's thoughts drifted toward his recreations, he was slow to process the subtle motion to his left. A figure had slipped from the darkness and nimbly mounted the side of the carriage. Suddenly a silhouette towered above him.

Before the driver could react, he felt a cold circle of metal press in against his temple, then a penetrating whisper, "Make a sound and you're dead!"

As the man froze, Early reached around with his other hand and dug into the coachman's shoulder blade. "Straight ahead, pal, and very quiet. Keep it that way, and you might come out of this okay."

Terror shot across the man's features. He nodded, then cast his eyes straight ahead, blank and robotic.

"Good, we understand each other. Now, I'm going to pay your boss a little visit. You keep driving. Nothing different, nothing rash. Mess with that and it gets pretty gruesome. Got it?"

The man nodded again, and Early released his hold. *Now for Quill.* Gun in hand, he silently negotiated his way down to the cab door. He was about to invade his adversary's deep cover. His presence alone might be enough to unglue the man. In fact, Early was counting on it.

Malcolm sat with his eyes closed, his head resting lightly on a pillow, his mind engorged with pictures. *Black stallions flowing beneath Prussian-blue archways ... beautiful women standing on the shore of an emerald-green lake, their long summer dresses pressed back by the breeze, clinging to the contours of their bodies ...*

Dimly, he became aware of something intrusive, something alien snaking into his sensuous collage. Thick and dreamy, he managed to force one eye open. The inside of the cab appeared misty and full of hostile shadows, intermittently lit by passing streetlights. Soon, a yellowish light washed through the cab. Malcolm gasped. A face had suddenly appeared across from him . . . then vanished.

Jostled against the creaking wood, Malcolm tried to sit up, strains of music still liquid inside his head. From the roadside, another brief sweep of a streetlight filled the interior. Three feet away, a hand flashed before him . . . then darkness. Malcolm struggled to assimilate the renegade images. *What the bloody hell was this? It looked like a hand pointing a gun!*

With fingers that felt like they were made of rubber, he peeled the headset from his ears. From somewhere close by, piercing his fog, a voice spoke sharply.

"Mr. Raines, we meet again. You didn't forget about our little appointment tonight, did you?"

Malcolm stared back without comprehension, his mind spinning helplessly. *The apparition looks like James Early. That's impossible!*

The voice came again as if the night itself were speaking. "You're an open book, totally predictable. I know every word on every page of your pathetic history. It's not a good read."

Malcolm began to squirm. *The drugs must have been cut with something! That was the only explanation.* But the phantom continued to undulate before him. This time, the words floated in the black space, stinging him like the tentacles of a Portuguese man-of-war.

"You remind me a lot of a guy named Patrick Wellington . . . lived in the eighteenth century. He was a big-time loser. He failed then. He'll fail now."

Malcolm blinked and dragged a sweating palm across his eyes. His mind wasn't functioning. His suit was soaked with perspiration, and his thigh was beginning to throb mercilessly.

Then he felt a pressure on his arm, a very solid hand digging into his flesh.

The face of his enemy was becoming huge, engulfing the tiny space. Against his cheek, he felt the heat of breath.

"If you think you're having a bad trip now, stick around. We're just getting started!"

The assassin heard the door creak open, followed by the parting words, "The party's on the Fourth, Mr. Wellington. Central Park. I'll be waiting."

Then the ghost melted away.

Malcolm gripped his head with both shaking hands. He was suffocating, the coach suddenly freezing and full of chattering voices. Leaning forward, he began to vomit.

THREE

WhiteMan's Penthouse Suite

The long ivory fingers gathered along the wrinkles of skin at his throat, then skittered around the collar of his robe as if seeking shelter. The Albino sat at his desk, waiting for the phone to ring again. Mid-conversation, he had just ordered a hysterical Mr. Raines to hang up and call back on a less traceable phone. He was through with taking chances. Raines was now a professional liability, and hotels kept records of outgoing phone calls. It was time to cut the line. In fact, two days from now, all his lines would be disconnected forever.

Now the fingertips forayed out along his face, pausing and darting, finally forming a protective cup around his aching eyes. Of late, the pinkish orbs seemed to be receding deeper and deeper into his skull. WhiteMan had been reluctant but finally made the obvious connection. Raines was the carrier. His contamination had somehow penetrated the clairvoyant's stronghold, affecting his state of mind, disturbing his work. Now *any* increment of light, even the faint glow from his tenwatt bulb in the bathroom, seemed to send his entire system into tremors.

Like most other psychics, WhiteMan had never been privy to his own future. Nevertheless, even a blind man would be hard-pressed to miss the signs. It was the feel of Pompeii just before the volcanic eruption or Hiroshima hours before the bomb. If he didn't get out now, he would be courting disaster.

There had been other ominous symptoms. Four times in the last ten days, he had been disturbed by anonymous phone calls. In each instance, the caller had blocked his psychic probe yet hadn't said a word. As WhiteMan listened, the ensuing silence at the other end had seemed to roar through his receiver as if the phone were being held up to the sea itself. Who was behind this? His number was unlisted. None of his clients knew he was leaving. The only consolation was that soon, none of this would matter.

The shrill sound of his phone ripped him back to matters at hand. The fingers stopped dead in their tracks. Steeling himself, WhiteMan picked up the receiver. "Now, Mr. Raines," he said disdainfully, "I will—"

"Now listen to me!" Malcolm interrupted savagely. Huddled in a phone booth outside his hotel, he began to vent. "Get rid of James Early, damn it! How the hell can I operate when he—"

"Quiet! You bore me to tears with these tantrums of yours!"

Malcolm slammed his fist against the booth's plastic wall. "I won't apologize! Once you were effective. Now you're a waste of my time."

"I assure you, the feeling is mutual," WhiteMan rasped. "You have paid for this consultation, so I will tolerate you for this last session. After that, you may consider our relationship to be completely terminated. Do I make myself clear?"

"Very," Malcolm said. He absently rubbed the soreness in his leg. "Answer my questions and I'll *gladly* remove every trace of you from my life!"

In the inky solitude of his room, the Albino leaned forward and placed his sharp elbows on the desk, his voice scraping through the wires like glass against stone. "I warned you. This man . . . this James Early . . . represents players who are far stronger than you. So strike soon! And change your tactics—from power to stealth. If they taunt you with *their* gauntlet, do *not* pick it up. Find an alternative approach that utilizes surprise. Do you understand?"

Malcolm's mind swept across the three possible strategies he had designed for Ellen's disposal. Number one was his favorite. It followed along his traditional lines of the spectacular. Now he felt unsure. Although time was running out, he did have a few days to make his final determination.

"I'll keep that in mind," he said flatly. "Now, before I—"

"Goodbye, Mr. Raines!"

Malcolm pulled the phone angrily away from his ear. The psychic had beaten him to the punch. The line was dead.

WhiteMan leaned back, sighed. It was over. *No more clients!* Instantly, the pale fingers became festive, a flurry of motion as they danced around the blotter. Tomorrow he would make a rare journey outside the barricaded confines of his home to see his lawyer. In that meeting, the final arrangements before departure would be concluded: the sale of his penthouse, the transfer of extraneous funds to his Swiss bank accounts. The following day, he would begin his emancipation by flying to Costa Rica, where a modest villa awaited him on the outskirts of San Jose. There would be no forwarding address, no way for his old life to adhere to his new one. If, by chance, it did, he would be well prepared. Accompanying him would be the black binder full of names, addresses, and incendiary details about the private lives of his clients. If he were ever threatened or needed some extra cash or even found himself wanting for a little excitement . . .

Feeling as though the worst was over, WhiteMan wrenched his feeble body to its feet. Straining and wheezing, he dragged himself across the carpet to a small air-conditioned closet that served as his wine cellar. Flicking on a tiny pocket flashlight, he studied the labels of his champagne collection, then selected one for the cooler. Not yet. But within forty-eight hours, he would uncork his best vintage Dom Pérignon. A fitting gesture to celebrate the hour of his freedom.

FOUR

Danny's Donuts

Early glanced around, then shook his head with disbelief. He used to push through the door, slide into a booth and feel like one of the boys. Now he felt out of sync. Outwardly, nothing had changed: the same scuffed white tile floors, the same red vinyl booths and tables, the same smudgy glass counters full of greasy donuts. Even some of the customers who greeted him were remnants of the old gang. Yet today, Early couldn't find the coordinates. For him, centuries had passed since he had last been here, sitting at the same table with Sam on the day after Greco, trying to reconcile the fact of his existence with the knowledge that he should be dead.

"A little surprised?" Desda asked, noticing that his initial expression of delight was sinking into something more complex. "You look like an alumnus who's come back to visit his alma mater and just realized it doesn't match the yearbook."

"Yeah, not better or worse. Maybe just a different perspective," Early mused. "Sam and I used to be hard-core regulars here. Ten years' worth. We were part of the scene—a couple of cops that everyone knew. Now I come back and I'm the outsider, one foot off the planet, trying to find my way back to just hang out and sip coffee."

"And the sad part is, after all that, the coffee still tastes like lighter fluid!" Desda grimaced, pushing her cup away. "How can you drink this stuff?"

They both laughed, and Early shoved back his sleeve to check his watch. "Listen, Sam'll be here in about five minutes. I had to twist his arm, but he'll show. Let's go over the basics. First, we need to convince him that we're not flipped out. In his book, right now, I'm suspect. Second, he's gonna want to know how we got our information. I'll have to try and sidestep him on that one."

"Stop me if I'm wrong," Desda said, "but we're walking a fine line here. I mean, we don't want to involve the police until you've had your chance to work the karma angle with Quill. But we can't mess around with Ellen's life either."

"Priority number one *is* Ellen. That's not going to change. That's why I've called Sam in. If it gets hairy, I want the NYPD within earshot. Right now, we have to wait and see if Raines takes my bait. In the carriage, I told him he's expected on Independence Day in the park. That might pump him up to go after Ellen on the Fourth of July. On the other hand, it could make him start thinking about alternatives. That's good for us. We want him to think *a lot*, get tangled up in his past. That's our best shot."

"You're talking about July second, Ellen's secret date?"

"Yeah. I checked it out. History books confirm it. The Declaration was ratified on July fourth but was approved by Congress two days earlier on the second. Quill was right about being held hostage by the colonists. They would have rubbed it in his face—hard. Somewhere below his consciousness, that date's gotta be stuck in his memory. So now we want to help it bleed through, make him do things we can anticipate. That's our only edge."

Desda mulled this over. "I keep thinking about Ellen's study. If the maid *did* tell him about it, he's gotta be tempted. It's a perfect setting, don't you think?"

"Absolutely. Ellen showed me her schedule book, the one Joanne copied for Quill. The entry for that day says something like 'home—final draft, practice speech.' It's also common knowledge that Billy's out of town, and the NYPD will pull some of the security. Except for us, they still think Billy's the target, so no one's going to be paying much attention.

"Considering the options, I still hope Quill takes the quieter approach. Not that the Burwells' place will be easy to defend, but I'll take it over Central Park any day. A hundred thousand people are supposed to show. It's gonna be a zoo."

They both lapsed into silence, contemplating the porous net with which they hoped to snare a killer who had never failed.

"I don't like our odds on this thing at all!" Desda finally mumbled.

Early nodded unhappily, his fingers drumming against the tabletop. "I just want to make sure NYPD is part of the mix. We're gonna need the backup."

A moment later, Sam Jenkins banged through the restaurant door. Spotting them, he made his way to their booth. "Well, well . . . James! Just like old times!" Then he looked at Desda and added, ". . . with a new twist."

"More than a twist, Sam. She's a complete direction." Early laughed and stood up to clasp Sam's hand. "Thanks for coming."

"Well, despite . . . whatever, you're still family," Sam conceded. "But I'll be honest, I don't have much time and this better be good. That said, I'm willing to listen."

Sam got his donut and coffee and sat down across from them. "Okay, shoot." Desda and Early exchanged glances, then Early gave his report: the fact that Ellen, not Billy, was the real target; the murder of Arlo Hensley; the likelihood of a showdown on the second or fourth of July. Included was a description and current location of a certain M. Raines.

When he was through, Early drained his cup. "No question, it's mostly circumstantial and undocumented. Stuff we used to chuck in the round file. I'm not giving you disclaimers, though. I wouldn't waste both of our time if I didn't think this stuff was vital."

Sam's expression had changed mildly, here and there, during the briefing. But the sum impact made little more than a small dent on the brooding machinery of his skepticism. Early knew the mindset well.

Sam chewed for a moment, sighed, then rattled off his list of responses. "Okay, one by one. Fourth of July? Yeah, we're tracking there and already on it. Ellen being the real target? Then why would he try to take out Billy? Out of character for Quill to use decoys. He's never done that kind of thing before, and there's nothing to substantiate it now. This Hensley guy, the horseman who got iced? Same thing. Why would Quill waste his time on some snotty little horse breeder who doesn't even begin to qualify as an American hotshot? It doesn't fit the profile."

Sam laid both beefy hands on the table. "Now, this hunch of yours about the Raines guy," Sam's eyes narrowed as he studied Early. "Look, my man, when you were a cop, you were real good. But let's face it, you're outta the fold now and maybe not all that popular with the guys. Even if I wanted to, I don't have the manpower to stake out some dude in a dark suit unless we've got something a little more concrete to go on. Sorry guys, I appreciate your efforts, but I'm gonna stay with what I got."

There was a moment of stubborn silence—one which neither man chose to mitigate with niceties. Eventually Early broke the stalemate. "Fair enough. I'd probably be taking the same stance if I were you. Just promise me *one* thing."

"And that is?"

"There may come a time when I'll need support—you and whoever else you can bring. I won't be crying wolf, and the evidence won't be soft. Swear to me you'll be there."

The former partners locked eyes, then Sam offered his hand. "Okay. *If* that happens, you call, I'll show."

They all stood up to go. Early reached across the table and gave Sam's forearm an affectionate punch. "Thanks, man. Thanks for coming."

"I owe you that much," Sam said with a half-smile. Pausing, he looked from Early to Desda and back, his round eyes softening.

"You guys look good together. Hope it all works out."

With a nominal wave, he turned and headed back to the wars of the NYPD.

"About what I expected," Early said after Sam had departed. "His hands are really tied. I guess it's down to you and me."

"Probably where it belongs anyway," Desda offered. "Speaking of you and me, got some time to talk?"

"Sure. I was just about to ask you the same."

Once outside, Early rested his hand lightly on Desda's shoulder. "This could all end badly. We may not—"

"I know," she cut in. "I don't want to regret that I didn't take the time . . . didn't say certain things when I had the chance."

Meandering east along Twenty-Second Street, both of them wondered how to begin. Desda spoke first. "Before I met you, I had gone pretty south on relationships. I guess I started out like everyone else—the hype, the expectations, the 'true love' thing. In my case, I hit the wall pretty young. I mean, the dream is great, but who's out there making it work? So after a while I went okay, just give me something real, something I could count on—a cigarette, a bottle of J&B, a great book, whatever—and I'd be okay."

She paused. "Then you come along, and it all breaks down. And it's not just boy meets girl, it's . . . Christ, I don't even know! And I want to be open, try again. But the truth is, the whole crazy thing scares me to death! We don't know *what* we are. I mean, look at our karma. We had a love affair that killed! What if it turns out we're evil together, that people around us die? What does that make us?"

"Doesn't make us anything," Early said evenly. "I've been up and down this thing from every angle. I always come back to the same place. What went down in the past will either split us apart or open us up together. Destiny has no hold on us. It's still our choice. Blessing or curse, we still decide.

"And what you were saying about relationships? I was there too. Probably just as bad. And the eight by ten glossy they all wave around in the name of love makes it worse. Not because it idealizes it, but because it trivializes it. Since I found you . . . "

Early suddenly felt his throat constrict. Before he could find his voice again, she had put her arms around him. In the middle of the frenzied tides of New York City, with pedestrians flowing by on either side, they became a small timeless island, wanting nothing more than to be with each other.

FIVE

He looked like a charcoal sketch, a nightmarish figure wrenched out of Edgar Allan Poe's mind. Despite the fact that it was a bright summer day, WhiteMan shuffled along Fifth Avenue in complete insulation: long dark overcoat, black silk muffler, and thick sunglasses beneath a broad-brimmed fedora.

He had just concluded his business with his lawyer. Now with the aid of a cane, he limped the short distance back to his apartment building. As people brushed past him, they glanced sideways, then quickly moved away. Nobody wanted to be caught staring. At best, he looked like Mafia, someone to avoid.

Thirty yards from his building, the cloaked albino suddenly felt a hand close tightly around the back of his neck. "Easy now, cretin. Keep it glued together, or I squeeze the pus from your soul," Trakker hissed against the startled psychic's ear.

Falling into stride, the poet began to march him along the sidewalk. "When we hit the doorman, don't squeak, don't whimper. This is a family thing. Poppa's been a bad boy. Poppa's gonna pay."

Once safely past the entrance guard, they boarded the elevator and rode silently toward the penthouse. Trakker relaxed his hold.

WhiteMan immediately coughed and gasped for air. Leaning forward, he attempted to steady himself on his cane. He was used to feeling weak. This time he was frightened for his life.

Beneath the thick glasses, his watery eyes studied his assailant's fingers. Confirmation enough. They were long, thin, and hyper—very much like his own. WhiteMan suddenly made the connection, understood who was behind all those anonymous phone calls. After all the years of covering his tracks, a piece of his own flesh and blood had come back to exact its due. The reunion would not be pleasurable.

"What . . . what is it you want from me?" WhiteMan stammered. "I have a little money saved for you. Maybe—"

Trakker pressed his finger against the Albino's lips. "It's over, old man. Over. Don't even try."

When the psychic's shaking hand finally managed to unlock his front door, Trakker shoved him inside. Aware that the room had no lighting fixtures, the poet left the door ajar, allowing the light from the hallway to provide tentative visibility. With one sinewy arm wrapped around his father's throat, he panned around the apartment, shook his head in disgust. "Fits you like a glove, old man. Darkness begets darkness."

The psychic struggled feebly against his captor. "This is uncalled for. You can't just barge in here."

"Oh, but I can, and I did. Terrorism runs in the family. Now we jam the broken parts together—abusive father and pissed-off son—and see what happens."

Taking hold of both of WhiteMan's wrists, he turned him around slowly. "Lose the shades. I want to see the face."

WhiteMan balked. "How did you find me, damn it! *No one* has ever done that before!"

"Don't you know? I have your gift. I travel. I listen. I trace nasty rumors right to the doorstep. Your daughter didn't fare so well. Right now, she's doing time in hell's halfway house. You torched her good—just like our mother."

The Albino began to bluster, "There was an unfortunate fire. I—"

"Zip it!" Trakker shouted. "You murdered my mother. Kicked two helpless kids out into the streets! And you were just getting started, weren't you? Scary how much damage one little black hole can do in the neighborhood."

WhiteMan's thin body began to quiver. "I'll make it up to you. I promise. Just let me go."

"No deal. One more time. Delete the shades!"

Slowly the Albino removed his sunglasses, revealing his runny pinkish eyes. For a moment, father and son stared at each other, WhiteMan blinking uncontrollably.

Trakker clucked his tongue in amazement. "Here I was expecting some kind of mountain of evil. What a joke! You're not even a man. You're a stick figure covered with phlegm!"

"I'm not well, son. I need rest. Please . . ."

"Shut up! Now we expose the slug. All the clothes—off!"

Before WhiteMan could object, the poet had ripped off the old man's hat and coat and tossed them across the room.

"The rest!" Trakker barked. "Shirt and pants . . . down to the nubs."

"What are you planning to do to me?" WhiteMan moaned, fumbling with his trousers.

"You're pale, Father, very pale. A little tan would do you good."

Numbly, the psychic undressed until he was reduced to an elongated skeleton. His translucent, splotched skin stretched unforgivingly across protruding bones that seemed almost phosphorescent, gleaming ghostly in the dim light.

Trakker jerked WhiteMan's arms behind his back and pushed him across the room, then propped him up in front of the black drapes that hid the massive windows.

WhiteMan was becoming frantic. He knew exactly what his son was about to do and was powerless to defend himself. And now all his carefully laid plans—the escape to Costa Rica, his freedom—were about to be incinerated in the fury of the sun.

Desperately, he tried one last time. In a whispery voice sugarcoated with warmth and sincerity, he turned his head and smiled at his son. "You were a handsome boy. Intelligent. I loved you and your sister very much. I was in a bind then. Please, give me a chance to make up for the lost years."

Trakker didn't speak. Standing behind his father, he slid his grip up WhiteMan's bony back until he seized the trembling shoulders.

"You don't have a conscience. So I'm gonna brand one into you. Open the drapes!"

The Albino's heart began to thunder loudly in his ears. "NO! Please! I beg you!"

Trakker dug his fingernails into WhiteMan's skin. "I could happily break your neck for what you've done. I'm giving you a chance. Now, before I'm tempted to kill you, grab the chord. Pull!"

The Albino flailed backward with his arms, trying to twist and scratch at Trakker's eyes with his sharp nails.

Trakker batted the feeble attack away and cut deeper into the Albino's flesh. "Do it!" he yelled.

Spiritually cornered, physically defenseless, WhiteMan took hold of the thin rope, his heart leaden with fear. With a shriek, he yanked down on the chord. The curtains parted, and the huge picture window burst into sunlight, hitting him like the flash of an atomic bomb. Shards of light ripped through his paper-thin eyelids and stabbed into his skin—his consciousness engulfed with searing volts of electricity.

Trakker clamped his hand over the clairvoyant's mouth as the body went into convulsions. After a while, the twitching diminished. The head slumped forward on the chest and the mouth fell open, a thin stream of drool seeping down from the corner of the parched lips.

Lowering the limp body, Trakker laid it out, spread-eagle on the floor—just outside the circle of blistering sun. Soon the eyelids became still. Now only the fingertips flickered with motion. As if trying to tap out a last desperate SOS in the air, they writhed and clutched, then went still. A peacefulness filled the room.

Trakker bent down and listened to the heartbeat. Faint but steady. The Albino wouldn't die from this exposure. Ultimately, his fangs had been removed. Nothing more. Nothing less. In a few hours, the poet would call the building manager who would send for the paramedics. By then, Trakker would be long gone.

The poet stood up slowly and allowed the coldness to drain from his heart. Horror mingled with sadness. He wiped his hands on his jeans and turned around slowly in contemplation. All in all, the punishment was a good fit for the crime. For the first time in a decade, light was allowed to reign in the silent rooms. The poet saw this and smiled. He had a few more things to do, then his payback would be complete.

Methodically, he began to search the apartment. In the desk drawer, he found a plane ticket and his father's passport. Trakker stuffed these into his back pocket. On the bedside table, he located a large black binder. This went under his arm. Both would be sent to the police.

Standing in the doorway, he glanced back at the prostrate figure, impaled on the floor by shafts of light. "What goes around has just come back to burn you. Tough love, but that's the law, Poppa dearest," Trakker called out from across the room. "Learn a lesson and try to get it right next time."

Paying homage for a moment to the great golden circle that sparkled through the window, he left his father's home. On a spiritual level, he could feel the difference. A tarantula had just been vaporized from the karmic web.

SIX

On July second, the anniversary of America's first raised fist of independence, the waters surrounding the island of Manhattan rose up as thick menacing clouds materialized above and stalked inland. In the early evening, the rain raked the pavement and buildings like machine-gun fire. Later, the storm settled into a fine drizzle giving way to mist, pressing against windows in homes, offices, and cars, making vision uncertain and troubled.

From the outside, the Burwell brownstone appeared to be in normal working order. Behind drawn curtains, however, Early, Desda, and Ellen prepared for a siege. Out of necessity and out of caution, the defense of the politician's life had been pared down to this irreducible trio. Billy was away, and the rest of the staff had been given the night off. Ellen had made it clear. There would be no extraneous moving parts, no innocent people caught in the middle if cross fire began.

Over the last few hours, guns had been cleaned and loaded, strategy discussed, and assignments nailed down. Now the talk was minimal and hushed. Every light on all three floors was on; each shadow accounted for. Although no one knew for certain, all signs indicated that Quill would make his move tonight.

Gun in hand, Early peered one more time through the crack in the drapes into the misty backyard, disquieted by the lack of visibility. *Advantage Quill*, he thought bitterly. Outside, nothing stirred . . . nothing audible beyond the steady drip of precipitation. Considering the assassin's stealth, this meant nothing at all.

Returning to the living room, Early quietly rallied his troops. "Desda, Ellen, let's have a quick one. I want us all in sync if it starts getting busy."

Desda lowered her weapon and reluctantly left her position overlooking the front yard. Ellen came from the landing above the staircase, holding her gun awkwardly in both hands as though it were something alive and unfriendly.

"Okay," Early began when his group had assembled. "First of all, Sam has been alerted. There are five phones in the house, and you all have his number. Again, we're not interested in heroics. We're interested in getting the job done. If anyone at any time wants to change our strategy—especially you, Ellen—just give the word, and we'll call in the NYPD. Understood?"

Ellen and Desda acknowledged. "All right. Now as far as Quill is concerned, we've gotta hope he's assuming it's a business-as-usual night at the Burwells'. He's counting on surprise, and we have to keep up the masquerade or he'll never set foot in our trap. That means we all stay downwind until the right time. When you're on lookout, don't be obvious. Keep your weapons out of view. As you know, Billy's absence has thinned down the outside security to two men—Tim in the front, Chuck in the back. Desda, got the portable radio?"

Desda patted the device stuffed in her belt. "Yeah, but I'm really worried about those guys. They're standing around out there in the open. Did you talk to them?"

Early's face became strained. "I tried, got in their face, the whole bit. But I don't like the odds either. It could be a very short night for them."

Desda frowned, then turned to Ellen. "How are you holding up?"

"I'll manage," Ellen responded. "I just want to make sure I pull my weight. You must understand, I feel responsible for this. I brought Quill to America, and you people are risking your lives to defend me."

"Bottom line, you're important," Early said, "and that's why we're here. But right now, I just want to solidify our plans."

"I'm sorry. Please go on."

"Okay. If our suspicions are correct, Quill's going to try to set you up in the study. That's been discussed. For him to get in there, there're three main entrance points he'll probably consider: the fire escape, the roof, and the tree outside the window."

Early studied Ellen's face. "As mentioned, if he gets that far, you'll be exposed for a moment before we move in. Are you really okay with this?"

Ellen nodded. "I don't pretend to understand how you've arrived at all of your conclusions. I'm just going to have to trust you."

Early shot a sideways look at Desda. "I appreciate that," he said. "Let's just say this case has huge implications. For all of us. We wouldn't be here if it weren't our battle too."

"He's right," Desda murmured under her breath.

"Any last questions before we hit it?"

Both women shook their heads.

"Okay, on we go. Ellen, do *not* engage in combat other than to defend yourself. Your job is to watch and warn. Desda, give it five minutes, then check with the patrol boys. Keep them on their toes. If anybody sees or hears *anything*, come get me."

Finished delivering his instructions, he walked up the stairs to Ellen's study and returned to his vigil by the window. The tension was palpable. If there were ever a time he needed to employ his growing powers of awareness, it was now. He needed to be so still inside, so attuned, that he could hear the sound of a psychopath's internal footsteps.

As he willed himself to relax and focus, he let his attention spread out around the environment. It would serve as his alarm system. At this stage, his perception was not advanced enough to pinpoint the exact location of entry—only the general impression of trespass.

A moment later, the first tiny tremor reached him. Faint but unmistakable. Somewhere in the near vicinity, the karmic field was beginning to strain with the weight of an ominous presence.

Barely discernible in the thick layers of mist, a shadow disengaged itself from the moonless night and quietly vaulted the backyard fence, then flattened against the grass. Dressed from head to toe in black, his face opaque with greasepaint, Malcolm lay still. For a moment, he luxuriated in the smell of the earth and the sensual feel of the wet lawn against his groin. In his gloved hand was the reassuring weight of his Smith & Wesson, impregnated with godlike powers. Against the muscular contours of his hip was the comforting pressure of his steel knife. At last! With WhiteMan out of the picture, he was in control again. Left to his own devices, he was a virtuoso with the instruments of death.

With reptilian grace, he slithered across the ten feet of lawn until he reached the back entrance of a small unlit greenhouse and crept inside. Rows of musty shelves were laden with flower and fruit bushes, the air pungent with herbs. Through a rain-blurred window, he gazed at the home of Ellen Burwell—now only twenty yards away.

From within, the warm glow of light seeped beneath the corners of drawn blinds, cozy and unsuspecting. Malcolm brushed the wet grass from his clothes and contemplated the building. He knew everything he needed to know. The little maid had been sucked dry before he had discarded her. Mesmerized by his prowess, she had prostrated herself at his feet. Eagerly and without reservation, she had complied with his sexual fantasies—and his espionage. Now he had an inch-by-inch description of the house's interior, particularly the candidate's study.

But it had been the maid's little foray into the cramped attic one night that would seal Ellen's fate. There, almost by accident, she had stumbled upon a trap door that opened down into Ellen's study. It was obvious from the layers of dust that it hadn't been used in years and was, in all likelihood, long forgotten. This one piece of information had made Malcolm's distasteful association with the American girl worthwhile.

Less than a week ago, she had lain naked in his arms, talking of Paris and Venice, twirling strands of his dark hair between her fingertips. In thanks, he had kissed her gently on both breasts. Soon the poison in her cabernet had taken hold, and the rhythmic rise and fall of her chest had been stilled forever.

The following day he had deposited her remains in the woods outside the Hensley estate. Regrettably, this was an incidental death, not worthy of his artistry. Ellen's execution, however, would afford him the opportunity to express his creative genius.

Letting his keen eyes rove from house to yard, the assassin contemplated his next hurdle. The phone lines were now dead, as was the policeman posted at the front of the house. Sometime tomorrow, he would be found lying facedown beneath a minivan on Twenty-Second Street. Soon the other sentry would be eliminated. Then . . .

A moment later, he spied the last cop stationed beneath the awning of the back door. Malcolm watched him with fascination—the stark visual poetry of the man's last few seconds on Earth. At that moment, he was cupping his hands to light a cigarette—the leap of flame, the shake of the wrist to extinguish the match, the exhale of smoke spiraling up into the veils of mist. Malcolm smiled inwardly. *How little they know. How little resistance they offer.*

Desda slipped into the study, stooped down beside Early, her face drawn and pale.

"He's here," Early whispered. "I don't know where, but he's here."

Desda took a shallow breath. "I hope this isn't related, but I just radioed Tim in front, and he's not responding. I have that sinking feeling."

Early's brows shot together. "Not good. Chuck?"

"I talked to him earlier. Nothing going on back there. I tried to jump-start him, but he's just being wet and pissed off, waiting for his shift to be over. No matter what I told him, he has *no* idea what's out there waiting for him."

"Where's the damn radio!?" Early demanded angrily.

Desda flew to get it and returned quickly.

Early flipped on the switch and tried Tim again. Nothing.

Beginning to panic, he called Chuck in the backyard. Now there was only the crackle of static.

"Shit!" Early grimaced.

"Maybe it's the rain . . . handsets shorting out," Desda offered. But the conjecture sounded hollow, and the same gruesome thought grew inside them. Unseen and unheard, Quill was advancing through the gloom, picking off their defenses, one by one.

"For Christ's sake, what the hell do we do now?" she asked, her voice growing strident.

"We stay put. Too risky to go look for them. And we can't leave Ellen unguarded."

Early turned to fully engage her anxious blue eyes. "Listen, whatever happens, you and I can't get cut off! If we can't actually talk, we've got to stay connected anyway. Keep the channels open. Understand?"

A look passed between them.

"Okay," Desda said resolutely and stood up. "I'm going back."

Fighting a sense of dread, she returned to her post. Once in the living room, she checked the front yard, saw nothing, then moved to a side window and peered through the curtains. She gasped. Was the mist playing tricks with her eyes? An outstretched hand lay motionless in the grass. Softly lit by the downstairs porch light, pale fingers curled upward, glistening with raindrops. She craned her neck further. Now the cap and shoulders could be seen. Panic threatened to overtake her. Chuck's corpse had been left out in the open for anyone to see. Quill was not just systematically dismantling their fortifications, he was taunting them.

Desda stumbled to get Early.

Shielded from view by a morass of tangled wet leaves, Malcolm stood on the wooden planks of the tree house. On a gnarled board, warped with time and neglect, were relics from the Burwells' past: a faded ball cap, a rusty hammer, an empty can of Coke. Pushing through the overgrown limbs, the assassin stepped over a soggy comic book and secured a vantage point where he could see the second-floor windows of the living room. Again, nothing seemed to stir.

Thick branches capable of supporting his weight rose up past the windows and ran parallel to the fire escape. These would be easy to spot and were not part of his design. From the far side of the trunk, hidden from view, another broad limb twisted upward, scraping against the attic window before rising above the roof. This fit his plan perfectly.

Shinnying upward along the branch, he vanished into the fog and foliage, his black clothing and darkened face making him disappear into the backdrop of night.

Early stood next to Desda, seeing for himself the lifeless form of the cop in the backyard. Grave and conscience-stricken, he looked away.

"I tried . . . I tried to warn him . . . both of them. Maybe I should have done more."

"No time to second-guess! It wasn't your fault. It's Quill, damn him!"

"I'm sorry, James, I know our plan—the karma and all. But enough is enough. This asshole needs to die."

"He will," Early said, grappling with his own rage, "but we have to stay with the big picture."

He suddenly signaled for quiet, cocked his head as if sniffing the wind. Something had just tripped off his invisible net. "Quill's real close now. Maybe in the tree house. I think it's time for our setup."

Motioning to Ellen, Early closed the short distance between them with quick strides.

Ellen waited uncomfortably, her jaw squared, her fingers grown blood-less where she gripped the revolver.

"Ellen, if you're ready?"

"I think so," the candidate said softly.

"You'll do fine."

Early placed an encouraging hand on her shoulder and felt the hard knots of tension. "This is going to be fast. In and out, okay? All we want is for Quill to think you're alone in the study. I'm going to be with you, but out of sight. Once we get inside, you're going to walk over to the window and peer out through the drapes. Look up at the sky like you're wondering about the weather. Then step away. After that, get the hell out and go lock yourself in your bedroom! Desda and I will take it from there."

"If he sees me, won't he just shoot?"

"We're betting that he won't—but that's why the bulletproof vest under your shirt. The point is, Quill has a certain . . . style. Part artist, part assassin. He won't kill until he's got his composition in place. The room is the key."

"The room . . . ," Ellen repeated.

"Let's just say that your colonial choices will have a particular impact on him. If we can keep him in there long enough and provide a . . . a little stimulation, he'll get confused. I know this all sounds like hocus-pocus, but believe me, we're work-ing on a solid premise."

The detective withdrew his arm. "All set?"

Despite the quaking in her legs, she nodded soberly. Before leading the way, Early turned back toward Desda for a final check.

She shook her head. "Nothing major. I thought I saw something move near the attic dormer. Probably just a squirrel. There's nothing up there."

"Well," Early began, "don't discount anything. Keep a lookout for—"

Suddenly out of the corner of his eye, he saw Ellen turn and bolt upstairs.

"Ellen! Wait!" he yelled. But she didn't look back. Desda's comment had just jolted her.

The ceiling hatch! She had forgotten all about it. After all the years, it may have been left unlocked. Because of her lapse in memory, all of their lives might be in jeopardy.

Early charged after her. Although he hadn't heard the soft thud of feet landing from a ten-foot height, he already knew. Quill had won the opening round. Over two dead bodies, he had managed to enter the house.

When Early turned the hallway corner, he spied her, one hand on the study doorknob.

"NO! Stop where you are!" he pleaded.

But Ellen had already decided. Fierce and determined, she flung open the door and disappeared into the room, gun thrust before her.

Malcolm stood with his back pressed against the study wall. He had heard the footsteps and the voices just outside. Now he was ready.

As soon as Ellen passed through the doorway, he struck with speed and force. Her gun clattered across the floor; her body hurled against the wall. Stunned by the collision, Ellen's shout of warning remained throttled in her throat.

An instant later, Early stormed into the room. Before he could assess the danger, he felt the side of his genitals bashed by the metal handle of Malcolm's Smith & Wesson. Floods of nausea and pain swept through him. Sagging forward, he crashed against the floor.

Unruffled, Malcolm calmly kicked the door shut, locking the deadbolt. "Now we wait. There's one more in your little party, I believe."

Five seconds later, the doorknob jiggled, and Desda's shoulder thudded against the unyielding frame. Malcolm raised his weapon and fired once into the ceiling, unleashing a shower of broken plaster. "That was a warning!" he called out to Desda. "If you persist, your friends will die immediately. Think back. Remember the scene in your apartment, little girl. Now go home. Your services are no longer required here."

Desda stood back from the door and cursed, her heart pounding violently. Now he had both Ellen and Early. This couldn't be happening! Caught in the twilight of indecision, she was completely unprepared when the door suddenly blasted open and Malcolm's fist exploded against the side of her skull. As blackness overcame her, she dropped senseless to the floor.

Satisfied, Malcolm stepped back into the room and relocked the door. Now all the pieces were neatly in place. With James Early out of commission, Ellen was completely at his mercy. It was time to put the finishing touches on his craft.

The assassin grabbed her by the collar, stood her up, and jammed her head back against the wall. "This moment has been hard-earned. Let's enjoy it together, shall we?" he said toyingly as he traced the point of his revolver along the swell of her breasts. "Now is the time to talk about art . . . and death."

Keeping Ellen immobilized with one hand, he scrutinized the room with the eye of a photographer, noting the details of furniture, artifacts, and lighting. "It's perfect!" he exclaimed. "I commend you on your decor."

Still savoring the possibilities, his attention became riveted on the antique flag on the wall behind them. "Yes . . . our theme," he murmured, "just as your maid described."

So saying, he seized Ellen's hand and cracked it back viciously against the display case. As Ellen cried out, the glass shattered, and the flag slid to the floor. Keeping his eyes pinned fiercely to her face, he said, "Look now, First Lady. This rag you revere," spitting on the cloth, "America be damned!"

Lips pressed against her cheek, he whispered, "Men were *never* created equal. Some of us were born to rule. You've been a whore to the masses. Time to die like one."

Pursing his lips, he made his final calculations. "You will be found on the rocking chair—legs parted, the stars and stripes stuffed between your thighs, one clean hole in the middle of your forehead. After which I will scatter your books of American history around your feet. Your country will eventually unravel, Ellen Burwell. It's already started. I will enjoy the headlines from afar."

Pleased with himself, Malcolm pushed her in front of him toward the chair, gun to her head. "Come, my pet. Let's begin our creation."

Ellen started to stagger forward but had ceased to listen. Early had managed to catch her eye from his prostrate position on the floor. The low blow had been slightly offcenter, and he had overplayed his condition. Now he was gathering his strength to fight back. Imperceptibly, he had given her a sign. *Get him near me!*

Two steps later, Ellen pretended to stumble and fell sideways against Malcolm's shoulder, bumping him toward Early before she hit the ground.

"On your feet, damn you!" Malcolm snapped as he leaned over and shoved the gun against her temple. "If you insist on groveling, I—"

Before he could finish, Early's hand lashed out like a whip, catching the assassin's ankle and yanking backward. Malcolm tumbled heavily, slamming his forehead against the floor.

Early scrambled forward. Arms wrapped around Malcolm's legs, he clawed his way up to the torso. Malcolm recovered quickly. Twisting his arms free, he pummeled Early's head and shoulders.

Furiously entwined, the two men rolled over and over—crashing against walls, breaking furniture in their wake. Early's weakened state could not withstand Malcolm's flailing fists and raging strength. Moments later, he lay face down on the floor—gasping for air, blood pouring from the gashes on his head.

Straddling the body, Malcolm caught his breath. A rib had been cracked, and one eye was beginning to swell. Yet, he had conquered.

He leaned back and placed his pistol firmly above Early's heart. "It's over," he rasped. "You've provided me with diversion enough."

Malcolm was just about to pull the trigger when a motion caught his eye. Turning slightly, he saw something that glinted—the blurred arc of a hand plunging downward. Suddenly a blinding pain tore through him, and his pistol tumbled across the floor, disappearing underneath the sofa. He shrieked and spun around.

Ellen trembled above him, her eyes burning with fury, her sleeve splashed with blood. She had grabbed the closest weapon available from her desk. Now embedded in his chronically tender thigh was a brass letter opener.

Moaning in anguish, Malcolm wrenched the blade from his leg and hurled it against the far wall. Before Ellen could step back, he staggered to his feet and seized her by the hair. "You bitch!" he screamed and rammed her face against the floor—then whipped her back up to her feet.

Early looked around, the salty sting of blood and sweat in his eyes. Dimly, he could make out the figures of Ellen and Malcolm weaving in front of him. As he tried to clear his vision, his thoughts raced ahead. The assassin still had the edge, but the odds were shifting. The killer's karma *was* kicking in. Ellen's fortuitous stab had honed in on Quill's ancient wound. Early had one last hope. Somehow, that old injury had to become completely infected—body and soul.

Early gave himself a command. *Calm now—sharp and decisive!* Steadier now, he looked past Ellen's frightened face to the man who stood behind her. He was hurt, vulnerable. For Quill, the personae of Patrick Wellington and Malcolm Raines were already entangled and confused. Now they needed to riot.

Malcolm had managed to limp with his hostage to a safe point eight feet away and stood facing Early with his back to the study window. His greasepaint had been smeared and revealed splotches of sweaty white skin. The scarlet outpouring from his wound was continuing to seep, a dark stain growing along the side of his trousers.

Malcolm barely noticed. With a shaking hand, he reached down and pulled his knife from its sheath, then laid its blade lightly across Ellen's throat. "There,

there," he said, breathing hard through his pain, "now we're all in place again."

Early pushed himself up to one wobbly knee and wiped the blood away with the back of his hand. "What place is that?" he challenged, his voice a blend of ridicule and exactitude. "Look around! It's very old, very familiar, isn't it? Where are you, Mr. Raines . . . or should I say *Wellington?*"

Malcolm glowered back. "Don't try your putrid psychology on me! I've won."

"What have you won? You have a bloodied thigh again . . . maybe from a handful of quills. Your musket keeps dropping to the floor . . . and a man keeps walking outside your window. You want to kill him, but he's getting away. He always will."

"Shut up!" Malcolm yelled. "She'll die and you'll be next. Your black magic can't help you!" But his countenance was riddled with agony and frustration. His side throbbed from the fractured rib, and his leg threatened to give way beneath his weight. Alien thoughts were starting to rattle through his mind, dragging old pictures: a *woman in a shawl with fury in her eyes, a fistful of quills plunging down like fangs . . .*

Around him, the room itself was beginning to pulsate with indecision. Two worlds merging, then breaking apart. His perfect setting was turning into a nightmare.

Sensing the beginning of a fissure, Early drove his wedge in harder. "Yes, your ghosts will always find you. I repeat, where are you, Mr. Wellington?"

Malcolm was momentarily speechless. His body shook, and his mouth had gone bone-dry. Something was gnawing from within—the prowl of old memories. Now the walls were closing in.

"You'll pay for this!" he bellowed, edging closer to the window.

Still holding Ellen captive with his knife blade, he reached to his left and grabbed a nearby floor lamp. One inflamed eye on Early, he shifted his weight and smashed the lamp against the window, sending fragments of wood and glass cascading out onto the fire escape. A moment later, he managed to pull Ellen through the gash and disappeared up the fire escape into the wet night.

Once alone, Early immediately thought of Desda. Stumbling forward, he flung the door open. A smear of blood on the floor, but she was nowhere in sight. Mentally he reached out to her, receiving back only vague impressions. *She had gone outside, maybe calling for help*. Early wiped the sweat and blood away from his eyes. Wracked with pain, he could only pray for her safety.

Next he contemplated Quill. The assassin's psyche was unraveling. Given a little more prodding, he could completely fall apart. Timing would be crucial. Too soon, and Early's "medicine" wouldn't have a chance to take hold. Too late, and the psychopath would start killing everyone in his path, starting with Ellen.

Early looked at the cracked face of his watch. He would wait a minute to let Quill's demons gather force. While exploring the killer's mind, he had also registered an important shift. Ellen's life was still in jeopardy, but Quill's priority had changed. Now, first and foremost, he wanted James Early.

Marking time, Early picked up his firearm from the floor and stuffed it into the back of his pants. If it became a question of Ellen's life, he would shoot to kill. Outside of that, he would follow where his options led.

Beneath the canopy of rain clouds, Ellen lay crumpled against the low brick wall where Malcolm had unceremoniously dumped her—dazed and battered but still conscious. She watched her assailant limp back and forth in the fog along the gravel rooftop—a wounded animal defending his lair. Disoriented and in searing pain, his expression seemed in constant warfare—features rebelling, turning into separate hostile factions . . . a haughty scowl giving way to bleak laughter, then transforming into utter terror. From time to time, he stopped and gazed out into the night—faces forming from the grey mist, then receding. "Leave me alone!" he cried out to them. "You deserved what you got!"

But the faces returned. Recent faces, faces from the past, faces from the living dead.

Ellen heard Malcolm's voice reverberating through the wet air and brushed the grime from her eyes. Pushing against the ground, she propped herself up against the ledge.

"You're sick," she wheezed, "you should turn yourself in."

Malcolm kicked a spray of gravel in her direction. "Turn myself in? Why yes, of course! Why didn't I think of that myself?!" he blurted, staggered slightly, then bent over in pain.

"I pity you," Ellen whispered.

"Pity? Pity? That's a dangerous word, hag. Will you weep for me when you and your friends are dead, the ground slick with entrails?"

Ellen tried to sit up. "Leave them out of this! Why don't you just kill me and be done with it?"

Malcolm wrenched his body to within a foot of where she sat and slapped her brutally across the face. "Your turn will come. Now . . . I want him."

Suddenly he stopped and listened intently. A malevolent smile played upon thin lips. Dragging Ellen to her feet, he crossed her throat again with his knife. "Come, my lamb, I have need of you," he said, pulling her off into the shadows.

Now she, too, heard the creak of the fire escape. From below, someone was approaching.

Slowly, deliberately, Early made his way up to the rooftop. To his dismay, the drizzle had not abated and obscured visibility. He paused, scanning up ahead. A moment before, he had heard voices. Now, a foreboding silence.

Once again, Early pushed his attention outward and collided with the killer's jagged state of mind. It had intensified, spilling out across the rooftop, gushing pain and madness. His prediction had been accurate. *Quill was losing his grip.*

Early began climbing again. Now it no longer mattered when the NYPD arrived. They were incidental to the process. What lay ahead was far bigger than two enemies in combat. In victory or defeat, Early now understood—the only thing that mattered was karma, the eddies of consequence shifting, spreading out to repurpose the future.

Soon he stood at the ledge of the roof. Throbbing with pain, he pulled himself over the low brick wall and tried to perceive through the gauzy film of mist and darkness. All about him, the landscape remained hushed and menacing.

Then abruptly to his right, a hoarse cry pierced the stillness.

"James Early!" Ten feet away, Malcolm emerged with Ellen slumped in the crook of his arm like a rag doll, his knife poised above her upturned throat.

Early took a measured step toward them. "You're a casualty, Raines. Why don't you quit?"

"I'll give the orders!" Malcolm barked. "Now, down on your belly!"

Haltingly, Early dropped to his knees, then flattened out, his face pressed against the wet gravel roofing.

"Good boy. Now crawl. Crawl all the way to my feet. Maybe then you will beg for forgiveness—or try something heroic. One way or another, our little play will have its climax."

Early clenched his teeth and began to crawl, the sharp bite of stones scraping against his flesh. A few feet later, however, he became aware of an anticipated presence. Desda was on the roof!

Telepathically, he tried to reach out to her. *Stay hidden! If I can get Ellen away from him, grab her and get her out of here.*

Praying she had received, Early stopped moving, raised his head, and looked up at the killer, now six feet away. The moment had arrived. All his training, all his hard-won knowledge of spirit and street, would be called upon to strike directly into the core of Quill. Somewhere below the killer's mental apparatus, the essence of the man could still be found—a light that could dim yet never be completely extinguished.

Early filled his lungs with moist air, then took the plunge. "You talk about courage. But you beat a defenseless woman then hide behind her. Very brave, Wellington, very brave."

Disoriented, Malcolm frowned, then lowered his knife. Balancing his weight on his one good leg, he seized Ellen and shoved her behind him. "Come," he invited, brandishing his weapon at Early. "You and me, then. Brute against finesse. A show of power—winner takes all."

"Power?" Early laughed contemptuously. "You had some, but you lost that centuries ago. Now you're nothing but a slave . . . a dime a dozen . . . totally run by your past."

"Crap! All of it. You're just—"

"Listen to me!" Early yelled, rising to his feet. "You're breaking down . . . you feel it. But part of you is listening—hard. That part knows *exactly* what I'm saying."

A sardonic smile creased the assassin's face. "Such conceit! I think you're actually trying to save me!"

Early shook his head. "No, that's *your* job. There's Quill, Raines, Wellington . . . and that's just for starters. Then there's *you*."

Just then, Early heard a noise coming from behind Quill's back—the sound of something being dragged away through the gravel. Although Malcolm was too obsessed and crazed to notice, Early was flooded with relief. Desda had gotten his message. Ellen was temporarily out of harm's way.

Knowing this, Early felt a surge of adrenalin. Now he could play his wild card. The gamble was enormous. If he lost, he would lose everything.

For a moment, he considered all that he cherished. He saw his beloved Palden, his robe blown back in the wind . . . Jori's kind weathered face . . . Desda, the soft blaze in her eyes . . . Sam as he leaned back in his chair with his forever cup of black coffee.

Each one, in different ways, had been an oasis for him. Each one had given him strength for the long journey home. If he were going to die, he wanted to go down holding their images next to his heart.

Early reached behind him and drew out his gun. Resting it in the palm of his hand, he offered it to Malcolm. "Go on, take it."

Incredulous, Malcolm stared at him, then ripped the gun away. As if to test it, he took aim and fired. His shot grazed Early's ear. The explosion ricocheted around the neighboring buildings, then was swallowed up by the night.

A warm trickle of blood immediately began to ooze down Early's cheek. He didn't bother to wipe it away. "Yes, Wellington, real bullets, real blood. And even those ghosts you see in your head are real people. Believe it all—it's not just a bad dream."

Malcolm went ballistic. "Are you a lunatic?! Am I supposed to be impressed because you want to be a martyr?"

"This isn't about me."

Early drew himself up to full height. "You wanted a climax, a tour de force. Here it is. Hand me back the gun . . . or blow me away. You decide."

As Early spoke, he felt somehow changed by his own words. Somewhere, somehow, beyond the gloomy rooftop, beyond the jarring soul who seethed before him, a piece of his own troubled karma seemed to be letting go and drifting away.

Watching his opponent, Malcolm felt utterly confused. For the first time in his life, he was experiencing the divided sensation of doubt.

Shuddering, his leg finally gave way. Still clutching the gun, he collapsed, slumping back into the rain-soaked roof. Inside his mind, voices demanded compliance: *You must kill! This man is your nemesis!*

But now the commands sounded oddly thin and synthetic. And there was another sound. A voice in the distance seemed to be calling to him. It was the echo of something from long ago and far away. A promise in the heart of a young boy .... somewhere back before the fall.

Early spoke again. "You have the power of choice. It's the only thing that breaks the chain. Use it now. Free yourself."

Malcolm didn't answer. Forces were pulling him in opposite directions, stronger and stronger, threatening to split him in two.

Early pressed one last time. "Kill me, or show your courage and do the right thing. There's nowhere left to go."

Malcolm stared back. The internal pressure had become unbearable—the walls around him giving way, cracking open. A wave of spasms racked his body.

Then, miraculously, the howling stopped, and a sudden quiet prevailed—the sense of virgin space, an indescribable warmth rising up inside him like an underground stream. Without warning, he began to sob. He could not go backward. He could not move forward. He could only be in this swollen moment—finally alone with himself.

He lifted the gun and pointed it directly at Early's heart. For a few endless seconds, he clenched it tightly in his hand, searching Early's eyes, an enigmatic smile seeping along the contours of his bruised face. Then he threw his head back to scan the charcoal sky above and appeared to murmur something to the heavens—so softly that only he could hear.

Before Early could react, Malcolm turned the gun around, guided it between his lips, and gently squeezed the trigger.

EPILOGUE

Dotting I's, Crossing Seas

Early sat on the floor of his Akashic office, eyes closed, his face honeyed by the light of the Fountain. With the Quill episode now officially behind him, this should have been a time to kick back and enjoy the afterglow. But he continued to feel oddly unresolved, almost skittish. After a few days of half-hearted celebration, he had decided to come back here and take refuge. All in all, there was much to consider.

The explosion on the rooftop was not just a shot heard 'round the world. It was a sound that carried to a realm beyond human outskirts where interested parties listened purposefully. For them, that single brackish note had positive overtones and a unanimous conclusion: James Early's big gamble had paid off in spades. Now Ellen Burwell would have the opportunity to fulfill her vision and give America a long overdue break from the reign of testosterone. Outside of that, the other ramifications were more intricate and less immediate.

Tracking the aftermath via the Fountain, Early had discovered that the soul once known as Malcolm Raines had reported to the Library of Souls, where his spiritual turning point had been registered. Quill's wall of justifications had shown cracks, replaced, in part, by a willingness to be accountable for his actions. The Karma Keepers were gratified. This one step was the most important on the journey to redemption.

Above all, the mission's experiment could be deemed a success. Early had proven that a mortal *could* handle the spiritual torque and be able to straddle the earth and the Akashic Realm. Some might have gone mad or pulled back. But Early had stood his ground and delivered—and would deliver again. He would teach others to do the work, with the hope that someday, perhaps hundreds of years from now, the karmic balance would be restored.

Although relieved and thankful, Early's heart was raw, the experience continuing to morph inside him. Sometimes the events and their meanings seemed resolutely clear and straightforward—at other times, tentative, riddled with uncertainty. Oddly enough, the image that haunted Early most was Malcolm's inscrutable smile before taking his own life. Amidst the blood and tears, madness and defeat, the killer had glimpsed something, then smiled. *What had he seen?* Early would have given anything to know.

He also struggled with the suicide issue, especially since he had been the catalyst. Some would say, by that action alone, the assassin had placed himself beyond redemption. Yet Early had not only studied the man, he had actually *been* the man for a few distorted hours. Viewed from that context, there was no clear-cut comfort zone of right and wrong. If Malcolm *had* surrendered to the police, what actually lay ahead for him? Execution was assured. But the utter humiliation of death row would certainly have undermined his recent hard-won growth. In the end, Early had to grant him respect for his final choice. Consciously and knowingly, Malcolm had chosen death as a beginning step toward integrity—not as an easy exit.

One point of irony did not escape Early's attention: *Quill's final work of art had been a self-portrait.*

Some inner clock sounded, and Early opened his eyes, instantly aware of the luminous presence of the Fountain. Another sensation crowded in. Despite his triumph, he felt abandoned. Jori had seemingly disappeared from the public library. When asked, neither fellow librarians nor library officials remembered seeing a man of his description, as if the whole adventure had been a mirage. Apparently the Karma Keepers had determined that Early was now capable of flying solo, his apprenticeship over. Early wasn't so sure.

Likewise, he was extremely disappointed that he hadn't heard from Palden.

Right now he craved this acknowledgment more than anything else in the world. A few appreciative words would bring spiritual closure and allow him to move on. But nothing had come down the line.

With no answers and many misgivings, Early rose to his feet and prepared to leave. One thing he had learned: after going as far as he could go on any given matter, he had to be willing to step back, let go of expectations, and experience whatever chose to happen next.

*   *   *

Early stood beside Desda on the Staten Island Ferry as she looked stoically out across the choppy waters. Even now, on the return leg of the boat's circuit, she was still being distant, still keeping up the tight little shield around her. Early remained perplexed.

When they had first met at the terminal, it was cheers and shouts, high fives and laughter. But when Early tried to hold her, he felt her body tense. Disappointed, he stepped back and studied her face. Her chin was pushed slightly forward, her brow creased. To Early's distress, he found her thoughts too complicated and dense to read.

With no alternatives, he extended her the right to define the space between them. When she was ready, she would talk. That had always been part of their pact. It still was.

With a somewhat heavier heart, he attempted to drink in the sun, the view, and the surging motion of the bulky vessel as it plowed through the waves. Seagulls followed their wake, shrieking and diving for food beneath the whitecaps, somehow mysteriously aware of life below the surface. Yachts and cabin cruisers motored by loaded down with weekend warriors with their ball caps and sunglasses, bathing suits and lotion, beer cans raised in greeting. Yet Early declined to wave back. Despite the fact that Desda stood less than a foot away, he found himself intensely missing her.

At that moment, she was leaning into the breeze, dark hair streaming behind her. Despite her agitated silence, she looked more striking than ever. More feminine, stronger, somehow more realized. Dressed in blue jeans and black T-shirt, she had her eyes closed, seemingly absorbed in the sunlight and salty air. Early knew otherwise. What she was really doing was finalizing the wording of something she was about to announce.

When she felt Early's attention squarely upon her, she slowly opened her eyes. Turning her face toward him, her blue irises managed a brief spark. Then came the first offering—a small apologetic smile. "You're very good with me," she said quietly. "It's unfair. It's your moment of glory, and here I am, stony and distant. Thanks for not pushing."

Early shrugged. "Whatever's going on, I want to understand. You know that."

"Yeah, I know." She paused and gripped the railing in front of her. "What to say? I used to be rock 'n roll. Hey . . . life's messy. Take a hit, fall down, get up and do it again. That's not me anymore. Probably never really was. But now I'm asking the questions. Karma . . . my path . . . what's next? You're a big part of it."

She turned around with her back to the sea and faced him directly. "I hate these scenes. Everything I want to say ends up sounding like a cliché. I mean, you're amazing. *We're* amazing. But I still feel *under* something . . . hemmed in. I know it's not you. It just . . . nothing seems to fit right now. Everything's slightly off."

"I'm working on that too," Early said with mounting agitation.

"I'm sure. But I think you've got a better handle on it than I do."

They lapsed into silence again. For the next few minutes, Desda retreated behind her walls, and Early looked out at the approaching skyline, trying not to know what he already knew.

"I'm going away for a while," she finally said gently. "Not to end anything—just to clean the palate before I start up again. God knows you're the most important person in my life. I just think it's best right now—for both of us."

The urge to protest welled up inside him, but Early batted it away. The timbre of her voice told him everything. She had worked hard for this moment, and he had to let it stand.

"Just tell me what you want to say."

Desda seemed embarrassed. "It's been a bitch coming to terms with this. I like to think we're really alike. But in some ways, we're very different. This karma thing came along, and you didn't second-guess. You hit the deck running. That's your style. I still have a lot of 'not yets' and 'maybes' going on. I can't just plunge into this with you. I'm not there yet. Maybe never will be."

Early looked down at the ship's worn boards beneath his feet, the old emptiness beginning to seep back in.

"I'm leaving today," she declared. "I'll be staying in a friend's guesthouse in Prescott, Arizona, so I'll be out of touch for a bit. No calls or letters. I'm not sure how long I'll be gone. The main thing is, you're totally committed to the mission now. I don't want to slow you down."

Tears began to cluster on her lashes. She wiped her face brusquely. "Maybe there's someone else out there, someone who can match your stride. You deserve that."

Early put an arm around her shoulders. "Desda, *hear me*. I don't *want* to keep my options open. You changed all that. The best thing about this whole damn circus is that I've seen that time doesn't matter anymore. You're part of me. Whenever you decide to come back, I'll be here, waiting."

This was all that was said out loud until the ferry made its clumsy arrival against the tar-stained pilings of the Battery Park dock.

Before they parted company, Early took her hand. "I'm with you. That's all you need to know."

Desda looked up shyly. "Someday I'll really let that sink in. When it does, I'll be on your doorstep."

*   *   *

Early crouched down beside his open apartment window and gazed out through the rusty grid of the fire escape. It was that transitional time of day when sun and moon call to each other from opposite ends of the sky. That night, their dialogue tented the earth in deep purples and cobalt blues.

With Desda's departure, he felt even more at loose ends. And what about the other characters who had recently touched his life—Ellen and Trakker, even Malcolm? When the dust settled, where would they end up? Closer in, what about James Early? Would the internal collision of Tibetan child and New York cop ever be reconciled? Most unnerving of all was the deafening silence of Palden. *What did this mean?*

After turning these things over and over in his mind, he finally came to a simple conclusion: He needed a new perspective. Where better to look than in the grit and unselfconsciousness of his own neighborhood? It seemed like many lifetimes had come and gone since he had last really said hello.

As he strolled uptown along Amsterdam Avenue, Early drank in the shops, styles, and faces. More than ever before, he absorbed the landscape—the changes and the constants, the themes and variations. And as if for the first time, he was struck by the competing undercurrents of spirit and flesh. These two passions seemed interwoven *everywhere!* Clashing and seducing, on and on they went, chasing after each other into the future toward some distant resolution.

Then suddenly, astoundingly, it fully hit him. *It was all a work in progress!* Himself, this city, this point in time—even the vast puzzle itself with all its rebel pieces—everything mid-negotiation. And if the state of Grace *did* exist somewhere up the line, all he could do for now was to know what he knew . . . and have the courage and openness to take the next step.

Early was about to cross the street when something out of the corner of his eye caught his attention. He did a double-take and began to laugh. Up ahead on Amsterdam Avenue, the elegant figure of the white Bengal tiger paused to look back at him, holding for a moment before setting off again, threading its way through the pedestrian traffic as it mingled with the afternoon sunlight.

Acknowledgments

First and forever, I want to thank my wife, Loy Whitman, who is always there for me, always my first responder in heart and soul . . . and her incredibly diverse skillset.

Also, a deep bow of gratitude to my editor, Joyce Walker, for her smart red lines and persistent help in curating my words until they spoke clearly and with my own voice.

And my appreciation for the expertise of Ashley Ess, who came to our rescue numerous times with her technological savvy and design execution.

I'd also like to acknowledge Don of DeHart's Media Services, Inc. As printer, he practiced the unusual blend of skill, patience, and kindness regarding this book that never seemed to follow normal routines.

Then there are the creative up-all-night warriors: Colleen Camp, Stephanie Dillon, and Anna Bogdanovich, who helped this project stay alive through all the shifting tides of the entertainment world.

With special thanks to The Visioneering Group and Tyler Ondine Whitman, who were there at the beginning for their contributions and encouragement in keeping the project moving forward.

Finally, a raised glass to all the generous people—too numerous to mention—who believed in *The Karma Factor* through the long, difficult years.